USA Today bestselling author ⬚⬚⬚⬚⬚⬚⬚ Texas with her very own her⬚⬚⬚⬚⬚⬚ beautiful children, a spunky golden retriever/standard poodle mix and too many books in her to-read pile. In her downtime, she plays video games and spends much of her time on or around a basketball court. She loves interacting with readers and is grateful for their support. You can reach her at barbhan.com

K.D. Richards is a native of the Washington, DC, area, who now lives outside Toronto with her husband and two sons. You can find her at kdrichardsbooks.com

Discover more at millsandboon.co.uk

RANCH AMBUSH

BARB HAN

LAKESIDE SECRETS

K.D. RICHARDS

MILLS & BOON

First Published in Great Britain 2024
by Mills & Boon, an imprint of HarperCollins*Publishers* Ltd
1 London Bridge Street, London, SE1 9GF

www.harpercollins.co.uk

HarperCollins*Publishers*
Macken House, 39/40 Mayor Street Upper,
Dublin 1, D01 C9W8, Ireland

Ranch Ambush © 2024 Barb Han
Lakeside Secrets © 2024 Kia Dennis

ISBN: 978-0-263-32237-8

0724

MIX
Paper | Supporting
responsible forestry
FSC™ C007454

This book contains FSC™ certified paper and other controlled sources to ensure responsible forest management.

For more information visit: www.harpercollins.co.uk/green

Printed and Bound in the UK using 100% Renewable Electricity at CPI Group (UK) Ltd, Croydon, CR0 4YY

RANCH AMBUSH

BARB HAN

All my love to Brandon, Jacob and Tori, my three greatest loves. I hope each of you knows how much joy and laughter you bring to others, and especially me. How did I get so lucky?

To Babe, my hero, for being my best friend, my greatest love and my place to call home. I love you with all that I am. Always and forever. That's a promise.

Chapter One

Can you ever go home again?

The question hit a little too close as Duke Remington parked his truck in front of the two-story farmhouse where he'd spent most of his happiest moments during childhood.

The white siding with green shutters, metal roof and wraparound country porch had seen better days, but his grandfather Lorenzo Remington was too proud to accept more help than he deemed necessary or could afford to hire.

Early October in Mesa Point, Texas, the weather was always a crapshoot. This year, the record-setting string of hundred-plus-degree temperatures fueled a drought that threatened to dry up the shifty soil and swallow homes whole.

As far as the farmhouse went, between Duke, his two sisters and three cousins, they could have the place spruced up in a couple of weekends. Grandpa Lor wouldn't hear of it.

The fact that Duke's beloved grandfather and grandmother were lying in separate hospital beds in the ICU instead of here at the paint horse ranch they loved hit him hard. His grandparents had defied the odds just by being high school sweethearts who went the distance. Could they do it again by surviving a horrendous car wreck? If ever there was a time for either one of their stubborn streaks to kick in, it was now.

Duke exited his truck as the sun began to climb. He'd driven from his home south of Austin to Mesa General Hospital the minute he'd received word about the crash. He'd been able to arrange leave from work first. He, his siblings and cousins planned to work out a rotation. Blinking through blurry eyes that had been open for over twenty-four hours straight, he caught sight of Nash Shiloh making a beeline toward him from the barn.

Nash, as they called him, had worked the ranch since what felt like the dawn of time but was more like sixty years. Hired at fifteen as a ranch hand before working his way up over the years to foreman, he'd been the only one permitted to hang around. Folks said all he needed to do was put his hands on a horse to hear its thoughts, which was a miracle in Duke's book. It was a gift he didn't have with horses or people, unless criminals counted. There, he seemed to excel at reading their minds and anticipating their next steps.

As a US marshal, Duke encountered his fair share of felons in need of capture and could hold his own thanks to his unique gift. At least, *gift* was the label his skill had been given by his fellow marshals. Was it what he would call it? No. There wasn't anything special about him. He couldn't read other people's thoughts. There was just a thin line between having the kind of mind that caught criminals and being one. A long time ago, Duke had realized he could stand on either side of that line. Doing good had been a choice, and he wouldn't have it any other way.

The older man's sun-worn skin practically hung on his bones at seventy-plus years old. Despite his age, Nash was still strong as an ox and could lift more hay bales than half the seasonal ranch hands four decades younger than him. But his age was starting to show in the slight limp in his right leg and the way his shoulders rounded on his six-foot frame.

Nash still had a full head of hair, and his mind was sharp as ever. "You're a sight for sore eyes."

Duke met the foreman halfway and brought him into a bear hug. "I should have been here so it didn't happen."

"You couldn't have known," Nash said with compassion. He was too quick to let Duke and the others off easy. Like when they'd painted stripes on one of the horses and then put a sign up in the barn that read Beware of Zebras. "Heck, I would have driven to pick up the new saddles myself, but the old man…" His eyes flashed at Duke. "Your grandpa wanted to take his wife out for a fancy lunch in town."

The words *fancy* and *in town* weren't something Duke thought he'd hear in his lifetime about Mesa Point. There wasn't much that would be considered extravagant about the small town. Not since the oil boom in the '70s and '80s when high-end stores brought merchandise to the ladies in town since most wouldn't set foot in a city.

Mesa Point had a small country club that barely survived the oil crash. Its green decor, complete with flowery wallpaper, was straight out of a different era. If the walls could talk, Duke had no doubt they would whisper scandals from back in the club's heyday. He'd heard of everything from affairs in the bathrooms to envelopes fat with cash being handed to golf caddies to "help" with a score or stand guard in front of a supply closet to make sure no one entered unless invited. Today, Mesa Point Golf and Social Club barely kept its doors open.

"How's the marshal business?" Nash asked in his characteristic excitement mixed with a favorite-uncle kind of warmth.

"Keeping me busy," Duke admitted before adding, "It's the reason I don't come home very often."

Nash shot him a look that meant Duke didn't have to explain. "You're here when it counts."

Duke nodded, trying to shake off the feeling that he'd let his grandparents down when they needed him most. What if they'd done that to him when his mother died after giving birth to Duke's younger sister and his father ran off?

Duke was the only son in a daughter sandwich, a middle child, except that he'd grown up with cousins Dalton and Camden who were like brothers to him. He and his sisters, Crystal and Abilene, were close as could be. His cousin Jules, or otherwise known professionally as Julie, was the middle child on her side of the family. Although, none of them ever thought of sides when thinking about each other. They were the Remington Six as far as anyone was concerned.

"Any change in their condition?" Nash asked, ushering Duke toward the back door of the farmhouse.

"Not yet," he responded in a voice that was probably too hopeful.

"They'll pull through," Nash said with a conviction that Duke didn't feel. "In the meantime, you should eat breakfast and get settled in." He paused, looking like he was trying to choose his next words carefully. "Have you decided how long you'll be staying on?"

"I took personal leave from work," Duke said, not loving the fact that he'd handed off several case files he'd been working on for weeks now. "I'm here to assess the situation and report back to the others so we can set up a rotation if needed."

Nash opened the screen door to the back porch, toed off his boots and then headed for the kitchen. "Scrambled eggs and sausage okay with you?"

"No. I'm fine. Don't go to any—"

"It's no trouble," Nash cut in with a hand wave, like he was batting a fly from a horse's behind.

Duke knew when he'd lost an argument, so he stopped himself from saying that he should be the one cooking breakfast for Nash.

Being inside his grandparents' home without them here sucked the air out of the room. Tears welled up. Emotion wasn't usually in his vocabulary. This seemed like a convenient time to remember he'd left his gym bag behind the driver's seat of his truck. His damn emotions had him thinking about someone else, too. But he didn't want to think about her after all these years.

"I'll eat whatever you put on the table as long as you let me clean up after." Before Nash could protest, Duke put a hand up and continued, "I need to get something out of my truck, so you're going to have to hold that thought."

Jogging out to the truck gave Duke a moment of reprieve from the tsunami of emotions threatening to suck him under and spit him out. Being home always reminded him of Audrey Smith, now Newcastle, and the summer she'd spent here. Then school started. She'd disappeared. But not without shattering his tender sixteen-year-old heart. For reasons he didn't want to examine, he had yet to forget that summer fourteen years ago.

Sure, Duke could blame his long memory on the fact a guy never forgot his first kiss, especially one that sizzled with the kind of promise that had been unmatched since. He'd chalked his past physical reaction up to teen hormones over finding real love when he was barely old enough to drive, let alone shave.

It had taken most of the summer for Audrey to warm up to him. Even then, she refused to speak about her past or what happened for her to end up needing a place to hide. He'd fallen fast and hard. And then she was gone. His grandparents had kept quiet about her whereabouts, asking him to respect her need for privacy even though he could hear the regret in their tones. They'd told him she left a message for him asking him to leave her alone. She'd said they were over and their relationship had been nothing more than a summer fling. With a nonworking cell number and no social media to follow, Duke had no choice but to try to forget Audrey Smith had ever entered his life.

A couple of years back, he'd heard a rumor she was back in Mesa Point as Audrey Newcastle. Married? Divorced?

He couldn't say one way or the other. He'd made a vow not to ask questions after her rejection.

Plus, Duke rarely ever visited his hometown except to spend an afternoon here and there with his grandparents, mainly doing work he worried they were getting too old to do despite his grandfather being too stubborn to admit it. True days off were rare because Duke loved his work as a US marshal and dedicated himself to searching for the most hardened criminals to lock them away and keep them from hurting other individuals. He sure wasn't planning to track down an old flame that sputtered out almost before it was lit.

Besides, during his visits to Remington Paint Ranch over the years, which weren't as often as they should have been, he never once ran into Audrey. Not at the feed store. Not at the post office. And not at the local diner where it seemed everyone passed through on the weekend to catch up on town happenings.

Audrey didn't want to have any contact with him after she'd disappeared, or she would have reached out at some point. She'd been clear about breaking up and there wasn't squat he could do about it then or now.

He'd come to understand she must have needed protection before. But now? She'd been back years and his number never changed.

Duke shook off the reverie. The morning sun beat down on him, indicating it would be another hot one. Texas heat had a bottom-of-his-boot-melting type of intensity. The summer had been brutal. Fall wasn't turning out to be much better. With sweat already beading on his forehead, he grabbed his gym bag and started toward the back door.

His cell buzzed. He fished it out of his pocket.

"What's up, Crystal?" he asked his older sister after checking the screen. Duke was the second born. Abilene, aka Abi, was the baby at twenty-eight years old. His sisters and cousins were US marshals. Each had their own reasons, but the seed had been planted long ago by their grandfather who'd been on the job to buy and support the ranch until he could work Remington Paint Ranch full time alongside his wife.

"First of all, how are they?" Crystal asked, referring to their grandparents.

"It's as bad as we feared," he admitted, raking his fingers through his hair. "They're both in comas and the road to recovery might be rocky."

"How soon do you need us there?" she asked.

"We can stick to the plan for now," he said. "I just updated the group chat so we're on the same page. Since we have to plan for the long haul, I think we should stick to the rotation we discussed."

That rotation would have Crystal taking leave next.

"I'll stop by as much as I can in the meantime," she stated, sounding as tired as he felt. Being physically tired was one thing. This was emotional draining, which was worse.

"Sounds good," he said on a sigh. Since he'd sent an update via the chat, this couldn't be the main reason for her call. "What else is going on?"

"Heard some chatter coming from the western district that I thought you might want to check out while you're in town," Crystal said. Her ominous tone added to the dark cloud overhead.

"What is it?" he asked, figuring he could make time for a pit stop after breakfast if work needed him to go somewhere. If this wasn't an emergency, he could use a shower and an hour or two of shut-eye.

Crystal hesitated, which caused Duke's blood pressure to rise. "It might be nothing, however…"

"Go on," he urged.

"You know the Ponytail Snatcher?"

"The guy who has been traveling around Texas targeting female deputies, and then torturing them before cutting off their ponytails, killing them and burying them in a shallow grave?" he asked. "What about him? He's been quiet for more than a month."

"An FBI agent tracked the perp down to a motel an hour from Mesa Point," she continued. "It's probably nothing more than a weird feeling on my part but I was studying the case, and the deputies have a lot of the same physical features as Audrey. I would feel better if someone checked on her. Since you're the one in town and our grandparents can't, I thought—"

"Do you have her address?" he asked, doing his level best not to give away his reaction—an emotional reaction that had no business rearing its head in connection with a work tip, no matter what their history had been. He'd heard Audrey had become a deputy and wondered why she'd chosen Mesa Point to live and work.

Crystal rattled off the location of a small cabin by the lake. He ignored the fact he'd kissed Audrey for the first time near that location before there'd been a development there. It couldn't have meant much to her, so it shouldn't make a difference to him, either.

"I got it," he ground out.

"Are you sure?" Crystal asked with more of that concern in her voice. Before he could answer, she said, "Never mind. That was a long time ago."

"Ancient history," he concurred.

"Check back in when you've had a chance to stop by?" Crystal asked, but she had to already know he would for work purposes. His sister wanted to check on him to make sure he was fine after seeing Audrey again all these years later.

He would be. No doubt in his mind. Even though a hand reached inside his chest and squeezed his heart at the thought. "Will do."

"Be careful," Crystal warned. Was she still talking about the perp?

"You know it," he confirmed. "And don't worry about our grandparents. I can cover."

"I should be able to drop in soon, but I'll have to leave just as fast," Crystal said. He could hear the guilt in her voice.

"We're a team," he pointed out. "All of us. And we got this. They won't be alone again."

Why did the word *alone* suddenly take on a new meaning to him?

LOUNGE CHAIR UNFOLDED to the perfect position. Check. Umbrella positioned to block the sun's unforgiving rays. Check. Good book to read on a much-needed day off. Check.

A sound in the tree line caught her attention, sent an icy shiver racing up her spine. Even after all these years, noise did that to her. Becoming a deputy was meant to face the monsters in the closet, as a manner of speaking. She'd taken self-defense classes to chase the nightmares away. So it frustrated Audrey to no end that her body still reacted to noises as if she was still that little girl hiding in her sister's closet being hunted by their mother.

The noise was just the wind, she determined.

Audrey Newcastle, formerly Audrey Smith, couldn't imagine relaxing after finding Lorenzo and Lacy Remington inside their banged-up truck in a ditch off Farm Road 12 yesterday afternoon, saddles splayed across the dirt. She couldn't conceive of what her life would have turned out to be without those lovely people intervening when she was sixteen years old and in more trouble than she knew what to do with. They'd shown her what real love looked like. All the credit for her turning her life around went to those two and not her pure evil mother and stepfather.

Leaving the hospital without knowing if the Remingtons would survive broke her heart, but she'd known better than to stick around and risk running into Duke. His grandparents gave her a heads-up every time before he visited, so she wouldn't accidentally run into him. They'd told her it was for the best if she stayed away while he was in town. She'd taken the not-so-subtle hint and made certain to keep out of sight every time. Even now. Walking away from Mesa Point and him all those years ago wasn't a choice she'd made lightly despite the message she'd asked his grandparents to give him. He would be too proud and too stubborn to forgive her for breaking up with him in that manner, but it had been the only way she could follow through with it.

Rather than go down the path of regret, she sat down facing the lake and opened her book. The glare from the water made her squint. The coffee she'd had a little while ago kicked in, causing her leg to twitch. Sitting still might not be her best move.

Getting up, she repositioned the umbrella but couldn't quite stop the glare from the water. This was her favorite lake, though, so she sat back down and looked across the surface that seemed to wink at her like brilliant stars on a clear night against a velvet canopy.

Audrey sighed as she picked up her book and opened to page one. Texas was known for its wide-open skies and sunsets that were postcard perfect. Today was no exception. Reading relaxed her.

The minute she got comfortable, her cell buzzed. Of course, it did. If not for the open kitchen window, she might not have heard it at all. Why did she always leave it inside?

Standing up, she debated answering for a half second. She'd lost countless days off covering for one of her co-workers while they attended back-to-school nights or last-minute trips to Galveston to get in more family time before school started. At thirty years old, she had no plans to become a mother, or wife for that matter. She involuntarily shivered at the thought. Parenthood wasn't for everyone.

Her stepfather was a prime example of that. Covering for coworkers was as close as she wanted to get.

By the time she got to her cell, the call had rolled to voicemail. The screen read Boss.

Her hunch that this was going to be a work-related call appeared to be dead-on. Rather than immediately call back, she waited to see if Sheriff J.D. Ackerman left a message.

Her work demanded her full attention. Being the only non-married deputy made her an easy target for helping out. But covering another shift for a coworker wasn't high on her list today. Not while she was still shaken from the devastating crash on Farm Road 12. After seeing the senior Remingtons in the hospital fighting for their lives, she was heartbroken.

Another noise outside caught her attention.

She surveyed the area, scanning the trees, searching for movement.

A deer? Some other wildlife? Wild animals were common in these parts.

Getting used to life in Mesa Point after growing up in Dallas was a big change, but she'd managed all right. And it mostly felt like home living here.

Audrey stared at the screen, tapping her fingers on the kitchen counter. Waiting. The voicemail icon lit up, showing the number 1. Audrey took a deep breath, steeling her resolve. She tapped the icon, then hit the speaker.

"I need to know a head count for the law enforcement versus fire department chili cook-off," her boss said. "Are you in?"

Audrey released the breath she'd been holding. That was easy enough to answer. As she started to send her response via text, a male figure showed up at her sliding glass door. Knocked.

Panic gripped her as she turned her full attention to the entrance. Had the noise in the trees been someone watching her?

She tamped down her nerves.

Someone out to get her wouldn't knock on the glass door.

She turned her full attention to the entrance. Her heart free fell the second she recognized the face. Duke Remington stepped inside the cabin.

Of course, he would show up in town for his grandparents.

But what could he possibly want from *her* after all this time?

Chapter Two

"Sorry to intrude," Duke said to Audrey as he stepped inside her home and then slid the door closed behind him. Her long auburn hair had fewer highlights now, but it still framed an oval face with big green eyes and a heart-shaped mouth with kissable pink lips. "Crystal asked me to stop by to check on you."

She checked behind him like she expected a rabid dog to ram itself into the glass at any moment. "Why?" she stammered as his gaze dropped to those lips—lips that were none of his business.

"Follow me," he said, figuring she needed to see what he was talking about before the evidence was recovered or destroyed. He turned toward the door, then said, "And lock up behind us." He exited the same way he came, forcing his thoughts away from how beautiful Audrey still was or how right it would feel to hold her again.

The sound of her footsteps signaled she was on his heels. Good. He'd only been half certain she would follow him.

Not ten feet into the tree line where they were surrounded by mesquite trees, he stopped. "Right here," he said, pointing to an area behind a tree trunk in the hard unforgiving dirt.

"Those are footprints," she said. "Looks like large boot prints. They're faint, but I can make them out in the dust covering the soil anyway."

"Someone stood here long enough to shuffle his feet," he continued, taking a knee. He noticed a curious leaf had blown into the scrub brush and stuck. He reached for it and almost shouted *eureka!* Holding the leaf by the stem in between his thumb and forefinger, he said, "Look at this. A perfect print on here to match the one on the ground."

"This one is much clearer," Audrey said as she examined the specimen.

He fished out his phone and took a couple pictures of the unmistakable shoe print on the leaf.

"I can't say for sure, obviously, but this looks like a standard work boot, maybe size thirteen," Audrey surmised, stretching her hand over the print on the ground for measurement.

"Agree one hundred percent." Duke snapped a few pictures of the prints on the ground from multiple angles without looking up at Audrey. Hearing the tension in her voice was enough to draw out all his protective instincts. But she may not want his help beyond making this discovery. "Of course, the prints don't prove anything in and of themselves."

"Except they are pointed in the direction of my home and I've had this creepy feeling recently someone was watching me," she said. Her voice still had a way of reaching parts of him that didn't need visiting. She planted her right fist on her hip and issued a sharp sigh.

"How long have you had this feeling?" He threw a mental wall up and shut down his emotions. It was the only way to do his job, and he'd become good at compartmentalizing so he could maintain focus on an investigation.

"A few days and again a few minutes ago before you arrived. Did you come out here before knocking?" Audrey crouched beside him. She was close enough for her shoulder to brush against his arm. Contact sent a surge of heat rocketing through him.

"Only to do a perimeter check. That's when I noticed the prints." Duke cleared his throat to ease the sudden dryness. Audrey exhaled and pinched the bridge of her nose like she was stemming a sudden headache.

"It's impossible to tell how long the person was here or how frequently he might have visited," he said. "Do you remember anyone hanging around or doing work out here with boots that could fit these prints?"

"No, but you know this can be a cut through to the lake," she admitted. They both worked in jobs where they were paid to notice things. It became habit and spilled over into a law enforcement officer's personal life, as well. "How did you... What are you doing here at my cabin when you should be at the hospital?" She shook her head like she was coming out of a fog.

That was a legitimate question.

"I got a call from Crystal with a tip that a perp might be headed this way," he admitted, standing up and taking a step away from her to get the lilac scent of her shampoo out of his nostrils.

"Oh," she said. "How does that apply to me?"

"Have you heard of the Ponytail Snatcher?" he asked. "You must have since everyone has been keeping an eye out."

The inside of her brain must look like a pinball machine right now based on the array of emotions passing behind her eyes. "Yes. Why?"

"Evidence of his work was found in a motel off the highway outside town," he stated. "Crystal pointed out the type this bastard usually goes for resembles you. She asked me to stop by since she had a bad feeling. That's as far as we got before I dropped my bag off inside the farmhouse and then headed over this way after being at the hospital."

"It's clear someone has been out here, watching my home," she said on a shiver.

"You're an attractive woman," he said, keeping his tone as level as possible. "You might have attracted teens, who like to sneak around in these woods."

"Or a voyeur who might escalate if he isn't caught before he moves onto the next-level crime of rape," she pointed out without making eye contact. It was difficult to get a good read on her. Even at sixteen, she'd kept secrets.

"Have you received an indication from anyone in town that you might be the object of an admirer?" he asked, his gut twisting at the thought of someone stalking her. No matter what she'd done to him, no one deserved to have their privacy violated and she sure as hell didn't deserve to become a victim of the Ponytail Snatcher. The thought caused his hands to fist at his sides.

"Not that I'm aware of," she said, rising to her full five-feet-eight-inches. She'd been tall and basically a stick back in high school, but now she'd filled out her frame with just the right amount of curves. The yoga pants and sports bra she wore highlighted those curves, as well as the fact she must spend some time at the gym. It was a shame her green eyes were hidden behind sunglasses. She'd slipped them on along with a pair of running shoes and locked the door in record time.

"Do you live here alone?" he asked, unsure if he really wanted to hear the answer. His shoulder muscles pulled taut as he waited.

"Yes," she said in a defensive tone.

"I'm not trying to overstep bounds here," he said, releasing his fists so he could fold his arms across his chest. "It's important for me to assess the threat level."

She nodded. "Living alone could make me an easier mark," she conceded. "However, I'm a law enforcement officer who happens to be good at her job and keeps a shotgun next to her bed. The person watching must realize that if he's been watching for very long."

"Could be the reason he's out here instead of coming in closer," he pointed out.

She visibly shivered. "We both know the profile of the kind of bastard who stalks and murders. But we might be jumping to conclusions here."

"Yes, we might and, yes, we do." Freaking her out was the last thing Duke wanted to do, but she needed to take the correct precautions.

Audrey crouched down again and studied the boot print. She snapped a pic with the cell in her hand.

Discreetly, Duke glanced at the home screen to see if there was a picture of her with someone. It would answer the question he needed to ask next despite not feeling like he had a right to. A breeze carried her lilac scent, which messed with his concentration.

"What about a relationship?" he asked.

"What about one?" Her fist came up to her left hip.

"Are you currently dating anyone?" he continued, pushing forward and doing his best to distance himself from caring about her response. It was good old-fashioned pride that caused the reaction. His ego had taken a hit and never recovered when it came to Audrey.

"No," she said. "And I'll save you the trouble of asking the next question." Her gaze bounced around from the ground to the trees to the sky and back. "I'm not currently seeing or interested in anyone. As far as I know, no one is planning to ask me out. So there's your answer. No need to waste time going down that line of questioning."

"I apologize for the necessity of asking," he said and meant it. His relief must have to do with getting her personal life out of the way and not because he still cared.

"You're just doing your job," she conceded.

He also noticed she gave away as little information about herself as possible. Meaning, nothing had changed.

"Are you divorced?" he continued.

"Never married."

"Your last name is different," he continued.

She flashed eyes at him. "You're a US marshal. Surely, you can figure out why."

"WitSec?"

"Not exactly but someone called in a favor," she said. "So, I was treated similarly. You do remember what your grandfather used to do for a living years ago to fund the paint horse operation."

Duke should have put two-and-two together a long time ago. At least some of his questions were answered for now.

The sunglasses came off, and those green eyes widened as they looked at him, which felt a whole lot like she was looking through him. "Why did you stop by instead of calling my boss?"

"SHERIFF ACKERMAN IS next on the list."

Audrey could scarcely make her mouth work. "Is there any additional intel?"

"These tracks could be kids," Duke reminded her after shaking his head. "A lot of teens come through these trees to get to the lake, like you pointed out."

"Right," she said. "Of course. However, you wouldn't be here if there wasn't a perceived risk." She of all people knew Duke Remington would rather poke his eyes out with branding irons than stand anywhere near her.

Begrudgingly, he nodded. "We should check this area thoroughly to see if the suspicious person left anything behind other than a boot print," he said, gripping his cell phone. "In the meantime, I'll send these pics to Crystal to see if they match up to anything."

Matching a boot print to another case would be the equivalent of finding a needle in a haystack.

"What do you know about my background?" she asked, wondering if he still hated her for breaking off their relationship the way she had.

"Nothing," he said with enough fire in his voice to set the woods ablaze during this awful drought.

She cocked an eyebrow at him. The man was drop-dead gorgeous. He could best be compared to Ryan Reynolds, if he had dark-roast hair and espresso-colored eyes—eyes that she'd gotten lost in as a sixteen-year-old while briefly living at his grandparents' ranch. At six feet three inches even back then, he'd already reached what looked like close to his full height. But, boy, had his body filled out since then. Even when he was young, he'd been solidly built. Now, it was obvious he was sculpted underneath his black long sleeve T-shirt and camo cargo pants—pants that looked a little too good on him from the back side.

Audrey mentally shook off the attraction that was still strong after all these years. One look at the face made of hard angles and planes was all it took to stir a desire to touch him. The word *off-limits* didn't begin to describe his vibe toward her, which was fine. She wasn't trying to re-kindle a summer fling, even if the kisses they'd shared had been the best in her life up to this point. She still had a lot of life left to go, or so she hoped, and figured the right person for her would knock those memories far out of reach.

Carefully stepping around the tree, giving a solid perimeter so as not to disturb the boot prints, she crouched down to see if there was anything else they were missing. The clay soil made it easier to see where someone had been standing. Another creepy-crawly feeling made her shiver, thinking about being watched from a distance.

The invasion of privacy stung. Thankfully, she had a habit of closing her blinds when the sun went down. Even in a safe town like Mesa Point, she never knew where danger might be lurking. She chalked it up to her line of work as well as her background—a background she didn't go into with anyone except for the sheriff's office during the hiring process.

J.D. Ackerman had taken a chance on her three years ago. She'd managed to put herself through school for a degree in criminal justice while working nights as a waitress at a honky-tonk. She couldn't count the number of times she'd been hit on by drunks. Enough to be convinced she needed to take self-defense classes at the local rec center for more reasons than the nightmares.

Despite those lessons and the training she'd received at the academy, knowing someone had been in her woods watching her took her back to a vulnerable place. Audrey, however, was no longer a kid who couldn't defend herself against violent parents who...

She couldn't even go there in her thoughts, except to say she vowed never to be so helpless again. Her gaze caught what looked like more boot prints. "Hey. Over here. I got something."

A few seconds later, Duke was by her side. His spicy

male scent filled her lungs as she breathed. Why did he have to smell so damned good?

"Tracks," she managed to say as her mouth dried up with him standing so close. Her pulse raced, too, as a warm flush crawled up her neck to her cheeks.

"Where do these lead?" Duke asked, his question rhetorical as he followed them.

The trail stopped at a spot off the road where folks parked their vehicles so they could go fishing in the lake. "I guess this is the end of it," she said.

"Tracks here are mixed together," he said on a sharp sigh.

Audrey glanced around. "Maybe we can set up a camera. Catch the bastard if he heads through the trees here."

"It's worth a try," Duke stated. "I have to head out to the hospital soon, but I could swing by on my way home and mount something up... Let's see." He walked over and tested a couple of angles before finding one that seemed to satisfy him. "This is a good place."

"I can do it," she countered. "Don't worry about this anymore. In fact, you should probably get going to see your grandparents. I've taken up too much of your time already today, and they need you more than I do."

Duke shot her a side-eye before nodding. "All is calm there right now and the nurses' station has my number taped to just about every monitor if anything changes. I'm on my way home to rest since I haven't slept in too many hours."

"I appreciate you for the warning, and for stopping by to investigate," she offered. He'd been tense the entire time, and she knew instinctively his reaction had a lot to do with their history and not just the current threat. "And I'm so sorry about your grandparents. Thank the stars I happened to be driving down the farm road to check on them."

"You're the one who found them?" he asked, shock widened his eyes to near saucers.

"You didn't know?" Should she be surprised no one told him? Probably not.

His expression morphed from shock to gratitude. "If you hadn't been there..."

His voice hitched on the last word.

"It's a good thing we never have to find out," she said.

"We owe you big-time," he continued.

"It's what people do for each other in Mesa Point." It was a large part of the reason she'd returned. "You being here is no different." She paused. "No matter what else happens, we help each other in emergencies."

"I'd like to stick around for a cup of coffee, if you'll offer one," he said without making eye contact. His demeanor toward her changed, though. "That would give me time to update Crystal on what we found and possibly get more information from Dallas. Not to mention I could use a caffeine boost for the drive back to the ranch."

Was he genuinely interested in the investigation or just plain ol' curious about her past?

Shame on her for thinking his motives were anything but pure. He'd given her no reason to believe that he had any interest in her other than figuring out if she could be a demented killer's target.

Another involuntary shiver rocked her body along with a renewed sense of purpose. Whoever this bastard was... he wouldn't win.

Chapter Three

Duke kept an eye out while he walked alongside Audrey back to her cabin. At this point, the tracks were the only visible signs someone had been there. "If you're uncomfortable with me coming inside, I—"

"No, it's fine," she responded.

Fine usually meant the exact opposite in his experience. But arguing seemed like a bad idea, and he could use another cup of coffee while he collected his thoughts, so he nodded.

While on the trail back, he texted Nash to find out if there'd been any change in his grandparents' conditions. The response came almost immediately: none.

"I'm guessing you already checked the perimeter," Audrey said to him as they approached her cabin.

"That's correct," he confirmed.

She stopped at the door long enough to unlock it and let them both inside. "I'm sorry about Grandpa Lor and Gram Lacy," Audrey said to him after he closed the door behind them. He'd forgotten she used to call them that, too.

Without her, they wouldn't have a fighting chance. He was surprised no one told him Audrey was responsible for saving their lives. "Thank you for finding them and rendering aid."

"It's my job," she said with a shrug. "Plus, I'm used to checking on them."

He wasn't letting her get away without some credit. "They're lucky to have you in their lives." He was still trying to figure out why they hadn't mentioned her visits. What else didn't he know?

A wave of disappointment washed over her features. Why? He'd just complimented her. Or so he thought. Then again, he had a lot to learn when it came to Audrey Newcastle.

"Initial report said Grandp... Mr. Remington swerved to avoid hitting an animal," she informed.

"He's getting older," Duke pointed out. Should his grandfather still be behind the wheel?

"I have those pods for coffee," she said, turning her back as she walked into the kitchen. He could take it as either a sign of disrespect or trust. In this case, he decided on trust. It also indicated he'd brought up a subject she wasn't touching. "Do you want to pick one out?"

If that meant standing in close quarters to Audrey, no thanks. "Whatever you're having is good with me."

"You like a darker roast," she said before catching herself. "At least, you used to even at sixteen."

"Nothing has changed on my end."

If he could reel that comment back in, he would. Everything in his life had changed since she'd known him all those years ago. He'd grown up, for one. He no longer trusted as easily, for another. It was probably just part of becoming an adult, and normal to be more guarded.

Rather than dwell on the changes in him, he glanced around. The place was cozy and comfortable even for a person of his size. The walls were a calming shade of white. Eggshell maybe? Hell if he knew. The couch was beige but not in a boring way. There were accent pillows that added color. Art on the walls showed off her taste in paintings. A stack of books on the coffee table pulled the whole scheme together. She had a modern but soft vibe that he could see himself getting used to.

Duke stopped himself right there. He wasn't here for Sunday supper or a date. There was nothing about this room or the kitchen that would make him want to stick around longer than he had to because every inch of it belonged to a person who'd had no problem stomping on his heart.

Call him a jerk, but he had no plans to get comfortable or appreciate the style of her home.

He pulled out his cell and took a seat at the small dining table in front of the glass patio doors. His call to Crystal went to voicemail. "I guess we'll have to wait."

"Why?" Audrey asked, concern in her voice.

"My sister isn't picking up," he informed her with a frustrated sigh. His irritation came from the fact they were stuck. He could also admit the condition of his grandparents weighed heavily on his mind.

They'd been everything to him after losing his mother after Abi was born. His father had split and was now remarried. The ranch had been a respite. There'd been rumors about his father cheating before Abi was conceived, but who knew what the truth was? Gossip could be cruel, and too many folks felt the need to be in each other's business as far as he was concerned.

His phone vibrated, causing a burst of hope to fill his chest that they were about to get some answers. Until he checked the screen. As it turned out, hell could freeze over. The incoming call was from dear old dad.

"What can I do for you?" Duke asked. He could hear the stiffness and formality in his own voice.

Stewart Remington had moved out of Texas with his second wife to raise her children in Colorado at her parents' dude ranch.

"How are they?" Stewart asked, clearly playing up his concern. It shouldn't gall Duke so much, except that he knew his father was a fraud when it came to the family he'd walked away from.

"I'm surprised you have my number," Duke said.

"Nash gave it to me," Stewart admitted. "I had to talk him into it."

"Still in the ICU," Duke informed him.

"I'll be on the next plane out of Denver," Stewart said with a whole lot of gusto. "There's nothing more important than family."

"Agreed." So why wasn't Duke believing the words coming out of his father's mouth? Must be all the evidence of missed birthdays, Christmases and pretty much every other day that worked against Stewart.

"I can drop everything and head that way," Stewart continued.

Duke didn't respond. Instead, he waited for it...

"Because nothing is more important than ensuring my parents are going to be fine," Stewart went on. If he kept at it, he might even sound convincing. "Oh, no. But..."

Here it comes...

"I just realized that I have a meeting this afternoon that I can't miss," Stewart said in a forlorn voice. "If I do, it could cost my business a whole lot of money. And what with the girls in college now."

College that his father hadn't seen fit to pay for Duke or either of his sisters. But also, the twins were long past college age. Who did Stewart think he was fooling?

"Do you think I should come now or wait until they're up and around?" Stewart asked. Before Duke could answer, his dad continued, "Because I think they'll need me the most once they're home. Am I right?"

"Do whatever you want," Duke said, not bothering to hide his disappointment. "They're your parents."

Leaving Mesa Point to go to college and then join the US Marshals Service was the best decision he could have made. There was nothing that could bring him back. A stab of guilt pierced his chest. Because he should have come back more to look after the two people who loved him the most.

"I'll wait," Stewart finally said after a dramatic pause. "If you think that's best."

Duke didn't remember having an opinion that mattered to his father. "If that's what you want to do."

"It's settled then," Stewart said like they'd just solved world peace instead of him getting out of visiting his own parents in the hospital. "I'll have my phone on me at all times. Text or call at any hour if there is any change in their conditions. Day or night."

"Will do," Duke said before ending the call.

He glanced over at Audrey, who was standing there with her hip against the granite counter, studying him intently. Their gazes connected. She jumped as if startled, then grabbed the cup from the machine and replaced it with a second one. After putting in a new pod, she brought his coffee over to him.

When he took the mug from her, their fingers grazed, causing electrical impulses to vibrate up his arm.

"I'm sorry about your dad," she said with those intense emeralds looking right through him.

"It's fine."

AUDREY RETRIEVED HER coffee as soon as the machine was done beeping and whirring.

She joined Duke at the table, thinking there hadn't been a day in three years since returning to Mesa point when she'd thought this moment might be possible. "I should inform the sheriff there could be someone in his town targeting one of his deputies."

"Good idea," he said.

Audrey excused herself and made the call. She relayed the facts about the motel raid and then mentioned the footprints. Ackerman mentioned teenagers but said he would inform the other deputies so everyone could be on alert just in case.

When the call to her boss was finished, she turned toward Duke. "How are you?"

"Fine," he said before taking a sip of fresh coffee.

Her gaze fell to the droplet of coffee in the corner of his mouth. Two *fines* in the space of a couple of minutes was a very bad sign when it came to Duke. She took in a deep breath and forced her gaze to meet his eyes. "I mean it, Duke. How are you really?"

He sat there for a long moment before responding. Then he issued a sharp sigh. "You want the truth?"

"Yes."

"I'm tired," he admitted. "I've been running on E for longer than I care to admit for reasons I don't want to explain, and this happening to my grandparents has reset my clock in ways that I'm not yet ready to examine but know I'll have to at some point."

Audrey was stunned at the honesty. She appreciated the fact he didn't sugarcoat the situation. So she made a confession of her own.

"I hate that your grandparents and your family are going

through this, Duke. I really do. If not for spending a summer with them years ago, I don't know how my life would have turned out." She didn't make eye contact with him. Couldn't make eye contact with him. "Because I learned how two people should treat each other that summer, and that was a foreign concept to me. I'd never met two people more in love or good to each other in my life. And that's why I still check on them. I owe them a debt of gratitude that they'll never allow me to repay because they believe this is just what people do for each other. Imagine that concept." She stopped long enough to take a sip of coffee, welcoming the burn on her throat.

"They always looked at you like one of their own," he said as his gaze intensified on the rim of his coffee mug.

"Without them, I have no idea where I would have ended up," she repeated. "Certainly not here in this cabin with a steady job."

Duke was silent for a long moment. "You never told me how you ended up in Mesa Point in the first place when we were sixteen."

She compressed her lips into a frown. "I don't talk about the past."

The hurt look in those brown eyes almost had her convinced she should change her mind.

What good would it do to dredge up those awful memories? The best she could hope for was to move on, focus on the future and try forgetting as much as possible. It had taken years for the nightmares to stop. Self-defense lessons gave her the confidence to be able to handle herself in almost any situation. Her job reminded her to stay vigilant.

And yet from the looks of it someone had been spying on her, and she hadn't had a clue.

Or was she being paranoid?

"Can you at least tell me why you don't talk about why you ended up here in Mesa Point the first time?" Duke asked, the rim of his coffee cup still holding his gaze.

Rather than go down that road again, she stood up and walked over to the kitchen cabinet. She pulled out a glass and filled it with water. From the window over the sink, she caught sight of someone in the tree line. "He's back."

Those two words sent Duke flying out the door.

She started after him but lost ground because she had to grab her keys and lock the door behind her. There was no way she was taking chances now that she was a target. By the time she reached the area where the boot prints were, Duke was long gone.

Also gone were the boot prints in the dry earth. Someone had come back to erase the fact they'd been there. Any hopes of a random Peeping Tom being responsible were dashed.

This just got real.

Chapter Four

The sound of twigs snapping underneath heavy footfall drew Duke's attention east. He glanced behind and realized he had lost Audrey. As long as the perp was somewhere in front of Duke, he wouldn't worry too much about the bastard circling back to get to her.

Duke pushed his legs to ramp up his speed. He'd always been a fast runner, and his job required him to stay physically fit to meet the demands of chasing felons while wearing a Kevlar vest. His perps had a habit of running. And shooting at him. Folks facing the rest of their lives in jail didn't have a whole lot left to lose. They tried pretty much everything in the book to avoid capture.

Adrenaline gave him a much-needed boost of energy, considering his body was dead tired from stress coupled with lack of sleep. Even so, the runner stayed far enough ahead Duke was having trouble keeping up.

The fact there'd been one set of footprints around the tree made Duke believe the perp was working alone. This guy might be a loner who had a grudge against law enforcement officers. Females. Similar in look to Audrey. Those details didn't exactly narrow the possibilities by much. Getting more facts would help narrow down what felt like finding a needle in a haystack. In Duke's line of work, he would usually have a case file with the felon's name on it. Tracking a perp down might be a challenge, but at least he knew who he was looking for and where their usual hangouts were. Flying blind carried a whole new set of challenges. He shouldn't get ahead of himself, though. Footprints weren't definitive proof Audrey was the next target.

Tree branches slapped him in the face as he tore through the wooded area by the lake. He knew this area like the back of his hand, which made following the perp a helluva lot easier.

Until the footfalls stopped, and he heard a splash coming from the lake.

Duke cut right toward the water as he shrugged out of his shirt. He toed off his boots at the tree line, then bolted toward the rocky shore. Sharp rocks lurked just beneath the surface of the water in this area of the lake. Keeping his boots on would slow him down swimming, so he wouldn't put them back on.

Breaking through the trees wearing only jeans and socks, Duke stopped at the edge of the water. The perp would have to surface at some point unless he could hold his breath for the ten minutes it would take to cross the water. Did he think he could outswim Duke?

Under different circumstances, that might be funny.

There was no sign of the swimmer. The perp must be able to hold his breath. Unless he hadn't jumped into the water like he wanted Duke to think. Duke spun around and searched the thicket. Movement to his left caught his eye.

Uncharacteristically, he hadn't holstered his weapon when he'd stopped by Audrey's cabin. In fact, his service weapon was currently locked inside his trunk along with the backup weapon he kept in an ankle holster.

Since he stood at the water's edge far from the trees, he couldn't exactly put a tree trunk in between him and the perp. The thick bark would have offered some protection against a bullet, and zigzagging through the thicket would have further reduced his chances of being shot.

Right now, he'd chased the perp right into a potential trap.

Duke bit back a curse that would make his grandmother reach for a bar of soap if he was still living under her roof.

A female figure emerged from the thicket as he tried to catch his breath. The run had knocked the wind out of him.

Audrey.

Duke turned toward the water again and scanned the surface for bubbles. The perp had to breathe at some point. It was then that he caught sight of the pool of blood that hadn't reached the shore. The gentleman in him wanted to tell Audrey to turn around so she wouldn't have to see all the blood. Except she worked in law enforcement and no doubt had seen this and much worse.

"What happened?" she asked, grabbing her side as she slowed her pace when she got about ten feet away from him. Those green eyes of hers searched his.

Rather than explain, he turned toward the water and pointed.

Audrey covered her gasp with a hand over her mouth. When she caught her breath, she asked, "Did you get a description of the perp?"

Duke shook his head. "He hasn't surfaced, either."

"This part of the lake has a lot of rocks and branches underwater," she said. Her eyes said she was thinking the same thing as him. The body of the perp had to have been pierced when he dived into the water. He was far enough out to be hidden by the dark water. "What if he's bleeding but still alive in there?" Audrey kicked off her shoes.

"He would have surfaced by now," he said, placing a hand on her forearm to offer some kind of reassurance. Instead of comfort, he got the equivalent of a jolt of electricity from the contact. He'd forgotten the physical effect Audrey had on him every time their skin touched.

If she felt the same energy, she sure hid it. Then again, they'd been away from each other fourteen years without so much as a word. Most attractions would dim given enough time.

Rather than get inside his mind about why his hadn't, he jogged over to slip his feet inside his boots and locate the shirt he'd chucked.

He found his clothing hanging off scrub brush. After shrugging into his shirt and pulling it down over his stomach, he rechecked the water. Red blossomed against the dark blue. At this point, he'd be tampering with evidence if he walked in to retrieve the body, so he didn't interfere. Besides, Audrey was already on the phone with her boss, explaining the situation and requesting assistance.

Duke squatted down next to Audrey after she finished the call, noticing some fresh prints in the dirt. "Tennis shoes," he noted.

"Doesn't necessarily mean it's not the same person," she said as he pulled out his cell phone and snapped a couple of pictures. Audrey did the same.

"True," he agreed. Only time would tell. He wasn't the same type of investigator as Audrey. His specialty was tracking known criminals.

"I guess we'll know the identity of my Peeping Tom, if that's what we're going to call him, soon enough," she said on an exhale.

"I can't imagine whoever is in the water knew the area, or he would have known this part of the lake is dangerous to dive into."

"Maybe. Did you ever watch the 911 World Trade Center tapes?" she asked, pushing off her knee to standing.

"Yes," he admitted, remembering the horror of witnessing the desperation in the women and men who'd been trapped inside the building.

"Those folks who jumped from a high floor to escape a burning building didn't see an immediate way out of the fire. They jumped without thinking," she surmised with a frown. "It was a tragedy unlike anything I've ever seen. Maybe this guy thought the water was safer than what chased him on land."

"The best place to dive into this lake is from the west bank," he reasoned.

"This person must have staked out the whole area if they were intent on watching me," she added. "Which wouldn't necessarily mean he would have known the terrain other than what he saw on a map."

"There must be a vehicle around here somewhere," Duke said, wanting to figure out if there was a way to identify the perp while they waited for the sheriff.

He wanted to go into the water to identify the perp.

Was this the person they were looking for?

Audrey examined the shoe print. Boots were larger, heavier and therefore made deeper tracks. Why would Tennis Shoes come back to cover Boot Print's tracks if they weren't one and the same person? It was the only logical deduction. The other looming question was whether or not their perp was here to kill Audrey.

Did he return to erase anything that could link him to

Audrey? All of this was conjecture on her part, but it was logical. Logic was usually right in investigations.

Then again, the Ponytail Snatcher was almost caught. He could be in Timbuktu for all anyone knew.

Would a determined killer risk getting caught?

She glanced up as Duke stood at the water's edge. His hands were clasped on top of his head, a runner's move that brought more oxygen into the lungs. However, his breathing had already returned to normal. Instead, this was a move she'd seen him do dozens of times over the summer in their youth. It was always a sign he was frustrated and unsure of what to do next. Something was percolating in that intelligent brain of his.

Seeing Duke again was harder than she imagined it would be.

The sounds of footsteps echoed from the thicket, growing louder. The cavalry was arriving. She realized that, after giving a statement, Duke would be able to leave. Would he go back home like he'd planned to do?

Audrey walked over to him. "I know you have to provide a statement but feel free to take off anytime. I can speak for both of us for now. You can always give your version to the sheriff at home. He won't mind the detour on his way back to his office."

Duke shook his head vigorously, like he used to do when he thought something was a terrible idea.

"Are you sure?" she asked, glancing over at the clearing behind them as voices became audible. "Ackerman won't mind, and you said you needed sleep."

"You couldn't stop me from doing what I want to do," he said with an edge to his voice that cut like a knife.

Rather than butt heads right here like she wanted to do, she reminded herself to calm down. Duke was right. He'd always been stubborn. If he didn't want to be somewhere, he wouldn't be. Audrey backed up a step and put her hands in the air in surrender. Before Duke could add insult to injury, she turned and walked toward her boss.

Along with the sheriff came another deputy and a pair of EMTs. The twins, as she called them, were the same age and had the exact same short curly brown hair. Each had a dotting of freckles across their noses. They had similar builds because they worked out at the same gym, together, on the same training regimen. Born six months apart, Clifford and Clinton had been best friends since the cradle. They grew up as neighbors, becoming and, even more unique, staying friends over the years. And they got a kick out of being referred to as twins. Clifford was an inch taller while Clinton had the biggest arms, according to him.

The twins threw on fly-fishing waders and goggles before heading into the water to investigate. Clifford came out first, his face pale. Clinton joined his buddy as they helped each other out of the rocky landscape.

Clinton ran to the tree line and grabbed hold of a tree before emptying the contents of his stomach.

"What is it?" Audrey asked as Duke joined her and the sheriff. "What did you see?"

Clifford shook his head. His skin tone had color but he appeared unwell. "It's the Napier boy."

"What?" Duke asked in disbelief. "No."

Audrey had lived in the town coming up on three years and knew just about everyone. The Napiers mostly kept to themselves, but they were nice enough folks. They had two high-school-aged kids, a boy and a girl.

"Jenson Napier?" Audrey asked for clarity.

"Yes, ma'am," Clifford supplied, looking green around the gills.

Questions flooded Audrey's mind, but the only person with answers was dead. That word sat heavy on her chest. Someone would have to inform this young man's parents he wasn't coming home today. Or tomorrow. Or ever. Audrey turned to her boss. "I'm going with you to speak to the family."

Ackerman was already shaking his head no.

"Yes," she argued. "I have questions."

"You're too close to the situation," the sheriff said. He wasn't wrong. And yet she wouldn't let that deter her.

"That very well may be," she said. "Jensen was a voyeur at the very least." She immediately ruled him out as a ruthless deputy murderer because his parents would have noticed him missing. "I'm wondering what his parents knew and whether or not they'll let us take a look at his room."

"What are you hoping to find?" Sheriff Ackerman asked.

"J.D.," she said, lowering her voice. The change in direction from being a potential target of a twisted murderer to being watched by a teenage boy was enough to give her whiplash. "I need to know if I'm his first mark or if there have been others."

"It's clear he's not going to pursue any of those activities again," Ackerman pointed out. "But it's probably worth speaking to his parents at least."

She couldn't argue that. Still, she had to know if this kid had been watching her for long or if this was his first time. Did he get spooked and come back to cover his tracks? This was personal. Ackerman, of all people, should realize the position she was in and why she would have questions.

"You're too close to this thing to be the one to investigate, Deputy," he said again. Calling her *deputy* instead of by her first name was the equivalent of her mother calling Audrey by her full name. It was formal and meant there would be no budging. Hearing *Audrey Lynn Smith* would make her cower to this day on instinct before she regained her senses, reminding herself that she was no longer a helpless little girl who feared her mother's wrath.

Audrey was no longer a child, and she had no plans to back down from the sheriff. Even if he was her boss and had the ability to fire her.

Chapter Five

Audrey was about to get herself into trouble with her job. Duke couldn't blame her. He also couldn't stand by and watch her ruin her career.

"Let's take a walk," he said to her, trying to catch her gaze.

She refused to look at him. "No, thanks. I'm fine right here."

"I can see that," he said, figuring he needed to take a soft tack if he was going to keep her from digging a bigger hole for herself. Sheriff Ackerman's face had already turned a darker shade of red, which wasn't a good sign. "All I'm suggesting is that we take a walk together and catch our breath."

Arms folded across her chest, she dug in further. "I'm breathing just fine right here."

When Audrey closed up in the past, Duke was the only one who could get her to open up again. Usually, he accomplished it by taking her for a walk, giving her the room to breathe while he was by her side.

A lot had changed since they were sixteen. His old go-to tactic failed.

Refusing to give up, he turned toward the sheriff. "Would you mind giving us a minute?"

J.D. Ackerman offered a nod before walking over to the water's edge where he began supervising Jenson's removal from the lake. Clinton and Clifford had shaken off their emotions and moved in a robotic manner that was a little too familiar to Duke. Watching someone else in that mode struck him as odd.

When Ackerman was far enough away for Duke to have privacy while speaking to Audrey, he moved toe-to-toe in order to face her and get her attention. Touching her would be a mistake, so he fisted his hands to stop himself from reaching out to her.

Slowly, she brought her gaze up to meet his.

"We can stop by the Napier home to offer our condolences to Jenson's family," Duke said slowly and quietly. "We can bring a dish or flowers, let them tell us everything they want to about Jenson. Believe me when I say his mother might need a shoulder to lean on, woman to woman. You'll get more information out of her this way without putting her off and causing her to turn quiet on you. His sister, Halsey, might know his habits. She might be willing to talk to us. As awful as this is, it's better than being watched by the person we initially feared."

Audrey studied him without giving away the slightest idea of what she might be thinking right now. Those emerald eyes could be haunting. This was one of those times that made him question whether he helped her all those years ago or not.

"Hey, I'm on your side here," he said, trying to ax his way through the brick wall that had come up between them.

She bit down on her bottom lip, a sure sign she was at least contemplating his idea.

"This kid wasn't a murderer," he continued, capitalizing on the fact she was giving him her full attention. Audrey knew when she'd had enough. If she didn't want him to keep talking, she would have walked away by now. "Let's find out what he was really doing watching you and if there have been others."

"J.D. thinks this is an open-and-shut case," she finally said. "He doesn't want to rock the boat with Jenson's family."

"I agree with what you said to him, by the way. You have a right to know the nature of why this young man was on and around your property as well as what his intentions were."

The tension muscles in her face relaxed ever so slightly. "Thank you, Duke."

"You gave your statement to him already, right?"

She nodded.

"How about the two of us get out of here and have another cup of coffee at your place?" he asked.

She held out her hand. It shook. "Coffee is not my best move right now and you need to get sleep at some point."

"Then we'll pick up some of that herbal tea you used to sip on at night," he said, realizing he'd been awake over thirty hours. At this point, he'd been fighting sleep for so long he doubted he could sleep if he wanted to after the adrenaline rush he'd just experienced. "What was that?" He made an attempt to pronounce the name from memory and failed.

At least the corner of Audrey's mouth turned up a tad in an almost smile. "Chamomile is the word you're searching for, Remington." Her expression changed when she said his last name. It was the way she used to refer to him when she was kidding around.

At least there was a glimpse of the Audrey she used to be hidden deep inside there somewhere. The spark had returned to her eyes, making her even more beautiful.

"Okay," she relented.

"Hold on a sec," he said, not wanting her to have to speak to her boss again. Intervening was no problem. He'd known of J.D. Ackerman for years. The two had a mutual respect for one another. Everything Duke's grandparents said about the man indicated he was a solid sheriff who cared about keeping his county residents safe. He had a reputation for being honest and fair.

Duke jogged over and asked the sheriff if he had a problem with Duke accompanying Audrey back to her place so she could slow down and process what had just happened. Ackerman agreed it would be a good idea.

Despite being a well-trained deputy—and this would apply to any law enforcement agent or officer—the shock of being the victim still hit hard. Being the one in the so-called hot seat, for lack of a better word, was usually more nerve-racking than anyone expected it would be. He could only imagine how violated she must feel. The feeling of a perp getting one up on an agent, deputy or officer was the pits. Not to mention embarrassing. After all, they were the ones who were supposed to protect and serve everyone around them, not be the ones in need of protection. Duke had encountered this phenomenon multiple times over the course of his career, having gone after criminals who'd shot and sometimes killed peace officers or judges. The ones who recovered carried a sense of shame—shame that was displaced if anyone asked Duke.

Anyone could end up a target or become a victim, even law enforcement officers. It happened. It was the reason they wore vests. And it was the reason they endured hours of training to learn how to make themselves less of a tar-get when walking into a hot situation.

Still. Things happened. Audrey needed to know she was not alone.

He had no plans to make a fool of himself by falling in love with her. Again. Pride overruled emotion. He would never fall down that slippery slope with her again. Not after the way his tender heart had been shattered years ago. He'd picked up the shards and moved on, figuring nothing good could come of rehashing the past. *Closure*, a little voice in the back of his mind said.

There was that.

Duke's heart wasn't young and naive any longer. He'd grown up. He'd learned to protect his heart at all costs. And he had been fine for a long time. Survival tip number one: don't get attached to anyone. Ever.

He could handle swinging by her home for a few hours until the dust settled and she regained her bearings. Maybe grab an hour or two of shut-eye if his mind would relax.

After thanking the sheriff, Duke turned around to make the short trek back to where Audrey was standing. Chin up, arms folded across her chest, all signs of vulnerability were gone from her stance.

Emotional distance was good between the two of them. But she needed to deal with her feelings about what had just happened, or she would carry it around in her profes-sional career for the rest of her tenure.

"THE SHERIFF AGREES it's a good idea to get you out of here," Duke said to Audrey.

She managed a nod, reminding herself this could have been a helluva lot worse.

Duke reached for her hand. Bad idea. She turned in time for him to miss the mark.

"My cabin is this way," she said, heading home. He was right about leaving the scene. She'd seen the footprints. She knew who the perp was. There wasn't much else that could be done here anyway.

The logical answer was that Jenson had been watching her. He'd visited at least once, staring at her from behind the tree line. An involuntary shiver rocked her body at the thought. He was a senior in high school. Testing the waters? Or had he developed a fixation on her? Talking to his parents and visiting his room, if they would allow it, might produce the answers needed for Audrey to have peace of mind again. For her to sleep at night.

Heat concentrated on the crown of her head as she walked from the lake to her cabin. For October, it was hot. She didn't need to look at a temperature gauge to realize it was in the high nineties. Unseasonably miserable and dry.

After unlocking the door, she left it open and walked inside without saying a word. At the kitchen, she turned around as he closed the door behind him. "You don't have to stay and babysit me. I'll be fine."

"I don't mind," he quickly responded. If not for the twinge of hope in his voice, she would have asked him to leave straight-out.

"Okay," she conceded.

"I wouldn't be bothered if you would allow me to heat up my coffee," he said, following her into the kitchen where he picked up his mug.

The kitchen was small, so he was being polite. All he had to do was look above the stove—she still wondered why anyone thought placing a microwave directly on top of burners was a good idea—to find what he was looking for.

Duke heated his coffee, and she followed suit for lack of anything better to do with her hands. She grabbed a small notepad and a pen from the junk drawer before joining him at the table. Tapping the pad, she collected her thoughts.

Duke retrieved his cell phone before taking a sip. He set the mug down and then sent a text. "Crystal will be interested in today's development."

"What about your grandparents, Duke? Has there been any change?"

He shook his head. "Afraid not. Nash has been good about updating the family. He's there right now, according to his latest texts."

"How about the others? Are they coming to town?" she continued before making a note about where Jenson was found and his activity before jumping into the lake.

"Yes," he answered. "I could get time off work first. I'm here for a few days before Crystal arrives. I'll be back and forth, of course, after that. And the others will pop in as their workload allows."

"Got it," she said, her thoughts immediately bouncing back to Jenson. Or maybe he acted out of pure panic rather than logic. Maybe he believed he could dive out far enough to miss the rocks and tree branches that made this area so good for catching fish but terrible for swimming.

Duke had educated her about this area years ago. Didn't people hand information down anymore? Teenagers spent more time on their phones than in nature, Audrey had noticed since returning. Naively, she'd believed rural areas were immune to big-city trends. Not true. Brutally hot summers kept kids inside, searching for ways to entertain themselves like video games and social media. The pandemic had made it worse, accelerating usage. Parents allowed their kids to use their phones and devices much more dur-

ing that period, probably expecting life to return to normal when everyone felt safe again. However, kids seemed
to have decided cell phones were more fun than playing
on a hot metal playground. The glued-to-a-screen trend
hadn't died down.

Was that the reason Jenson didn't know about the rocks?

"Why me?" she asked.

"Did you ever notice the teen trying to speak to you
while you were on duty or in town?" Duke asked.

"No," she said. A voyeur wouldn't necessarily stalk her
down grocery store aisles. "I never really ran into him,
which also strikes me as strange." His parents would be
receiving the news of his death soon. Their lives would be
forever changed after the sheriff's visit.

"I asked Ackerman to shoot a text once he told the family, by the way," Duke said.

"I was just thinking about them," she admitted.

"Your forehead wrinkled," he pointed out. "I guessed
you might be considering his parents."

"I had a sibling once," she continued. "Losing my sister
changed everything."

The look on Duke's face said he had no idea she had
brothers or sisters. Then again, she'd been told never to
mention her sister or anything else about her family. So
she didn't. How her parents had explained the death to social services and managed to keep custody of Audrey was
anyone's guess.

"I'm sorry," Duke said with the kind of compassion that
threatened to break down carefully constructed walls.

"It was a long time ago," she said, unable and unwilling to go there. If she could reel the revelation back in, she
would. What she needed to do now was change the sub-

ject. "How soon do you think we can head over to the Napier house?"

"Let's give the sheriff another hour or two," Duke suggested.

Audrey had no idea how she was going to survive being in her home with Duke for several hours. Food came to mind. There was no way she could eat, but perhaps he could. "Are you hungry?"

He shook his head.

"We could head over to the hospital to give Nash a break if you want," she said. Anything would be better than hanging around her cabin where she felt most at home. The lake might be surrounded with memories of a summer with Duke, but her cabin was her own. She liked being close to the lake in her own space. Being here had always comforted her.

Until now. Until Duke Remington sat at her kitchen table. And until her sense of safety started unraveling again.

"We can head out after we finish our coffees," he said.

When she risked a glance at him, she realized he'd been studying her. "What is it?"

Chapter Six

Duke shook his head. "Nothing."

Questions brewed but this wasn't the time. After finishing his coffee, Duke drove to the hospital and parked in the lot. He turned to Audrey, who'd been understandably quiet on the ride over. "Does Jenson's mother still work at the hospital?"

"As a matter of fact, she does," Audrey said after a thoughtful pause.

"Any idea if she'll be on shift?" he asked.

"Your guess is as good as mine there, but I assume she has been called by now by the sheriff so he can inform the parents together," she supplied.

Running into Stephanie Napier while on shift wasn't exactly his version of a good idea. Audrey's emotions were still running high, this was personal, and she might lose her better judgment long enough to ask questions that didn't need to be asked before a mother was informed of her son's death.

"Whatever you're thinking that's causing you to sit here and idle the engine rather than go inside, don't," Audrey said, surprising him.

"I'm good," he said. "Are you?"

"I can be," she responded with raw honesty. "If Mrs. Napier is on shift, I'm not going to quiz her if that's what you're worried about." Now, she sounded offended. "Give me more credit, Duke."

Duke cut off the engine. "I apologize if I offended you." He meant it, too. "Keep in mind that I haven't seen or spoken to you in almost a decade and a half. Believe it or not, I'm hesitating because I remember the kind of heart that's beating inside your chest. You would be upset with yourself if you accidentally crossed a line with Jenson Napier's mother."

Audrey kept her gaze on the vehicle in front of them. She gave a slight nod and then exited the truck before he could come around and open the door for her. He knew full well she could open a door for herself, but it was a common courtesy that had been ingrained in him from birth. At sixteen, she used to like it when he circled around the front of his Chevy truck to get the door.

Had she changed, or was she making a statement that she could take care of herself?

Duke shoved those unproductive thoughts aside along with the small part of him that was disappointed. He made a mental note that she liked to do those things for herself now and got on with it. No sense dwelling on the past.

In fact, Duke followed Audrey into the hospital rather than take the lead. Damn. In all the activity, he'd lost sight of the fact she'd been the first responder on the farm road making sure his grandparents were okay. Now that he had her for the next couple hours, it would be nice to have a few of his questions answered.

The only reason he was sticking by her side right now through the Jenson boy ordeal was because his grandparents would tan his hide if he walked away from Audrey after the trauma of the afternoon.

Inside Mesa General, the white sterile tile caused him to tense up. Hospitals and funeral homes were the two places he generally liked to avoid. But this couldn't be helped.

They breezed by reception with a nod from Flo, who worked behind the counter. She was as good at reading people's moods as his grandmother was. One look from Lacy Remington, and you were an open book.

They walked straight to the elevator bank. Audrey pressed the button, and almost immediately a set of doors opened. They stepped inside where she pushed the number three. Three thirteen was his grandmother's room. Grandpa Lor was next door in three fifteen.

The second the elevator doors opened, Duke's stomach dropped. Based on the flurry of activity at the nurses' station, someone on the floor was coding.

"Grab the crash cart and follow me into three thirteen," one of the nurses demanded. She flew right past Duke so close he had to take a step back.

Three thirteen? Duke bit back a curse. Grandma Lacy.

Audrey's hand pressed against his forearm in a show of support. Duke took off behind the last nurse as Audrey kept pace by his side. Grandpa Lor was hanging on by a thread as it was. Losing the love of his life would certainly be a blow. Would he be able to survive? Would it set him back? Duke couldn't let himself think about losing his beloved grandma.

As the team reached the door, he tried to scoot in behind the last nurse, a male. The guy turned around to close the door, ran smack into Duke's chest and bounced.

The nurse shot him a look of sympathy. "Sorry, man. Only personnel past this point when a patient codes."

Duke welled up to argue but stopped himself. He didn't want to take critical seconds away from his grandmother's care by delaying one of her nurses. He took a backward step.

"We'll take good care of her. I promise." With that, the door was shut.

Duke could hear a flurry of activity in the room. All he could think about was his grandfather's reaction should the worst occur.

"They're doing everything they can, Duke." Audrey's voice broke through the noise in his head.

"I know," he conceded before raking a hand through his hair. "I just hope it's enough. You know?"

The question was rhetorical, but Audrey's hand on his arm kept him from losing it. None of this was fair. His grandparents were two of the nicest people on earth. They didn't deserve to have this happen to them. This was the longest they'd slept in separate beds in their entire lives together.

Nash came running down the hall with a look of concern. He motioned toward the steady beeps coming from the nurses' station. "What's happening?"

A nurse was hot on his tail. "Sir, please go back to the waiting room." She didn't catch on there wasn't a chance in hell Nash was turning around to go back to that room without knowing exactly what was going on.

"Grandma coded," Duke said. Hearing those words come out of his own mouth was the equivalent of a punch to the solar plexus. Not being able to do anything except stand in a hallway was the worst feeling he could imagine. It gave him a whole new respect for victims' families who paced halls just like these while waiting to find out if their loved one would live or die.

"Did they say why?" Nash's face showed his age from lack of sleep and worry. The wrinkles were deeper now. Much more so than from years of too much sun working outside.

Duke shook his head.

"What will it take to get the three of you to move to a waiting room?" the nurse asked. Her name tag read Mitzy. "We need to keep the hallways clear. I promise someone will provide an update as soon as possible."

Duke didn't want to make her job more difficult. However, he wasn't leaving. Which basically meant they were stuck. Except...

"We'll step into my grandfather's room if that makes it easier," he said to her. "But we need to be close by in case..." He couldn't bring himself to finish the sentence.

Mitzy's face morphed from stern to compassionate. "Go ahead. It's visiting hours. I just can't have you clogging up the hallway making noise since I do have other patients and families to consider."

Duke nodded his understanding before ushering his group into Grandpa Lor's room. The three of them huddled in one corner. Seeing his stronger-than-an-ox grandfather laid up in bed with tubes running out of him and machines beeping gutted him.

"Should we let the others know what's going on?" Nash whispered.

"They'll abandon their lives and still potentially not arrive in time to see her before she goes if that's what we're dealing with," Duke reasoned. "I'd rather give it a few minutes first."

"I suppose you're right," Nash agreed.

"There isn't anything anyone can do right now," Audrey

interjected. "Except maybe send up a good thought that she'll pull through this all right."

No one spoke the truth that everyone knew. If Lacy Remington was going to die from her heart stopping, it would be in the next few minutes. And that was only if it hadn't happened already. The thought caused Audrey's knees to buckle. She grabbed tighter on to Duke's forearm to steady herself. She couldn't imagine a world without Lacy Remington in it.

Audrey hated that the family was going through this. Duke had been her first thought when she'd found his grandparents. She knew how much he loved them.

The group would need to discuss how they wanted to handle moments like these in the future.

This was still too new to all of them to have come up with a good plan. Audrey had called Nash instead of Duke at the scene while EMTs worked, figuring she was the last person Duke wanted to hear from again after his grandparents warned her it would be best to keep her distance once she moved back to Mesa Point.

Being here at the hospital, witnessing Duke and Nash react to what was happening in the next room, reminded her of the task the sheriff had ahead of him. Talking to Jenson Napier's parents was going to be one of his most difficult jobs. Period.

Despite the teen watching her, which gave her the creeps to no end, she would never have wished him dead. She didn't wish that burden on his family. They were not only about to find out their only son was gone but that he was engaged in criminal activity to boot.

As far as days went, this one topped the Worst list.

Hang in there. You got this. Audrey wasn't a praying

person, so that was all she could think to say on Gram Lacy's behalf.

It seemed all kinds of wrong that Lorenzo Remington was in this room rather than with his wife. Would that help? Did they realize they weren't together? The doctor had said no when she'd asked, but something deep within said he was wrong. She believed the Remingtons knew they were apart, which was why she'd stayed with them until Nash arrived at the hospital and why she wouldn't have left if anyone other than Duke had been the first to show.

Audrey had no idea how the others viewed her since she hadn't stayed in touch with anyone other than Lor and Lacy. And she always steered clear of the paint horse ranch when one of grandchildren visited, respecting their time with their family. All of the Remingtons worked as US marshals and were busy with their careers. Between the six of them, visits were often short.

Audrey took a deep breath. Being in the hospital flooded her with bad memories—memories that made the simple act of breathing difficult. The image of her baby sister, all red hair and freckles, on a gurney, all pale, bruised and helpless, assaulted her.

Other memories accompanied the image. Memories she'd spent a lifetime trying to block out.

She strained to listen for noise in the next room. What was happening in there?

"I should check on the horses," Nash said. The older gentleman twisted a ball cap in his hands. He looked uncomfortable, out of place even, away from the barn and the horses he loved so much. Nash was as much a part of the land at Remington Paint Ranch as the dirt and structures that made up the place.

"I'll call the minute I hear word," Duke promised after embracing the man in a bear hug.

Nash gave a slight nod before walking to the side of Lorenzo's bed. He took his best friend and boss's hand before saying something Audrey couldn't quite pick up. Lorenzo was breathing through tubes, unconscious. Watching Nash squeeze Lorenzo's hand and ask him to wake up was enough to cause tears to spring to her eyes. The ranch foreman was every bit a part of the Remington family as Duke and the others.

Audrey was the only one truly out of place despite the summer she'd spent with them and how much they'd made her feel welcome. Audrey didn't belong anywhere. Not in Dallas. Not in Mesa Point. Not at the ranch.

Not since leaving Duke.

Audrey mentally shook off the reverie as the door opened and closed behind Nash.

Duke turned to face the window. He raked a hand through his hair again. It was the move he always did when he was at a loss. Her chest squeezed as she wished there was something she could do to ease his pain in the way he had hers all those years ago.

When nothing came to mind, she did the only thing she knew: she walked over to him and wrapped her arms around his midsection before resting her forehead on his muscled back. She feared she'd gone too far when he tensed, but then he slowly turned to face her, looping his arms around her.

For a long moment they stood there, holding each other. It was as though time warped, and she was caught in the wave. Memories bathed her in warmth. Memories of her first kiss.

Duke had parked out at the lake not far from where

she lived now. They'd walked hand in hand to the bank as they'd done a dozen times before. That night, the stars shone brighter than she recalled ever seeing them. His hand was warmer, moist. She chalked it up to being hot, but later looking back, she realized how nervous he'd been. He came across so cool and mature it hadn't crossed her mind that night that it was his first kiss, too. It wasn't until weeks later, right before she left, that he'd admitted it to her.

By sixteen, she believed she'd experienced the worst life could hand her and that she could handle everything else. She'd lost everyone and everything she ever loved. Keeping everyone at arm's length had kept her safe, kept her standing straight as the world around her crumbled time and time again.

No amount of rationalizing had prepared her for the pain of walking away from this man. Sixteen shouldn't have been when she was introduced to the best person she would ever know.

In some ways, though, it made life easier. Less painful. Because nothing since had compared to that particular depth of heartache. At the time, she'd been convinced she had contracted some kind of life-threatening sickness. Every part of her body ached. She wanted to throw up every time she managed to push herself to standing. The room would spin.

Child services had located an uncle who was willing to take her after she left the ranch. The bastard kept her for three months before she ran away. She scrounged enough money to buy day-old bread and peanut butter by offering to clean or babysit. She found a couple willing to provide a roof over her head and meals in exchange for babysitting services. At one point, the owners of two different restaurants took pity on her and gave her leftover food if she waited at their back doors around closing time once the babysitting job ended after the husband was offered a job in Colorado.

One of the owners had pure intentions. The other did not.

Audrey had fought owner number two off by ramming her knee where no man wanted to be hit. It gave her enough advantage to loosen his viselike grip around her arms so she could run. She ran all the way home that night, begging her uncle to take her back, and never returned to either restaurant again.

Audrey involuntarily trembled at the memory. He'd called her names, told her she was ungrateful, and then treated her like his personal servant all the while collecting checks to "take care of her" until she turned eighteen when he happily booted her out.

"What is it? What's wrong?"

"Nothing," she responded, taking a step back. Trusting anyone, especially a man, wasn't something she could see herself doing. Not even Duke.

Chapter Seven

Duke felt the tension in Audrey's body a second before she pulled away. He got the message. She'd reached the end of the line when it came to offering comfort. When it came to Audrey, an end was inevitable.

It was a good reminder to keep his distance.

Turning away, he caught his grandfather's hand twitching. Duke immediately moved to his bedside and took a knee. He held Grandpa Lor's hand in his as he studied the older man's face. A bandage covered a gash high on his forehead. The bruising on his cheek where it hit the steering wheel looked the same as earlier. At least there wasn't any additional swelling since he was last here.

Calling a nurse might take resources away from his grandmother, so he watched his grandfather for signs he was waking up out of his coma.

"Hey, Grandpa Lor. It's Duke," he whispered as hot tears pricked his eyes. Did his grandfather know his wife was in trouble? Did he somehow sense it?

Those two had the kind of connection others aspired to but rarely achieved. One of their sons found it but died young, and the other one gave up on family life after having three kids.

"The doctors and nurses are taking good care of Grandma Lacy," Duke promised. "She'll be all right." One of those tears broke loose and ran down his cheek, leaving a hot trail in its wake. "Come back to us whenever you're ready. We'll be here waiting for you. In the meantime, they're taking good care of your girl."

How's my girl? was the way Grandpa Lor would greet his wife every morning when she joined him in the kitchen. He knew the exact time she woke up and had a cup of coffee waiting for her with a splash of milk, just the way she liked it.

Duke had asked his grandfather once how the two of them had kept the spark up all these years.

We finally got the hang of marriage after about the fifteen year mark, he'd explained with a laugh. The early years, he'd said, were about figuring each other out and compromise. Something he admitted to being bad at until he found his wife sitting in a chair looking out the window with a suitcase open on the bed. Tears streaked her cheeks.

Right then and there, I realized how much of a jerk I'd been. She wasn't asking for much but deserved the world. I asked myself why on earth I would treat the love of my life the stubborn way I had been.

Grandpa Lor had said from then on, his thinking changed. He wanted his wife to know how much he loved her and needed her. His change had been overnight, but it took time for her to trust it would stick.

"Show me a sign you're still in there, Grandpa Lor," Duke whispered. It struck him as strange how small and frail his grandfather was lying there instead of just looking like he was peacefully sleeping. Duke had no idea how someone in a coma was supposed to look, to be fair. Still, he hadn't expected to see the man who had no problem throwing a fifty-pound bag of feed over each shoulder looking like this. "Squeeze my hand." *Do something*.

Watching his grandfather lie there motionless with a breathing tube sticking out of his mouth had to be one of the most unnatural sights Duke had ever seen.

For a second, he debated checking the nurses' stand to ask about the tremors in his grandfather's hand but decided against it now that they'd stopped. There were no other signs of him waking out of the coma, so Duke let it be.

Waiting was the worst. Not sleeping for almost two days wore his nerves thin.

"What's happening in there?" Audrey finally asked in a voice slightly above a whisper as she took to pacing around the room.

"Your guess is as good as mine," he admitted. "Part of me wants to attempt to slip into the room but I'd end up being a distraction."

"I feel the same," she said. "I'd use my badge if it would help, but I highly doubt it would and the last thing I want to do is take attention away from where it needs to stay, focused on your grandmother."

"We could go downstairs and grab more coffee," he offered, figuring a walk might do them both some good.

"Yeah, okay," she said. "But maybe water this time."

There was a time when he believed he could read her mind. Of course, he'd been wrong or he would have seen her disappearing act coming. He should have known the perfect summer wouldn't last and neither would the perfect girl. Whatever temporary magic they'd had at sixteen had disappeared. Too many years had passed. They'd become different people.

Duke stood up as he released his grandpa's hand. He

stalled for a second, wishing the older man would reach for him. He didn't.

It was too early to give up hope. His grandfather could wake up any minute. The first person he would look for was his wife. Once the emergency passed in the next room, could Duke pull some strings to get his grandparents moved into the same room?

He followed Audrey out of the dimly lit room into the bright hallway with rows of fluorescent lighting in the ceiling. They took it slow as they passed Grandma Lacy's room. Activity still buzzed inside, which he took as a good sign. Leaving the floor was more difficult than he anticipated, but he forced himself to get into the elevator anyway.

The cafeteria was on the first floor. It was a bright room with a wall of vending machines offering everything from lattes to brisket sandwiches. The art on the walls was what could only be described as cheery with yellows and oranges.

Duke bought a hardboiled egg to go with his coffee. Audrey picked out yogurt to go with her water. Neither spoke false reassurances that his grandmother would magically be all right, and he appreciated it. Life didn't always work out the way folks wanted it to. People died, sometimes at the hands of cruel individuals. Life wasn't always fair. Period. Duke's family was no different. They weren't special. Life could deliver a blow to them just as easily as it could anyone else. And just to prove a point, it had many times over, beginning with Duke's parents.

"How about sitting here for a minute while we eat?" Audrey asked, motioning toward a four-top table near to the door.

"Okay."

The cafeteria had a view to a courtyard outdoors. It was

too hot to sit outside, so he wouldn't suggest heading out there even though fresh air sounded good to him about now.

Duke took a seat across from Audrey at the square table. They positioned themselves where both could see the door. Being in law enforcement had trained him never to sit with his back to a door. The habit carried over into his off-duty time, as was the case with every other law enforcement officer he knew. Audrey was no exception.

Two bites later, he'd polished off his egg. Eating wasn't high on his list right now, but it would put something in his stomach to balance out the coffee. He fished out his cell phone and checked to see if word had spread to any of the others about their grandmother. Relief washed over him when there were no emergency messages or requests for information. The minute he had information to share, he would provide an update to his cousins and sisters. Mesa Point was a small town, and word could spread like wildfire if it wasn't contained. His family would hear the news from him first.

A woman entered the cafeteria. Stephanie Napier. Her gaze locked onto Audrey, and a concerned look wrinkled her forehead.

The encounter Duke had been hoping to avoid was about to happen. Dammit.

"I HEARD YOU were in here," Stephanie said to Audrey. The woman's laser focus caused Audrey to sit up a little straighter in her chair. As far as nightmares went, this one was right up there.

"We should go," Duke said as he pushed to standing.

"Do you have any idea what the sheriff wants?" Stephanie asked Audrey, undeterred by Duke's statement. "I just got the message that he wants me to meet him at my home, but he won't say what for."

Audrey could lie and say she had no idea except that her name would certainly come up as the target of Jenson's infatuation, if it was one.

"I'm sorry to interrupt," Duke continued, unfazed. "But my grandmother coded upstairs, and we were just heading up."

Audrey appreciated him trying to spare her the inquiry from Stephanie.

Jenson's mother was five and a half feet tall, give or take, with long straight hair tied back in a low ponytail. Her face was oval, her ears a little too big for how thin it was. Eyes were a deep shade of cobalt blue. Stephanie had brackets around her mouth and fine lines above her lip from years of smoking despite covering the smell with a strong breath mint. She wore scrubs and her name tag marked her as an RN. Other than scrubs, she had on tennis shoes and very little, if any, makeup.

"I just thought maybe we could clear up whatever it is he wants," Stephanie said on a shrug. "Nothing surprises me anymore with two teenagers, but they're good kids. I got the sense this was something urgent."

"Go home," Audrey gently urged. "Speak to my boss."

Stephanie stood there for a long moment. "Should I be worried?"

"You should get in your car and drive home as safely as possible," Audrey said, dodging the question as best she could. "I'll stop by after in case you have any other questions."

A thinly tweezed eyebrow shot up. She opened her mouth to speak, but Duke came up beside Audrey and placed his hand on the back of her arm.

"I'm afraid we really do have to go now," he said to Stephanie. "My apologies for being rude, but this is urgent and we need to get back upstairs."

"Yeah. No. Of course." Stephanie shook her head. "Sorry. I just thought maybe I could avoid a trip home, but it sounds like I need to clock out."

Before Audrey could say another word, Duke ushered her out the door.

"Thank you," she said out of the corner of her mouth once they were inside the elevator.

"You're welcome," he said as they rode up the lift.

Heart pounding inside her chest as the doors opened, she wasn't sure if she should breathe a sigh of relief when the nurses' station was full of nurses again. She scanned their faces. No one came across as distressed. Was that a good sign? Or were they too used to losing patients? So much so, it had become almost routine? Although, she knew deep down the loss of life would never be routine. Not for law enforcement officers and not for nurses or doctors. They all developed their own unique coping mechanisms, but losing someone on their watch would always be personal.

"My grandmother," Duke said to the first nurse they came across. Audrey reached for his hand, and he immediately linked their fingers and gave a little squeeze.

"Lacy Remington," the nurse said. "Is that who you're referring to?"

"Yes, ma'am," he confirmed.

"As you already might know, she went into cardiac arrest," the nurse said with compassion. "The team was able to revive her, and her heart is beating just fine now on its own." She gave them a warning look not to get too excited. "Her case is still very much touch-and-go, but she won this battle."

Audrey didn't realize she'd been holding her breath. She released a slow exhale at the news of Gram Lacy's condition. It was enough to provide hope for a meaningful recovery. Both of the Remington grandparents needed to get better soon.

"I have to ask a question," Duke began, and she knew exactly where he was about to go.

The nurse gave him a tentative nod.

"My grandparents have been together for most of their lives. Seeing them in separate rooms doesn't seem right," he explained.

Duke had a way with people. Audrey would bank on the fact the nurse wouldn't still be listening if Audrey was the one doing the speaking. He put people at ease. In fact, the nurse was leaning toward him. It didn't take a body language expert to figure out she was really listening to him.

"I have no doubt in my mind they would do better if they were together in the same room," he said. "Hell, push their beds as close together as they'll go. I promise you both of them will improve. It'll give them a fighting chance."

"I'm sorry," she said, shaking her head as her face twisted in regret. "Hospital policy."

She wore the standard issue blue scrubs—a color that said she meant business. Audrey appreciated having a serious nurse look after the people she cared most about. Could he convince the woman to put his grandparents in the same room against hospital policy was the question.

"As much as I'd like to help, we can't make special arrangements—"

Duke glanced down at the name on the ID badge sewn above her pocket. "Arlene," he started, catching her gaze, "doesn't it make sense to do what's right for each individual case? I can see in your eyes that you care about your work more than most."

She nodded and made a face that said she agreed with that statement more than anyone could realize.

Duke Remington was a smooth talker. His natural good looks and easy-going charm were addictive.

"I know you want to help my grandparents, Arlene," he continued in the easy way he had with people.

Arlene stood there for a long moment, almost transfixed as she stared into his eyes. Then came, "I'll call the floor supervisor."

Chapter Eight

Duke argued his case to the floor supervisor, a nurse by the name of Jenn. Jenn didn't look ready to budge on the issue.

Audrey, who had been quiet up to now, intervened. "Hi, Jenn. Look, I'm going to be honest with you here. This family is very important to me and the rest of the community. Do you know the Remingtons personally?"

Jenn nodded. "We don't have Sunday supper together if that's what you're asking, but I run into Lacy Remington at the grocery from time to time."

"Sweet people, aren't they?" Audrey continued.

"As a matter of fact, yes, they're the best," Jenn agreed. Her stance softened. "I'll see what I can do."

Jenn disappeared down the hall before returning a few moments later. "We can make an exception this time."

"I can't thank you enough," Duke stated.

"Don't mention it," Jenn said as she stared at Lacy and Lorenzo's rooms. "I don't believe I've ever seen two people more in love than your grandparents." She shook her head and blinked a couple of times. Duke glanced over at Jenn's ring finger and saw a tan line where a gold band was at one time. He didn't know if it was divorce or death, but Jenn had lost her husband in one form or another.

"They had...*have* something real special," Duke agreed.

Jenn sniffed and then coughed. "I'll see to it these two are moved into the same room before I leave the floor."

Now that his grandparents' situation was settled, Duke could turn his attention to taking Audrey to the Napiers' house. Stephanie Napier would have had plenty of time to get home and receive the news about her son by now. Audrey had laid the groundwork for their visit in the cafeteria. All that was left was for them to stop by her home and see if they could find some answers as to what Jenson was doing hiding in the woods, watching Audrey's place.

The teen was probably doing what they believed, peeping, but Audrey would sleep better at night if she had her questions answered. And, honestly, Duke wanted a few answers, as well.

The sheriff's text, as he'd promised, confirmed he'd delivered the news.

"We should probably head over to the Napier home," he suggested, hating that he was the one to remove the smile from Audrey's lips. They were in the shape of Cupid's bow, he noticed, and he burned with the memory of how they felt moving against his. "I just got word from the sheriff that they're finishing up."

It was probably all this focus on true love that was softening his heart—a heart that Audrey had shattered a long time ago. Even though they'd been together for hours now, he still had no idea why she'd left or where she'd gone.

The past was best left there as far as he was concerned.

AUDREY STAYED QUIET on the ride to the Napiers'. No matter what she believed about Jenson Napier, or believed him to be might be a better way to put it, his mother truly had had no idea what the sheriff might want to say to her.

Parents rarely saw their teens as they were. Then again, young people at that age were trying to figure themselves out, so it would be impossible for their parents to know them. Puberty changed most everything about them for a few years at least, or so she'd been told time and time again by surprised parents. Surprised because she was at their door with their once-sweet-and-innocent child who'd been caught breaking into a vehicle or with an illegal substance. The first time it happened was always a shock, even when the parents admitted their child had become withdrawn and they'd been worried about them. There was a fine line in the teen years between giving them space when they became sullen and too introspective, and realizing they'd gone to a dark side and needed to be pulled back.

For this and many other reasons, Audrey had no plans to become a mother. Becoming a parent was a terrible thing to do to a child, in her opinion. If anyone had doubts, they could take her family as living proof.

Duke parked in front of the small ranch-style house in a tree-lined neighborhood near the hospital. Chain-link fences encased front yards, and a cracked sidewalk reflected the damage from too-hot summers and too much sun.

He checked his phone. "The sheriff left five minutes ago."

Any excuse to turn around and bolt was gone, too. So Audrey took in a deep breath and exited the truck as Duke came around the front to open her door.

She used to like when he opened doors for her. Not now. It reminded her too much of how they used to be with each other in a more innocent time. She remembered too easily how sweet he'd been with her and how hard she'd fallen for him in a matter of days after arriving at the Remington ranch.

Audrey remembered how timid she'd been like it was yesterday. She'd hid her bruises under makeup and refused to come out of her room the first few days after arriving at the ranch. Crystal, Jules and Abi tried knocking on her door at different times to check on her, which she appreciated. But it was Duke who sat next to her door and told her to take her time.

He'd reassured her there was nothing to be afraid of, that no one could get to her while he was sitting outside the door. He slept sitting up those first few nights, sensing she'd come from a dangerous situation. One night, she sat on the opposite side of the door with her back against it, hugging her knees into her chest, talking. She didn't say much at first. He opened up, though. He acquainted her with everyone on the ranch, giving her the ins and outs of everyone's personality. He shared his favorite color, light blue like the sky on a spring morning. He shared his favorite food, slow-cooked brisket. And he shared his fear that he would grow up and be just like his own father.

The last admission resonated. The raw honesty struck a nerve inside her that gave her the courage to open up a little bit to him. The next night, she kept the door cracked when they talked, with only the moonlight pouring in her window. It took a week to work up to being in the same room.

Eventually, Duke sat on her floor, his back against the dresser and hers against the bed frame as they got to know each other. Audrey wished she could tell him everything, all the horror she'd been through and how much she blamed herself for the abuse she'd suffered at the hands of her parents after her sister's death. By the end of the summer, she'd been close to being able to open up that part of herself.

The Remingtons asked no questions. They welcomed a stranger into their home. In three months, they showed Audrey what unconditional love meant.

And then, Audrey had to leave. She had to walk away from the temporary sanctuary and back to a life she never wanted.

"Hey." Duke's voice broke through the dark heavy cloud of thoughts.

Audrey realized she'd stopped in front of the gate at the Napier home. "Sorry."

"Where'd you go just now?" Duke asked, his forehead creased with concern.

"Nowhere," she quickly said. Too quickly? She probably just gave herself away, but she couldn't talk about those memories with him, and she sure as hell didn't want to lie. That would betray everything they'd shared. She shook her head. "The past. Sometimes it rears its ugly head, and I..." She flashed her eyes at him.

"It's okay," he reassured her, but there was distance in his tone.

It was fine. Necessary. For the good of both of them. Getting too close would be touching a hot stove twice. Because this time, he would be the one to leave, and it would break her. Audrey couldn't, wouldn't go there again. Losing him once was enough for one lifetime.

Audrey mentally shook off the fog, reached for the handle and pushed the gate open. "After you."

Duke's smile didn't reach his eyes when he said, "Not a chance. You go first." He put his hand on the gate to keep it from automatically closing and then held out his free hand to usher her inside the yard.

Several of the yards in the neighborhood had toys littered around. There was a dump truck in one, and a bright orange-and-blue plastic slide that stood about four feet high in another. In the Napiers' yard, there were no such signs of small children. They'd had two teenagers...*had* being the operative word. And they had just received the life-altering news no parent should ever have to endure.

It was impossible to be mad at Jenson for what he'd done even though Audrey still felt violated by the young man.

Standing in front of the Napiers' front door, she had a moment of hesitation about knocking. She'd been so certain this visit would make a difference in the way she slept at night. Would it? Would it make a hill of beans' difference? Or would it just rub salt in a wound?

Based on Stephanie Napier's reaction at the hospital, the woman still fell into the camp of blissfully unaware parents.

Before Audrey could change her mind, the door swung open, and Stephanie stood on the other side. Her red-rimmed eyes and tearstained cheeks confirmed the sheriff had already paid a visit just like his text had said.

"Come inside," Stephanie said before turning around and walking away, leaving the door open.

Chapter Nine

Duke placed his hand on the small of Audrey's back as gentle reassurance before they walked inside the Napier house. She glanced up at him with a look of appreciation that stirred a place deep inside. She'd always done that to him, from the first time they met face-to-face in her hallway under the moonlight to now, years later, despite all the baggage between them.

Morris Napier stood five feet eleven inches if Duke had to guess. He was thick with muscular arms and tree trunks for legs. Funny how this man had seemed so big to Duke when he was just a young buck back in middle school and Morris was twenty years old. Morris was known for making a living by cutting firewood. He'd buy slabs from sawmills, then bring 'em home to cut in his shed. When Duke, his sisters and cousins came into town for trick-or-treating, Morris built out a full-fledged haunted house inside his shed, complete with gooey slime for brains and jump scares. That was a long time ago.

"Mr. Napier," Duke said, extending a hand to the bearded man. His defeated demeanor wasn't at all like the normally good-natured person Duke recalled. To be expected, though, after hearing devastating news.

The broken father took Duke's hand and still gave it a vigorous shake. "I'm guessing you're here about my boy." Morris's voice hitched on the last word.

"Yes, sir," Duke said, hating to do anything that might add to the Napiers' pain.

"Can I fix either of you a cup of coffee?" Stephanie asked after perfunctory greetings.

"No, thank you," Audrey said.

"I'm good," Duke added. "If you need one, go ahead. We'll wait."

Stephanie shot him a look that was a mix of gratitude and sorrow. It was one of the most pitiful expressions Duke had ever witnessed. It was the look of a mother who'd just lost her young son and was still trying to process the news.

"We can sit here at the table," Stephanie urged, twisting her hands together.

The Napier home looked like almost any other in the area with a circular recliner-style couch directly across from an oversize flat-screen TV. There was an oval-shaped coffee table in between, with stacks of magazines and books on top along with a few porcelain figurines. A basketball sat to one side of the room. Duke wanted to ask if it belonged to Jenson but figured it wasn't important under the circumstances. He was curious about the teen's life and his habits that might have led him to think peeping on women was a good idea.

The adjacent dining room housed a large mahogany table with six chairs and a matching hutch filled with plates and trinkets.

"First and foremost, I'd like to offer my condolences," Audrey said to Stephanie and Morris after they took seats beside each other at the table.

Duke and Audrey sat opposite them at the oval-shaped six-seat dining table.

"Thank you," Stephanie said. All the nurses he knew were tough on the outside. They'd seen more than most and had watched folks take their last breaths while in their arms. They knew how to do hard things. Stephanie was no exception. Her eyes had deep lines carved underneath, and her mouth had deep grooves.

Morris, on the other hand, was a big teddy bear. A steady stream of tears leaked from his eyes. The tip of his nose was red, and his shoulders were hunched forward.

There were no signs of abuse or neglect in the home, but that didn't always mean what it should. Even teens who were well cared for went astray, got involved in illegal substances or bought prescription pills from friends to dabble with because it looked cool or they thought it might make someone like them more. Some of those kids ended up addicted, and what happened from then on always broke their families' hearts. It happened in good families. It happened in bad families. Duke had heard enough stories to realize no one was immune.

Stephanie reached for Morris's hand as though to steel herself against what was coming next. "You came here for a reason."

"Yes, we did," Audrey began, leaning forward and clasping her hands on top of the table. "I'd like to hear more about Jenson's known activities."

"What do you mean?" Stephanie asked with a perplexed look. "Was he in some kind of trouble?"

It was Duke's turn to lean forward. "He was hanging out—"

Before he could finish his sentence, the front door swung

open and a teenage girl burst into the adjacent living room. Halsey, Jenson's sister.

"Mom. Dad," she said as she scanned everyone's faces, looking barely able to contain her emotions—emotions that were the equivalent of a volcano about to erupt. "Is it true?"

"Sweetie, come sit down," Stephanie said, motioning toward the nearest empty chair.

"No," Halsey said. "Not until you answer my question."

Stephanie took in a slow breath. "Yes, I'm afraid it is."

"Jenson's gone?" Halsey continued as the first sob tore from her throat.

"Yes, honey," her mother said, pushing up to standing as the teen came barreling toward her mother.

How did Halsey hear the news?

Duke had been forced to deliver bad news to families. It was all in a day's work. He had been fortunate never to have to do this with anyone he knew. And although he wouldn't exactly say he knew the Napiers well, he'd seen them around town his entire life, and the situation hit hard. He could only imagine what it must be doing to Audrey, who called Mesa Point home.

Stephanie guided her daughter to the table after a long embrace and then introduced her to him and Audrey. He reached for Audrey's hand under the table to find it trembling. She calmed down after he linked their fingers.

Duke leaned forward and clasped his hands together. "How did you find out?"

"My best friend is Clifford's cousin," Halsey said. "He called to check on her when we were together and told her what happened. Told me that I should get home but, like, I couldn't believe it."

Duke nodded.

"I was just telling these nice people about your brother,"

Stephanie said to Halsey before turning her attention toward Audrey. "You were asking about…"

"Known activities," Audrey clarified when Stephanie couldn't pull up the answer.

"Right," Stephanie said. "Well, he goes to school and does his homework."

Halsey blew out a loud breath as she crossed her arms over her chest. She shook her head. "That's what you guys think. He's been forcing Landry to do his homework all year."

"Landry Pickens?" Stephanie asked, clearly shocked at this development.

"Yes," Halsey continued in a defiant tone. "I know you guys think Jenson is perfect, but he wasn't."

"Halsey," Stephanie admonished.

"Ma'am," Duke said with as much respect and courtesy as he could muster. This was going to be tricky territory, and he would have to navigate it carefully. "Would you mind allowing your daughter to explain?"

Stephanie looked lost for a moment. But then she nodded. "Go ahead. Maybe we'll all learn something new about my son."

"All I'm saying is that Jenson wasn't the perfect kid you and Dad believe he was," Halsey said like that explained everything. She sat there in a leather bomber jacket, looking more street-smart than she probably was.

"Do you have examples other than forcing someone to do his homework?" Audrey asked, her voice calm.

A picture of a bully was emerging.

"I mean, yeah, my brother wasn't exactly a nice person," Halsey continued. "Like, everybody knew he was getting into bad cra—"

Halsey stopped long enough to glance at her parents.

Shoulders hunched forward, she apologized for almost swearing in the tone only a teenager could pull off. "I'm sorry, but it's true. Jenson became a real jerk last year."

"Do you have any guesses as to why?" Audrey asked.

"I don't know," she huffed. "He started liking a girl who was trouble, and she treated him like cr—"

Once again, she stopped herself in time.

"Her friends picked on him after they found out he had a crush on her," Halsey explained. "My brother was already hanging around with the wrong crowd. The boys from Hardeeville were being bused to our school. Jenson wanted to be cool, I guess." She shrugged. "And now he, like, what... How did it happen?"

"No one is certain until the report comes back but he was found in the lake with blood on the scene," Audrey said as Stephanie winced. The sheriff might have explained his hypothesis on method of death. Of course, he would.

Halsey's face wrinkled. "How did that happen? He never went into the water. He didn't know how to swim to save his life." She seemed to catch those last words too late as they left her mouth. The teenager shot a look of apology to her parents.

Being rejected by a girl and ridiculed could have caused Jenson to resent females. It could have been motive enough to lurk in the shadows watching Audrey, who was a beautiful woman. There might be any number of reasons he would have targeted her. She might have been nice to him at some point during an interaction that was routine for her but caught his attention. Made him feel like he might have a chance with her? Made her a target?

It was a logical progression that couldn't be ignored. Also, it wasn't uncommon for kids who were bullied to become bullies themselves.

Audrey released her grip on Duke's hand underneath the table and made a motion like she was about to get up. She stopped herself and turned to Halsey. "What kind of shoes did your brother wear?"

She was smart to ask his fashion-conscious sister. The girl would notice these things.

"Vans," Halsey supplied. "All the time. He doesn't even own a skateboard."

"What about boots?" Audrey pressed.

"Like cowboy boots?" Halsey's face puckered like she'd crammed her mouth full of Sour Patch Kids candy.

"Work boots," Audrey corrected. "Does he own a pair?"

Halsey laughed. That was the thing with teenagers, their emotions were all over the place and could change as easily as flipping the light on. "My brother wouldn't be caught..." She stopped, and then shook her head rather than finish her sentence.

Duke figured now was as good a time as any to ask the all-important question. "Mind if we take a look in his room?"

STEPHANIE BALKED, and for a minute, Audrey thought they'd lost her.

"Is that really necessary?" Stephanie asked. "To disturb his room? I mean, tell me what you're looking for, and I'll go check." Her gaze bounced from Duke to Audrey and back. "Boots? Is that what you're trying to find?"

"Yes. I'm looking for a certain kind of boot." Audrey had taken note that Morris wore cowboy boots. Actually, he had on socks and no shoes, but his boots were stationed at the front door where she suspected he usually came inside.

Could he have work boots? Yes. Could they be some-where else in the house? Yes. Did most men have more than one shoe? Yes. However, the shoe worn the most was either on their feet or kept near the door in her experience.

Jenson Napier fit the mold of a Peeping Tom since he wasn't accepted by the opposite sex and was bullied for liking a female then became a bully himself. Based on what Halsey had said, he was a loner. But Audrey was still trying to pull an interaction out of her brain between the two of them and couldn't. Could the young person who'd shamed him resemble Audrey in some small way? It could be as simple as that. Often times, the easy answer was the right one.

Of course, despite the circumstantial evidence, Jenson might not be the person they were looking for. He might have innocently been in the woods and then been spooked by a noise or realized they were coming for him.

No, it didn't follow logic. Why would he be there except to watch her? Why would he run if he didn't have something to hide? Did he know they'd figured out someone was watching her? The boot prints had been smeared, which would indicate Jenson might have intentionally blurred them.

Stephanie crossed her arms over her chest. "Can I ask what this visit is really about?"

"Isn't it obvious, Mom?" Halsey chimed in. "Jenson probably committed a crime or something, and they're trying to, like, prove it was him."

"I get that," Stephanie stated, her tone clipped. "But why? He's gone. It isn't like he can be brought up on charges anymore. My son is dead."

Morris wrapped an arm around his wife. "This conversation is upsetting her. Is this really necessary?"

As unlikely as it might be, Audrey had to make absolutely certain there wasn't someone else out there watching women. Peeping Toms escalated. Always. She had to be certain it was over or risk it happening to someone else all over again. Someone who wouldn't figure it out before it was too late.

A small voice in the back of her mind reminded her that she was doing this for herself, too. She was attempting to gain some peace of mind. Because no one got to make her feel unsafe again.

"I'm afraid so," Audrey said with as much sympathy as she could muster. She felt it, too.

"Why didn't the sheriff ask any of these questions?" Morris asked. The man was clearly protecting his wife.

It twisted Audrey's heart in her chest to tell these parents their son wasn't the person they'd believed him to be. His sister had caught on. She'd assaulted his character. But her comment about him being rejected and made fun of by females his age made him a good candidate for becoming a Peeper.

"Sheriff Ackerman had to deliver the worst possible news to parents," Audrey explained. "He didn't want me here to say that your son might be implicated in a crime."

"I'll ask again," Stephanie interjected. "What does it matter now?"

"Because if by some chance it wasn't your son, there's someone out there who needs to be locked behind bars before someone gets hurt," Audrey said as calmly as she could muster.

Stephanie winced like she'd just taken a physical blow while Morris hung his head. Halsey huffed a few breaths out.

"I don't know if my brother did what you think he did, but I can guarantee you that he wouldn't be seen wearing work boots," Halsey said, matter of fact.

"Then it shouldn't be a problem if we take a look in his room," Audrey hedged. It was a long shot at this point, but one worth taking.

Chapter Ten

Morris Napier stood up and looked Duke dead in the eye. "I think you'd better leave."

Audrey opened her mouth to respond, but Duke knew when they needed to head out. He touched her arm to signal they should listen.

Clamping her mouth closed, she stood up. When she did speak, it was to apologize for the intrusion and to offer condolences once again. The Napiers' emotions were still too raw to listen to reason, and they clearly rejected the idea their son might be a criminal.

Wasn't that always the case? It was always the folks who swore their child would never do anything wrong who ended up being the most surprised when they found out otherwise. But this wasn't the time to push this family while they were processing their son's death.

Duke followed Audrey out the door, which was shut behind them. They weren't exactly kicked out, but the Napiers definitely weren't sad to see them go.

"Thank you for keeping me in check in there," Audrey said as they walked to the truck. "We were so close that I overstepped. I pushed when I should have pulled back."

"There's a reason folks don't work on investigations

when they're too personally involved," he said. "You're not the first person to lose objectivity."

"That may be so, but I pride myself on being good at my job under normal circumstances," she said as he opened her door.

"You don't have to convince me," he said before closing the door. After reclaiming the driver's seat, he added, "Seeing you at work is impressive. You maintained your temperament when too many others wouldn't have kept their composure. You're being hard on yourself if you think you didn't do an amazing job in there."

"Thank you," she said quietly. "That means a lot coming from you. And I don't normally overstep my bounds or insert myself into an investigation that I'm not officially involved in or that my boss has specifically asked me to leave alone."

He started the engine and put the gearshift into Drive before easing down the street. They needed a change in topic, something to lighten the intense mood. "What are the odds we would both end up working in law enforcement?"

Audrey blew out a breath as she eased back into her seat. His attempts to redirect the conversation were failing. They were both tired. It had been a long day, and they'd barely eaten anything. The thought of dropping her off at her cabin and leaving her there to chew on the day sat like lard in his gut. "Do you want to grab something to eat?"

"No," she said. "I don't think I could get much down anyway." She rubbed her temples. "Did you see the looks on their faces?"

"Yes," he said. "If I was a betting person, I'd put money on this being the worst day of that family's life. But that wasn't your fault."

Audrey gave a small nod. "Why do I have a nagging feeling we somehow have this wrong?"

"Was it the boot comment from Halsey?" he asked.

"That didn't help," she said. "Jenson is dead. He literally ran from the exact spot where the perp stood. Why is there part of me that believes this is too easy?"

"You know the first rule of an investigation," Duke reminded.

"The easy answer is usually the right answer." There was no enthusiasm in her voice.

"It's also a mistake to make a final judgment this early in the case," he reasoned.

"The evidence led us to Jenson Napier," she conceded. "The evidence is never wrong."

"It's still early, though," he pointed out. "And everything we have is circumstantial. As far as I know, the sheriff hasn't located any binoculars or a phone with pictures of you on it."

"I seriously doubt Ackerman is going to go to those lengths, considering he didn't ask the family if Jenson owned a pair of boots."

A few beats of silence passed as Duke pulled up to Audrey's cabin.

"I guess this is where we say goodbye," she said before exiting the truck in a hurry. She rushed to her door before he could roll his window down and shout at her.

Was their time together over? Was that the thing that had him riled up? Or was it something else?

Jenson was dead. She was safe. Shouldn't that be the end of the story?

They didn't have definitive proof Jenson acted alone, if in fact he turned out to be responsible. He might have done this on a dare. Was that possible? Could Jenson have been spying instead of peeping? It would make a huge difference in the severity of his crime. Halsey already said he was trying to impress the so-called cool group of kids. Would that include taking a picture of a beautiful—and less clothed—female deputy?

Now that Jenson was gone, would the prank die out?

Seeing a family's heart collectively break would never become easier. As law enforcement, Duke had become good at compartmentalizing. It was a job necessity. Anyone who couldn't wouldn't last in his chosen profession. Audrey was no different. He'd been paying attention to her reactions to the family, to what questions she'd asked and the manner in which she asked them. Then there was the scare with the Ponytail Snatcher. Would he act so close to where he'd almost been caught by the FBI?

Realizing he hadn't updated the family, he put a note on the group chat to let them know what had happened and that everything was stable now.

Duke didn't realize he'd been sitting in front of Audrey's cabin for a solid fifteen minutes until the door swung open again and he checked the time on the dashboard of his truck. Her head popped out the door first, then she came walking out with a confused look on her face. He hit the button to roll the passenger-side window down.

"Are you planning on sitting here all night?" she asked.

"Didn't realize how much time had gone by, to be honest." It might be a bad explanation, but it was the truth.

"You asked if I was hungry before," she said, glancing over to the general area where someone had stood and watched her. She trembled before regaining her composure. "I didn't think I could eat a bite after the day I've had until my stomach reminded me food is a necessity. What I'm saying is that I could eat something if the offer still stands."

"It does," he said, as relief he had no right to washed over him.

"Okay." She tapped the windowsill a couple of times with her palm. "I'll run inside, get my purse and be right back."

It was probably for the best she hadn't invited him inside to eat. The less time he spent in Audrey's house, the better. Getting too comfortable would be a mistake he wouldn't make twice.

"What sounds good?" he asked after she returned to the truck and climbed into the passenger seat. He noticed her gaze trained on the trees. "Everything okay?"

"I just keep getting this creepy feeling someone is watching me," she said. "But I don't see anyone out there. I don't see any movement. I'm starting to think my imagination is running wild."

"It happens," he reassured, trying to soothe her nerves that were fried.

"Chicken-fried steak smothered in cream gravy with some fried okra and mashed potatoes," she said after a pause. "And peach cobbler with a dollop of vanilla ice cream for dessert." Her lips compressed.

"Sounds like a visit to Mesa Café is in order," he decided. Mama Bea's place had the best chicken-fried steak in the county, hell in the state.

"She swears business was ruined after the restaurant was featured on that Food Network show about small-town diners," Audrey said with a chuckle.

It was good to hear her laugh even if it was just a little and tightly contained. He missed the sound of her laugh.

He should have known she wasn't going to stay at the ranch forever. On some level, he probably did. What he hadn't expected was for her to break up with him and cut off all possible lines of communication with no way to know if she was all right.

Maybe the last part had haunted him the most. She'd clearly been through some kind of trauma in her life. At six-teen, he'd noticed the bruises she covered up with makeup despite never calling her out on them.

But for tonight, he would set aside his questions because Mama Bea's food demanded full attention, and he couldn't think of a better person to share a meal with than Audrey.

"The meal you mentioned is Grandpa Lor's favorite," he said to Audrey.

"I bring it to him the first Monday of every month." She practically beamed when she said it.

"I didn't know that," Duke responded, surprised by the admission.

"Oh," she said, clearly keeping something else from him.

"You can't leave me hanging like that," he said as he pulled into the parking lot and found a spot way off to the side.

"Not to change the subject, but there sure are a lot of cars in this parking lot," she noted, the stress back in her voice.

"Yes, there are," he agreed.

"Mind if we order on the phone for pickup and just eat in the truck?" she asked.

"We can do that," he said, figuring there was a story be-hind the reason she didn't want to be around folks right now. Was she worried about being tied to the Napier boy's death? And how others might react to her because of it? Or were her tingly, being-watched senses being triggered again?

AUDREY PULLED HER phone out of her purse and put in her order after searching the vehicles in the lot. "What'll you have?"

"The same as you," he said. "It's Bea's specialty."

"I'm holding off on dessert until after dinner," she said, focusing her attention on the screen while hoping he didn't decide to push her on the reason she wanted to sit in the truck. "Can't have the ice cream melt."

"I didn't know Bea opened her business up to online ordering," he said, sounding impressed.

"Progress," she chirped. "Businesses had to change up over the last few years if they wanted to survive. Bea's place was no different."

"I'm glad she did," he said. "Survive, that is. I can't imagine a Mesa Point without Bea's place."

"The food scene would definitely suffer," Audrey agreed, hearing the note of tension laced her own voice.

As much as she wished she could relax and forget, she couldn't.

"So what happens now that the order is in?" he asked.

"They'll bring it to the truck if we park in a designated spot," she explained. "Or I'll get a text and one of us can run inside to pick it up."

"I'll do it," he quickly said.

"You don't mind?"

"No reason to," he answered as he cut off the truck's engine and cracked the windows. He leaned his seat back like he was sitting at home in a recliner. "At least the evenings are starting to cool off. We won't fry in here with all the windows cracked."

"That's the only thing I don't like about living in Texas," she admitted. "The heat."

"Ever think about moving somewhere else?" he asked. "Somewhere cooler?"

"Me?" she asked, surprised he would even ask. "No. Texas is home despite its imperfections."

She fixed her seat to a more comfortable position so she could look out the windshield up at the stars. The velvety sky seemed to go on forever. It was one of the many things she loved about living in Mesa Point. She saw the vastness of the sky, and it reminded her that she was just a speck in a bigger, broader universe. That as much as her problems seemed insurmountable at times, she was insignificant by comparison.

"How about you?" she asked, turning the tables. "Ever see yourself leaving the state, living anywhere else?"

"I have a lovely home in Austin," he supplied. "I'm close to Lake Travis where there are rolling hills and wineries. Restaurants have moved in. I have every kind of food I could want at my fingertips. But I can't say the place feels like home. I haven't felt that since I moved away from the ranch, to be honest."

"Ever think about coming back?" she asked, wanting to know the answer to that question more than she wanted to admit.

Her cell buzzed, indicating a text. She checked the screen before turning it toward Duke for him to take a look.

"I'll be right back," he said, putting his seat up but keeping it far back from the steering wheel. "Hold tight." He opened the door and then paused. "You'll be all right in here alone, right?"

"I'm fine," she said, realizing it had become her favorite new word to describe herself despite being far from the truth. It wasn't exactly a lie. More like wishful thinking. Could she wish it into reality was the real question. "What I mean to say is that I'll be fine."

Duke turned back and smiled in a show of perfectly straight white teeth. He'd always had the kind of smile that lit campfires in her belly. It worked years ago. It worked now. And she couldn't imagine a time when it wouldn't. "I'll be back in a snap."

Audrey returned the smile and nodded. "I'll be right here."

Here was where she'd returned when she couldn't force the Remingtons, or more specifically Duke, out of her thoughts. She'd almost slipped earlier and told him that his grandparents asked her to stay away while he visited, figuring it would be easier on him.

They didn't make her feel shame for how she'd left things. They hadn't judged her.

Because they knew. They knew everything.

A vehicle turned toward where they were parked and turned the high beams on, practically blinding her. *What is that all about?*

Jerk!

The vehicle's engine idled. Her retinas burned when she tried to see who was behind the wheel. She had to put a hand up to shield her face from the light.

The tingly sensation returned, pricking the hairs on the back of her neck.

Jenson Napier was dead.

Who was this jerk? As she reached for the door handle, fear gripped her.

It couldn't be the Ponytail Snatcher. Could it?

Rather than open the door, she locked it instead as she slid down in the seat. It was then she realized she'd forgotten to strap her ankle holster on.

She had no weapon. No way to protect herself here on the backside of the lot.

The horn.

Sliding over toward the driver's seat, she laid her palm on the horn.

The vehicle backed away, kicking up a dust storm.

More of that panic gripped her as the cloud enveloped the walkway to the restaurant.

Duke.

Chapter Eleven

Duke stepped out of a dust cloud holding a bag of food in plastic containers. Audrey exhaled as he returned to his seat on the driver's side, which caught him off guard.

"Someone was here," she said, before adding, "Maybe. I think. It felt like maybe I was being stared at. Challenged?" She gave a quick rundown.

"By the jerk who did this?" He motioned toward the dust.

"Yes," she said.

Duke handed over the bag and then started the engine. "I'm guessing he went that way."

"Yes, but I have no idea which way after he left the parking lot," she admitted before reaching over and touching his arm. It was a move she'd done before to get him to stop and think. "I don't even know what kind of vehicle we'd be going after other than the fact the headlights were high enough to be a truck's. We'd be looking for another needle in a haystack."

Duke clenched his back teeth, wanting to go after the bastard. At the very least, he was a jerk.

"I could be way off base," she said. "Maybe we should just stay here and eat. See if he returns."

It took a few seconds for him to commit, but he finally nodded.

"The smell alone is making my mouth water," she said. "As much as I doubted I could hold any food down, let alone eat in the first place, I had a feeling Bea's would do the trick."

"She's a miracle worker in the kitchen," he agreed, surveying the lot as the cloud broke. "She also said to tell you hello."

He skipped the part about Bea telling him to give Audrey a huge hug from her. There was no way he was fulfilling that request. Getting close to Audrey physically was a bad idea. Years might have passed, he wanted to be over her, but she was still a beautiful woman who'd only managed to get better as she reached her thirties. She'd always been what folks called an old soul. He wouldn't disagree.

They took a minute to organize the plates and cutlery, balancing the plastic containers that reminded him of school lunch trays but cooler looking and with much better food. But he couldn't let it go that someone might have been trying to intimidate her?

"Can I ask a personal question?" Audrey asked in between bites.

"Shoot," he said.

"I thought surely you would be married by now. No wife?"

"You weren't kidding with the personal question," he quipped. He held up the third finger on his left hand. "No wife. No tan line. No desire to get married."

"Really?"

"Why do you sound so surprised?" he asked, keeping a watchful eye as folks entered and left Bea's.

She shrugged. "You just always struck me as the marrying type, I guess."

"Because of my grandparents?"

"Maybe," she said after taking another bite.

"What they have is special," he pointed out. "Not many folks get that. And the few who do, sometimes it gets ripped out from underneath 'em. Take my parents for instance. Now, my father is alive but abandoned his own children after our mother died giving birth."

"I knew you, your siblings and cousins lived with your grandparents for personal reasons, but I had no idea why," she admitted, sounding astonished. "You don't have anything to do with your father?"

"Why would I?" he asked.

"Point taken," she said. "I was dealt a terrible hand in the parent department." She blew out a breath. "Believe me when I say that my life would have been better off without knowing them. I come from the worst kind of evil, Duke."

Was she about to open up to him? Give him the reason she'd had to hide out?

Audrey visibly trembled. "I can't go there. Not even now." She shook like she could shake off whatever feeling had gripped her. "How did you guys turn out to be normal? People who don't walk around with a chip on their shoulders?"

"Living with our grandparents helped," Duke said, not sure that was completely true. The chip he'd carried had to do with losing her and not knowing why. Now, he realized she'd been surviving the best she could. Why was it still so hard to shake off the rejection? Bruised ego? It was clearer to him now that she'd had no choice back then. "We knew what it was like to be loved."

"I had no idea how horrible that must have been for you

and your sisters," Audrey explained. "Losing your mother and then your father taking off must have been awful to live through."

"Honestly, I was so young that I don't have any memories of either one," he admitted. "Just my grandparents and the six of us plus a bad taste in my mouth for the father who donated his DNA to me." He set his fork down. "All in all, I can't complain. I wouldn't change my childhood for the world."

Did he have a few emotional scars from losing his mother? Probably. But he'd tucked those away in a little box, too, and had no plans to revisit something that could only cause more pain. That would be like stepping into the boxing ring with a strong opponent and without training or gloves. Could he get in a few punches? Sure. Would he take more hits than he wanted to? Absolutely.

Why torture himself when he could keep that box closed and forget it ever existed?

"Your grandparents are amazing people, Duke. You definitely hit the jackpot there," Audrey said. "Do you ever wonder what your mother was like? Did you guys ever talk about her?"

"No, but I know exactly what kind of person my father is," he stated. "He's the kind of person who can walk away from an infant and two other children who just lost their mother. Not someone I particularly care to keep in touch with, if you know what I mean."

"It's understandable," she conceded, but there was a note in her voice that struck a chord in him, a chord he didn't want to acknowledge. It was curiosity.

"Look, I spent too many years thinking that man might show up at the ranch on my or one of my sisters' birthdays or Christmas," he explained, for reasons he had no plans to examine. "I literally sat in the front yard one day on my little suitcase because I built up a story in my head that he was coming for me when I got mad at my sisters. It took my grandmother to convince me to come back inside and be her taste tester for an apple pie she was baking. I didn't want to give up. Call me stubborn, but my eight-year-old self had decided this was the day my dad would return to the ranch. To this day, I still don't know why that day, of all days, I dug my heels in and decided he would show if I believed it enough."

"You didn't deserve to be abandoned," she said with compassion.

"He called," Duke continued. "I told him about the accident and the guy pretended to care for a minute but then decided he was too busy unless him visiting the hospital was absolutely necessary. Jerk."

A tidal wave of emotion crashed into him, catching him off guard. He turned his face toward the window and coughed. Tucking the memories back in its place, he resumed eating dinner. "Food's getting cold. We should probably just eat instead of talk."

"Okay," Audrey conceded when he expected her to fight. The look of compassion on her face spoke volumes, though. She picked up her fork and took another bite. "This is so good. I should probably come here more often just to remind myself why I live in Mesa Point on bad days."

"Not a half bad idea," he said.

"We can move on," she hedged. "But I just want you to know that your dad leaving had everything to do with him and nothing to do with you or your sisters. It wasn't your fault."

"Yeah?" he asked, but it was more statement than question. "It sure never felt that way."

A surprising amount of emotion flooded him at the thought of his dad. Anger. Hurt. Betrayal. Those were fierce and the ones he held tightly to his chest. Others joined them. Curiosity. There were times when he did want to talk to his father, to get answers to some of his questions at the very least. Like how he could have pulled a stunt like that when his children needed him most. Not to mention leaving Duke's grandparents with six children to raise, even though they never seemed to mind.

"I won't pretend to know how that feels, Duke. All I do know is that you, Crystal and Abi deserved better from your dad."

"We had our grandparents," he said. "We weren't missing out." As much as he wanted to believe those words, they felt like a lie. His grandparents had been the best surrogates he could have hoped for. But despite that love and kindness, every child still wanted love from their parents.

They'd talked enough about him for one evening.

"What about you, Audrey? In all our late-night talks in your bedroom, you never opened up about your family situation. What you said a minute ago is the most you've ever shared about them. Why is that? Didn't you trust me?"

She tensed like he'd thrown a punch, which made him feel like the worst kind of jerk.

"If you're done eating, you can take me home," Audrey said. She didn't talk about the past with anyone. Not even him.

She'd wanted to at sixteen but just couldn't put the horror into words. There'd been the all-too-real fear he would want to intervene or come to her defense. She'd had a lot of wild ideas back then. Talking about it now wouldn't change the past. It wouldn't change what had happened.

It wouldn't bring back her sister or stop her mother from putting out cigarettes on Audrey's back or her stepfather from attempting unspeakable acts of horror.

"Today has been hell on wheels," Duke explained, softening his tone. "I wasn't ready to talk about my mom. Bringing her up at all does nothing but cause pain even after all these years. I'm a grown man, and I don't need a mother. Our conversation struck a nerve, and I'm sorry that I turned the tables without warning. Since I can't take it back, all I can say is that I hope you'll forgive me for being a jerk."

"I'm the one who should apologize," she argued. "You obviously don't want to talk, and I pushed when I should have stayed out of it." She wanted to say that all she wished for him was that he could forgive himself when he'd done nothing wrong in the first place. "It's not my place to needle in your personal life, Duke. I'm truly sorry."

"Hey," he started. "Let's just forget the whole conversation happened and move on. Deal?"

"Okay," she agreed, even though her heart wasn't in it. She wanted to know more, dig deeper, find out what made him tick. But that wasn't an option on the table right now. She'd seen the hurt in his eyes when he looked at her. His grandparents had been right about one thing: she shouldn't try to cross paths with him while he was in town.

But she couldn't exit on that note. "Do you want to swing by the hospital on the way to dropping me off at the cabin? We could check on your grandparents."

"I thought you wanted dessert," he said.

"Maybe next time," she said, even though there wouldn't be another next time. She couldn't afford it with the way her heart betrayed her, wanting to be as close to Duke as possible. It was too hard, and besides, what would being close accomplish at the end of the day? Duke would go back to his job, and she would go back to hers. He wasn't the kind of person she could downshift and just be friends with no matter how much she wanted that option to be true.

"Since you asked me, turnabout is fair play," Duke said, breaking into her thoughts.

"What do you mean?"

"Why aren't you seeing anyone special?" he asked.

"There have been people in my life," she said, a little more defensively than intended. She wanted to add no one had been as special as him, but that wasn't the right thing to say under the circumstances. They were different people now. She was still in love with that sixteen-year-old, but time changed everything and everyone.

Duke's eyebrow shot up and a look of disdain crossed his features. Was it wrong she got a rush of satisfaction from his response? Probably. Still. She enjoyed it for a half second and the change in topic offered a break in the tension causing her shoulders to pull taut.

"Was I wrong about now?" he asked.

"No," she admitted. "There isn't anyone in my life I'd call special at the moment." She'd walked away from her last relationship after he became too clingy, demanding to move a few of his bathroom items into her cabin to make it easier for him. Len had no idea that she didn't allow sleepovers. He assumed that would be the next step in their relationship, but he'd assumed wrong.

There was no sense in getting used to having someone sleeping in the bed next to her unless it was...

She stopped herself right there.

There might not have been anyone since Duke that she could see herself with long-term, but that didn't mean there would never be. In fact, maybe she should ramp up the search for someone to fill the shoes he'd left empty without ever knowing years ago.

"You got quiet on me," he said.

She didn't respond.

"That used to mean I touched on a sensitive topic," he said. "If there's someone in your life, you know you can tell me. Right?"

"Sure," she said, wishing it was true. All of it. The part where she had someone special in her life. The part where she could say the words out loud to him. And the part where she didn't go home to an empty house every day because she couldn't find anyone who came close to the person she'd been in a relationship with at sixteen.

Hearing herself say those words in her head, they sounded ridiculous. No one found the love of their life at sixteen.

Okay, maybe she should change that to *most* people didn't. The Remingtons were the exception, not the rule. If she looked it up, she was certain the statistic for couples who met in high school and went the distance would be grim.

"There hasn't been anyone in my life for a while," she admitted. "I've come to prefer it that way, and I just keep thinking something might be wrong with me because of it. Isn't everyone supposed to long for that special someone? Isn't that what we're trained to believe we're supposed to need?" She paused for a beat. "What if people go through their whole lives searching for 'the one' and never find it? Not every couple is in love."

Case in point, her parents. *Codependent, addicts* would be better words.

"When I look at my mom and stepfather," she went on, "it's easy to see some people are codependent rather than in a loving relationship. Mine couldn't live with each other, and they couldn't live without each other, which makes no sense to me. I have no intention of dragging another human being down by forcing them into a legal binding contract saying we have to work out our problems long after anything we felt toward each other is dead. Is that horrible of me? Does that make me a bad person?"

Chapter Twelve

"No," Duke said to Audrey after listening to her confession. "In fact, I couldn't have said it better myself."

"Which explains why we're both still single," she quipped, but there was a subtle note to her voice that rang hollow. Almost like she was trying to convince herself everything she'd said was true.

Or maybe he was reading way too much into it.

It had been a long day, and they both needed rest. "Are you sure you want to stop by the hospital before I drop you off?"

"I won't sleep without seeing them together in the same room," she admitted.

Again, he couldn't agree more. Except that he'd adjusted his plans and wanted to sleep at the hospital tonight instead of going back to the ranch. He figured he could hand over his keys to Audrey so she could drive herself home.

Not five minutes later, Duke located a spot in the hospital parking lot and cut off the engine. He rushed around the front of the vehicle, fully expecting to lose the race. Audrey had developed a habit of beating him to the punch when it came to opening her door.

He was pleasantly surprised when she didn't.

On the way over, there'd been no sign of the vehicle that had stressed her out at Bea's place while he was inside. She was keyed up. Was she afraid of her own shadow at this point?

They walked into the hospital side by side, and then to the familiar elevators. She pushed the buttons, and before he knew it, they were standing in front of his grandmother's room.

The beeping noises inside had doubled, which brought a smile to his face. Knowing the two of them would be together no matter what else happened gave him comfort. Would it make them stronger, too? The orderly had gone so far as to push their beds close enough together that Duke would have to turn sideways to walk in between them. The room was dimly lit. His grandparents finally looked like they were resting instead of fighting for their lives.

As Audrey walked to the foot of the bed, she froze. "Hey. Come here."

Duke joined her.

"Look." She motioned toward the space in between the beds.

The sight brought tears to Duke's eyes. Somehow, they'd managed to find their way to each other. His grandparents were holding hands.

"They're good," he whispered to Audrey, taking her by the hand before walking her out of the room. He kept going to the end of the hall and into the waiting room. "I figure I'll stick around here for the night." He reached into his pocket and produced the key fob to his truck. "Feel free to head home."

Audrey stared at the key in his hand for a long moment. "Is it strange that I feel like I'm exactly where I want to be? I only left before because I didn't want to intrude on your time with your grandparents."

"What makes you think I wouldn't want you here?" he asked as he fixed a cup of coffee. He handed the first one to her, which she took before thanking him, and made a second one for himself.

Audrey was silent as she took a seat. The mental debate as to whether or not she should tell him what was going through her mind was visible in her expression.

Duke kept one seat in between them, sensing this wasn't the time to invade her personal space. "You don't owe me any explanations, Audrey. We're adults who've gone their separate ways. Whatever it is, I won't judge you for it."

"It's not related to me." Her eyes widened like the admission caught her off guard. She issued a sharp sigh before blowing on the top of her foam coffee cup. She took a sip and then cleared her throat. "Well, it is but there are others involved."

"Then who? Because you managed to avoid running into me the entire time you've been back in Mesa Point despite me returning several times over the last few years, which clearly took some effort on your part," he stated, trying to mask the hurt at the snubs.

"I never wanted that," she admitted. "But I was told that it would be for the best if I didn't come around when you visited."

"How would you know when—"

It dawned on him. She took food to his grandparents every first Monday of the month. She was the one who'd found them after their wreck.

He pinned her with his gaze. "My grandparents asked you to stay away, didn't they?"

She gave a hesitant nod as she studied his reaction.

How could the two people who loved him the most betray him like that? For three years, Audrey had been actively avoiding him at the urging of his grandparents.

"Please don't be mad at them," she urged. "They were right. Seeing each other again would only lead to more pain."

"Is that what you think?" he asked. "Because I've been over what happened in the past for a long time now. Haven't you?" It was a lie that he wanted to be true.

Her face twisted, and he could read her expression. "We were kids back then. What did we know about true love?" She stood up and gripped the strap on her handbag. "This is probably a good time for me to say good-night."

He fished his key fob out of his pocket again, but she was already shaking her head.

"No, thanks," she said, stabbing her hand inside her purse before coming up with her cell phone. "I'll figure out a ride on my own."

"Hey," he started as she turned her back toward him. "Don't walk away like this."

Audrey stopped, but she didn't turn to face him.

"You're welcome to stay," he continued while he had her attention. "In fact, I would very much like the company."

They were the only two in the waiting room on this floor. Audrey folded her arms across her chest.

"I would very much like *your* company," he corrected. "We've grown up. We're different people than we were at sixteen. Maybe we take tonight to get to know the people we've become."

Had he ever really known her? Back then, he believed he did, especially after all those all-night-long talks and promises of a future together. And yet, she always held back. There was always this huge piece of her that was out of reach. He'd naively believed she would open up all the way at some point if he was patient enough. She'd been like a wild animal that had been deeply wounded. Approach too quickly, they panicked and attacked. A scared animal would claw your eyes out if you weren't careful.

People were far more complicated, he'd learned. They could make you believe you'd broken past barriers when, in fact, you hadn't even scratched the surface.

Duke had a bone to pick with his grandparents when they woke up from this nightmare. With his grandmother crashing today, she seemed the worst off of the two. It couldn't have been a good sign, and he wasn't ready to consider what that might do to her recovery.

"I'm going to go, Duke. I think it's for the best."

Before he could argue, Audrey rushed out of the room.

DUKE HAD BEEN right about one thing. It had been one helluva day. Audrey needed to go home and take a shower to wash the day off. It was late, and being near Duke probably wasn't the best idea when she was feeling so vulnerable. He had a way of stripping her defenses without even trying.

Audrey wasn't sure if she would be able to sleep after Jenson's death, the visit to the Napier home and the prickly feeling of being followed that haunted her. She would replay the conversation in her mind dozens of times if she closed her eyes. That much was certain. If her visit got back to her boss, she might be in trouble.

No matter what else happened, a shower and pajamas would go a long way toward making her feel human again.

Right now, though, she needed to figure out a ride home. Maybe she should have accepted Duke's truck offer. Except then she would be bound to see him tomorrow. His grandparents had one thing right. Seeing him again dredged up a painful past. The only part they'd been wrong about was that it affected her far more than it seemed to hurt him.

Duke came across as not being bothered at all. Good for him.

When she was rested and had a chance to process the fact someone had been watching her and that person was now dead, she might be able to get there, too.

Walking out the glass doors that swished open, she stepped into the night. Everyone she knew was most likely asleep. There weren't exactly car services out here available at the tap of a screen like in Dallas or Austin. The slower pace came with fewer conveniences and was part of the charm of small-town living.

She should have brought her own vehicle, though. No buses ran this late, either. At this point, she might have to walk home. She pulled up the map feature on her phone to see how long she was about to be hoofing it home. Pride kept her from turning around and going back inside the hospital to ask for Duke's key.

But the lake was far and the high beams from the parking lot a little while ago caused her to think twice.

Face turned down, she was caught off guard when the doors swished open behind her.

"Hey, don't leave like this," Duke said. His voice had matured to a deep timbre that stirred places deep inside her.

Audrey turned around to face him. "Would you give me a ride home? You can just slow down, and I'll jump out. You don't even have to stop."

"I'll stop," he said, holding out his hand to reveal the key. "I wasn't going to let you walk. As far as I remember, this town rolls up the streets past nine o'clock on a weeknight."

"Thank you for not making me beg," she said. "I would have, though." She left out the part where she couldn't bring herself to go back inside the hospital. At least this way her pride stayed intact.

"The nurses seem to think it'll be a quiet night, and I sent out another update to everyone, so I'm good to leave for a bit." Duke started toward his truck after splaying his hand on the small of her back.

He used to do that same move all the time when they were sixteen. His hand was large then and covered most of her lower back. His touch always brought a sense of calm over her as though he could reach the depths of her from this very spot.

"If you're sure you don't need to be here," she said to him. She wouldn't be able to stand the thought she'd dragged him away from the hospital if something bad happened while he was gone. He was the one in the family who'd agreed to take leave from work to be here for their grandparents.

"Trust me, I'm good," he reassured her.

Audrey had seen that look on his face before. Arguing would do no good at this point, so she wouldn't. Instead, she would let him take the lead and give her a ride home. She should be able to rest easy tonight, knowing the perp couldn't repeat his crime. He couldn't do anything to her or anyone else.

And yet her heart broke for the family. She had an unsettled feeling in her chest, a tightness that was probably residual from a traumatic past that never seemed to let go of her. It was the reason she'd gone into law enforcement. Every officer has a story, and she was no different.

For Audrey, the idea started as a seedling when she was young and felt helpless against her parents' wrath. Their cruelty knew no bounds. Her younger sister had taken much of the brunt of their tempers. Making Audrey watch while helpless to stop them had given them an extra thrill. Disgusting.

They were pure evil. At some point, they shifted their focus despite her sister's attempts to draw their attention away from Audrey. Her sister would pull a stunt like slamming a book closed or "accidentally" dropping a glass while doing dishes.

Clara might have only been three years younger, but she'd seemed so wise to a young Audrey. But the guilt was real, too. Audrey carried it around with her because she was the one who lived when her sister hadn't been so lucky. Why? Clara was the better person. She was good. Whereas Audrey clung to the leg of the kitchen table, hiding, while Clara was being hurt by their parents.

"You're quiet again," Duke said after they climbed into the truck and he got on the road.

"I keep thinking about Jenson's family and how tragic this is for them," she said. "I can't stop wondering if he died because of a practical joke or because he was headed down a dark path like Halsey thought." She put her hand up before he could respond. "And I do realize he's gone and maybe none of this should matter anymore."

"It does matter," Duke stated with the kind of confidence that left no room for doubt he meant those words. "Because he made you feel unsafe."

"Thank you, Duke. I've been thinking the same thing, which makes me feel guilty now that he's gone. How messed up is it that part of me feels sorry for this lost kid? After hearing Halsey talk about him being bullied then in turn bullying others, it breaks my heart things would end for him this way."

"You're not messed up," he countered. "The world might be off, but you're a good person, Audrey. Don't let anyone convince you otherwise. You care about someone you never met because he was being bullied despite the fact he violated your privacy."

The thought he might have been out there taking pictures of her that he intended to share or *did* share caused bile to rise up in the back of her throat. The only way to find out what he'd been doing was to subpoena his phone records, which she highly doubted her boss would approve. Part of her decided she should almost be grateful her voyeur had been Jenson and not the Ponytail Snatcher like she'd feared after being told he might be in the area.

Duke pulled in front of her cabin and idled the engine.

"That's strange," she said, looking at her porch.

"Did you forget to turn the light on?" he asked.

"It's automatic," she said. "Turns on by itself when the sun goes down." She let her hand hover next to the handle and saw that it was shaking. "What are the odds the light needs to be replaced on the day Jenson Napier dies?"

Chapter Thirteen

Duke exited the driver's side of the truck before coming around the front of the vehicle to open Audrey's door. She waited for him and then took his hand to climb down. The jolt of electricity shouldn't catch him off guard considering it was exactly as he remembered it. But it did. Somehow, it had grown stronger than ever, or maybe his memory had weakened instead.

The dead lightbulb sent up a red flag. "Do you want to wait inside the truck?"

"I'd rather stick with you if that's okay," she said. He could hear the shakiness, the fear in her voice.

He flipped on his phone's flashlight as Audrey did the same. Side by side, they walked up her porch stairs and onto the concrete slab. She checked the bulb, screwed it around a couple of times.

The light came on.

Audrey bit out a few muttered curses as she scanned the ground with her flashlight. She walked over to the edge of the porch, stopped and bent down. "Duke, take a look at this."

There were boot prints.

He immediately scanned the area around them, behind

them with the phone's flashlight. Between crickets and the wind whipping through the trees, his danger radar clicked onto full alert.

"The question is whether or not these were made before or after this morning," he said.

"I haven't thought to check around the perimeter of the house today with everything that's happened," she said, standing and following the boot tracks around her home. They consistently seemed to stop in front of windows, making a circle around the house.

"I checked the perimeter when I first came by this morning and I didn't see these prints." Investigations often stopped the second a perp was dead, so these prints had to be newer. Unless Jenson had walked around her home to figure out where her bedroom was just before he'd been caught and took off running. It was a likely explanation. No. That didn't make sense when Duke really thought about it. Jensen was found with tennis shoes on, so these prints could not have been made by him. Did that mean he hadn't been working alone?

"Again, we have boot prints while Jenson wore tennis shoes," Audrey said. Her fixed gaze on the tracks suggested she was thinking out loud. She still got the same look he remembered from that summer. Her gaze narrowed and her lips compressed into a frown when she was seriously considering something.

"It's impossible to tell if Jenson planned to escalate tonight or if any of these prints belong to him," she said with an involuntary shiver. "But it would explain the light bulb being unscrewed."

There was another explanation. One he didn't want to consider but had to. Ponytail Snatcher.

From the corner of his eye, Duke caught movement in the trees.

"Stay with me," he said, bolting toward it, pushing his legs until his thighs burned.

He might be chasing wind or an animal but he intended to find out.

"Stop," he ordered, running with the barrel of his Glock leading the way toward the trees.

A male figure came into view.

"Stop, or I'll shoot," Duke shouted, gasping for air as he tried to catch his breath.

The man stopped as Audrey caught up. She shined her phone app at the tall, muscular man.

"Morris?" Duke asked, astonished as the man's hands went up.

"Don't shoot," Morris practically begged.

"What the hell are you doing here?" Duke asked as Audrey wasted no time calling her boss.

"He was my boy," Morris said as his face morphed to the kind of sadness that would break anyone's heart. "My son."

"You better tell me exactly what you're doing here in the next two seconds because the sheriff is about to be on the line," Duke warned.

"I had to come see what he was doing for myself," Morris said as the big man wiped at his eyes before returning his hand to their previous position. "I had to know what he was up to and why this happened."

"Does your wife know you're here?" Duke asked.

"No," Morris stated. "Please don't tell her. She's been through enough already, which was the reason why the sheriff pulled me aside and told me privately."

Audrey stepped closer to Duke as Ackerman answered. She gave him the quick rundown about the vehicle at the restaurant and then briefed him on who they found near the scene before telling her boss she'd call him back if there were any new developments. "No, I don't need anyone to come here. False alarm."

Morris had on a pair of jeans, a dark shirt, and work boots.

"Toss me one of your boots," Duke said.

Morris complied.

Duke checked the bottom against the print. The two didn't match. "Catch." Duke tossed the man his boot back. "Go home, Morris."

"I'm sorry," he said with the kind of sadness in his voice that threatened to rip Duke's heart in two. "I'm not trying to cause any trouble. I just needed to see for myself and I didn't want to worry my wife. She wouldn't want me here. But I had to see where it…"

Morris broke into sobs.

"How did you get here?" Duke asked.

"My truck's parked down the road," Morris admitted.

"Get back to it and go home before anyone starts asking questions," Duke said.

"I will," Morris said before turning and running. He disappeared into the trees.

And then, he and Audrey headed back to the cabin.

"He could have been testing the water," Duke said as a niggling feeling ate away at the back of his mind once they'd caught their breath and were back standing in front of her home. "Checking to see if you would notice the light bulb." It wasn't the most likely story, but he wanted to offer an alternative theory. It was always good to consider every angle. The other side to the story was that Jenson wasn't acting alone. Duke was bothered by something he couldn't quite put his finger on. He'd made a career out of honing his instincts, and they told him to keep digging in this instance.

Fortunately, they could do most of the investigating on their own. They'd have to move forward without subpoenas and official channels, but between the two of them, they had enough combined experience to give her the peace of mind she searched for.

"Do you have a guest room, or should I crash on the couch?" He yawned, realizing it had been almost forty-eight hours since he last slept.

She was already shaking her head before he finished his question.

"I'm not leaving you alone while there are questions about whether or not Jenson acted on his own," he explained.

"Well, I can't let you get distracted on my account while you're supposed to be up at the hospital with your grandparents," she countered.

"Compromise?"

"If you can come up with one that satisfies both of us, I'll consider it," she reasoned.

"How about we get cleaned up here, and then we can sleep at the hospital?" he asked. "I'm not expecting a change with either of my grandparents, but you can never be too sure. We can brainstorm other possibilities while we're there. They have coffee and a cafeteria if we get hungry. And I'm sure they can find recliners for us when we need sleep." He wouldn't need more than fifteen or twenty minutes of shut-eye every few hours. He'd trained himself to survive on little sleep while he worked on a case.

Her gaze stayed on the ground as she stood there, contemplating. She glanced at her cabin and then back at him. He had no idea which way she was leaning.

"I'LL GO," AUDREY SAID, not wanting to spend the night at her cabin alone. She hated the feeling of weakness that almost made her turn Duke's offer down. The truth was that she wanted to stay at the hospital anyway. She was glad he hadn't suggested the ranch because it held so many memories. She was feeling too vulnerable to stay there tonight. And this most recent scare had her unnerved.

She did her level best to convince herself that last part was true because her heart argued she wanted to spend time with Duke. She wouldn't deny it. She missed him. The times she'd known he was coming home had been the hardest days to endure.

At least he knew the truth about why she avoided him when he was in town. His grandparents had been right. Seeing him for the first time had been harder than hell. At least he no longer believed she actively avoided him on her own accord. That was something.

"Do you want to wait on the porch while I grab my overnight bag?" he asked.

She probably didn't want to know why he had one so readily available in his truck if it wasn't for law enforcement purposes. "I'll wait." Going inside her home without backup didn't seem like the smartest play.

He retrieved his backpack while she fished the key out of her purse. Moving to Mesa Point should have meant leaving doors unlocked and keys inside vehicles. It was more of that small-town charm that had drawn her. Except that she would never be one of those people who could leave the back door unprotected. Or windows open, for that matter. Even though she'd learned a long time ago the ones closest to her could cause the most damage.

The people you loved shouldn't be the ones who hurt you. Period. Age didn't matter. The statistics were plain sad. Women were hurt more often by the man who was supposed to love them the most. How was that for messed up?

But Duke and his sisters and cousins were the furthest things from abusers. They were taught love and respect. Duke put her on a pedestal when they were dating. One she wasn't so sure she deserved.

He, on the other hand, had been the perfect boyfriend. He was then, and she imagined he would still be now, honest and honorable.

A hot tear spilled out of her eye and ran down her cheek.

Duke hopped onto the porch, took one look at her and stopped in his tracks. "Hey. Hey. Hold on there. What's this?" He closed the distance between them and thumbed away her tear.

She turned away, sniffed and unlocked the door before entering.

The snick of the lock behind her confirmed he was inside, but she could already feel his presence. It was just that way with Duke. His presence filled a room. There was never a need to announce him. Her skin tingled, and the tiny hairs on the back of her neck danced whenever he was near. It had always been like that, even the times he sat in the hallway at sixteen. She'd known he was there without checking.

Before she could disappear down the hall, Duke's hands were on her shoulders gently turning her to face him. "Hey," he said.

"I'm not a crier," she defended, even though he hadn't asked the question or made an accusation. She was telling him so they would both believe it.

"I know," he said. "But even if you were, it's not a sign of weakness."

Her chin quivered, but she didn't respond.

"It's a sign of trying to be too strong for too long. It's a sign of standing alone on a mountaintop with no one to have your back. But that's not the case anymore, Audrey. I'd like to be there for you if you're willing to let me in."

It would be so easy to let Duke be her comfort right now. Was it smart?

The air shifted the minute her eyes met his. It crackled with a very different kind of tension. She dropped her gaze to those thick lips of his—lips that made hers burn to touch them again.

"All I need from you right now is a kiss," she said, surprising herself. "Or is that off the table?"

"Do you think it's a good idea?" he asked. "Because I've wanted to do just that far too long." His gaze lingered on her lips and left a sizzling trail.

"No," she admitted. "But that isn't stopping me from wanting to do it anyway."

The corners of his lips turned up in a sexy little grin full of mischief that weakened her knees. Just for a few minutes, she wanted to lean into his strong body. She wanted those muscled arms to wrap around her and that voice to promise everything would be all right. And she would believe it, too. Because the Duke she'd fallen for all those years ago wouldn't say it if it wasn't true.

"Well then, maybe we should test the waters a little bit," he said. With that, he dipped his head down and kissed her so tenderly it robbed her of breath.

Audrey brought her hands up to Duke's shoulders to anchor herself. It dawned on her that he might need this escape every bit as much as she did. And it occurred to her that Duke might be spending time with her to distract himself from the nightmare in his own life, his grandparents' accident.

Shoving those thoughts far out of reach, Audrey slicked her tongue across Duke's bottom lip. She gently bit down, capturing his full lip in her teeth before releasing him. The move elicited a guttural groan from somewhere deep inside him.

His hands came up to cup her face, positioning her mouth for better access. But first, he feathered kisses along her neck. Then her jawline. He moved to her ear where he tugged at the lobe.

Warmth coursed through her as heat pooled between her thighs.

Audrey dug her fingernails into Duke's shoulders. He gave another groan against her lips. Her breath quickened, and her heart raced in perfect tempo with his. The memory of the last time they kissed was stamped in her memory. It was burned into her lips to the point no one had even come close to matching it since Duke.

And then he pulled back, resting his forehead against hers as he tried to catch his breath.

"Not one kiss has come close to yours," she said low and under her breath. The fact she'd said those words out loud caught her off guard and caused her cheeks to flame.

"What am I supposed to do with that?" came his breath-less response.

She had ideas, but this probably wasn't the best time to share them. Or should she?

Chapter Fourteen

"You should go first in the shower," Duke urged, needing to think about something besides the feel of her lips as they moved against his. Because they felt a lot like home.

He chalked the deep connection up to muscle memory. He'd loved intensely at sixteen. Age and experience had a way of taming him.

"There are two bathrooms," Audrey said when she took a step away from him. She brought the back of her hand up to her mouth. "You can take the guest bathroom." She motioned right as she moved away, flipping lights on. "Let's make sure all the blinds are closed first."

"Okay," he agreed as she shivered, no doubt at the thought of having had someone invade her privacy.

The perp had been watching her from the woods, but if he worked alone—which was the current assumption since there was no proof otherwise—he'd also gotten close enough to leave tracks a foot from her foundation. The trail circled her home. He was responsible for unscrewing her light bulb on the porch enough to keep it from illuminating the dark. Did he intend to breach her home using the back door? Many criminals walked right through a door with an easy lock. If they had the kid's cell phone or laptop, would his search history reveal he'd been learning how to pick locks?

Working without their usual tools, like access to records and the like, made the investigation more challenging. Since Duke had never shied away from a challenge, he wouldn't let the current limits set him back by much. It might take longer, but there were other ways to explore.

Plus, they were continuing the search for facts mainly for Audrey's peace of mind. That, and dotting every *i* and crossing every *t* in order to ensure there wasn't someone out there working his way toward her.

The boot print versus tennis shoe bothered Duke. It was inconsistent with one person working alone. Could be nothing. Or it could be the key to unlocking a bigger case than they originally thought.

Either way, Audrey being able to sleep at night once he was gone was his main concern.

He made his way into the guest room. Audrey's home had an open-concept living, dining and kitchen space with cathedral ceilings. A wood beam ran the length of the space. The island provided separation between the living and kitchen areas. Bar chairs rather than stools were pushed up to one side of the granite island. Hers was a kitchen of whites. White flooring. White cabinets. White granite countertops. Rather than leaving things feeling cold, she'd warmed the place up with green plants and candles.

The guest bathroom mirrored the rest of the house with light fixtures that weren't the least bit sterile. He set his backpack down, pulled out his travel kit complete with a razor, shaving cream and toothbrush and set them on the counter.

A ten-minute shower was all he needed to feel human again. Also in his backpack was a change of clothing down to his boxer briefs. Changing into clean clothes was the closest thing to heaven. Duke brushed his teeth and changed inside of fifteen minutes, complete with a shave. He was the in-and-out type when it came to spending time in the bathroom.

In the kitchen, he located her pod-style coffee maker along with everything else he needed for a fresh cup within arm's reach. They still planned to make the drive back to the hospital tonight. And even if they didn't, sleep wouldn't be an option. Not for him. He was too keyed up to think about any real shut-eye for several hours at a minimum.

As he took the first sip of coffee, Audrey appeared wearing yoga pants and a form-fitting cotton shirt. She had on tennis shoes and was carrying an overnight bag that she set down next to the granite island.

"Coffee?" he asked.

"Sure," she said. "But let's make these to go."

Duke nodded. "I hope you don't mind I helped myself."

"Not at all," she reassured him. "In fact, I meant to tell you to make yourself at home before I took my shower."

He did his best not to stare at the droplet of water rolling down the silky skin of her sleek neck where her pulse thumped. Fixing another cup of coffee after locating two to-go mugs helped keep his mind focused where it needed to stay. He couldn't go there with the whole having-feelings-for-Audrey again and end up getting his heart stomped on twice. Duke considered himself to be tough as nails when it came to most things, but his foolish heart didn't cooperate. It was the one weak spot that could be shattered over and over again without ever learning its lesson. His brain had the job of constructing high enough walls to keep emotions from taking the wheel.

"Here you go," he said as he handed over the to-go mug.

As their fingers grazed, an electrical current vibrated through his hand and up his arm straight to his heart. *Great job keeping distance, dude.*

They double-checked the window and door locks before heading out. The night was black as pitch as they made their way to his truck. He'd locked his doors so there was no worrying someone would jump at them from behind the seat. Locking his vehicle doors was a habit he'd picked up in the marshals service. He carried weapons in the trunk that he didn't need used against him or anyone else by the dirtbags he was after.

The ride over to the hospital was quiet.

Audrey was thinking. Overthinking? She used to have a tendency to do that. He'd noticed the habit years ago. He used to love being the one to help her relax. She would sit in front of him, lean her back into his chest so he could wrap her in his arms. She'd rest her arms on his knees as they watched a sunset from the back of his truck. In fact, when he thought about it, the cabin was part of a new development on the east side of the lake. They'd watched countless sunsets less than a mile from where she lived now.

Duke didn't want to notice those things or read too much into them. The cabin development was nice. The fixtures and plumbing were all new, so she'd probably picked out all her cabinets and colors at some point during the building process. Her home suited her, but he didn't want to get too used to being there.

Not that it mattered much. He didn't get back to Mesa Point very often. When he did, it was to work the ranch. Speaking of which, Nash wouldn't be able to handle the place on his own. Duke would need to call a meeting tomorrow with his relatives so they could figure out a rotation plan.

As much as he hated to admit it, there was a possibility his grandparents might be in the hospital for a long while. When he first spoke to the ER doctor, he'd explained people coming out of a coma wasn't a straightforward process. There could be wide swings with big ups and downs. At this point, anything was possible. One of them could be sitting up talking one day and then back unconscious the next. Their ages complicated the situation but their general wellness and fitness should help. Then there would be a recovery period to think about. The notion he would be able to swing into town and handle all that needed to be taken care of in a matter of days was long gone.

Duke had to face facts. His grandparents might need time to recover from the accident. The doctor had been honest even though Duke hadn't wanted to listen. He couldn't allow himself to believe a bad outcome was possible. Hope was all he had, and he intended to cling to it like a life raft in the middle of a hurricane.

"They're going to be okay," Audrey said.

He parked and then cut off the engine. "I know."

"I mean it," she insisted, not at all fooled by his attempt to agree. "There's no other possibility."

He couldn't agree more. Rather than reply, he gave a nod and then exited on his side. Audrey waited for him to open her door and then she took his hand when he offered to help her out of his truck.

Duke didn't risk looking into her eyes. She had a way of seeing right through him.

Walls up, he turned toward the hospital.

AUDREY WALKED NEXT to Duke as they made their way to his grandparents' floor. Visiting hours were long over, so they checked in at the nurses' station, confirmed nothing had changed since they were last there and then headed to the waiting lobby. Nash had gone back to the ranch hours ago.

A nurse brought pillows and blankets, explaining the chairs along the back wall were recliners and should be decently comfortable. Audrey might be tired, but she doubted she could do much more than rest her eyes.

After thanking the nurse, they picked out side-by-side recliners. Audrey positioned hers as flat as possible, turned on her side and hugged the pillow. Duke sat perched on the edge of his seat, sitting in the most upright position.

"Hey," she said, wondering if she should go down the path of apologizing for the way she left things between them all those years ago. The kiss they'd shared at her cabin was literal wildfire burning her from the inside out.

Would him knowing change the past? No. Would it open the door for him to forgive her? Maybe. Was she willing to try? Yes.

Based on their interactions so far, he was keeping emotional distance. There was no mistaking the mistrust in his eyes despite the fact he was trying to hide it. Duke turned his head toward her.

"Why didn't you reach out at some point later?" he asked.

"Honestly?" She hesitated in bearing her soul.

"I think I deserve the truth, Audrey. Enough time has passed."

"Okay," she started, taking in a slow, deep breath. Where to begin? Since there were no magic words, she decided to go with whatever came. "You've probably figured out my life was in danger."

"I thought you left and then avoided me for all these years. I tried to find you, but it was impossible with the resources I had back then."

"My folks were responsible for my sister's death," she said through the frog in her throat and the heavy pressure bearing down on her chest. "They beat me and threatened me within an inch of my life if I told anyone."

"The bruises," he said quietly. "They were from your parents?"

"Yes," she said, chin up even though it quivered.

"I thought maybe you'd been running away from a boyfriend," he admitted. "It never occurred to me that your own parents would have done that to you."

"You should have seen what they did to..." A sob escaped before Audrey could suppress it. She shook her head, trying to shake off the emotions threatening to suck her under.

Duke reached for her hand and linked their fingers. "I'm so sorry. That should never have happened." He whispered other reassurances that gave her the will to continue.

"I thought leaving Mesa Point would break me," she admitted. "Leaving you was by far the hardest part. Or that's what I thought at the time. Turned out, it was a lot worse not to be able to pick up the phone and call you or text. I blocked all social media so my parents wouldn't be able to find me and my uncle could continue to collect a social security check on my behalf. They tried to move heaven and earth to find me. It wasn't like they loved me. Not in a way any reasonable person would recognize."

"Why couldn't you just stay here at the ranch?" he asked.

Remembering was harder than she expected it to be. The emotions that came with those memories had been tucked away in a dark place she never wanted to revisit.

"This is too much," she conceded. "I can't." A few rogue tears rolled down her cheeks.

"You don't have to," Duke reassured.

As much as she wished she could keep going, she couldn't. The past was in the past, and talking about it wouldn't change the many nights she'd cried into her pillow, missing him so much it was a physical ache.

At least he knew that she hadn't walked away without looking back on purpose. At least he knew the situation was out of her hands. And at least he knew she hadn't wanted the summer to end that way.

Being here in Mesa Point, coming back, was supposed to give her a fresh start. Being so close to Duke's grandparents without being able to talk to him had cut deeper than she expected.

Time to suck it up, buttercup.

Audrey had made the choice to come back here and start a career here. A part of her had needed to rectify the past. Come to terms with the time she'd spent here and the people who'd helped her during her darkest days.

Now?

She didn't see the need to stay in Mesa Point. Once Duke's grandparents were up and around, back to their old selves—which was the only outcome she could allow herself to consider—it was time to move on.

"Hey," Duke whispered. "You don't owe me an explanation."

Why did it feel so much like she did, though? They'd both grown up and moved on. She'd been in a few relationships, nothing that stuck. Then again, that had more to do with her messed-up parents than anything else, despite how much it felt like she might never be able to replace what she'd had with Duke.

Even if she found the perfect person to spend the rest of her life with, how could she trust it?

Chapter Fifteen

Duke sat still, contemplating. A nurse stopped in to give an update an hour after they arrived at the hospital. The waiting room gained visitors as the sun began to rise. A young couple came by to pour cups of coffee and wait for visiting hours to open. They were dressed like they were going to work. She had on the kind of scrubs hygienists wore at the dentist's office. The guy wore jeans and a flannel shirt.

The female was a short brunette. She kept glancing over at Duke and Audrey, who'd drifted off to sleep after their conversation, a conversation that had taught him Audrey hadn't disappeared without a word on purpose. He'd known on some level at least that she must have been in danger and felt guilty for resenting her disappearance. The selfish part of him that wished she'd trusted him enough to find a way to contact him should have died out years ago. He was embarrassed to admit, even to himself, that he'd carried it around for so long.

There was a small sense of satisfaction having his suspicion it had been out of her control. Call it his ego talking, but knowing she'd been just as upset about the way she'd disappeared gave him relief. The brunette must have decided she recognized him even though he drew a blank on who she was. She started tentatively walking toward him. Her lips pursed, and she held on to her coffee cup with both hands.

"Hi," she said, keeping her voice low so as not to wake Audrey. "My boyfriend and I were just wondering if you're related to Lorenzo and Lacy Remington?"

"As a matter of fact, I'm their grandson," he said. "Why? Is there something I can help you with?"

"Oh, no," she said, looking at him with admiration he didn't deserve. "They sold us our first horse, a paint by the name of Calico. They've been so sweet and still check up on us to this day." Her gaze softened. "We actually stopped by to check on them for a change. How are they?"

Duke probably shouldn't be surprised someone would feel this way toward his grandparents, and yet the brunette had caught him off guard with her comment. "They're together in the same room now," he said, standing up to stretch his legs. "Nice of you to come by and check."

"We wouldn't miss seeing them for the world," she said. "We wanted to bring flowers or something, but we weren't sure if they were awake or flowers would be permitted in their rooms."

Duke shook his head.

The brunette reached out and touched his forearm. Her contact didn't give him the same reaction as when Audrey touched him. She was special.

"I'm real sorry for what happened to them," the brunette said. "They are the sweetest people you could ever imagine. Bobby and I feel the same. He insisted he stop by to see them with me before he dropped me off at work."

"I'm Duke." He extended a hand. "And you are?"

"Jeannette Calier," she supplied, taking the offering with a small but vigorous handshake. "As you've probably already figured out, I just love your grandparents." She sniffed back a tear before bringing her hand up to wipe her eyes. "I can't imagine two kinder people."

"Thank you," Duke said. "That means a lot. I'm sure they feel the same way about you and Bobby."

Bobby, who'd been sticking close to the coffeepot, waved as the two of them looked over at him.

"I guess I better go before I'm late to work," Jeannette said. "Will you let them know we stopped by if they wake up today?"

"Will do," Duke reassured her. It was strange to think how many people his grandparents had touched between living in this town their entire lives and their business. They supplied horses to many a family who had children who loved to ride. They sold to farmers and business owners alike. A pair of brothers had made a solid business out of offering tourists trail rides around several area lakes. "I'm sure they'll appreciate your kindness."

Jeannette offered a heartfelt thank-you.

Guilt washed over Duke that he'd had no idea who these nice people were.

Him, his siblings and their cousins had moved away the minute they were old enough to graduate high school and then started careers that kept them away from Mesa Point.

The strange part about it, Duke thought as the couple left, was that he'd had a great childhood here in Mesa Point. His grandparents had been the best. Was it true that successful child-rearing meant the kids felt safe enough to move far away once they grew up? Or had he abandoned the people who'd sacrificed the most to make sure he had a roof over his head, food in his belly and love in his life?

As the couple disappeared and an elderly woman walked into the room, he realized he'd been a jerk for not thanking his grandparents every day for taking him in, loving him. They'd made his life good when it could have turned out horrible.

He glanced over at Audrey. Who had her back? No one from the sounds of it. Although she'd shut down the minute they started diving into difficult topics. On some level, he appreciated the fact she'd talked to him about the past at all, about the way she'd left.

He needed to come to terms with the fact he might never know the whole story. Audrey may not be able to go any further than what she'd already said. It wasn't a complete explanation, but at least she'd offered something.

"Excuse me," the older lady said, pulling his attention to her and out of his reverie.

"Yes, ma'am," he said, standing up to stretch his legs again. He'd sat back down after the couple walked out the door. "Is there something I can do for you?"

"Aren't you one of the Remington boys?" she asked, straining to get a better look at him. The older woman's hair was all white. She had it piled in a bun on top of her head. She wore one of those smock dresses with pockets that she stuffed her hands into.

"Yes, ma'am," he responded, figuring it didn't matter which one he was.

"I thought so," she said with an aha tone. "You look just like your grandfather when he was a young boy."

This seemed like a good time to put a name to the older woman's face. Yet, he couldn't. "I'm sorry, ma'am, but who are you again?"

"Right," she began, "of course you don't remember me. I was much younger when you last saw me." She held out a hand. "I'm Ms. Apple."

"My first-grade teacher?" he asked.

"That's right," she said. "You've grown into a fine young man."

Duke wondered if anyone would notice if he ended up in the hospital or worse. His siblings and cousins were obvious choices. But who else? Without a family of his own, was there anyone who would care enough to sit by his side?

Why did the thought suddenly derail him?

AUDREY BLINKED HER eyes open. Disoriented and still foggy, she panicked as she glanced around the room. The lights in the room were bright, and the sun was high enough in the sky to indicate it was midday.

Hospital.

Scanning the room, she noticed Duke standing at the window, staring outside. He was nursing a coffee and had a serious expression. Her mind immediately snapped to something being wrong with his grandparents.

"Hey," she said as she sat up. "Everything okay?"

He immediately twisted his neck around to look at her but didn't move. "There's no change. They're still holding hands, though. The nurses thought maybe I did it, but we both know I didn't."

Her chest squeezed, and warmth filled her.

"No change is better than a change for the worse," she admitted.

Duke agreed with a nod. He held up his cup. "Coffee?"

"How did you end up with a real mug?" she asked.

"My first-grade teacher stopped by and brought a few supplies. Apparently, she was stocking a donation shelf for visitors." He walked over to the coffee area and picked up a small box. "She baked oatmeal cookies and called them breakfast. And there's banana bread slices, too. Care for anything?"

"Banana bread and a cookie sound pretty amazing to me right now." She hadn't napped long enough for her breath to qualify as morning breath. Thank heaven for small miracles. "How long was I out?"

"A few hours."

That explained the foggy brain. It wasn't anything a strong cup of coffee couldn't cure. She pushed the button to bring her seat up from fully reclined. Then she pushed up to standing, shook out the sleep in her legs and crossed the room to the coffee maker. "Is there another mug inside that magic box?"

He was fixing her a paper plate of breakfast treats by the time she sidled up beside him. "Right there." He picked up the blue-brown swirly mug and handed it to her.

Audrey had to face facts. She'd given Mesa Point three years of her life, hoping to find a place to call home. What she'd been looking for wasn't here anymore. The feeling she'd had at sixteen that she would have a future with someone. Duke had moved on and so should she.

She'd saved enough money to get by until she figured out a new line of work. She could check up on Grandpa Lor and Grandma Lacy from her next stop.

She'd mistakenly believed a career in law enforcement would finally make her feel safe again only to realize that wasn't the case. Anyone could get to her. She might have a few more tools to work with but a determined criminal could find a way to watch her, target her.

Hell, a teenager caught her off guard.

"Every time you get lost in thought, you get a little wrinkle on your forehead." Duke pointed just above her eyebrow. "Right here."

"Is that so?"

She hadn't noticed. Then again, she wasn't exactly staring at herself in the mirror throughout the day, checking for reactions as she spoke.

"Yep," he quipped. "It shouldn't be sexy." He said those last words so low she almost didn't hear them. The effect they had on her was instant. Warmth encircled her as need welled up from deep inside. Duke's deep, masculine timbre caused goose bumps on her arms. Thoughts of the kisses they'd shared assaulted her, making her wish for more.

Before she could fall too deep into that rabbit hole, a figure emerged in her peripheral view. Young, female. Halsey? What was she doing here?

Audrey turned toward the door to the waiting room as Halsey knocked. The waiting room had emptied out so it was just Audrey and Duke inside.

Halsey stood at the door, unsure as to whether or not she should enter the room.

"Come on in," Audrey urged, trying to put the teen at ease. "Someone dropped by with cookies if you're hungry."

"No," Halsey said, checking behind her like she was afraid of being followed. The reason dawned on Audrey right away. Halsey's mother worked at the hospital. Surely, she would have taken today off after receiving news her son died. But small towns had eyes everywhere. Her mother's coworkers would recognize Halsey in a heartbeat, possibly ask what she was doing at the hospital or at the very least mention seeing her when they called to offer condolences.

Halsey's paranoia made sense.

"Do you want me to close the door so no one else can come inside without us knowing?" Audrey asked, meeting the teenager halfway across the room. Duke was right behind Audrey, his hand resting on the small of her back. Memories of their interaction with Morris last night were still fresh. The panic she'd felt when they realized some-one was watching from the woods was still a little too real.

"Um, no, it's okay," Halsey stammered. "I have to get back home before my mom realizes I took the car." The teen twisted her hands together.

"Do you want to sit down?" Audrey motioned toward chairs outside the view of the hallway.

Halsey shook her head and started working her hands double time. "I saw my brother talking to some, like, old guy."

"When you say old, do you have a guess as to the man's age?" Audrey asked.

She shrugged. "Probably like thirty or forty."

"What did he look like?" Audrey pressed, her deputy skills kicking into gear.

"Not really. He was too far away to get a good look. I didn't recognize him. All I could tell was that he was older and I got a bad feeling about him. Like, my brother had no business talking to him," she continued.

Although it wasn't exactly illegal for a thirty-year-old to speak to a teen, the conditions would matter. "How long ago did you see them talking?"

"A week and a half ago," Halsey stated.

"Did you ask your brother what the man wanted?" Audrey continued.

"Yes, but my brother blew me off. Said I was seeing things that weren't there and that he wasn't talking to any-body." Halsey looked put out. "Jenson became a real pain in the a—"

Halsey stopped herself as her cheeks flushed bright red.

"Was the man as tall as your brother?" Audrey asked.

"Um, I'd say he was a couple inches taller," Halsey

stated. She glanced over at Duke. "Closer to his height and maybe a little smaller in build."

"Dark hair or light?" Audrey asked.

"Seemed dark but it was nighttime and I was on my way home. The guy glanced over at me, handed something to my brother and then Jenson took off running. The guy disappeared around the corner."

"You didn't follow?"

"No, ma'am," Halsey said with a headshake, as though punctuating her sentence. She bit down on her bottom lip. "What was my brother really doing at the lake?"

"That's what we're trying to figure out," Audrey admitted. "It's the reason we stopped by your house yesterday."

"Drugs, right?" Halsey's shoulders hunched forward, defeated. "Had to be. Why else would he run away when I caught him talking to the older guy?"

This wasn't the time to explain the situation or what they believed the real reason to be. She didn't need to be told their suspicions.

Audrey chose her next words carefully. "We're interested in finding out the truth as much as you are."

"The man gave my brother an envelope full of money," Halsey blurted out. "I checked in his pocket when he was in the shower. I saw Jenson take something white from the guy, and it was money. A lot."

A lot could be a wide range. There were teens who would think twenty bucks was a fortune while others wouldn't bother to bend down and pick a twenty up if it was lying on the curb. It was all about perspective.

Halsey shook her head. "I heard the faucet turn off, so I didn't have time to count but I wouldn't be exaggerating if I said there could be a thousand dollars inside. The envelope was thick with twenty-dollar bills and barely folded."

It made sense why Halsey believed her brother was selling drugs with a bankroll like that. Jenson wasn't popular but seemed to want to hang out with the so-called cool kids. Would dealing drugs make him look "cool" to the others? Little did he know how uncool those insecure kids actually were. Anyone who felt the need to belittle those around them or put someone down was a jerk. Hurting someone because you believed they were beneath you was the lowest form of low in Audrey's opinion.

Audrey wished they could have access to Jenson's room. She might just be able to find the missing puzzle pieces for this unauthorized investigation to blow wide open. However, she knew for a fact his parents wouldn't give it to her, and she couldn't ask Halsey to go behind their backs. She would just have to figure out another way.

With this new information, she needed to go to her boss to bring him up to date and open an investigation. Or at the very least ask permission to dig further into it. A warrant to search Jenson's room would be helpful to get.

Halsey might be right about her brother being involved in drugs. Unfortunately, it was the path kids like him often went down when they were rejected by their peers or trying to appear cool. Once a kid started taking drugs, many didn't stop. Drugs didn't discriminate, either. They hooked rich kids and poor kids alike.

An envelope full of cash being handed to him rather than the other way around without any type of exchange was suspect. Could Jenson have started dealing? Become a middleman between dealer and the person who sold them on the street?

It didn't scan.

So what had Jenson really been doing?

Chapter Sixteen

Duke had kept quiet up to this point. "Where is the money now?"

"I have no idea," Halsey admitted. "Believe me, I turned his room upside down because I planned to take the money to my mom. But I couldn't find it."

Which meant Jenson had either hidden it or had it on him when he died. But why would the sheriff hide that? Duke casually glanced at Audrey, who'd picked up on the same thing he had. Wouldn't the sheriff have checked the kid's pockets?

Of course, the fact an older man was seen talking to Jenson and handing him an envelope full of cash could mean something else was going on besides a drug deal. Jenson might have picked up an odd job, except the amount was staggering if Halsey was correct. She also couldn't put a finger on who the man was, which might mean he was from out of town.

Access to Jenson's phone records could clear up any confusion. Would the sheriff agree?

Duke and Audrey needed to stop by his office. He'd insisted Audrey take a couple of days off to regroup after what happened yesterday. He'd said finding the boy would mess with her.

As far as Duke knew, Ackerman was a competent sheriff. Duke had a feeling they were about to find out if what he knew was true.

"I should get back home," Halsey said, checking the door for the third time in a few seconds.

"Thank you for stopping by," Audrey said. "I know you took a risk in coming here to your mom's work to speak to us, and I speak for both of us when I say we appreciate your bravery."

"This was the only place I knew I'd find you," Halsey admitted. "I called first and disguised my voice to find out if you were here. Plus, my brother's personality changed, but my parents are so blind." She rolled her eyes. "They refused to see anything negative when it came to him even when his behavior was as plain as the noses on their faces." She issued a frustrated sigh. "It's the most ridiculous thing. Like, I love...*loved* him, too, but that doesn't mean I didn't see him treating us like we weren't worth the dust on his tennis shoes."

"I get it," Audrey agreed, her voice a study in calm. She had a way of putting folks at ease. "Parents put blinders on sometimes. I see it all the time in my work."

Duke didn't like the sound of someone being able to find out where he and Audrey were with something as simple as a phone call. Although, small-town folks usually didn't worry about giving out information in the way people in the big city did. Folks from places like Dallas and Houston protected their privacy like they were holding on to the last piece of gold in the world's market. He didn't blame them a bit, considering how easy it was to spy on someone using the internet.

"My brother was in big trouble, wasn't he?" Halsey asked after chewing on her bottom lip. The teen looked ready to jump out of her skin if someone shouted *boo*.

"We're not certain but this new information is going to be very helpful," Audrey said, skillfully sidestepping the issue without lying. They weren't a hundred percent sure about anything when it came to Jenson's intentions.

Of course, there were easy answers. Jenson might have gotten mixed up in taking or selling drugs or both after being bullied or to prove he was cool. A surprising number of young people became addicted. And parents spent years trying to find their kid, or get him or her the help needed, or both. It always made Duke sad to come across those situations. Drug addiction hurt far more people than the addict themselves. It hurt everyone around them, everyone who loved them, especially the people who cared for them most.

"Okay, well, I better get home," Halsey conceded.

"Be careful on your way out," Audrey said.

In a surprise move, the teen hugged Audrey. She probably wouldn't agree, but she would make an amazing parent someday.

Duke thanked Halsey, too, hiding his concern at her last revelation.

"Did you catch how easy it was for her to locate us?" he asked Audrey once the teen was out of earshot.

"I know," Audrey responded. "But that's not the biggest issue right now." She pursed her lips together as she retrieved her cell. "We need to meet with Sheriff Ackerman. Ask him to open an investigation and allow me to lead."

"He would see you as too close to the case," Duke pointed out.

"Yeah? Well, that's not okay with me," she declared. "This is my life, and this investigation affects me."

"Are you buying the fact the money might have come from drugs?"

Now it was Audrey's turn to chew on her bottom lip. Her tongue darted across, leaving a silky trail. Duke didn't want to remember the kiss they'd shared when he needed all his powers of concentration for this case. Because it was more complicated than they first believed. He was certain of it.

Audrey issued a sharp sigh. "I want to believe the drug story. That might be wrong of me, but I'd like it to be that easy."

Duke knew the reason. If it wasn't about drugs, then someone might have been paying Jenson to work for them. Folks paid in wads of cash for one reason—to keep their dealings under the radar. In Duke's experience, ninety-nine percent of those transactions were illegal.

"You should stay here for your grandparents," Audrey said after a thoughtful pause. "I'm a distraction that you don't need right now."

"Until we get to the bottom of this, consider me your shadow," Duke argued.

"You don't have to do that, Duke. I know how much you love your grandparents, and the real reason you came home was to be with them, not me."

"As long as they're in a coma, there isn't much I can do to help," he stated. "Stopping in periodically throughout the day is just as good as sitting here. Actually, better. I feel useful out there."

"I know, but—"

"If you don't want my help, that's another story," he interrupted. "I won't push my services on anyone. However, I'd like it very much if you'd allow me to continue to assist you. It gives me something worthwhile to do instead of climbing the walls in this hospital."

"You know how much I appreciate your help, right?" She set her left fist firmly on her hip. "I can't imagine doing any of this without you."

"It's settled then," he confirmed.

"But if you have to beg off, I'll understand."

"I'm not walking away..."

Audrey shot a defensive look. He didn't mean it that way.

"This seems like a good time to tell you that once Grandpa Lor...*your* grandfather and grandmother are out of the woods, I'm moving away from Mesa Point," she informed him.

"Can I ask why?" There'd been something comforting about knowing she was back in town.

"I'm done here," she stated. "I came here three years ago looking for something that I couldn't quite put my finger on."

"So you found it and then that's it? You're bolting again?"

"No," she said, shaking her head for emphasis. "As a matter of fact, what I was searching for was already gone. Turns out, I'm wasting my time. But I did love being here with your grandparents."

Was she giving up on them having a full recovery? No one could blame her if she was. Duke, on the other hand, couldn't afford to think that way. Not with the two of them laid up in the hospital.

It was looking like he needed to call a family meeting to discuss how to care for the ranch moving forward. He had to face a fact he wasn't willing to consider before even though the ER doctor had laid it out: his grandparents might not be in any condition to keep their business going for a long time, if ever.

Duke couldn't stand the thought of either one of them waking up to learn the business they'd built together was no longer.

Whether Audrey stuck around or not, it didn't change the fact his temporary leave was going to have to turn into an indefinite one.

The idea of sticking around town after Audrey was long gone shouldn't feel like the gut punch it was. Weren't these the memories he'd been doing his level best to avoid?

"It's your life, your choice."

AUDREY SUCKED IN air as though she'd been punched. "I'm sure it'll make it easier on everyone. Right now, though, I need to call my boss and see what else he knows or if there is information he's keeping from me."

With that, she stepped out of the room. Staying would have been a mistake. Tears threatened, and she didn't want Duke to see her lose control. Besides, stepping away was good when she could feel her blood pressure escalating.

Hands shaking, she managed to tap the screen and get the ball rolling on the phone call. Sheriff Ackerman picked up on the second ring as she trekked to the opposite end of the hallway. A quick glance behind her revealed Duke stayed put. Good. She didn't need him on her heels anyway.

"What can I do for you, Audrey?" her boss asked.

"I'm curious about what you found on the Napier boy's body when you searched him," she said, getting right to the point.

"The best question you can ask yourself right now is how much time you need off to regroup," Ackerman said, his voice overly kind. Which meant he most likely found something.

"Why is that, boss?"

"Because you've been through a traumatic event," Ackerman said, softening his tone.

She couldn't argue his point there. Yesterday had been one for the books. "I'm trained to handle these kinds of events," she countered. "And I think we both know finding out the truth is the best way to put my mind at ease about what happened."

Ackerman was quiet for a long moment. Was she gaining ground? Possibly changing his mind about allowing her to be involved? "Audrey, you're a very good deputy," he finally said. "Which is why you need to take a step back from this one as I asked. So, you don't cross a line that can't be undone."

Audrey filled the sheriff in on the visit from Halsey.

"She came to me on her own, boss," Audrey said. "She trusted me with the information and now I'm telling you."

"You're doing the right thing, Audrey." The sheriff paused. "Still need you to step off this case. Let me do my job."

"Does that mean you're opening an investigation?" she pressed, knowing full well she was pushing her luck.

"I'm not discussing my plans with you," Ackerman said firmly. It was the tone he used when she'd crossed a line, and he was warning her to proceed with caution. "But you have introduced new information and I wouldn't be good at my job if I didn't follow up." Ackerman blew out a frustrated breath. "We're on the same team here."

"I know," she said. "Did you find the cash on him?"

Again, she was met with silence on the other end of the line.

"I'm good at being a deputy because I'm stubborn," she said, trying to influence his position. "You've praised those qualities before."

"Can't say that I'm not regretting that choice right now," he admitted, still with the warning tone.

"You probably are," she said, easing off the gas pedal a bit. "But I think we both know the department is better off for it. And all I'm looking for here is confirmation about the money. Can you give me at least that much?"

"Did you visit the Napier home?"

She could deny it, but he could easily find out. Plus, she hated lying. "Yes, sir, I did."

"Did you ask the Napiers to give you access to the suspect's room?"

"Yes, sir." She figured Halsey was right about their parents keeping their heads in the sand about what Jenson had become. Especially their mother. Stephanie Napier most definitely had blinders on when it came to her son. Morris did not.

Even if Morris knew something, he wouldn't say it in front of his wife. He came across as the loyal type. He wasn't likely to say it behind her back, either, for fear word would get back to her. No, Morris wanted to protect his wife from any potential harm even when he needed to find out what his son was up to, and he would see nothing to gain by exposing his son. In his mind, it was over.

"They lost their son, Audrey," Ackerman said. "This hasn't been easy on them."

"I can't imagine it would be." Was that it? Was her boss trying to protect folks he'd known for the better part of his life? Small towns gossiped, and small towns protected their own.

Didn't she qualify?

"They don't deserve to have their names dragged through the mud without concrete proof," he continued.

"Halsey came forward. We have to respect her for that."

She wanted to point out that she clearly wasn't the only one with a personal interest in the case. But this didn't seem like the right time for the reminder.

A flurry of activity down the hallway caught her attention. And then Duke came bolting down the hallway toward his grandparents' room. Had he been standing at the waiting room door or taking a walk after their tense exchange?

"I have to go, sir," she said to her boss. She got the okay before ending the call and rushing toward a distressed-looking Duke.

Chapter Seventeen

"False alarm."

Duke heard the words, but they were taking a minute to seed. His heart had dropped as he'd been walking the halls before hearing his grandmother's room number being called out as in distress.

"What happened in there?" he asked the nurse blocking his entrance to his grandparents' room.

"The good news is that your grandmother moved," the nurse said, holding a hand up to stop Duke from charging right through her. She couldn't stop him if she wanted to, but he didn't think it was a good idea to get on the wrong side of the nursing staff when it looked like his grandparents might be in here for a while. "She jiggled her IV loose which caused the alarm to sound."

"Everything okay?" Audrey asked as she came up beside him. Those concern lines were back, creating deep grooves in her forehead.

"Seems like nothing," he said, his words consoling her. She'd walked out of the waiting area in a huff. "An IV."

"You'll do your grandparents the best favor if you go back to the waiting room," the nurse urged, taking a step forward while her hand was still planted on Duke's chest.

It caused him to take a step back. His first instinct was to charge forward, but experience and getting older was bringing more patience.

Still. He had limits.

"We'll be in there if anything else happens," he said to the nurse before turning to Audrey. It dawned on him that she might not be so willing to go back with him after having words a few minutes ago. He dipped down to whisper, "I'd be honored if you'd come back in the waiting room with me."

Audrey's muscles were tense. He had to flex and release his fingers for fear they would take on a life of their own and reach to comfort her. She hadn't invited touch, so he wouldn't cross the line.

Thankfully, she didn't head toward the elevator bank. For a second, he thought she might be returning to the waiting room to grab her purse before leaving. When she sat down on the recliner, he knew she planned to stay for a minute at the very least.

"What did Ackerman say?" he asked.

"He didn't want to tell me much, but I informed him of Halsey's visit," she said. "He didn't come right out and say he was already investigating the case but came close enough."

"Information being withheld from you is frustrating as hell," he admitted. "But he might have his reasons."

Audrey blew out a breath, and her shoulders deflated like a balloon. "I get that he's trying to protect me and the Napiers, but I still feel like I deserve to know what's happening, especially if there's the slightest possibility I could still be in danger."

"I couldn't agree more." In fact, they wouldn't make progress here in the hospital. They needed to get out of here. "Nash is on his way. He texted when you were in the hall and I stepped out of the waiting room to stretch my legs."

"Does that mean we can leave?"

"I don't see why not," he conceded.

"I'd like to go home," she said. "Have a home-cooked meal."

He got it. After folks experienced traumatic events, doing something like cooking or cleaning gave them a sense of normalcy. They could take a break. He hadn't slept, and fog was settling over his brain anyway.

Maybe an afternoon would do them both good.

"Mind if I come with you?" he asked, not taking for granted that she might want him to join her. He hadn't meant what he'd said a little while ago about her leaving. He'd popped off at the mouth. Being tired wasn't an excuse, but it was the reason. An hour or so of shut-eye would do him good.

"I was hoping you would," Audrey said quietly.

"We can stop off at the grocery to pick up steaks and all the fixin's," he said.

"Sounds good," she said without giving much away in the form of emotions. She had a way of shutting down when she was overly stressed. He'd seen it when they were kids more often than he cared to admit in those first few weeks of summer. But he'd always been able to get her to open up again with a comment or his touch.

Right now, though, she would slap him if he tried physical contact, and he didn't trust himself not to say the wrong thing like he'd already done a few minutes ago. He'd take the words back if he could. It was too late.

The last thing he wanted to do was put more emotional distance between them. He could use a friend to lean on, and he guessed she needed one, too. Just like when they were younger, and he was trying to figure out why his own flesh and blood could walk away from the family he'd created with a woman he was supposed to love who died. And Audrey had been running from her own demons—demons that had eventually taken her away from him.

Could they get past them to be there for one another for one evening?

He hoped so.

Nurses reassured they had Duke's number at the ready in case either of his grandparents' condition changed.

On the way back to the cabin, Duke stopped off at the grocery. He was amazed at how many folks paused to offer a kind word about his grandparents and how proud they were of him and his siblings and cousins.

Being back in Mesa Point reminded him of what he'd loved about the ranch in the first place. It felt like home.

THE STEAKS TURNED out amazing thanks to Duke's finesse with a grill. Audrey was duly impressed and wasn't shy about telling him so. The man had skills.

She didn't want to let herself think too much about the other skills he had, like being the best kisser she'd ever experienced. Those thoughts wouldn't do any good and only managed to make her lips burn to touch his.

"I'm on dishes," she declared, searching for a distraction and wishing she'd picked something else the minute those words came out of her mouth.

"Mind if I take a seat on the couch while you clean up?" Duke asked.

"Go for it."

He gave a nod and a smile that pierced her heart.

Washing dishes didn't take long as he got settled in the

living room. Still, by the time she finished, Duke had practically sunk into her couch with his eyes closed. His steady, even breathing said he'd dozed off.

The sun was descending and shining brightly through the mini-blind slats. Audrey scooted across the living room and closed them. The man hadn't slept since they'd been together and probably not for a minimum of twenty-four hours before that when he arrived in Mesa Point. She thought she remembered him saying something about being on a case prior to his trip home that had kept him awake.

Audrey needed her sleep. She had no idea how he managed with so little and still functioned like a normal person. Then again, *normal* wasn't exactly the word she would use to describe Duke Remington. He fell into the superhero category as far as she was concerned. There was something quietly reassuring about having Duke in her home, like he belonged there. And he was the only reason she could be there right now too after all that had happened.

Audrey had been back in Mesa Point for three years already—wouldn't Duke have come back a whole lot sooner if he wanted to see her?

In truth, he did visit his grandparents. She respected their wishes and stayed away, but he could have asked about her. He could have stopped by her cabin, a cabin located almost exactly at the spot they'd shared their first kiss. The fact had not been not lost on her the first time she was shown this place. As a matter of fact, she knew the exact spot where it happened.

The time had come to move on. Her lease was coming up next month. She needed to give her landlord thirty days' notice. Then again, with the way word traveled in this town coupled with the lack of privacy, maybe she would be better off paying for an extra month rather than give a heads-up too early.

Audrey had never acquired a taste for lying like her parents, but she didn't welcome unwanted questions about her private life. Questions that would surely come if she turned in her notice. What would she do next? She wanted land and plenty of space between her and her neighbors. Animals, too. Raising alpacas sounded good to her. She might be able to work someone else's herd to learn the ins and outs before diving into running her own place.

Patience.

After making a cup of coffee, she started toward the kitchen table where her laptop was charging. The sun had dipped lower in the sky. Metal sparkled on the grill. She'd forgotten to grab a pair of tongs smothered in steak juice. Leaving those out overnight would invite all manner of unwanted creatures.

Audrey headed outside to retrieve the dirty tongs, leaving the door unlocked behind her. She was literally stepping ten feet outside her home and then coming right back in.

As she reached for the tongs, something sharp slammed into the back of her head. The earth tipped off its axis, and her knees buckled. Before she could scream, a hand came over her mouth. Suddenly, another wrapped around her in a viselike grip, and a voice whispered in her ear, "Think you can get away from me, bitch? You're just like the others. You like to fight. I'll punish you for that. You haven't been nice to Trey. You hurt me, so I'm going to make you pay."

The voice was low, guttural, and the words came out in between grunts. She didn't recognize the male gripping her from behind.

Audrey tried to open her mouth to bite his thick fingers

but failed. His hand wasn't the only thing over her mouth. He held a cloth that had a chemical smell. Chloroform?

She wriggled her body. At least, she attempted to. The man's grip held her steady. A second blow to the back of the head caused the world to spin as though she'd just taken several tequila shots. As much as Audrey fought against losing consciousness, she was no match for a head injury.

Bile burned the back of her throat as everything went dark.

AUDREY PUSHED THROUGH the fog and the darkness, struggling to wake up. She didn't know how much time had passed but she *had* to open her eyes if she wanted to live.

Forcing her eyes open wasn't working, so she tried a different tack. Maybe she could scream. Nope. Opening her mouth was next to impossible. Did she have something covering her mouth? A rag? Duct tape?

Where was she? How long was she unconscious?

Audrey forced herself to calm down and listen. She was being walked through the woods, caveman style. With every step, her body bounced. This sonofabitch took her from her own home. The cabin was the one place she'd felt safe after leaving Remington Paint Ranch.

Fighting back right now would give away the fact she was alert. She must not have been out for too long. It wasn't too late to find a way out of this.

The element of surprise was her best chance of beating this bastard.

Thinking hurt. It felt like her skull was cracked, no doubt a result of being hit in the back of the head with something hard. A rock? A brick? Hell, it could have been a hammer for all she knew.

Panic gripped her.

Every step he took produced another wave of pounding, like the hammer was inside her trying to whack its way out. Audrey had been in a few scuffles since becoming a deputy, but she'd never been abducted.

Why hadn't he shot her already and got it over with?

This had to be the man who'd handed over a wad of cash to Jenson and got the kid killed in the process. It dawned on her the bastard might have paid Jenson to come cover his tracks. It would explain the boot prints versus tennis shoes and the fact Jenson wouldn't be caught dead wearing work boots.

She forced her eyes to open a crack. Thanks to the caveman carry—some called it a fireman carry—she could see the man's backside.

He was a large guy. Tall and thick, like a football player. Since he was carrying her without so much as breathing heavily, he was also strong as an ox.

And he had on a pair of work boots.

How was she going to get away from him before he took her to an isolated location where he could do as he pleased with her?

Leaves slapped the backs of Audrey's thighs and feet as her arms dangled. They weren't bound. Neither were her ankles. She hadn't put on shoes since she was only supposed to be stepping outside for a few seconds.

A creepy-crawly feeling came over her at the thought this guy wanted to kill her so badly that he kept watching her home despite having Duke there.

Of course, the Ponytail Snatcher must have been lurking around. Those had to have been his footprints around her home. He was too quick to seize the opportunity when it presented itself to have been far away. Had he been camping in the nearby woods?

Was he taking her there now?

Chapter Eighteen

Duke rubbed eyes that felt like someone had slipped sand-paper inside them. The room was dark. How long had he been out? Sitting up, he listened for signs of Audrey moving around the house. The last thing he wanted to do was catch her off guard or scare her. She'd been through a lot and was jumping at little sounds, so he cleared his throat and checked the time.

It wasn't late. Only half past six.

Where was she?

Duke stood up and stretched his arms out. His right leg had fallen asleep, so he pounded his thigh a couple of times with his fist to wake it up. There was no sign of her in the kitchen, so he listened for shower water. Didn't hear that, either.

Was she taking a nap?

He walked across the room to the main bedroom.

"Hey," he whispered in case she was up reading and didn't want to disturb him. No response came, which jacked his heart rate up a couple of notches. She could have ear-buds in, playing music.

None of those thoughts rang true. He was grasping at straws.

Gut instinct told him that something was up. He had a bad feeling. He turned tail and checked outside to make sure his truck was still there. It was parked on the pad right where he left it. Her vehicle was in front of his, blocked. She couldn't have driven to the store. The back door was unlocked, and the porch door was open.

His cell buzzed in his pocket. He fished it out of his pocket and glanced at the screen, didn't recognize the number. He decided to answer in case it was the hospital calling. "Hello?"

"Mr. Remington?"

"Yes, ma'am," he answered. "May I ask who wants to know?"

"This is Cybil from Mesa General," she said. Hearing those words alone made his chest clench. "You're listed as the emergency contact for Lorenzo Remington, is that correct?"

"Yes, ma'am," he said, not liking where this was going one bit.

"I'm afraid your grandfather has had a cardiac event," she stated with sympathy in her voice. "You might want to head this way in case the doctor needs you to sign off on any paperwork."

"Paperwork?"

"For procedures," she clarified. "It's precautionary."

"What happened to my grandfather's heart?" he asked.

"He was resuscitated from cardiac," she continued.

"Is he conscious now?" he pressed.

"No, sir," she answered. "It's not uncommon for a patient not to regain consciousness. Recovery could take hours or weeks, or longer."

"Does that mean he could stay as a vegetable forever?" he asked, needing to know if he was facing one of the worst possible scenarios. He couldn't even consider the other one, death.

"It's too early to tell," she said. "The doctor hasn't figured out why he went into cardiac arrest in the first place, and he would like to run a few tests."

"Tell him to do whatever is necessary to save my grandfather's life," Duke instructed. At this point, he didn't care what that entailed.

"I'm afraid insurance only approves certain procedures," she explained.

"I'll pay for whatever he needs to have done," Duke insisted. "Put me down as financially responsible."

He didn't care if it took the rest of his life to pay the hospital bills if it meant getting his grandparents back. The rest could be figured out later.

"I'll pass along the fact we have verbal commitment, but everything has to be done in writing, Mr. Remington," she informed.

"Okay, fine," he said. "Send the forms to me electronically. I'll sign whatever you need."

"It should be so easy," Cybil sympathized. "I'm afraid we're not there yet. We need your signature witnessed by a hospital employee."

Duke issued a sharp sigh. "I'm on my way as soon as I can get there," he promised. He needed to get to Audrey.

More than that, he found that he wanted to talk to her about what was going on. Talking to Audrey brought a surprising amount of calm over him. Not being with her had the opposite effect, and his stress level hit the roof during this call.

Quickly ending the call, Duke grabbed hold of his keys and made a beeline for the back door.

Duke bent down and pulled his SIG out of his ankle holster. His backup weapon came in handy more times than not and he'd strapped it on after not having it last night. The SIG was small in his hand, easy to maneuver. He searched the home, cleared every room in a matter of minutes. Her service weapon hung inside her closet.

Audrey's purse strap hung around the back of a dining room chair. Her laptop was charging. Her cell was sitting on the kitchen counter.

He moved to the patio door. Noted that her shoes were next to the door. If she'd gone outside barefoot, she wouldn't have gone far.

Moving outside, he noted the dirty tongs he'd used to flip the steaks were still sitting beside the grill. Had Audrey stepped outside to grab the tongs while she was cleaning dishes?

Damn that he'd nodded off and couldn't remember much past dinner. Exhaustion had taken hold, and he'd closed his eyes seconds after sitting down on the couch with a full stomach.

Anger ripped through him, heating his blood to boiling. Someone must have been watching, waiting.

But where did they take her?

Duke tapped the flashlight app on his cell phone and used it to check the ground around the grill. Sure enough, there were boot prints similar to the ones from yesterday leading away from the grill.

From the looks of the dusty dry soil, there'd been a scuffle. Good for Audrey for fighting back.

The boot prints were set deeper in the ground as they left a trail leading away from the house and toward the wooded area where they'd first been discovered the other morning. One set of deeper prints most likely meant the bastard carried Audrey. She wouldn't go down without a fight, so that led Duke to believe she'd been knocked out.

Duke searched for signs of blood as he followed the tracks, covering his light so he wouldn't advertise to the abductor that Duke was onto him. Deeper in the woods, scrub brush covered the boot prints.

At this point, it was anyone's guess which way the bastard had taken her. Duke released a string of swear words underneath his breath. The perp wouldn't have shot her near the house because he must have realized Duke was there. Had he seen Duke asleep through one of the windows?

A picture was emerging with Jenson, as well. They'd had the kid wrong. He'd been slipped the cash to cover the perp's tracks once Duke arrived in town. The hunch made perfect sense. Had the perp known Duke was going to keep an eye out for Audrey?

More of that anger welled up. He couldn't lose her again. Where the hell was she?

AUDREY'S BEST MOVE at the moment was to play dead. Trey—she'd repeated his name several times so she wouldn't forget—had carried her far enough away from her cabin, he must be confident he could get away with murder because he dropped her off his shoulder.

Her body thudded on the hard dry earth. Her hip slammed into a rock, but she didn't dare make a sound as she crumpled onto the ground in near fetal position. This way, she could reach into her xHolster. She might have taken her shoes off once she was home, but she'd trapped on her holster.

Risking a peek, she saw Trey reach for something... A weapon? It was too dark to make out his face clearly. She didn't recognize his voice when he'd half whispered, half grunted at her a few minutes ago.

How far from her house had he taken her?

One thing was clear as the full moon: Trey didn't intend to let her leave this area alive. Audrey figured he was taking her far enough from everything and everyone in the area so he could kill her and leave the body.

What did he plan to do then? Go after his next target?

Squinting, she made note of all that she could see. Her eyes had thankfully adjusted to the darkness enough to make out some images. Trees were thick here. The ground was littered with rocks—one had slammed into her hip hard enough to leave a bruise. That was going to hurt for a long time to come.

Moving slowly so as not to draw attention, she reached for the backup weapon in her ankle holster. Came up short. Could she stretch her fingers enough to release the weapon from the holster and palm the gun?

A glance at Trey caused her blood to run cold. He'd palmed his weapon and aimed it directly at her.

With no time to lose, Audrey made a play for her weapon. The metal felt cool against her warm palm. She came up with it, lifted the barrel to aim directly at Trey's chest and fired. The second she pulled the trigger, she rolled in order to get out of the way of the bullet zooming toward her.

Did she make it in time?

THE CRACK OF a bullet split the air. Not one, Duke corrected himself, but two. He adjusted his position and bolted toward the sound. He killed his phone's flashlight so he could move in the darkness.

Thankfully, he knew this area like the back of his hand. Now that he had a direction, he knew exactly how to get there. The question was whether or not he'd be too late. Two gunshots fired close together weren't a good sign. He had no idea if Audrey had a weapon on her.

Duke pushed his legs until his thighs burned, then slowed down, not wanting to announce his arrival by making too much noise.

Sounds of a struggle caught his attention.

And then he heard a bloodcurdling scream. *Audrey.*

Muttering a string of curse words under his breath, he bolted toward the distress calls. Another shot fired.

Please let her be all right.

He broke into a harder run, panting as he pushed through the thicket. Scrub brush tangled around his shoes, tripping him every other step, but nothing could stop him from reaching Audrey. He forced his way through the overgrown vines and weeds.

By the time he reached Audrey, she was gasping for air on her side.

Duke's training taught him better than to run toward an injured person, so he slowed down and surveyed the area before dashing to her and taking a knee by her side.

"Duke," she gasped, immediately looping her arms around his neck. "He took off that way." She released him and pointed northeast, talking through gasps. "Go. You might be able to catch him if you hurry."

"I'm not leaving you here alone," he insisted as he fished his cell out of his pocket. "We'll call for help."

"He said his name," she said. "It's Trey."

He muttered another curse when he realized there was no cell coverage at this spot. Audrey, however, managed to sit up. She winced in pain with movement as her hand immediately came up to the back of her head.

"Where are you hit?" he asked, hoping for the best while

fearing the worst. His grandfather was in trouble. Audrey was shot. To say this day had gone to hell in a handbasket was an understatement.

"I don't know," she admitted. This close, he could see the whites of her eyes in the moonlight. Her adrenaline must be pumping through her veins, and she most likely was in at least a mild state of shock.

Blood wasn't gushing out of her as far as he could tell.

"Can you get up and walk?" he asked, holding out his hand, ever aware the perp could be behind a tree setting up his next shot.

They needed to get out of here. Now.

Chapter Nineteen

Audrey managed to stand up with Duke's assistance. She had no idea where Trey had disappeared to. He could be anywhere out here. Duke wasn't able to call for help. Even if he could, it would take time for another deputy or the sheriff to get out here. At this point, they were sitting ducks.

They needed to move no matter how much pain it caused. Reaching up to touch the back of her skull, she felt something wet. Most likely blood. She wouldn't be surprised, given the couple of whacks she'd taken on the crown of her head. She remembered Trey tried something else, too.

"That sonofabitch put a rag over my mouth soaked with chloroform," she said to Duke as they started back toward the cabin.

"It doesn't work in real life like it does in the movies," he said, but they both knew that was true already. Very little did work the same. "It does give us an idea that he's maybe using crime shows as inspiration."

Audrey limped, moving as quickly as she could. There was no obvious blood gushing out of her anywhere. Was it possible she'd literally dodged a bullet, even at close range?

"I'm certain I hit him," she said to Duke. "It looked like

I took off a piece of his shoulder, but he dived once he realized I had a weapon. He wasn't exactly in point-blank range, but I'm usually a better shot than that." Her hand had been shaking as she raised it to shoot, which hadn't helped matters.

"You're alive," he reminded her. "You did good."

"Thanks, but he's still out there so I'm not exactly safe," she pointed out.

"He's not coming back tonight," Duke stated. "We're too aware of him now."

"Still, I don't want to stay at the cabin anymore," she said, firm on her stance. Being there, knowing someone could so easily walk up and watch her through her windows gave her the creeps.

This wasn't the time to dig her heels in and insist on staying home.

"You're more than welcome to stay at the ranch," Duke offered. "I'm the only one in the house right now, but that might change."

There was a note in his tone that concerned her. "What's going on? What happened?"

He shook his head. "Not now."

"I can handle whatever it is, Duke." Granted, her head pounded like someone stood behind her and played drums with a hammer. Still. Whatever was happening, she wanted to know.

And then it dawned on her. She sucked in a gulp of air. "Your grandmother?"

"Grandfather," he corrected.

"Oh, no," she said. "What is it?"

"Grandpa Lor went into cardiac arrest," he said in a low whisper.

"We need to get to the hospital," she stated. "Immediately."

"We do," he admitted. "But not just for the reason you think. You need to be checked out, Audrey."

"I'm lucid," she said defensively. Realizing how that sounded, she softened her tone when she said, "While we're there checking on Grandpa Lor, it wouldn't hurt for me to see the doc on call. You can run up to your grandfather's floor. I'll check in with emergency and meet you up there as soon as I'm cleared."

They broke through the clearing of her yard. The cabin was in view now. He would have bars on his phone.

"We should call this in," she said to Duke. "This one hit way too close to home." Literally and figuratively, as far as she was concerned. It was a bold move, attacking her at her own home while a US marshal was inside. The perp might have figured out that Duke was asleep but still. He had to get close to the windows to learn that information. Audrey distinctly remembered closing the blinds in the living room so Duke could rest better.

Duke made the call to her boss as they walked into the cabin. He set her down on the couch so she could assess her injuries and then cleared the home to make certain the bastard wasn't hiding somewhere inside.

"You told the sheriff we'd meet him at the hospital?" she asked, lost in her thoughts while he'd made the call.

"That's right," Duke said, grabbing her purse and cell. He tucked the phone inside and then threw the strap over his arm.

"I can help." She started to get up, but gravity gave her a hard no in return. She plopped right back down on her backside. Her head felt like it might actually explode when she tried to move, which made her dizzy.

She also noted there was blood on Duke's shirt where his side had been pressed up against her. She checked under

her arm and realized she'd been nicked by a bullet fragment. Thank heaven it wasn't much more than a scratch
that might not even need stitches. Maybe a butterfly bandage and a little glue would do the trick.

"You were hit," Duke said as he helped her up. He did
most of the work of getting her on her feet.

"I got lucky," she admitted with a small smile meant to
reassure him. "It could have been a lot worse."

He took in a slow deep breath and mumbled something
that sounded a whole lot like, "I can't lose you twice."

Audrey slipped through the front door he opened, her
weapon still in her hand. He managed to hold her up while
at the same time he held her handbag and locked the front
door.

She scanned the area for any signs of movement.

Duke fished keys out of his pocket and hit the button to
unlock his truck as they neared the passenger side. With
effort and a whole lot of help, she managed to ease onto
the seat and buckle in. Most of the pain was coming from
her skull. So much so, she hadn't noticed the bullet graze
on the inside of her underarm.

The idea of staying at the ranch for the night brought
back a flood of memories. So many of them were the best of
her life. Little did she know at sixteen years old she would
have her absolute best three months. No other season or
time in her life would live up to that summer.

Duke claimed the driver's seat, started the engine and
secured his seat belt.

Getting a dog sounded like a good idea if she ever wanted
to feel safe again in her own home, wherever home ended
up being. It wasn't supposed to be like this. She worked in
law enforcement. She was trained.

She'd worked hard to overcome her past.

Not feeling safe in her own home brought back all the helpless feelings she'd experienced most of her young life. Would talking about the horrors she'd experienced help when training to shoot a gun hadn't?

"My parents killed my sister and blamed it on me," she said to Duke out of nowhere. "I was so young and so horrified that I lost the ability to speak. The psychiatrist I was ordered to see called it traumatic mutism. Only she believed I was traumatized by accidentally killing my sister when in reality I was terrified of my parents. They didn't know I was hiding in her closet when they came in that night and roused her from bed. I was, though. They got fired up about something she was supposed to do around the house but forgot. The long and short of it was that they ran a bath and then basically waterboarded her until she was exhausted. I sneaked into my room, but they came for me, too. Forced me into the bathroom and told me to watch her. My job was to scream if she climbed out of the tub."

Tears streamed down Audrey's face at the memory.

"She was so tired, she sank to the bottom of the tub," Audrey continued after catching her breath. "I thought she was playing a game and holding her breath. I wasn't watching because I was curled up in the corner, shaking like a leaf. I didn't offer help when I could have saved her."

"You were a child," he said with the kind of compassion that made her want to believe those words. "You couldn't have known what was going to happen."

"So why haven't I been able to let myself off the hook ever since?"

DUKE'S HEART BROKE at hearing what Audrey had been carrying around all these years. He wished there was something he could say to ease some of her pain. Rather than try and fail, he reached across the truck and squeezed her hand while stopped at a red light. "I'm sorry for everything you've gone through, Audrey. I really am."

Her hand relaxed in his, and she managed a smile that didn't reach her eyes. "I'm damaged goods, Duke. You're better off staying far away from me."

There was no way in hell he was letting her talk about herself in that manner. "You're a survivor, Audrey. And a damn good one, too. Not many folks could endure what you did and still come out willing to help others. You've been taking care of my grandparents when it should have been one of us."

"You guys had places to go," she argued. "Your careers took you away from home, but that didn't stop you from coming back to help out when the need arose. Your grandparents are lucky to have such loving people in their corner."

He wasn't so sure they'd done everything they could, but this conversation wasn't about him, so he guided it back on track. "When you came to live with us that summer, you didn't say the bruises were from your parents."

"That's right," she confirmed. "They did a number on my face."

"How did you escape?"

"They locked me inside my room," she said quietly. "I set the house on fire with matches I found, so they'd have to let me escape. That was after going two days without water and three without food. I was desperate."

"And then what happened?" he asked.

"A favor was called in from one of Grandpa Lor's old friends at the marshal's office and I landed at the ranch to 'stay with a friend' until their trial." Her voice took on a detached note. It was almost as though she had to distance herself from reality as far as possible in order to talk about it. He'd seen the same thing with other crime victims during his career.

"And that's how you ended up in Mesa Point with my grandparents." One positive from this difficult to hear conversation was that Audrey was finally opening up to him and talking about something significant from her past. She usually redirected the conversation when he asked questions about what happened.

She nodded. "The thing is, when I acted in desperation back at home and set the place ablaze, I lost the ability to speak again."

"But you spoke to me at the ranch," he said.

"I know," she admitted. "You were the first and only person who made me feel safe enough to speak, is the best I can figure. It was most likely having someone my age to talk to that did the trick." She shrugged.

It was probably wrong of him to want to be special in her eyes. To want to be the reason she opened up at all and not just because they happened to be the same age and in the same place.

"It was easy to talk to you," he admitted. "You were an old soul even back then. More mature than your age dictated."

"Thank you, Duke. That means a lot coming from you." She tapped her index finger on the armrest. "Your friendship has always meant the world to me."

Duke didn't argue her word choice, but they'd been a couple planning a future back then, not merely friends. Could they become friends moving forward? All he knew for certain was that he wanted her back in his life.

"I've decided to turn in my notice at work," she said. "I'm moving out of Mesa Point, but I don't want you to think it's because of the perp. No one gets to take my power away again. It's important for me to stand up for myself. You know?"

He nodded, trying not to give away the fact her news was the equivalent of a gut punch. "Standing up for yourself is important," he said. "And I know you'll do it the right way. You won't go off half-cocked at the perp."

"No, I won't," she said. "This bastard needs to rot in hell."

"The sheriff might be able to get a DNA sample from the woods," Duke stated. "It'll take a while to get results back, but you never know when you'll get lucky. It could help ID the bastard. Plus, you got a first name."

"True," she said. "But I only plan to stick around long enough to see your grandparents wake up." She sounded so certain they would. "And then I'm packing up and getting out of Dodge."

"Do you have to go so soon?" he asked, realizing she may have started the process before he arrived home. "Is there a job waiting?"

"No," she said. "I think it's best if I leave and clear my head. Coming back to Mesa Point, to the only place I've ever felt like I belonged, wasn't the same this time around. Once I was here, I started working almost right away."

"Speaking of work, doesn't the sheriff need you here?"

"I guess," she said. "Honestly, I don't think Ackerman and I see eye to eye. And I'm considering buying land at some point. This job isn't what I thought it would be."

"Don't let that jerk take this away from you," he argued.

"The perp? He couldn't. I've been thinking along these lines for a while," she admitted. "I wanted to help people while feeling safe. But I don't. I'm just as vulnerable as everyone else."

"You're trained and good at your job," he countered. "But if it's truly not what you want, then you're smart to get out before you have too many years invested."

A heavy feeling settled in his chest as he parked at the hospital. A sense of urgency moved him to exit the truck and then come around to Audrey's side to open the door for her. He couldn't imagine Mesa Point without her now.

With his grandparents' conditions worsening, there was change in the air.

Chapter Twenty

Audrey walked beside Duke, leaning on him as they cleared the parking lot and hospital doors. She broke off at the ER where her boss sat waiting in one of the blue plastic chairs.

Sheriff Ackerman immediately stood up and walked to her. His gaze inspected the blood spots on her clothing.

"Will you be okay here?" Duke asked as he helped her sit down. Her boss took the seat beside her. "I need to sign consent forms."

"I'll make sure she's all right," Ackerman said. "I know I haven't done a great job so far but that changes here and now."

Duke nodded, then disappeared down the hallway. Audrey gave a quick rundown of what happened to the sheriff. Two of her coworkers were on scene in the woods, searching for the location Duke had described on the phone.

"Did you get a good look at the person who did this to you?" Sheriff Ackerman asked after listening carefully to the rest of her version of what happened. He would naturally be concerned about one of his own being attacked. He also had a bigger problem, in that a dangerous criminal was running around in his county. The Ponytail Snatcher targeted female deputies around the state, cutting off their ponytails. That had to be significant.

"It was dark, and my vision was blurry after being hit in the back of the head," she admitted. "He was tall and strong as an ox. Thick, like football-player-type muscles."

Ackerman shook his head as he took notes. His face pinched. "Your quick thinking saved your life. I didn't mean to let you down by not giving you access to information. I was following protocol meant to protect law enforcement. In this case, it did more harm than good."

"How many deputies has he killed?" she asked.

"Five, according to the FBI agent on the task force hunting for him," Ackerman supplied.

"I was so close," she said. "I let him slip out of my hands."

"You lived," Ackerman countered. "You're the only one."

She didn't respond.

"You got further with the family than I did too," he admitted. "Any other details come to mind while the attack is still fresh?"

"I couldn't get a good look at his facial features except to say he had dark hair," she admitted. "I know tall with dark hair in Texas doesn't exactly narrow the field. He's injured, though. That should help. I got a good piece of his shoulder."

"Matches the general description Halsey provided," he pointed out.

"True," she agreed. "He might have been paying Jenson to forget he ever saw him or cover his tracks."

"I checked the hospital, and no one has come in with a GSW to the shoulder. We might not have an exact description to work with, but that won't stop me. I'll put out a BOLO either way," Ackerman said. "This perp is armed and dangerous. He's nursing an injury. Word needs to spread immediately in case he shows up in another county seeking medical aid."

He spoke quietly into the radio clipped to his shoulder as Duke rejoined them.

The sheriff made a good point. Audrey had already gone down the path of the perp most likely finding a shed near the lake to hole up in rather than leave a trail of blood everywhere or be seen in his current condition. That should make it easier to identify the man if someone came across him and knew to look for an injured person.

Audrey glanced up in time to see a wheelchair being pushed toward her by a concerned-looking nurse.

"Deputy," the nurse said to her as she came around to help Audrey transition to the wheelchair. Without another word, she was wheeled into the hallway and then through a door that led to an open room with several curtains closed while Duke gave the sheriff his quick-and-dirty version of what happened.

An ER doctor met them in a small room behind a curtain. The badge on his white lab coat read Dr. Garcia.

The doctor immediately went to work, checking her over as he asked her to point out every spot she'd been injured. Garcia seemed to know better than to ask Duke or the sheriff to leave.

He stood there looking more bull than man with his muscled arms crossed over a solid wall chest. The doctor gave a nod of acknowledgment to Duke after he pulled the curtain closed. It occurred to her the two most likely knew each other.

Dr. Garcia worked methodically, cleaning and bandaging Audrey's wounds. He gave her two shots to numb under her arm where he said she needed a handful of stitches. The numbing agents did their jobs. She felt nothing while he sewed her back together.

"Are you good to stay?" Ackerman asked Duke.

"I won't leave her side," he reassured.

"Well, then I'll take off so I can jump into the investigation before anyone else is attacked in my county," the sheriff said. "The task force trying to lock this bastard behind bars is sending an FBI agent."

After a concussion test, Audrey was advised that she'd been lucky. She wasn't showing any signs there. The back of her head had a small cut.

"Heads are bleeders," Dr. Garcia said. He was almost completely white haired, with good bedside manners. Considering he was hit with all manner of emergencies at his job, the man was a sea of calm. "The cuts aren't as bad as I first feared."

"That's good news," she agreed.

"I'd like to keep you overnight for observation, but I'm guessing that's not going to be an option," Dr. Garcia said.

"A hospital is no place for rest," she said with a smile.

"I'd have to agree with you there," he said with a wink. "Unfortunately, you have people coming in and out of your room all night poking and prodding."

The thought of anyone being able to walk through those doors and into her room caused an involuntary shiver to rock her body. No, thanks. Could she go back to the ranch with Duke? Could she face his family home with him without stirring up all those memories?

"As fun as that sounds, I'll have to take a pass," she said, offering a small smile.

"Can't say that I blame you," Dr. Garcia said, returning the gesture. "Someone will be in with your discharge papers in a minute."

"Is it possible to have those sent upstairs?" she asked.

The doctor glanced from Duke back to her as recognition dawned. "I can arrange that." He removed his gloves and then walked over to Duke. "I'm sorry to hear about your grandparents. They're nice folks."

"I appreciate the kind words, Doc." Duke offered a handshake, which the doctor took. "And thank you for taking care of Audrey so fast."

"The sheriff called ahead and gave me no choice," Dr. Garcia said with another wink. "We take care of our law enforcement around here."

A nurse popped her head inside the curtain. "Doctor, you're needed in room five as soon as possible."

He nodded before turning back to Audrey. "Take it easy and take good care of my stitches."

"Will do, Doc." She mock saluted, which seemed to amuse him. The break in tension was much needed. Audrey finally exhaled before locking gazes with Duke. "Let's head upstairs."

"Whoa there," Duke started. "Is it too soon for you to walk?"

"You heard the doc," she said with a self-satisfied smug. "I'm good to go."

"What I heard from Dr. Garcia was that you should be spending the night here, but he realizes how stubborn those of us who wear a badge are, so he didn't ask," Duke pointed out. It was his turn to look smug. He took the ball and ran with it, putting her attempt to shame.

"I'm not getting pushed around in that thing, if that's what you're hinting at," she said, digging her heels in.

"Is Stubborn your middle name?" he teased.

"Might be," she retorted. "Who wants to know?"

The playful exchange broke some of the gravity of the

situation. The reality was that she'd almost been killed. Duke had almost been too late. Between quick thinking and fast fingers and Duke arriving, Trey had been spooked. He'd also been shot in the shoulder. She was certain of that. There would have to be fibers in the woods that could be matched once his identity was discovered. Those fibers would be enough to convince a jury to send the bastard to jail for the rest of his life, for the murder of five deputies.

Audrey shivered at the thought others were dead while she'd survived. For the second time in her life, she couldn't help but wonder why she'd been spared.

With Duke's help, she pushed to standing. Thankfully, her underarm was still numb from the shots. Her head was a different story, but she didn't want to take anything for the headache. It might be extreme, but she'd had a ringside seat to people who relied on pills. No, thanks. She steered away from them. All she needed was a big glass of water to feel better. On top of everything else, she was probably dehydrated.

"If this gets to be too much, you'll tell me, right?" Duke asked.

"I promise," she responded as they left the small room separated from the others around it by nothing more than something that looked like a shower curtain.

Duke helped her out of the ER, into the elevator and up to his grandparents' floor. Audrey stopped at the nurses' station while he kept going. He only managed a few steps without her before he turned to face her. His forehead wrinkled like it did when he was confused.

"You coming?"

"I thought I'd give you privacy with your family," she said, not wanting to intrude. Part of her couldn't stand to see the Remingtons in those beds. They didn't look peaceful or like they were sleeping. They appeared motionless, like they were wasting away.

"As far as my grandparents are concerned, you are family," he said to her, causing warmth to surround her like a blanket, cloaking her in strength.

"Okay then," she said, joining him once again.

He reached for her hand as they neared the door to his grandparents' room.

A nurse came out, essentially blocking the door. "I'm sorry, Duke, no visitors are allowed right now," the older woman said. Her name was Tabby according to the metal pin affixed to her scrubs. "We just got him stabilized but it's still touch and go at this point."

"Can I pop my head in at least?" Duke asked.

"Okay," Tabby agreed. "But make it quick so I don't get into trouble. The patient needs rest after an event like the one your grandfather had."

Tabby's expression sent panic coursing through Audrey. She held tighter to Duke's hand.

DUKE DIDN'T SEE how hanging around the hospital would do anyone good after he saw his grandparents. He was grateful for the minute he had to see how they were doing with his own eyes. "We'll head home."

"You know we'll call if there are any changes," Tabby said with a nod. He knew the doctors and nurses were doing everything possible to take care of his family. Knowing didn't make him relax or assume the road would be easy.

The nap he'd had at Audrey's had been enough to keep him going for a few hours. Maybe once they were back home, he could grab real sleep.

Nash would take over at the hospital. Duke checked the group chat and saw that Nash planned to head over soon. They would probably pass each other on the street without realizing.

He rubbed the scruff on his chin. He could use a real shave, too, before he looked like one of the wild animals on ranch property. *Tired* didn't begin to describe him. He'd let his guard down falling asleep at Audrey's cabin. He wouldn't make the same mistake twice.

Calling in reinforcements from the family would be his next move along with Nash. He, and everyone else, had naively hoped this would be a blip in their grandparents' lives. They all thought Duke could come home for a couple of days, a week tops, to handle the ranch and make sure Grandpa Lor and Grandma Lacy could function fine at home when they were released from the hospital.

Audrey squeezed his fingers, a reassuring move.

Decisions that might be coming, like taking one or both of their grandparents off life support, needed to be made with clear minds. His family would want an update, which didn't make him dread giving one any less.

With Audrey safely by his side, he could deal with anything.

Of course, this seemed like a good time to remind himself her presence in his life and in this town were temporary. She'd made it clear that she planned to leave as soon as his grandparents improved. Would she just disappear in the middle of the night once again? Would she pack up and leave without so much as a word? Duke let go of her hand, reminding himself that he shouldn't get used to her being there.

The look of hurt that crossed her features at the move

caused his chest to squeeze. He didn't like hurting her any more than he wanted to drink battery acid.

But she would walk away again. And he needed to protect his heart this time.

Chapter Twenty-One

The drive to the ranch was thankfully uneventful. Audrey settled into her old room in no time. A soft knock at the almost-closed door drew her attention. The hall light clicked off and then she heard Duke slide down the wall to sit on the floor.

She moved to the opposite side of the wall near the door and did the same.

"Hey," he said in a whisper. There was something about the deep timbre in his voice that traveled over her and through her at the same time.

"Hey," she returned.

"Can I ask a question?" The hesitation in his voice made her nervous.

"Go ahead," she responded, tensing as she readied herself for what might come next. She had no idea what he was about to ask, and it worried her that she couldn't read his mind.

"Why didn't you find a way to contact me all those years ago?" he asked. "I thought we had something special. Didn't I deserve an explanation? Didn't I prove that I was worthy of your trust?"

"I couldn't."

"That isn't good enough, Audrey. Not for me. Not for what we had together."

"It's simple," she said, blood pressure shooting through the roof at what she was about to admit.

"Is it? Then why didn't you tell me already?"

"I didn't say it was easy, but you're right about one thing, Duke. You deserved better from me."

"Then why won't you tell me now?" he pressed.

Was he sure he wanted to know?

"Why don't you trust me now?"

"How I feel about you has never been the problem, Duke. But I knew then like I know now if I heard your voice or saw a message from you on my phone that I would change my mind. I would turn around and come back. And then what if my parents found me here in Mesa Point?" She could feel herself trembling now. "My parents weren't good people, Duke. They would have wanted revenge against anyone who took what they believed was theirs…me. And it didn't matter that they didn't really want me. My uncle was a nightmare but even he knew to cut off contact with them years ago. They were messed-up individuals, and nothing would have stopped them from coming down here and lighting the barn on fire to prove a point." She could hear the shakiness in her own voice. "At sixteen, I couldn't handle doing that to you or rationalizing that you might be able to defend yourself. Plus, there was no way I could reach out to you even if I thought it was safe. My uncle took me in, and I had a whole other life. Not that it was a good one, but my plate was full trying to survive every day."

Duke didn't immediately speak, which meant he was processing her response. She hadn't meant the words to tumble out of her mouth like an outburst, but that was exactly what happened.

The stillness should stress her out, but it was oddly comforting, like two companions who didn't need to fill the space between them with words.

"Given my line of work, I understand the position you were in," he finally said. "Personally...it hurt like hell."

"I never meant for that to happen," she explained. It didn't or couldn't change the past, but maybe it would help him forgive her and move on. "I was confused and caught up in a hailstorm dealing with the trial and my parents. Thankfully, they were convicted and sentenced to life in prison. But not before threatening to find me wherever I went. I believed them too. I thought they would find a way to escape just to punish me."

"I tried to look you up on the internet," he admitted on an exhale. "The fact you'd used a false last name while you were here didn't dawn on me until years later when I started looking into working for the US Marshals Service."

She wished she'd been able to suppress the memory of Duke. For her, everything she saw reminded her of him. "Despite everything, I couldn't forget you."

She'd tried. Shutting Duke Remington out of her mind altogether had been impossible. At best, she'd learned to distract herself. She dated around once she turned eighteen. Anything before that wasn't an option. Child Protective Services hadn't been much help. They'd offered to put her in a group home. Now, she realized how short they were on resources. But going from bad to worse didn't seem like the right play, which she feared if she'd told on her uncle. Plus, the devil you knew always seemed better than the one you didn't.

"Part of me didn't want to forget," she admitted to Duke. She understood why he would want to suppress the memories. He'd had no idea what was really going on. She couldn't find a way to explain how jacked up her family had been. Not when he grew up with his grandparents in a loving home.

She had no concept back then of how he could have understood her situation.

"I would have helped you," he said quietly with a voice filled with regret.

"There was nothing you could have done, Duke."

"You couldn't know that unless you'd given me a chance," he contradicted.

"What could you have done against parents intent on punishing me?" she asked.

"I would have done anything for you, Audrey. Including run away if it meant getting you to safety."

"Don't you see? That's exactly the reason I couldn't let you in on what was going on at home," she said. "You are the kind of person who wouldn't have given up. Believe me when I say my parents wouldn't have let you get in their way. Besides, where would you be now if we'd run away together?"

Those words seemed to strike a nerve. Duke's eyebrows knitted together like they did when he was seriously contemplating something. At least he was thinking about what she said. He might resent her for the rest of their lives for her actions, but he might finally understand why she did what she did. And that was something.

"You're right," Duke conceded. "I wouldn't have stopped until I'd figured out a way to help you. And I would have gone off half-cocked at that age, which might have made life worse for you with your parents. I can't say my life would have been better off without you, Audrey. It might have looked different today, but we would have figured out a way to make it work."

"That's the problem," she said. "I couldn't let you settle. You would have helped me, and then your honor would have forced you to stick around. The thing is, I had to learn how to help myself first. And I was lost back then."

"What about now?" he asked.

"I know who I am, if that's what you're asking," she answered. She figured she needed to change the subject before they really went down a rabbit hole. "Are you tired?"

"No," he admitted. "I thought I would be. But I got a second wind."

Second, third or fourth at this point since he'd barely napped in the past few days, but she got what he meant.

"I need to go check the barn since Nash is at the hospital," he said. "The horses need to be checked on. We have a newborn foal to keep an eye on."

"Can I come with you?"

The thought of seeing new life gave her a burst of hope for the future. Hers might be uncertain at this point. Witnessing the miracle of a foal walking around would do her heart good.

Duke hesitated. Was he trying to keep her at a safe distance? She wouldn't blame him for it even though it shredded her heart.

"HOW ABOUT THIS?" Duke started, trying to find a way to tell Audrey she should rest. She'd been whacked on the back of the head a couple of times. Even though she'd been cleared by the doctor at the ER, she didn't need to expend more energy than necessary. "You get ready for bed, and I'll check on the foal. You can come down and help feed her in the morning. After a good night's sleep."

"Does that mean you don't want me to come with you?" she asked.

"I never said that," he admitted. He was trying to look out for her. Would she see it that way, though? Or would she think he was rejecting her? "You should know by now that I've always enjoyed your company."

"Does that mean I can come with you?" she pressed.

He would ask if she was always this stubborn, but he already knew the answer to that question. All capital letters *Y-E-S*.

If he was being honest, he would admit it was one of her more attractive traits. He imagined she'd learned how to survive her childhood and parents by digging her heels in and not allowing any other outcome. She'd done it. She'd survived. And yet, he couldn't help thinking she was still in survival mode. "Can I stop you?"

Her laugh was downright magic. It had the ability to soothe his soul and lift his spirits, like that was the easiest thing in the world to do. He had news for her, it was next to impossible. To say he lived a closed-off life was an understatement. Duke was beginning to realize just how much he'd shut down parts of himself after losing Audrey. The stubborn part in him decided not to ever feel that kind of pain again.

Duke was realizing that had also stopped him from loving anyone else, too. He'd been living a half life since he was sixteen years old.

That was the good thing about realizing your shortcomings—it meant you could fix them.

Pushing up to standing, he held his hand out, palm facing up, in the doorway. "Madam. Care to join me in witnessing the miracle of a foal walking around the barn?"

Duke was mildly concerned he hadn't heard from Nash yet. The ranch foreman had promised to text an update once he got to the hospital and he should have arrived by now.

Which most likely meant there wasn't any news to report or Nash would have sent word. There was another explanation, as well. Nash's cell battery was notorious for running low. It was highly possible his cell died, and he forgot to bring in his charger. Grandpa Lor had joked about Nash being bad with his cell too many times for Duke to panic.

But considering recent events, Duke was unsettled.

If he didn't hear anything after he went down to the barn, he could always call the hospital and talk to a nurse at one of the stations. Speaking of phone batteries, his own needed a charge.

Audrey took his hand and waltzed, not walked, out of the bedroom and into the hallway. He played along, twirling her and remembering how many times they'd done the same thing out in the barn when they were alone. They'd spent a lot of good time among the horses, which despite living in Dallas, she'd seen very little of. He shouldn't be surprised. Some folks still had the impression Dallas was all barns, open spaces and tumbleweeds, but it was a metropolitan city known for its sushi and shopping. It wouldn't be wrong to say shopping was considered a sport in Dallas.

Duke liked shopping malls about as much as he liked the thought of eating raw chicken.

Audrey took the lead for the rest of the trip down the hallway and then the stairs. To say his grandparents' house was large was a lot like saying Texas was big. They'd joked the eight-bedroom home with guest quarters had always been too big for the two of them and their pair of sons. Despite Duke's father's many shortcomings, there was still a picture of him along with his brother on the fireplace mantel. Even though he'd walked out on his children, and they shook their heads as to why he would do such a thing to young impressionable kids when they'd just lost their mother, they never spoke an ill word about him.

Duke's father didn't deserve their kindness. The fact didn't matter to them. They loved their sons. And if they didn't, it never showed. Duke, on the other hand, had always been vocal about thinking his father was the biggest jerk for running out on him and his sisters. His baby sister entered this world and immediately lost the two people who were supposed to care for her the most. Their mother couldn't help it. But their father...

Considering the man had called recently, there must be a significant amount of potential inheritance. It was the only reason he would come sniffing around after all these years. Bastard.

Duke didn't want to go down that slippery slope of anger and frustration about the non-father he'd had. Instead, he wanted to check on the foal with Audrey.

He kept hold of her hand, linking their fingers, as they walked outside. It was a miracle she could walk unassisted already. But then nothing should surprise him when it came to Audrey Newcastle.

Nash's truck was parked around the side of the barn where it was hidden from view from the house. Well, the lack of a text made even more sense now that Duke realized Nash hadn't left yet. Was the filly in trouble? Duke picked up the pace, holding on to Audrey's hand like a lifeline.

"What's wrong?" Audrey asked.

"Maybe nothing," he said, stopping a good fifteen feet from the barn's door. "Maybe it would be a good idea for you to stay out here while I check on the foal just in case." He had no idea what he would be walking into and the last thing he wanted was more stress for Audrey. She'd been through enough for one lifetime, let alone what had happened over the past couple of days. "Something feels off in my gut and I can't explain it."

"Whatever it is, I can handle going with you, Duke," she reassured.

Could she?

Chapter Twenty-Two

Duke turned to Audrey and locked gazes with her in a manner that melted any walls she'd constructed. Fine. She still had feelings for the man. Why wouldn't she when no one had measured up to him? She'd dated around, too, trying to find someone who could even come close to holding a candle to him. No one, and she meant no one, did.

"Okay," he said to her. "I trust you to stick with me."

Those words, spoken with conviction, brought tears to the backs of her eyes. Funny, Audrey would never classify herself as a crier. Normally, she would be offended at the urge. And yet that was exactly what she wanted to do. Tears no longer felt like weakness to her but seemed like sweet release instead.

But before she let her emotions take the wheel, they needed to check on the foal. She had a bad feeling creeping in.

"Okay then," she said to Duke. "Let's do this."

Duke dipped his head down and pressed a kiss on her lips so tender it nearly robbed her breath. "And then let's talk once the dust settles."

Her heart leaped at those words, at the implication. Could they figure out a friendship? Because she would settle for that if it meant never losing Duke again. After spending these past two days with him, she couldn't imagine her life without him. She remembered, though. It had felt like living in a cold dark cave. She was fine. She would be fine. She could survive without him. It wasn't like she needed someone else to complete her.

He made her want to be a better version of herself. He drew that out of her. And she loved him for it.

Friends?

Good luck with that one, Audrey.

A noise that sounded like a grunt came past the door as Duke slid it open.

Audrey gasped at the sight of Nash on the hay flooring, lying on his side with his hands tied behind his back. The perp had on a dark hoodie. She was certain it was the same bastard.

He kicked Nash again.

That one movement was all it took for Duke to make a run toward him and Nash.

The smile on Trey's face caused Audrey to instinctively reach for Duke's arm to hold him back. He had thick, black eyebrows that curled down over his black eyes. His nose looked like it had been broken. She saw the look in his eyes—eyes that held pure evil.

Running at Nash was exactly what the bastard wanted Duke to do. The smirk on Trey's face would haunt Audrey's dreams for a long time to come.

Her reach wasn't long enough for how fast Duke bolted toward the injured man.

Trey ran in the opposite direction toward the other end of the barn. At the door, he stopped, turned and held up something in his hand.

"No, Duke," Audrey managed to get out.

"I said you would pay, bitch. Now, you can go to hell and take these bastards with you!" Trey tapped the detonator.

The explosion knocked Audrey back several feet. The ambush had been successful, and all she could think about was the fact she might have just lost her best friend a second time. And Nash was innocent in all this, and it might have just cost his life to protect her.

No one was safe around her. There was always someone in the background trying to strip everything away from her. *Not this time, bastard.*

She managed to sit up and take inventory. She'd momentarily lost hearing in both of her ears. It sounded like she was being held underwater. Everything around her happened in slow motion. The blast had caused a small dust storm in the barn.

On a second look, that was smoke, not dust. The barn was on fire.

Somehow, she wasn't exactly certain how, Audrey managed to stand up and run toward the growing blaze.

Thick smoke slammed into her the second she entered the barn doors, making her eyes burn and her lungs hurt. She pulled the top of her cotton shirt over her nose and mouth to stop from chugging so much smoke.

Coughing, eyes watering, she scanned the area to find Duke.

She didn't immediately see him.

Nash, however, was still crumpled on his side. The older man hadn't moved as far as Audrey could tell. Was he already gone? She forced tears back as she kept searching for Duke.

When she found him, he was already trying to crawl toward Nash. Audrey bolted toward the older man, figuring the best way to get both him and Duke out of the barn was to get Nash out. It wouldn't do any good to run to Duke first. There was no way he would leave. He would only go toward Nash.

There was no time to see if Nash could open his eyes or speak. If he was alert, wouldn't he be trying to get out of the barn, too?

Audrey reached his boots and grabbed him by the ankles. With great effort and a rush of adrenaline, she started dragging Nash out of the barn, ever aware the bastard who did this could be lurking anywhere. Tray had all but disappeared into the smoke, like some kind of freak phantom.

The fact he'd figured out who Duke was and where he lived to set up this ambush wasn't lost on her. He might not have recognized present-day Duke asleep on her couch, but he could have been watching the hospital, knowing they would end up there.

That had to be it. He had to have been hiding among the vehicles when they parked at the hospital. He had to know that Duke would come check on Nash if the older gentleman stopped texting. This perp watched and waited before striking. The boot prints near her home at the cabin proved he studied a situation before he acted.

White-hot anger roared through Audrey, giving her the boost of power she needed to get Nash out of the smoke-filled barn. She checked his wrist and got a weak pulse. At least his heart was still beating.

That was as much as she could do because she needed to run back into the building and save Duke. This was exactly the kind of situation she was trained for, running into danger. Except she hated to leave Nash alone, vulnerable. Trey was somewhere around here. She'd bet money on the fact he was watching, lurking.

By the time she returned to the barn, a noise caught her

attention. White foam sprayed next to her. She jumped to one side to get out of the way of the stream only to realize Duke was standing up, battling the blaze with a fire extinguisher.

While he had that under control, she needed to free the horses from their pens. Unfortunately, she was going to have to guide them out the opposite end where Work Boots had disappeared. One positive was that it also directly led them to the practice arena out back. Another was that the smoke hadn't filled this side of the barn just yet, so the horses should be okay.

Quickly and methodically, she released latches and guided the paint horses toward the proper exit. Twelve stalls later, she'd removed all the animals, along with a barn cat that had been hiding high up in the wood beams. She'd managed to coax it down after some trying and all the horses were out. The stubborn kitty had been too scared to jump down, so Audrey climbed up to meet it halfway.

By the time she turned back to Duke, the last bits of flame were extinguished. Thank heaven for small miracles.

"Nash," she said to Duke, struggling to be able to speak. She could barely hear herself, and apparently, Duke was in the same boat. He gestured toward his ear.

Audrey motioned toward the exit where she'd dragged Nash a few moments before. At this point, she could only pray the horses were all right. The foal had followed her mother. They'd all been spooked.

Duke nodded before turning toward the ranch foreman, who hadn't moved. If anything happened to him because of Audrey, she would never forgive herself. Duke made a beeline for Nash before dropping down to his knees at his side. He was careful to scan the area first.

"Is he breathing?" she asked Duke as she came up beside him, phone at the ready. It dawned on her they were extremely vulnerable right now. She turned so that they would be back to back as Duke performed emergency life-saving measures on Nash and she called 911.

Was any of it working?

DUKE PUMPED NASH'S CHEST, careful not to break the older man's ribs. He stopped, cleared Nash's airway, pinched his nose and tilted his head. As Duke lowered his face to perform CPR, he saw his eyelids flutter.

Nash gasped in a breath and coughed. He almost immediately turned to his side. The ranch foreman shook his head like a dog shakes off water, and then blinked up at Duke.

"Were you trying to kiss me, big boy?" Nash's serious expression broke into a smile.

The joke meant that Nash was going to be fine. Duke returned the smile and sat back on his heels. "You scared the hell out of me."

"Big sucker jumped me from behind," Nash shouted. His hearing must be compromised from the blast, too.

He turned around to check on Audrey, who'd been right behind him, only to realize she was gone. Duke bit out a curse. He scanned as far as he could see, which wasn't much. It was too dark outside to see very far. Did she go after Trey?

After fishing out his cell phone, he hit the numbers 911. He wouldn't be able to hear Dispatch, but the person on the other end of the line would be able to hear him. So, he shouted out for the sheriff and fire department, stated his name and location and asked for medical aid.

In these parts, help could take half an hour to arrive, so he didn't get his hopes up the cavalry would show up anytime soon. He was still angry with himself for being ambushed in his grandparents' barn.

Nash could use a bed at the same hospital even though he was able to force himself to sit up. A pack of Pall Mall cigarettes fell out of the front pocket of his shirt. He'd quit smoking five years ago, but carrying around a pack was habit and reminded Duke that old habits died hard.

Where the hell was Audrey?

Chapter Twenty-Three

Running off half-cocked and without backup wasn't something Audrey would normally do. This was an emergency. Trey was getting away and would kill again. She came around the back of the barn to check on the horses, turning the corner with caution so as not to be taken by surprise again. She was still frustrated with herself for letting Trey get the drop on her earlier.

The horses were spooked but doing better than expected. Heads high, ears back, they were on full alert. It always struck her how intuitive these majestic animals were. There was such a thing called horse sense. It was real. She'd witnessed it.

Her hearing hadn't returned to normal. It still felt like her head was underwater. She checked behind her. Creeping up from behind would be even easier now. Was that part of the perp's plan? Maybe he thought he would wipe all three of them out with the bomb.

Guess what? Audrey wasn't going down like that. She intended to fight tooth and nail until only one of them was left standing if that was what it took to nail this bastard. She didn't want to kill him. No. That would be too easy of an out. Work Boots needed to spend the rest of his life behind bars with plenty of time to think about his actions and feel their repercussions. The man had killed five officers and attempted to murder one more. He couldn't be allowed to run free. He wouldn't stop now.

The tiny hairs on the back of her neck pricked. She got the feeling someone was watching her.

Where are you, sonofabitch?

Audrey rounded the corner to a concerned Duke. He jumped to his feet and ran over to her, bringing her into an embrace.

"I thought I lost you again," he said to her, making eye contact and ensuring she could read his lips as he spoke. This close, she could hear him okay.

"I'm here," she said. "I'm okay. I told you I was checking on the horses."

"I called 911." Duke's gaze shifted to a spot behind her and to the right. He locked on like a missile to a target.

"I did the same," she said. Two calls were even better than one.

"Stay here with Nash," he said.

She shook her head vigorously. "I'm not letting you go after him without backup." This perp might not be superhuman, but he sure seemed that way. Besides, it was good law enforcement practice to go in with reinforcements. She realized, however, Duke was most likely used to going after felony perps alone.

In her world, backup was essential. Neither one of them was armed.

Duke hesitated for a second before giving a quick nod. He took off in the direction he'd been staring at a moment ago. Audrey's heart rate kicked up a few notches. At least Nash was sitting up on his own. Help was on the way.

Audrey ran behind Duke. She realized he put his body in

between her and the threat. At least, he must believe there was a threat because he'd spotted something on the other side of the pen. She trusted his judgment as they crouched down low to stay under the top fence railing.

At this point, she wouldn't argue, but she took a lot of pride in pulling her own weight at work. Since she and Duke didn't work together and his protectiveness was personal, she would see it for what it was, a compliment rather than a message that she couldn't handle her own.

Moving as stealthily as they could manage without grunting from pain with every step, they rounded the back end of the pen, making a circle.

Duke slowed down considerably. Were they getting close to whatever he had seen?

Audrey thought about how this perp liked to watch from the trees. If she and Duke stayed near the pen, they might end up right where the bastard wanted them. She put a hand on Duke's shoulder, urging him to stop.

He did. Then he craned his neck around to see her.

She motioned with two of her fingers on her right hand to indicate eyes might be on them from the trees.

Duke nodded. It appeared he was having a similar thought. At this vantage point, could they get to the perp without him seeing them? It was dark enough in this part of the property. Except Trey's eyes had no doubt adjusted to the darkness. Another bright full moon wasn't helping. It would be fine once they entered the tree line. They could end up shot.

Risks had to be taken. This was one of them. She locked gazes with Duke for a few seconds. He gave an almost imperceptible nod before starting toward the trees. He broke into a sprint, running in a zigzag pattern to make it more difficult to shoot him.

Audrey did the same, keeping pace as best she could.

By some miracle, she and Duke made it to the tree line without a shot being fired at them. There was no time to stop and count their blessings. They bolted toward the spot Duke had in mind.

Branches slapped her in the face and torso as she ran. She tore through something that felt a whole lot like a spider web. Spitting and swiping at her face, she kept pushing. The very real knowledge Nash was back at the barn all by his lonesome was enough to keep her running.

At this point, she was almost one hundred percent certain she'd busted Dr. Garcia's handiwork with the stitches. He wasn't going to be thrilled with her, but that was a future problem. Right now, she needed to make an arrest more than she needed to breathe.

Duke ran smack into something that seemed like a brick wall, considering the way he bounced backward. He'd managed to get far enough ahead for her to stop and duck behind a tree trunk.

Had she been seen? Heard?

She had no idea. The ringing noise in her ears was starting to subside, and she could hear, if not see, a fight unfolding not far from her.

Rather than run into it and end up right where the perp wanted her, she made a circle around the fight. Giving them a wide berth hopefully kept her below the radar. Based on the grunts and commotion, Duke and the perp were engaged in a tough fighting match.

This was the time Audrey wished she had her weapon. She'd removed her ankle holster inside the house because her SIG Sauer had been taken in for processing after she used it in the woods. Was there something here she could use? A rock? A sharp stick?

With no time to waste, she palmed the first solid rock she could find. It would make her punches much more effective.

Audrey slowed her pace as she neared the struggle between the ox of a man and Duke. One minute they were on the ground wrestling, and the next they were on their feet throwing punches. Duke had just been blown up in the barn, so he was probably operating at sixty to seventy percent strength. Otherwise, ox or not, Duke would be waxing the trees with this dude.

Trey's back was to Audrey. It was now or never.

Like a wild banshee, she came out from behind a tree and jumped on the perp's back. One arm hooked around his shoulder, she pounded his skull with the fisted rock, throwing punch after punch in rapid succession.

The move caught the perp off guard. But she was nothing more than a fly on his back, despite wrapping her legs around him and squeezing her thighs as hard as possible. Trey wriggled, almost tossing her off.

In the nick of time, Duke came at the perp like a prizefighter. He threw a punch that connected with the Trey's nose. Blood squirted as his head snapped to one side. Duke threw a few kicks aimed at the perp's shins, but the monster of a man fought back hard.

An idea came to Audrey. He had another weak spot: the shoulder she'd put a bullet in. She'd shot him while holding the weapon in her right hand, and the fragment took off a piece of his left shoulder.

Gathering as much anger and force as she could, she dug her fingers into the approximate spot as Duke landed an almost knockout punch.

Trey dropped to his knees and screamed as the cavalry arrived, surrounding them and shining bright lights to illuminate the area.

Audrey was still clinging to the perp's back as he fell facedown with his arms out. She tossed the rock out of his reach, just in case, as Deputy Roark traded places with her. Her coworker was a tank in and of himself. He was more than capable of restraining the perp.

Trying to catch her breath while searching for Duke, Audrey's legs gave out. Before she hit dirt, two strong hands were guiding her upright.

"Hey," came Duke's voice in her ear, piercing through the bubble. He helped Audrey sit against a tree as the twins, Clifford and Clinton, came rushing over.

Audrey tried to slow her breathing, in through her nose and out through her mouth, like she'd been taught in the yoga class she'd forced herself to sign up for a couple of years ago.

Clinton knelt down in front of her. "How are you doing, Deputy?"

"I've been better," she said, cracking a smile.

"You're looking good to me," Clifford joined in.

"I got this one," Clinton reassured him as Duke took a seat beside her.

She immediately reached for his hand, and he linked their fingers. She was certain this simple act dropped her blood pressure by serious degrees. They both sat there, panting, trying to catch their breath while a twin worked on each one of them.

"It's over," she said to Duke as relief washed over her. "He'll go to jail for the rest of his life."

She didn't have enough energy to speak as emotion washed over her. It was over.

"Justice will be served for the deputies who lost their

lives," Duke reassured her. "And this bastard won't see the light of day or be able to harm anyone else ever again."

Clinton snapped fingers in front of her eyes and then asked her to follow his index finger. "You're bleeding. Can I take a look at your underarm?"

She cooperated, allowing him to stitch her up while the piece of trash they'd called Work Boots was forcibly removed from the property.

"What about Nash?" she asked Clinton.

"He's on his way to the hospital now," Clinton reassured. "He was giving lip about taking him in the back of her ambulance."

She smiled. Sounded about right for Nash.

Soon, they would give statements to the sheriff, and then this ordeal would finally be over. Audrey could turn in her resignation and then move on.

Why did her heart break in half at the thought?

DUKE'S PATIENCE WAS running low by the time the EMTs worked on him and Audrey, but he appreciated the fact they carried her to the house instead of taking her to the hospital. He'd used up most of his strength in the fight and had about enough left for a shower and to make it upstairs to crash after a house visit from the doctor.

But there was something else niggling at him that would come before both of those things.

After depositing Audrey in the main house, the EMTs left. Duke locked up behind them and brought a couple glasses of water over to the couch where Audrey lay down with her feet up.

A knock at the door interrupted their peace and quiet. Audrey sat up.

Duke answered after checking to see who it was. "Sheriff, come in."

Sheriff Ackerman joined them in the living room. He surveyed the room. "I won't take up much of your time. I thought you deserved to know first. Trey Hoffman was identified by his prints."

Audrey shrugged. "The name doesn't ring any bells."

"Nor should it," Ackerman continued, wringing his hat in his hands after taking it off. "He's from Haltom City where his stepmother used to be a deputy."

"A deputy? The ponytail," Audrey said in little more than a whisper. "We all wear them while we're on shift. Almost all females wear them."

Ackerman nodded. "Apparently, he's been a suspect for a while due to the abuse he suffered at his stepmother's hands after his biological father died. But no one could find him. After interviewing her, it was surmised that she felt 'stuck' with Trey from the age of eleven after his father died while on a ride-a-long. The stresses of the job grew. She started drinking after coming home from work." He paused. "And abused this kid beyond belief. Enough to make your stomach turn."

Audrey winced. She knew firsthand what that was like. She also knew the choice every person got to make just like Duke did. Good or bad. It was a choice. The irony would bite hard that she'd pointed her compass toward good after being here at the ranch. Who'd done that for Trey?

Would she have ended up bitter? Lawless? Vengeful?

Somehow, he doubted it.

Audrey was just good. She was the light.

"We see this in our line of work, but it still makes me

sad every time," she admitted with a frown. This one must hit a little too close to home for her.

"Agreed," Duke said.

Ackerman nodded. "Well, it's over now. You're safe. Take all the time off you need to heal. I'll hold your job for as long as you want me to."

"I appreciate that," Audrey said. "More than you know."

Sheriff Ackerman excused himself, so Duke saw the lawman out. He locked the door behind him and returned to Audrey.

"Now that this is all over, I guess I'll start making plans," she said to him as he joined her.

"What kind of plans?" he asked, handing over a glass.

She accepted the offer and immediately drained the contents. "Well water on your family's ranch is literally better than wine."

"I'm not much of a wine drinker, so I can't comment on that, but I'll agree the water out here is special." He managed a small smile. "But then, the water isn't the only thing."

She nodded, and he realized she thought he was talking about his grandparents. The sheriff had reassured him on the way out there hadn't been any changes in their condition and that he would personally set up shifts or whatever it took so Duke and Audrey could get some rest.

Funny thing about his mood. He was beginning to feel restless instead. The reason dawned on him. Audrey lay down on his grandparents' couch.

Duke perched on the edge next to her and cleared his throat to ease the sudden dryness. His clothes smelled like smoke and there was dirt on his face. This was probably the least romantic time to say what he was about to. Except that he couldn't wait another minute for Audrey to know how he felt about her. She'd said she was ready to start making plans. He wanted to be part of them.

Taking in a breath to fortify his nerves, he started, "Being home has been special despite the stress of what my grandparents are going through. Because of you. In fact, I wouldn't want to go through this with anyone else by my side as my equal partner and best friend."

She stroked his arm, her touch like magic to his body.

"I don't have the right words, so I'm just going to come out and say it." He locked gazes with her. It was the only way he could pluck up the courage to say what was on his mind. "I've loved you since I was sixteen years old. Time should have changed the way I feel about you. I mean, we spent three months together and then didn't see each other for fourteen years. But no one, and I mean no one, ever came close to holding a candle to you. I'm in love with you, Audrey. Still. And I hope, no pray, you feel the same way. Because I hope you'll do me the great honor of marrying me."

Audrey didn't immediately speak, which caused his heart to nearly stop beating in his chest. The first hint she might feel the same came in the way of tears leaking out of her eyes.

"I love you, Duke. I never stopped. Even after all these years, I feel the same way about you as I did when we were sixteen." She blinked back a few tears. "My answer is yes. I'll happily spend the rest of my life with you. If that means marriage, I'll do that, too. I can't imagine my life without you, Duke. I had no idea how I was going to leave this ranch." With effort, she lifted her arms to wrap them around his neck. "Or leave you. It nearly killed me to do it once. I never want to know that awful feeling again."

"Then, we're on the same page because I love you with my whole heart." He dipped his head down to kiss his future bride, the love of his life, his Audrey.

And he was finally home.

* * * * *

LAKESIDE SECRETS

K.D. RICHARDS

Prologue

There's no need to panic. Karine Eloi will probably stay in Carling Lake just long enough to put the house up for sale then she'll return to that godforsaken city where she lives. After all, she's some kind of big-shot financial person in Los Angeles. Nobody would trade that life for Carling Lake.

Marilee Eloi's killer just had to keep a clear head.

The killer had been lucky, damned lucky, for more than twenty years. No one had even thought to connect them to Marilee's murder. Besides, folks in this town wanted to believe Marilee had died at the hands of an outsider, that one of their own couldn't have done something so evil. And they'd had the perfect scapegoat. Jean Eloi. Even his name was snooty.

Jean had snuck right in and married a hometown girl and the Carling Lakers hadn't liked that one bit. It hadn't taken more than a few well-placed rumors, the best kind if you asked the killer, to get people casting suspicious glances and talking all about how Marilee's highfalutin husband must have been the murderer.

If the killer had known she'd been in the house with her mother, little Karine might have fallen prey to the big bad burglar that night too. Why leave a witness when you didn't have to? Karine wasn't a witness, though. She'd slept through the whole thing and that was what had saved her life all these years.

But now she was back in town and that was bound to kick up memories that the killer would rather stay buried. That new sheriff was far too progressive for the killer's liking. What if he decided to show off by delving into a more than twenty-year-old murder?

One problem at a time. The killer would have to keep a close watch on Marilee's girl. Maybe give her a reason not to linger in Carling Lake. And if there was any cause to worry…well then, the killer would just have to finish the job that was started twenty-three years ago.

Chapter One

It was far too quiet in Carling Lake, New York. That was the problem, Karine Eloi thought as she turned onto her back and stared up at the ceiling, willing sleep to come. She was used to the sounds of Los Angeles. The ever-present car horns, shouts, music and other assorted fracas of the city. The high-pitched squealing and fervent scratching coming from the attic above her was one thing that did remind her of Los Angeles. Or rather, the dump of an apartment she'd lived in when she'd first moved to the city. She made a mental note to put mousetraps on her shopping list and tried to tune out the sounds.

When she'd arrived in Carling Lake earlier that evening, she'd stood on the sidewalk in front of the house, looking at the place that had been her home for the first twelve years of her life. It looked familiar, but time and tragedy had dulled her memories of the place. But while the town and house she lived in had faded in her mind, the boy who'd lived next door never had. Omar Monroe had been her best friend since they were five years old. Even after her father had moved them three hours away to Springtree, Connecticut, she and Omar had remained close. Not even her move across the country to Los Angeles for college, and her subsequent decision to stay on the west coast, could break the bonds of their friendship.

Karine had hoped to see him when she reached town, but traffic had put her behind schedule and the house next door to the one she now owned, the house Omar had lived in his entire life, was dark by the time she'd arrived. She knew that as the only full-time state park ranger assigned to the Carling Lake area, Omar often had to work late, but she was excited and more than a little anxious to see him; it had been six months since he'd come out to visit her in Los Angeles. She remembered the punch in the gut she'd felt when she dropped him off at the airport, how difficult it had been to watch him walk away, knowing she wouldn't see him the next day.

She turned onto her side and closed her eyes. She was sure she'd see Omar soon enough. Right now, she had to get some sleep. But her mind wouldn't shut off. Coming back to her childhood home had opened up a Pandora's box of emotions that wouldn't be quelled by slumber.

The two-story home was an imposing mix of brick and clapboard. But it had been well maintained, just as Mr. Hill, the lawyer who had managed the family trust, had told her. The home had been in Karine's family for nearly sixty years, built by her grandfather, Wayne Barstol, who'd had the forethought to pass it to his daughter, Marilee, and then on to her, his granddaughter, via a trust so that it would remain in the family. After her grandfather had passed away, Karine and her parents had moved in. She may have been young when she'd lived here, but she remembered how much her mother had loved the house and Carling Lake.

A memory floated to the forefront of her mind as she'd stood on the sidewalk, peering up at her childhood home. Her, her mother and her father sitting on a swing hung from the porch ceiling, cuddled under a blanket on a starry night. And laughter. Lots of laughter.

There'd always been a lot of laughter when her mom was alive. Not after though.

Karine couldn't remember what her father's laugh sounded like or the last time she'd seen him smile.

She swallowed the tears that rose in her throat. Her father hadn't wanted her to ever return to Carling Lake. After her mother's death—her murder—twenty-three years earlier and the suspicion that had swirled around him, Jean Eloi had packed their bags and moved them to Connecticut, never looking back. He'd wanted Karine to do the same.

Never look back.

But Karine couldn't just plow ahead like her father had. She'd been there. She'd seen…something. Her dreams, her nightmares really, made that quite clear. But what had she seen?

Her dreams had never been clear enough to answer that question. For her father, it was tough enough dealing with the reality that his beloved Marilee was gone. The who and the why wouldn't bring her back, so he'd pressed on, remarried and gotten on with his life.

For her, it was the opposite. Each year, each moment lately, the need within her to know who and why grew stronger. Why had her mother been taken from her? Who had shattered her childhood and changed her life so irrevocably? Two months ago, she'd turned thirty-five and, by the terms of the trust left by her grandfather, become the outright owner of the family home. She'd known what she had to do. Go to Carling Lake and get justice for her mother.

She'd made it to Carling Lake. Now what?

She was a financial analyst without the first idea of where to start investigating a murder.

Her mind churned through what she knew about her mother's murder. Twenty-three years ago, while Karine had slept upstairs and her father was at a faculty function, someone had broken into the house. The then sheriff had theorized it was a burglar who hadn't realized anyone was at home. Her mother must have awakened and confronted the intruder. The confrontation had ended with her mother being bludgeoned.

There was so much about that night and the days after that was foggy for Karine, but she remembered talking to a policeman with bushy gray eyebrows and kind eyes. Telling him she hadn't heard or seen anything after her mother had put her to bed for the night. She remembered, too, hearing the police officer speaking to another cop.

I don't think she saw anything. Small blessing.

For more than twenty years, she'd also believed that, but now she wasn't so sure anymore. As her thirty-fifth birthday approached, the dreams had begun. Vivid dreams. Her mother lying on the floor in the hallway. A red river around her. And a figure over her mother's body.

In the dream, the figure was never clear enough to tell who it was or even if it was a man or a woman. At first, she'd thought it was nothing more than a dream, but each time she had it, the details became clearer, sharper. The fireplace poker was on the floor next to her mother. The red river, she realized, was blood encircling her mother's head. The back door to the house was standing open. She could see it all as if she was there. Or had been there. Everything except the face of the person who'd killed her mother.

Karine had all but given up on the police ever naming a suspect, much less convicting anyone, until a few weeks ago. That was when she'd received an email from Amber Burke Spindler, one of her mother's closest friends.

She remembered Amber from when she was younger, even though Amber had made no attempt to reach out to Karine after she and her father had moved to Connecticut. No one from Carling Lake had made any effort to keep up with her or her father, except Omar and his parents.

She gave up on sleep and reached for her phone on the nightstand. She scrolled to the opened email chain from Amber.

Karine,
You may not remember me. My name is Amber Burke Spindler, and I was friends with your mother. Good friends at one point. There is something I need to speak to you about. It's important. About your mother. It's too much to type out and too dangerous to put on paper. I need to tell you in person. Please get back to me. And tell no one.
Amber Burke Spindler

She'd thought about the email for weeks before she'd finally responded. Her father had never liked talking about her mother or the way her mother had died. Whenever she'd attempted to bring it up, he always said it was a tragedy and that she should try not to think about it. But the older she'd gotten, the less she'd heeded his advice. She'd searched the *Carling Lake Weekly* online for news on the murder and, talking to Amber, someone who'd known her mother and been around during the time of her murder, just might get her the answers she needed. Karine knew the police theory was that her mother had surprised a burglar. But something about that explanation just seemed off.

She hadn't told anyone about the email from Amber. Not even her best friend and Carling Lake resident, Omar Monroe. She knew he'd have pressed her to tell the authorities about Amber having reached out to her, and she didn't want to do that until she knew what Amber had to say. She'd tried to convince Amber to disclose whatever it was she wanted to tell her via email and had even offered to call or video chat, but Amber hadn't budged.

In the end, curiosity had won out. She'd used some of the vacation time she had banked from years of early mornings and late nights at her investment firm and headed to Carling Lake. She hadn't told Omar about Amber's email, but he was aware that she hoped to convince the sheriff to reinvigorate the investigation into her mother's murder. She'd also known her father would try to talk her out of it if he realized the truth, so she'd told him only that she was coming to Carling Lake to ready the house for sale.

She'd arranged to meet Amber the next afternoon at Amber's house in an upper-class section of Carling Lake where lots of the rich part-time residents lived. Amber could afford to live there having married then divorced Daton Spindler, heir to Spindler Plastics.

Karine was anxious to hear what Amber knew about her mother's death that was so important she couldn't tell her in an email or video chat and why, if it was so important, she hadn't told the police.

She set the phone aside, swung her feet over the side of the bed, and rose. She was too wired to sleep. What she needed was a cup of chamomile tea to help settle her nerves. Luckily, she'd arrived in town with just enough time to drop off her suitcases and head to the supermarket before it closed since 24/7 shopping hadn't seemed to have made its way to Carling Lake just yet.

She padded down the stairs; the moon providing more than enough light to guide her. In the kitchen, she hit the switch for the penlight that hung over the stove, but left the brighter recessed lighting off. She'd found an old-fashioned stainless-steel kettle in the cabinet next to the sink earlier that evening and filled it now. While the water in the kettle heated, she stepped over to the sliding-glass doors that led from the kitchen to the back porch and slid them open.

Mr. Hill had rented out the house over the years and it had been several months since the last renter had vacated. She'd left the windows open for several hours after dinner, yet the air inside the house was still stale and heavy.

Karine turned back to the floor-to-ceiling pantry and reached inside for the thin can that held her favorite brand of chamomile tea leaves.

A muscular arm clamped around her waist, yanking her backward. The can clattered to the tile floor, spilling tea leaves at her feet. The scream that ripped from her throat was cut off by a gloved hand.

OMAR MONROE DIDN'T know how anyone could choose to live in a place where they couldn't see the stars. He'd bought his childhood home from his parents when they'd decided to move to Florida and now he looked up at the dark blue sky rimmed with purple and dotted with twinkling stars. It was breathtaking. He glanced over at the house next door. He had hoped to be home by the time his best friend, Karine Eloi, landed in town, but when he'd arrived, the lights inside the house next door had been out. He knew Karine had arrived, though, by the rented sedan parked in the usually empty driveway.

As a state park ranger, he spent the day just how he liked to spend every day: protecting and preserving the Carling Lake Forest. He'd lost track of time when he'd been out on patrol today. It wasn't like him, but since he'd earlier discovered several dead birds along a stream and creek feeding into Carling Lake, he'd been taking even more care on his patrols, on the lookout for any abnormalities or animals that appeared to be in distress. He'd noted some concerning issues, enough so that he'd been authorized to conduct water samplings of the stream and creek, looking for pollutants. But those samples had come back clean and, as far as his boss was concerned, that had been the end of it.

But that wasn't the end of it. Not for him. He knew this forest as well as he knew himself. He'd grown up in Carling Lake, playing in these woods, fishing, camping and hiking with his father. He'd known from a young age that he wanted to become a state ranger. Protecting this particular forest was a job he took seriously, and he'd been overjoyed when the position had opened up four years earlier and he'd been able to transfer from his then position in Buffalo, New York, to his hometown of Carling Lake.

But something was off inside his forest. The town's economy depended on tourism, but some of Carling Lake's visitors didn't realize how delicate the forest's ecosystem was. Any introduction of outside contaminants, even accidentally, could throw that system out of balance. And if it wasn't an accident? Ecoterrorism was more prevalent than a lot of people realized. Without knowing what he was dealing with, Omar couldn't pinpoint a motive or know what corrective steps might have to be taken. He needed to figure out what was going on, and fast. Before irreversible damage was done.

He glanced again at the house next door, determined to make time to spend with his best friend while she was in town. As much time as he could finagle.

He let out a frustrated sigh. It had been six months since he'd last seen Karine. Waiting one more day wouldn't kill him.

A little ping of awareness in the center of his chest argued the opposite. That ping had been happening more and more frequently. Whenever he talked to or texted with Karine. Whenever he thought about her, which was, he was willing to admit to himself, more and more often. He loved being a park ranger, but it was a solitary profession. He spent a great deal of time in his truck or out patrolling through the forest. Plenty of time for a man to think, and lately the only thing he could think about was Karine.

Karine, his friend, he reminded himself not for the first time. It was only natural that, lately, his mind had turned to her more. She'd turned thirty-five and announced she was coming back to Carling Lake for the first time in twenty-three years to take up her own investigation into her mother's murder. As happy as he was to have his best friend next door instead of three thousand miles away, he was worried about her desire to delve into her mother's death.

Omar didn't pretend to understand what she must feel, having been in the house when her mother was murdered, but he knew she'd struggled with nightmares over the years. Marilee Eloi's homicide hadn't been solved, and although it was technically still an open case, there had been no new leads in nearly two decades. He wasn't sure what Karine hoped to find, but he hoped it wasn't trouble. No matter what, though, he planned to be by her side through it all.

He took a deep breath of crisp, clean mountain air and tried to settle. The night was quiet, like most nights in Carling Lake. Just how he liked it. Every so often, he'd hear a small animal scuttle across the undersized yard that separated the back porch of his house from the forest beyond.

He swallowed a sigh, burrowing deeper into his lounge chair and taking a long sip from the half-empty beer bottle in his hand.

Relax. You'll see Karine in a few hours.

His phone buzzed and he knew without looking who it

was. Only a few other people in town worked crazy hours similar to his, although his friend was supposed to be packing for his vacation in Maui, which was to start the next day.

Karine has arrived?

Sheriff Lance Webb was his closest friend in town and he'd heard all about Karine, although the two had never met. Unfortunately, Lance and his girlfriend, Simone, were going to be on a long-awaited vacation for most of Karine's visit.

Shouldn't you be packing for your trip?

I'm multitasking. And don't change the subject.

Lance hadn't said anything explicitly, but Omar suspected he had picked up on his growing feelings for Karine. Ever since Lance had coupled up with Simone, he'd been pushing Omar to find a nice woman and settle down. The idea wasn't unappealing, but there was only one woman who came to mind wherever Omar thought about making a commitment.

Karine has arrived. I had to work late so I haven't had a chance to welcome her home yet.

Join you for a nightcap?

How sweet of you, but I'm exhausted.

Not me! Her. Ask her to join you for a nightcap.

I think she's already gone to bed. The lights in the house were off when I got home.

The sound of something crashing jolted him from the text conversation with Lance.

A scream, loud and terrified, had him on his feet, tucking his phone into his pocket as he did, jumping over the porch railing and darting for Karine's house in an instant.

It only took seconds to assess the scene in front of him. A masked man. A terrified Karine clawing at the arm around her neck.

"Let her go," Omar growled, stepping through the open sliding-glass door.

Karine's eyes widened, fear radiating from them.

The masked man's eyes narrowed. He locked his arm tighter around Karine's neck, drawing a pained squeak from her.

It was only the possibility that Karine could get hurt in the scrum that kept Omar from launching himself at the intruder.

He'd rushed over without stopping to grab his gun, but no matter, he was well versed in hand-to-hand combat. There was no doubt in his mind that he could overpower the intruder, who was only about five-eleven and thin, maybe a hundred and thirty pounds. He just needed to get Karine out of harm's way first.

"Let her go," he repeated.

"You want me to let her go?" the man said in a voice that sounded as if he was trying to disguise it. "Fine."

The masked man gave Karine a hard shove, propelling her forward unsteadily.

Omar caught her before she fell headfirst into the countertop. The intruder darted from the kitchen and back toward the living room and front door.

He steadied Karine, studying her for injuries. Even in bare feet and pajamas, she was statuesque. Her long, light brown hair was disheveled from the attack and her toffee-colored cheeks were pink with fear and exertion. "Are you okay?"

"Yeah. Yes," she said, shaken, but with no obvious injuries that he could see.

"Okay. Stay here," Omar ordered before taking off after the man.

The front door was open. He ran outside onto the porch, looking up and down the street, but saw no one. Whoever had broken in was gone, lost in the shadows.

Omar walked back into the house, locking the front door, then doing the same for the rear sliding-glass doors leading from the porch to the kitchen.

"Are you sure you're okay?" he asked, joining Karine on the sofa, pulling her in close. She wasn't the only one shaken by the intrusion and he needed to feel her warmth to assure himself she hadn't been hurt.

He pulled away enough to look down on her while still keeping his arms around her. "Not much of a welcome to town, is it?"

She gave him a tight smile. "So far, I'm not impressed." She pulled out of his arms. "How did you—"

"I was out on my back porch, having a beer and unwinding from the day, when I heard you scream."

"Thank goodness you did. Who was that guy? I guess the house has probably attracted a lot of vagrants sitting here vacant like it's been for the last couple of months."

"Actually, I have been keeping an eye on it for you. I

didn't get a good look at whoever attacked you, but no one's been hanging around here. At least, not that I've seen."

"Oh, well…"

"We need to call the sheriff's office and file a report."

"Oh, I don't think all that is necessary. It's late and—"

"It's definitely necessary." Omar pulled his phone from his pocket. "You might want to take a look around and see if anything is missing while we wait."

"I wouldn't even know if there was anything missing. The trustee rented out the house as a furnished rental, and while everything here is technically mine, none of this is really mine. Everything I brought with me is upstairs in the master bedroom."

It was just as well. He didn't want her leaving his side, and he didn't think whoever had broken in had done so to rob the place. The house had sat empty for the last several months, giving any burglar the perfect opportunity to ransack the place well before Karine's arrival.

He reported the attempted burglary and was told a car would be sent right out, then he called Lance and conveyed what had happened.

"This was not exactly the way I imagined my homecoming."

"I'm just glad you're here." Omar put an arm around Karine's shoulder and pulled her to him. "And that I was close by."

And that was exactly where he planned to be until he was sure she was safe in Carling Lake.

Chapter Two

When the doorbell rang a short time later, Omar went to answer it. Karine had never been so relieved to see her best friend. She wasn't sure what would have happened had he not bounded through the sliding doors. She was no shrinking violet, but the intruder had caught her off guard.

A pinch that was more attraction than relief hit her. She watched him stride into the room. His six-foot frame packed all the muscle one would expect of a man whose job included frequent hikes through the woods and daily physical activities. But it wasn't just Omar's physical attributes that turned heads. He had a presence, a warmth and intelligence that he exuded wherever he went. It was a charm that naturally drew people to him.

Omar led a uniformed sheriff's deputy into the living room where she sat.

The deputy took off his hat as he entered the house, revealing blond hair that was rapidly going gray and thinning, but his dark brown eyes were shrewd. He was in his late forties, with a round midsection that hung over his waistband quite a bit.

"Mr. Monroe," the deputy said, earning a nod from

Omar before he turned to Karine. "Ma'am, I'm Deputy Shep Coben. I don't believe I've had the pleasure."

"Karine Eloi," she said, pushing to her feet and offering her hand.

Deputy Coben studied Karine through narrow eyes. "Eloi? Any relation to Jean Eloi?"

"He's my father." She gave the deputy's hand a quick shake before dropping it.

"Then you must be Marilee Barstol's girl."

"Marilee Barstol Eloi was my mother, yes."

"Huh." Deputy Coben sniffed, his gaze traveling over the room. "Guess it makes sense to find you in the Barstol house. That's what we natives call this place."

She bristled at the way the deputy's eyes swept over her and the house as if they were specimens for him to inspect and dissect. He struck her as a man who did that a lot. Inspected and dissected, looking for a person's weaknesses and ways to exploit those weaknesses.

"Technically, it's the Eloi place now," Karine said sharply.

Shep smiled without warmth. "It'll always be the Barstol place to native Carling Lakers, ma'am. I was new to the department when your mother died, but Marilee, rest her soul, and her daddy, Wayne, your grandpa, were part of our community."

The space between them weighed heavily with the implication that Karine and her father, Jean Eloi, were not a part of the Carling Lake community.

Jean Eloi had always been resistant to talking about his late wife and the years the family had lived in this town. Whenever Karine had asked about her mother or the break-in that had led to her death, her father would become visibly upset and change the subject as quickly as he could.

She knew he had terrible memories of this place, not only because of her mother's murder, but also because he was a suspect.

Her father had been a struggling new professor working at the nearby community college when he'd met Marilee, the town sweetheart. Karine had gotten her father to open up enough that she knew he and her mother had met at a workshop on conservation at the community college and they'd fallen for each other hard. "Love at first sight" was how her father had described it. They'd married three months after meeting, much to the chagrin of Grandfather Wayne and many others in town. Eleven months later, Karine was born, which had done little to soften her grandfather's dislike of her father. It was commonly rumored around town that Jean had only married Marilee for the home and extensive land holdings she was set to inherit when her father passed away. It was why her grandfather had set up the trust to ensure that her father would never get his hands on any of Marilee or Karine's inheritance. Even though he'd technically inherited very little because of the trust, there had still been whispers that he'd killed his wife for her money.

"Why don't you tell me what happened here tonight?" Deputy Coben pulled a small notebook from the pocket of his coat, along with a stub pencil, and turned to a clean page. "Who wants to go first?" His gaze danced between Karine and Omar.

Omar made a gesture in her direction, indicating she should go first. She recounted the night's events, from being unable to sleep and rising to make tea, to seeing Omar bound through the sliding-glass door.

Shep turned to Omar with suspicion in his eyes. "That's

mighty convenient, Omar. How did you know this young woman was in need of assistance?"

Waves of irritation flowed from Omar, but he kept his tone polite. "You know, I live next door and Karine and I have been friends since we were children. I was just home from my shift and having a beer on my back porch when I heard a scream. I figured I should check it out."

Shep scowled. "You know you're nothing but a civilian within the town limits of Carling Lake. Your jurisdiction is limited to the trees," he said condescendingly.

"I know where my jurisdiction ends, Shep," Omar responded, his tone sharpening. "But Karine is my friend. If she needs me, I'll be there, jurisdiction or not."

"And I, for one, count that as a good thing." A tall Black man in a sheriff's uniform strode through the front door that Shep had left open when he'd been let into the house. "I think we all ought to be thankful Omar was nearby. This could have ended much differently if he hadn't been."

Shep shrank back with a pronounced grimace on his face as the man joined them in the living room.

Karine shivered. She thought again about what could have happened if he hadn't been close by. What had happened in this very house years earlier?

Omar must have sensed the direction of her thoughts. He wrapped his arm around her and pulled her in close. She inhaled his piney scent and sank into his arms.

The man held out a hand to Karine. "Sheriff Lance Webb."

"Karine Eloi," she said, giving Lance's hand a firmer shake than she'd afforded the deputy.

"I've heard so much about you from Omar. Once you're settled, we'll have to have coffee and you can tell me all of his secrets," he teased.

The sheriff smiled, and she relaxed a touch more, which she suspected had been the sheriff's intention.

Sheriff Webb turned to Omar. "Omar."

"Lance. Thanks for coming." The men shook hands.

"Sheriff, I was just finishing up taking these witness's statements," Shep interjected.

Lance turned to his deputy. "Good. Why don't you go canvass the neighbors and see if anyone is awake? Maybe someone saw something."

Shep's mouth turned down into a frown, but he closed his notebook and pushed it back into his pocket. "Yes, sir."

Deputy Coben turned on his heel and left through the door the sheriff had entered.

Omar's brow rose. "You've got a problem with that one."

Lance swiped his hat from his head and wiped his brow. "I know. It's been brewing since I was voted in as sheriff over him. I'll have to deal with it at some point, but not today. Right now, I want to make sure you are both okay."

"I'm fine," Karine said.

"I'm good. The guy ran off almost as soon as I came through the door," Omar added.

Karine chewed her bottom lip. "Omar doesn't think this was a robbery attempt. Do you?"

The sheriff shared a look with Omar, but neither answered her, which she guessed was an answer of a sort.

"Miss Eloi—" Lance started.

"Karine, please."

"Karine," he began again with a tight smile. "I'd like to gather all the facts before I make any determinations."

"That's very diplomatic, Sheriff. I take it you know about my mother's murder in this house twenty-three years ago?"

He nodded. "I'm familiar with the circumstances. It remains an open case with the sheriff's department."

"Omar doesn't want to scare me, but I know him too well. He's concerned my burglar wasn't a burglar at all. That whoever broke in here was targeting me and that it might have to do with my mother's death."

Lance glanced at Omar.

"I didn't say that," Omar said quickly.

Karine rolled her eyes. "You didn't have to. I've known you since we were five. You don't think I know what you're thinking?"

"Karine, I'm sure it's difficult to not have answers to your mother's murder…"

She pushed her shoulders back, stepping away from Omar. "It's not just difficult, Sheriff. It's excruciating. It's been years and still no one has been held to answer. Well, I just officially inherited the house, and I plan to find out why my mother was murdered."

She took a deep breath then and let it out slowly. "Twenty-three years ago my mother was killed in this house. Her murder was never solved. I've come back to Carling Lake to find answers. And to finally get justice for my mother."

OMAR WAS NOT what anyone would call a morning person and getting up at six thirty was not his idea of a good time. Especially not when he'd spent the night before tossing and turning, worried about Karine. He'd wanted to stay over at her place, but she'd declined his offer. Usually, he admired her fearless independence, but not when someone might be targeting her. Since it had been late, Lance had suggested they all get some rest and meet for an early breakfast before he headed to the airport to begin his vacation. Thus, his early-morning wake-up call.

He had hoped to catch Karine that morning so they could head over to Rosie's diner together, but he'd hit the snooze button one too many times, it seemed. By the time he made it out of his house, Karine's car was already gone from her driveway.

He ignored the anxiety that bubbled in his chest as he drove to Rosie's. Carling Lake was generally a safe town, although it had seen its fair share of crime recently. But no one would attempt to harm Karine in broad daylight.

He was sure she was perfectly safe. Still, his anxiety didn't abate until he pulled the door to the diner open and stepped inside. He scanned the L-shaped space, his eyes falling on Karine almost as if pulled by an unseen force. She looked across the room, meeting his gaze and sending his heart into a gallop. Dark circles rimmed her light brown eyes, telling the story of how her night had gone after he, Lance and Deputy Coben had left her. But she was still beautiful.

He slid into the chair next to her at the table.

"About time, Monroe," she said, bumping his shoulder playfully. She knew about his aversion to early mornings.

"I'd planned to catch you so we could head here together, but I couldn't stop hitting the snooze button."

She laughed, and something in him lightened. "Between the jet lag and the adrenaline, I couldn't go back to sleep. I went out for a run, showered and made it here early."

Omar frowned. "You shouldn't have gone running by yourself. We don't know if last night was a one-off or something more serious."

"I'm not going to hide out, Omar."

Now was as good a time as any to bring up a subject he knew she was going to hate. "Before Lance gets here, I wanted to talk to you."

She held up her hand. "If you're going to try to talk me out of searching for my mother's killer, you can just save it."

"You should leave this to the professionals."

Her forehead creased. "No offense, but the professionals have had twenty-three years and they haven't been successful at finding my mother's killer. I have to ask myself if that's on purpose or merely incompetence."

A waitress arrived to take their orders before Omar could rally a response. He ordered an egg white omelet and Karine ordered the French toast.

As the waitress left to put their order in with the kitchen, the door to the diner opened again, letting in Lance, followed by James West, a newly minted Carling Lake resident.

James West owned an art gallery on Main Street, but despite his career change, he still looked like the marine he'd been four years before moving to Carling Lake. He was a large man, a few inches over six feet tall, and he was muscled, as if he were still keeping himself ready in case he was called up for combat once again. He was an intimidating presence, but he wore a smile when he entered the diner. The two older men sitting closest to the door called out hellos as James and Lance made their way over to the table.

James's eyes scanned the patrons in the diner quickly and efficiently before landing on Omar and Karine.

Lance exchanged greetings with Omar and Karine and took a seat across from them at the table.

"Omar." James nodded hello, sitting next to Lance. "And Miss Eloi, I presume. It's a pleasure to meet you. I'm James West."

In the year or so since James West had made Carling Lake his home, Omar had gotten to know him pretty well. James and Lance were close, and the three of them often got together to watch a ballgame or just hang out. James had seemed like a decent enough guy. He'd have to be for Lance to have befriended him.

"I asked James to join us. I hope you don't mind, Karine," Lance said.

"Lance thought I might be of help to you two," James added.

"Uh, sure," Karine said hesitantly.

The waitress returned with Omar's and Karine's breakfasts and poured coffee for each of the new arrivals. James and Lance declined to order breakfast.

"I'm curious, Mr. West." Karine spoke when the waitress left again. "Why would the sheriff think you could help me?"

"Because he's a West of West Security and Investigations," Omar said.

Karine stared blankly.

"West Security and Investigations is one of the premier private investigations and personal security firms on the east coast," Lance offered.

"We're expanding to the west coast too," James added with a cheeky grin.

Omar rolled his eyes. James was charismatic, he'd give him that.

"I see." Karine bit her bottom lip.

"You won't find better help than West private eyes," Omar conceded.

"Why don't you explain your situation and then we can figure out how to be of service?" James brought his coffee to his lips and sipped.

Karine's gaze bounced between Omar, Lance and James then, seemingly deciding she could trust them, or maybe just that she had nothing to lose, she began to talk.

"When I was twelve, my mother was murdered. The

sheriff back then believed the culprit had to be a tourist or one of the seasonal workers in town, but no suspect was ever officially named. I say officially because, even though the sheriff had chalked it up to a home invasion gone wrong, my father became the prime suspect, at least in the minds of a lot of the people in this town. He had an alibi, but that didn't stop the gossip. He was ostracized."

And so was she, Omar recalled. Some of the kids at school had been cruel. Picking on Karine, calling her father a murderer. Someone had even started a rumor that Karine had killed her mother.

"The people in this town pretty much made his life unbearable," Karine continued. "A few months after my mother's murder, Dad found a teaching job at a community college in Connecticut and we moved away. My mother's case went cold."

"You say your father had an alibi?" James questioned.

Karine nodded. "Yes, he was an assistant professor at Pinewood Community College back then."

Pinewood Community College was about forty minutes north of Carling Lake and many of the local youth began their higher education there in order to save money for a four-year university.

"My father taught botany. He still does, actually. He was at a faculty dinner with twelve other professors from his department the night my mother was killed."

"So why was he a suspect?" James questioned.

"Because he was an outsider. The popular theory was that he'd hired someone to kill his wife and make it look like a break-in. Or that he had somehow snuck out of the dinner. Since it was nothing but a rumor, it didn't have to make a lot of sense even though it decimated my father's reputation," Karine added bitterly. "My mother's family, the Barstols, had been in Carling Lake for generations. My grandfather, Wayne, was a prominent citizen and my mother, Marilee, was beloved by all, according to what little my father will tell me. Grandfather Wayne never liked Dad, and that was enough to poison the town against my father even years after Grandfather's death. But there's no way Dad would have been involved, not just because my mother was the love of his life, but also because he would have never put me in harm's way. He knew I was home with Mom."

"I read the investigation file this morning," Lance said. "You were in the house at the time of your mother's murder."

Karine nodded. "Yes. Asleep in my bedroom. At least, that's what I've always thought."

Omar leaned forward, his eyes narrowed on Karine's face. "What do you mean that's what you'd always thought?" This was news to him. He thought Karine had told him everything about that night.

"For the last twenty-three years, I thought I'd slept through my mother's murder, but I've been having these dreams for the last several months. Vivid dreams where my mother is lying on the floor of our house with blood all around her and someone is there, next to her, but I can't make out their face."

Omar shared worried glances with James and Lance. "You think you saw your mother's killer?"

"I do. I think I blocked it out when I was younger, but it's coming back to me now. Maybe because I've finally inherited the house where she died, but whatever the reason, I have to know the truth. If I can identify my mother's killer, the sheriff—" Karine nodded at Lance "—can reopen the case and she can finally get the justice she deserves."

"You realize these memories could put you in real danger?" Lance said.

"It's a good thing a real-life ranger lives next door." James took another sip of his coffee.

Omar frowned. Next door wasn't nearly close enough. If Karine was truly in danger, it was best if she returned to Los Angeles.

Karine straightened in her seat. "I'm grateful that Omar stepped in last night, but I can take care of myself."

Omar growled. "You're planning on going after a murderer who has gotten away with his crime for decades? You need all the help you can get, not the least of which is someone to watch your back."

"And would that someone be you, Omar?" James questioned.

Omar shifted in his seat to look at Karine directly. "I think the safest thing would be for you to go back to Los Angeles. If you remember anything, you can always call Lance."

She shook her head. "No, I'm not running. Not anymore. I can handle myself, like I said. That guy last night caught me off guard, but it won't happen again.

"I don't need anyone to protect me, but I wouldn't mind help identifying my mother's killer." She turned to look at Lance pleadingly. "Sheriff, I'd like to see the police report from the investigation."

Lance was already shaking his head. "Technically, it's still an open case. I can't risk having you compromise it."

Karine threw her hands up. "Compromise what? Correct me if I'm wrong, but you have no leads and no suspects. When was the last time you even thought about the case before last night?"

Lance pursed his lips.

James tilted his head. "It is unorthodox, Lance, but Karine doesn't have any incentive to compromise the case. Quite the opposite. And maybe something in the file will jog a memory. Give you a fresh lead to follow up on."

Lance glared at James.

"I don't think this is a good idea," Omar offered.

Now Karine glared at him. "Well, I do. And I'm going to investigate no matter who likes it or who helps me."

Omar sighed. He knew that tone. He wasn't going to win this argument.

Lance glanced at his watch. "I have to go. The car is coming in twenty minutes to take me and Simone to the airport. She'll kill me if we miss the flight. Look," he said with a sigh, "I can arrange with my deputy to let you look at the file later today."

Omar watched a brilliant smile bloom across Karine's face and felt something else bloom in his chest.

"But," Lance cautioned, "you can't take anything out of the station."

"Absolutely not, Sheriff. You have my word." Karine smiled.

Lance looked like he already regretted his decision, but he rose and, with hurried goodbyes to each of them, left the diner.

"I guess I should get going too. Karine, it was a pleasure meeting you and, please, if I or West Investigations can do anything to help you, don't hesitate to call. Omar has my number or you can feel free to drop by the gallery or the B and B. I'm usually at one place or the other."

"You are really going to do this then." Omar turned to Karine after James left.

She took his hands in hers. "I know you worry about me, but I have to do this."

"You know your mother's killer could still be out there. You could be drawing the attention of a murderer."

"I hope I do," Karine said with a note of ferocity. "I hope I scare whoever killed my mother so much they make a mistake and reveal themselves."

That was the last thing Omar hoped for. A scared killer was a very dangerous killer.

He couldn't let her do this by herself. No matter what she thought, she was putting herself squarely in the line of fire of a murderer. She needed someone to watch her back.

He leaned back in his chair, resigned. "Okay then. Where do we start?"

Chapter Three

Karine and Omar finished breakfast with a frisson of tension running between them. She knew he wasn't thrilled about her plan, he'd made that clear from the moment she'd told him why she was coming to Carling Lake, but something inside her was pushing her to do this now.

The waitress had just cleared away their plates and left the check when Omar's phone buzzed. He pulled it from his pocket and read the screen. "Lance works fast. He says we can meet Deputy Clarke Bridges at the station to review the file whenever you're ready."

Karine wiped her mouth then tossed the napkin on the table, standing. "I'm ready now."

Omar paid for their breakfast and they stepped out of the diner into the cool morning air. It was late September and it seemed that fall was intent on making itself known.

Karine hurried to her car then turned back, calling out to Omar, who'd parked a few spaces away. "I just realized I don't know where the police station is."

"You can follow me. It's not far."

Omar led the way, and he was right. The station was less than a mile from the diner. Sometime, sooner rather than later, she'd have to take a drive around town and reacquaint herself with Carling Lake. It had been dark when she'd pulled into town last evening, but even in the light of day, nothing they passed on the drive from the diner to the station seemed familiar. She followed Omar into the parking lot, anxious to get a look at the investigation file and happy to be able to do so before she met with Amber.

A pang of guilt ran through her at not having told Omar about the email from Amber yet. But Amber had been clear that she shouldn't tell anyone. Karine would tell him everything as soon as she'd spoken to Amber and found out whatever information she'd been hiding for all these years.

Omar parked in the lot in front of a boxy, white, two-story building with a sign in front of it declaring it was the sheriff's station. She found a parking space a couple of feet closer to the building's entrance and waited for Omar to dismount from his shiny black pickup and join her.

They entered the building together. Omar gave their names to the desk clerk and, after several minutes of waiting, a stout man in a deputy's uniform with thinning brown hair pushed through the doors separating the front reception area from where the deputies sat.

"Clarke." Omar shook the deputy's hand.

"Omar, how are you? It's been a while."

"Oh, same old. Busy."

"I see." The deputy's gaze moved to Karine.

"Deputy Clarke Bridges. Karine Eloi."

Deputy Bridges extended his hand to her. "Ms. Eloi. A pleasure."

"Karine, please."

"So…" Deputy Bridges clapped his hands. "You two can follow me. Lance told me that I should let you see the file on Marilee Eloi. I understand she was your mother," he said, looking at Karine.

"Yes."

"I'm sorry for your loss."

"Thank you. It was a long time ago, but I think it's about time her killer was brought to justice."

Deputy Bridges gestured for them to precede him into a small interview room. "Well, certainly everyone here at the sheriff's department would love to see a killer brought to justice. Now, I've got the file here for you." Deputy Bridges patted the top of a thick accordion-style file folder. "You guys can take your time, but of course, nothing can leave this room." The deputy shifted from foot to foot nervously.

"What is it?" Omar said.

"Shep will be in soon. I know Lance gave you the okay to be here, but while he's on vacation, Shep is technically in charge and, well…"

"It would be best if we weren't here when he got here," Omar said astutely.

Deputy Bridget shrugged. "You know Shep."

"I do know Shep," Omar grumbled. "We'll do our best to get out of your hair before the curmudgeonly deputy arrives."

Deputy Bridges grinned. "I sure would appreciate it."

Deputy Bridges left them to it, closing the door behind him.

Karine took the seat at the table in the room, in front of the file. "I'm glad to see all of the Carling Lake deputy sheriff's aren't like Deputy Coben."

"No, Coben is in a league of his own. He thinks Lance's newfangled city ways of policing are ruining Carling Lake."

"Ah…"

"We've had a bit of trouble in the last year or so, but none of that has been Lance's fault. A lot of it has been festering for years, well before Lance became sheriff. Shep knows that, but he has to blame someone for his loss."

"I see. Well, maybe Lance can redeem himself in his deputy's eyes if he's finally able to bring charges against my mother's killer."

"I doubt it," Omar said. "But you're not doing this for Lance, and certainly not for Shep."

That was true. She was doing this for her mother and her father. And for herself. They all deserved answers.

Karine slid the papers out of the file and passed the reports on top to Omar. "Why don't you start with this top half and I can start with the bottom half."

They dug into their respective files, reading quietly for the better part of an hour. From all appearances, the investigation into her mother's death had been thorough. The sheriff had talked to several of her mom and dad's friends, neighbors and coworkers. No one had seemed to have any idea who could have attacked her mother, or why.

It was also clear from the file that the police had suspected her father. They'd questioned him multiple times and looked into his finances. Although there was never any evidence that he'd had a hand in his wife's death, some of the handwritten notes by then sheriff Edward Sampson revealed an open skepticism. One word in particular caught Karine's eye.

Affair.

"Does the former sheriff still live in Carling Lake?" Karine asked Omar.

Omar shook his head. "No. He moved to Phoenix when he retired. Why?"

Karine pointed to the word *affair* in the notes she'd been reading. "I'd like to ask him what he meant when he wrote this note. 'Affair.' Probably another one of the rumors going around about why my father would have killed my mother," she said disdainfully.

"Do you know if your father was having an affair?" Omar asked gently.

"It's not exactly a topic that's come up between me and Dad. You know he doesn't like to talk about Mom, her murder, or Carling Lake at all, really."

Omar set the report he had been reading aside. "You know, if you really want to get to the bottom of things, you're going to have to find a way to get your father to talk to you. He's the only person who knows what was going on inside his marriage at the time your mother was killed. And he probably knows much more than he realizes."

She knew Omar was right. Over the years, she'd tried half a dozen times or more to get her father to open up about her mother's murder. Each of her attempts had only led to an argument and hard feelings. She loved her father; he was the only parent she had left, but his refusal to answer her questions about her mother's homicide had put a wall between them, especially since there was so much she couldn't seem to remember about that night herself.

Karine flipped to the next page in the sheriff's notes. It was a hand-drawn map of the first floor of her childhood home. Squares marked where the furniture had sat twenty-three years earlier. An X marked the spot where her mother's body had been found in the hallway between the living room and the kitchen.

Karine put the notes aside and reached for another file from the accordion folder Deputy Bridges had given them, regretting it almost immediately.

Inside were photographs of the crime scene. She gasped.

Omar looked over and, seeing the photos in her hand, reached for them. "You don't have to look at these."

Karine pulled the photos away before he could take them from her hands. "No. I want… I need to see them."

There were several photos of her mother's body from various angles. If she had known any better, she might've convinced herself that her mother had simply decided to take a nap on the floor. But the dark purple marks marring her neck and the blood put truth to that lie. She couldn't imagine what her mother must have felt as she'd faced her killer. Had she known she only had moments left to live? Had she feared her daughter, asleep in her bed upstairs, would be next? She knew that her mother had fought for her life. The police report had indicated Marilee had several chipped fingernails. So far, Karine hadn't found a DNA report in the file, leaving open the question of whether one had been ordered.

After a moment more, she stuffed the photos back into the file folder and slid it across the table. "I don't need to see any more."

Omar ran a hand down her back. "We can leave whenever you're ready. You don't have to do this all today."

She knew Omar wanted to say she didn't have to do this at all. She couldn't really expect him to understand, even if he was her best friend. It wasn't something anyone could understand unless they'd been through it themselves.

The door to the room crashed open.

Omar was on his feet in a flash, putting his body between her and the interloper.

Karine leaned around Omar to see who had burst in, although she had a feeling she knew who it was before her eyes landed on the person. She was right.

Deputy Shep Coben stood in the doorway, his face red. "What the hell do you two think you're doing?"

"We're looking at the file on Marilee Eloi's murder. The sheriff gave us permission," Omar responded.

"I don't care what Lance gave you permission to do. I'm in charge until he returns from his vacation." Shep spat *vacation* as if it was a dirty word.

From what Karine could see, he was a man in desperate need of some time away to unwind.

"And as long as I am in charge, I'm not gonna have any civilians in here compromising my investigations. It's time for you to leave unless you want me to put you in handcuffs."

Omar held up his hands. "If that's what you want, Shep, we'll leave."

Karine took the hand that Omar extended to her and let him pull her up from her chair.

Shep stepped back out of the room to let them pass. He stopped them before they got all the way out. "You two need to listen to me, and listen to me good. Stop this investigation of yours. Your mother is gone. There's nothing you can do now to help her or bring her back. I won't let you rip this town apart over something that happened more than twenty years ago."

Karine looked the deputy square in the eye. "I think a lawman would want answers to an unsolved murder that happened in his town. But whether you want answers or not, Deputy Coben, I plan to get them. And if I have to rip this town apart to do it, then so be it."

OMAR AND KARINE stepped out of the police station and headed for the parking lot.

"Well, that went well," Karine said with a heavy dose of sarcasm. "We didn't learn anything that could help us."

Omar placed a hand on her back and steered her toward

their cars. "You know my job doesn't just involve finding lost campers and fining tourists for littering. There's
an investigatory component too. Right now, I'm working
on an investigation into possible illegal dumping and it's
not going well. That's kind of how investigations are. You
follow a trail and sometimes it leads to a dead end. Or nowhere. Then you have to find another. You're looking for
answers that have remained hidden for twenty-three years.
It's going to take time."

Karine chewed her bottom lip. "I don't have time. I only
took a week off of work and you don't know how hard that
was to get."

Omar hesitated to tell her how unlikely it was she'd find
anything at all in a week.

"Mr. Monroe."

Omar turned to see Daton Spindler hurrying toward him
and Karine. The man's sudden appearance was as much of
a surprise as the fact that Daton knew his name.

Daton was the CEO of Spindler Plastics, a major em-
ployer in the surrounding area. Omar had seen him around
town at various events, but the two had never spoken.

Daton came to a stop in front of them. "I'm glad I caught
you. I heard Miss Eloi was in town and I'd planned to stop
by and say hello."

"I'm sorry, but I don't believe we've met," Karine said.

Daton pressed his palm to his chest. "Please forgive me.
We've never met, but I knew your mom. You were so young
the last time I saw you, it's no surprise you don't remember
me. My name is Daton Spindler. Your mom and I grew up
together, and we were good friends once."

Omar shot a glance at Karine. He could tell from the look
on her face she knew nothing about a friendship between her
mother and Daton.

"I'm sorry, Mr. Spindler, but I don't remember much about my mother's life and Carling Lake."

"Of course not, and I don't mean to spring myself on you. Your mother was a good friend to me and I just wanted to let you know that if there is anything you need while you're in town, you just let me know."

"That's very kind of you," Karine said.

"Daton is the CEO of Spindler Plastics. His family has been a staple in Carling Lake for many generations."

"As has yours, Monroe."

Omar nodded in acknowledgment of the compliment. His family had been in Carling Lake for more than three generations, but they hadn't achieved anywhere near the social status of the Spindlers.

"It's hard to imagine you and Miss Marilee as friends," Omar said, unable to keep the suspicion out of his tone.

Daton chuckled. "I guess it is. Marilee, Amber and I went to the same primary and secondary school. We were the only two kids from Carling Lake to go to the private school in Stunnersville. It was an unlikely pairing, but it worked."

"Spindler?" Karine said, her forehead scrunched. "Were you married to Amber Burke Spindler?"

Daton shot Karine a look of surprise. "She's my ex-wife. Do you know her?"

Omar knew the look on Karine's face. There was something she didn't want to say.

"No. Not really. I just heard her name somewhere... Mr. Spindler, I'd love to sit down and talk to you sometime about my mother," Karine said, changing the topic back to Daton's friendship with her mother. "That's part of why I'm here. To learn more about my mom."

Omar was glad she hadn't added the piece about finding

out who'd murdered Marilee. He was sure the news would make its way around town, but the fewer people who knew, the better, as far as he was concerned.

"Anytime," Daton said, reaching into the inside pocket of his suit and pulling out a business card. He passed it to Karine. "And please, it's just Daton. Everybody just calls me Daton."

"Daton then. I'll give you a call soon."

"I'll be looking forward to it," Daton said with a wide smile. "Mr. Monroe." Daton nodded then turned on his heel and strode away.

"That was…" Karine started.

"Strange," Omar finished.

"Yes. Strange. He doesn't seem like the type of man my mom would have been friends with. She was very artsy and into nature. I can't see her being friends with someone who's built a fortune on producing plastic."

Omar watched Daton get into a black Porsche parked at the corner.

"To be fair, Daton Spindler simply inherited the company. His family had probably assumed from the moment he was born that he'd take over the reins of the family business. He may not have felt like he had much choice in the matter."

"Maybe," Karine said, dropping the business card into her purse. "I still find it interesting. And I definitely want to sit down and talk to him soon."

"Hey, what was that about Amber Spindler? How do you really know her?"

Karine fiddled with the automatic door opener for her car and avoided his gaze. "What do you mean? I said I heard her name somewhere."

"You've been in town for less than a day."

Karine remained silent.

"Karine—"

"Okay, look…" She looked at him. "Amber emailed me a few weeks ago. She said she had something to tell me about my mother."

"I can't believe you didn't tell me."

"Amber asked me not to tell anyone. I'm meeting her at her house this afternoon."

"Not without me."

She put a hand to his chest. "Yes, without you. That's the way she wants it and I'm not going to do anything that could make her change her mind about telling me whatever it is she wants to tell me."

He frowned. "I don't like it."

"You don't have to. I know you want to help, but I have to do this part on my own."

He let out a frustrated sigh. "You'll call me as soon as you leave her house, and if you get a negative vibe at all, you'll get out of there immediately."

She grinned. "Negative vibe. Run. Got you."

He didn't respond to her attempt to inject some levity into the conversation. "Karine, I'm serious. Until we have answers, you can't trust anyone in Carling Lake."

Chapter Four

Omar followed her back to her house.

Karine opened her front door and they stepped inside, her nerves prickling. It had been dark and she'd been tired when she'd gotten to the house the night before. She'd stayed downstairs long enough to make herself a quick PB&J and then headed up to grab some shut-eye. Of course then she'd been attacked and she hadn't slept much at all after Omar and Deputy Coben left. When she'd woken this morning, she had been in a rush to make it to the diner to meet up with Lance and Omar.

But now she took in her childhood home. The furniture was completely different, and although she couldn't remember the days and weeks surrounding her mother's death, she could remember the many happy years she and her parents had spent together in the house before the tragedy. She closed her eyes and could almost smell her mother's famous cinnamon-and-sugar cookies baking in the oven. Her father hadn't had a proper office. Instead, he'd pushed a desk into the far corner of the living room, where she would often find him reading his botany journals or grading papers.

They'd had a big brown sofa that sat in the middle of the living room opposite an old boxy television set. Her mother had loved having family Friday movie and popcorn nights.

Even her always-serious father had seemed to loosen up on movie night.

All the furniture now was functional and neutral. Perfectly acceptable for the renters who'd lived in the house in the ensuing years and nothing that anyone would get upset about if it got broken.

Now that she had seen the photos of the house as a crime scene, she couldn't get the picture of her mother lying in the space between the living room and the kitchen out of her head.

"Are you okay?" Omar asked.

"I knew my mother died in this house, but those pictures... Now I can't get the image out of my head."

Omar turned her to face him and lightly grasped her shoulders. "You know you don't have to stay here, right? You can stay at my house. I have a guest room."

Karine shook her head. "No, I need to be here. Hopefully, being in this space will jog my memories. I need to know what's real and what's not."

"You know, we've spoken generally about the night your mother died, but you've never spoken to me about the details of that night." Omar led her to the sofa and they sat. "I don't want to push you, but it might help."

"You're not pushing me. And you should know at least as much as I know if you're going to help me get answers."

"I plan to be right by your side," he said, wrapping an arm around her shoulder.

A warmth pushed through her at his touch. It gave her the strength to resist the memories of the worst day of her life.

"Like I said, I don't remember much. At least, I didn't remember much before the last couple of months. I'd been starting to have dreams, dreams where I saw my mom lying on the floor and the blood, a lot like in the photos we saw at the police station. But the dreams are much more vivid."

"You think you saw your mother that night?"

"I'm not sure. My dad never told me much, but he did tell me that when he came home and found my mom, he went straight to my room and found me still asleep. He said he threw a blanket over my head so I wouldn't see anything while he carried me down the stairs and out of the house."

"Maybe the blanket slipped? Maybe you did accidentally get a peek at your mom before your dad got you out of the house?"

Karine pulled away enough to look up at Omar sitting next to her. "I don't think so." She shook her head. "In my dream, I see my mom lying on the floor in the hall, but there's also someone else there. A shadow."

She could tell from the look on his face he wasn't sure.

"Our minds can play tricks on us. Just because you see a shadow in your dream doesn't mean one was there."

She stayed quiet.

She understood where he was coming from, and certainly with his law enforcement background and experience, he was probably right, but her gut told her that the shadowy person she saw in her dreams was her mother's killer. But Omar wasn't wrong. Her gut wasn't evidence. "All I'm saying is that we have to keep an open mind if we want to get answers."

"What do you plan to do now?" Omar asked, rising from the sofa.

She stood too.

"I'm not sure. I'm meeting Amber Spindler this afternoon, but I don't have anything I have to do until then. Don't you have to go to work?"

"I do, but I want to make sure you aren't going to get yourself into any trouble."

Karine eyeballed the ceiling. "I'm not planning on getting into any trouble. Actually, I think the combination of jet lag and drama is starting to hit me. I want to take a nap and I haven't had a moment to unpack fully and settle in." She was emotionally and physically exhausted from the last couple of days.

Omar cupped her cheek. "Going through that file had to be emotionally taxing. Why don't you take a break? Unpack. Unwind. And let me take you out for dinner tonight. We can catch up."

She felt the corners of her mouth edge up and excitement buzzed through her. "Unpacking and rest will have to wait. I'm meeting Amber Spindler at her place this afternoon."

Omar's hand dropped to his side. "Are you sure it's a good idea to meet Amber alone?"

She smiled. "I'll be fine. She was my mother's best friend. But dinner sounds great."

He returned her smile. "It's a date then."

Chapter Five

The ranger's station was located in a long, narrow clapboard structure topped with cedar-shake shingles. It was just after noon and Omar stood in the station's conference room, next to Ranger Emmanuel Pearson. Emmanuel had been hired recently in a part-time capacity, which had helped ease Omar's ever-increasing workload. Carling Lake Forest State Park was three hundred acres of forestland that saw thousands of tourists each year. As a ranger, he dealt with everything from bear sightings and lost hikers to the occasional small-time drug bust.

At the moment, he and Emmanuel were staring at a map of the forest that Omar had pinned to the bulletin board and which denoted areas where he suspected an unknown contaminant was polluting the water source. Colored pins marked areas where he'd found dead birds and smaller woodland creatures. He'd highlighted in yellow the streams that had been tested and come back clear of any outside pollutants. There didn't seem to be any rhyme or reason to what he'd been seeing, and yet his gut told him there was something there. If some sort of contaminant was working its way through the forest and he didn't find its source,

there was a good likelihood that larger animals could become affected and then, possibly, humans.

"I'm thinking maybe I'll take a trip up here on my day
off this week." Omar pointed to the northernmost section
of the forest on the map, where there was a cluster of pins.
"See if I find anything suspicious or unusual."

"Haven't you already been up there looking for clues?"
Emmanuel questioned.

"Yeah, but I only tested these water bodies here." He
pointed to the highlighted areas. "John only authorized
enough money for limited testing and I had to make a
judgment call about where to test. Maybe I chose wrong.
I want to run tests on water bodies further away. See if
anything pops."

His theory was that something was tainting a water
source, obviously not the streams he'd already had tested,
but there were dozens of little creeks and streams that ran
through the forest, not to mention the ephemeral creeks and
streams. Maybe one of those smaller water bodies was the
source of the toxin. Based on the placement of the clusters
on his map, contaminated water was going to be the most
likely source. Assuming he was right about a pollutant at
all and that he'd identified all the affected areas. Big as-
sumptions, he knew, but he had to start somewhere.

"What is going on here?"

Omar and Emmanuel turned. Their boss was standing
in the doorway of the conference room.

Emmanuel visibly gulped, shooting a nervous glance
at Omar.

Omar and John Huyton had gotten off on the wrong foot
from the first day Omar had transferred to Carling Lake.
At his last post, his regional supervisor had trusted the
rangers on the ground to know their territory. Whenever

there'd been a problem, his supervisor had provided whatever resources and support he could to the rangers to solve
it quickly and with as little upheaval to the environment as
possible. He'd let the rangers do their jobs. In fact, Omar
couldn't remember a single time when his prior supervisor
had showed up at the station unannounced.

But John was the opposite. His unannounced visits were
close to becoming a habit, and he seemed to think his sole
job was to keep an eye on the budgetary bottom line. Omar
knew that the overall budget for state parks was perpetually
on the chopping block and grew smaller and smaller each
year. But his job wasn't about money. It was about preserving the beautiful, majestic land that was the Carling Lake
Forest State Park for the generations that would follow.

John didn't see it that way though.

Omar had fought tooth and nail to get John to authorize the initial testing of the four streams he'd identified
as potentially contaminated. When those tests had come
back showing no problem, John had considered the matter closed. No amount of discussion had convinced him to
authorize more testing of the water bodies and the continued search for an answer for what Omar was seeing on the
ground. The last time Omar had broached the topic of a
possible pollutant or contaminant affecting certain of the
small creatures in the woods, John had yelled that the matter was closed, that there was no way more testing would
be approved, and that Omar should stop wasting his time.

So he'd gone rogue. Paying out of his own pocket for
water testing was expensive, but he'd resolved to do it,
and it didn't cost him anything to keep his eyes open and
map out the areas where he was finding the affected animals. Nor did it cost him anything to ask a few discreet
questions. There was a mining operation about forty miles

west of Carling Lake, and although the regulations around
mining were strict, it wouldn't be the first time a big cor-
poration had sought to cut corners and, accidentally or on
purpose, caused damage to the surrounding environment.
So far, though, his questions had turned up nothing useful.
And now it looked like he was going to have to answer for
ignoring his boss's order to stand down.

John plunked his hands on his hips. "I asked what's
going on here? What is this?" He gestured toward the map.

"It's a map of the areas where I've found the remains of
several small birds, squirrels, and other small animals,"
Omar answered resolutely.

John's face pinked. "I want to talk to you in your office,
Monroe. Now." John spun on his heel and marched from
the room toward Omar's office.

Emmanuel gave him a sympathetic look, but made no
move to follow.

That was fine. Omar was the senior ranger and this off-
the-books investigation was his baby. If someone was going
to get called out over it, it should be him.

John was pacing the small office when Omar entered,
which basically meant he took two steps forward before
he was forced to turn and take two steps back. It hardly
seemed worth the effort, but John had always struck Omar
as more show than substance.

"I thought I made myself clear that you needed to drop
this idea that there was some sort of contaminate affecting
the Carling Lake Forest." John ceased pacing, but he blocked
the path to the desk and forced Omar to stay standing.

Omar stood by the door, his back straight. John was, at
best, five foot six, which meant Omar had about six inches
on him. He used that advantage now, literally looking down
on his boss.

"You did. But part of my job is to identify and document abnormalities in my coverage area. That's what I'm doing. My job," he emphasized.

"Abnormalities," John snapped. "You did the tests. Expensive tests, I'd add, and they came back clear. There are no abnormalities."

"Maybe not in the water that was tested, but something is going on here. I want to make sure I stay on top of it."

A dark red hue climbed up John's neck. "You are bordering on insubordination here, Monroe. I told you to drop this and that's what I meant. Drop. It. Now. Or I will write you up."

"Sir," Omar said through clenched teeth, "I don't think you understand—"

"I understand perfectly," John boomed. "And I am in charge. Now, have I made myself clear on this issue?"

Omar's temper festered, but he kept it in check. John may be a bureaucratic hack who only cared about money, but he was still the boss.

"Understood."

"Good." John gave him a weasely smile. He took a step forward and Omar moved out from in front of the door so he could get by. With his hand on the doorknob, John turned. "I'll check in with you later this week. I want to see things back on track in this office or I'll have to take more serious measures."

John walked out, leaving Omar staring after him, wondering if his supervisor's eagerness to nip his investigation in the bud was solely due to budgetary concerns or if there was something else, something more nefarious, behind his threats.

Chapter Six

Karine drove to Amber's house, passing through downtown Carling Lake. The town had changed over the years, but there was enough left of the Carling Lake that she remembered to conjure a sense of déjà vu. She came to a stop at an intersection at the center of town. The storefronts had been modernized, and there were several shop names that she didn't recognize, but the ice cream shop was still there, as was the *Carling Lake Weekly*, although the art gallery next to it had not been there when she was a kid. "The West Gallery" she read on the discreet lettering scrolling across the bottom of the glass window. James West's place. She would have to make sure she stopped in.

The car behind her honked and she pressed down on the accelerator, driving through the intersection.

She reached Mockingbird Estates and made a right into a newish upper-class neighborhood. Each of the houses was two to three stories and set far enough apart from one another to afford the occupants quite a bit of privacy. Despite the size and undoubtedly the cost, many of the homes looked to be unoccupied, which didn't surprise her. The heart of Carling Lake was its dedicated year-round citizenry, but the town relied on its seasonal residents and tourists for survival.

Karine turned onto a wide cul-de-sac and parked in front

of the address that Amber had given her. There were no lights on in the house, but a Lexus SUV was parked in the driveway.

She checked the email from Amber: 2:30 p.m. She was right on time.

She got out of the car as a gust of wind, whooshing off the nearby lake, blew past. She yanked her arm clear of the car before the door slammed shut on it and pulled the collar of her light jacket tightly around her. It was mid-September, but she'd forgotten that fall came more quickly in the mountains. The heavy, dark gray clouds overhead didn't help. They cast a melancholy pallor over the morning. It smelled like rain, as her father often said. She still didn't know what rain smelled like, but she knew she'd have to put "buy a heavier jacket" on her list of things to do.

She made her way to the front of the house and rang the doorbell.

No answer.

A chill that had nothing to do with the wind engulfed her. Something was wrong. The house was too still.

She peeked through the front window to the left of the door. The dining room was empty.

She moved to the window to the right of the door and spied a couch, coffee table and television set. A leather handbag sat on the coffee table. So, Amber was home. No woman would go anywhere without her purse.

Karine rang the bell again. Minutes passed and still no answer.

She debated leaving, but Amber knew she was coming, and her email had been so imploring. Maybe she was in the shower or… Amber lived alone and hadn't Karine read that most household accidents happened in the bathroom? Or was that the kitchen? Either way, Amber could need medical attention.

She bounded down the porch steps and rounded the house. The side door into the garage was locked, so she kept moving toward the back of the house.

The front porch on the home had been just big enough for one person to stand there while waiting to be let in. But Amber had gone all out in building the back porch. It extended a good nine feet and ran the width of the house. She had set one side up as an outdoor living room while the other side resembled an outdoor kitchen, complete with a built-in barbecue and pizza oven. A series of French doors ran across the back of the house, letting in an abundance of natural light.

Karine climbed the porch steps and peered through the glass in the door.

Nothing looked out of place in the kitchen. Her gaze traveled to the adjacent den, which had been decorated with a nautical theme. Blues and greens abounded—the sofa, the rugs, the walls. A painting of the ocean hung over the fireplace, and an intricate model boat held a prominent place on a center table.

She was just about to admit defeat and head home when her eyes fell on something that froze her in place.

A hand hung off the side of the sofa, fingers skimming the ocean-blue rug.

Her heart raced. "Amber! Amber, it's Karine Eloi. Amber!" She banged on the French doors.

The figure on the sofa didn't move. In fact, whoever was lying there was unnaturally still.

She tried the door's handle, unconcerned with the impoliteness of simply walking into Amber's home.

The doorknob turned, and she let herself into the house, rushing to the sofa.

Any hope she'd had that Amber was just a very heavy sleeper was immediately dashed.

Amber's eyes stared, unseeing, at the seafoam-colored ceiling. A bottle of vodka and a glass sat on the coffee table in front of the sofa. A small orange pill bottle peeked out from under the sofa. Diazepam, she read on its label.

Whatever Amber had wanted to tell her, she'd taken it to her grave.

Her heart still pounding furiously, Karine reached for her phone. On instinct, she called the one person she knew she could count on.

"Karine, hey." Omar's deep baritone carried over the phone. "Are you done with your meeting with Amber Burke Spindler already? What did she want to tell you?"

"I don't know... I..." Karine fought to catch her breath.

"Karine? Are you okay? What's wrong? Where are you?"

"Amber's house. She's... Omar, she's dead."

"Are you still in the house?"

"Yes, I'm... It looks like she overdosed."

"Karine, get out of the house. Get back in your car and lock the doors. Do it now."

She backed away from the sofa and hurried through the French doors and across the yard, back to her car. She could hear Omar on another line talking, requesting an ambulance and the sheriff's deputy be dispatched to Amber's house in the Mockingbird Estates.

"Omar, I've got her exact address," she said, locking the car doors while rattling off the address.

Omar repeated the address to the person he was speaking with, then came back on the phone line. "Karine, I'm on my way. Stay in your car until the sheriff's office gets there."

"Okay." The little shred of sunlight that had managed to pierce the dark skies suddenly vanished. Thunder rolled in the distance as a fat raindrop landed on her windshield. "Omar, hurry."

OMAR BARELY SLOWED long enough to tell Emmanuel where he was headed. His state-issued pickup didn't have flashers and sirens like the sheriff's department vehicles, but it was the offseason and midafternoon traffic was light. The rain seemed to be helpfully holding off for the most part. Only a few stray raindrops fell as he raced toward Amber Spindler's house.

He made it to Mockingbird Estates in record time, but not fast enough to beat Deputy Coben.

He turned the corner leading onto Amber Spindler's cul-de-sac and spied the deputy talking to Karine next to her car.

He was out of the truck and racing to her side a split second after throwing his pickup into Park.

"Are you okay?" He pulled Karine into his arms, completely unconcerned about interrupting the conversation between her and the deputy.

"I'm okay. Shaken, but okay." He bet. Given what she'd told him about her recently resurfaced memories of finding her mother, finding another body had to have been traumatic.

"Excuse me, Mr. Monroe. I was interviewing a witness. You can wait over there—" Shep pointed to the pickup "—until I'm done."

Omar kept one arm wrapped around Karine and glared at the deputy. He wasn't going to leave Karine's side.

Shep glared back.

After a long moment, Karine sighed. "Deputy Coben,

can we please just get on with it? I'd like to leave some-time today."

Shep shifted his glare to Karine. "Fine." He looked down at the notepad in his hand. "I believe you'd just gotten to the point in your story where you arrived at the house when we were interrupted."

"Right, I rang the doorbell, but Amber didn't answer. I could see her purse in the living room through the front window, and her car was in the driveway."

"So you just traipsed around to the back of her house? You really must have wanted to speak with her."

"Amber asked me to come over at two thirty. She had something important she wanted to tell me. I thought she might have been in the shower or maybe she'd fallen or something and couldn't get to the door."

Shep harrumphed. "Well, that wasn't a bad theory. Everybody around these parts knows that Amber imbibes too frequently for her own good and that she has a problem with pills. Chews them like candy."

Unfortunately, the deputy wasn't exaggerating. Amber had been on a downward spiral ever since Daton had left her for a much younger executive at his plastics company three years earlier. The gossip mill had long churned around the fact that Amber hadn't been able to give Daton the heirs he'd so desperately wanted. The new wife's pregnancy and the birth of twin boys last year had only seemed to accel-erate Amber's decline.

"What did Amber want to talk to you about?" Shep pressed.

Karine shot a look at Omar. After a decades-long friend-ship, he didn't need to say anything to convey a message.

Karine turned back to Shep. "I don't know. She didn't get a chance to tell me."

The deputy's eyes narrowed to slits. He had undoubtedly surmised that whatever Amber had wanted to tell Karine might have to do with Marilee's death. And since Shep had made no secret about how he felt about Karine's investigation into her mother's death, it made sense that Karine would want to keep as much information as close to her vest as possible.

"Okay." Shep eyed them both with unabashed hostility. "Continue."

Karine recounted how she'd gone around back, had seen a hand hanging off the sofa through the French doors and, after finding the doors unlocked, had gone inside to see if she could help the person. But Amber had been beyond help.

"We'll have to wait for the medical examiner to know for sure, but I've seen a few overdoses in my time on the force. It looks like there was nothing you could have done for her," Shep said in a rare show of sensitivity. "She probably expired sometime last night."

Karine shook her head. "It doesn't make any sense. I mean, she knew I was coming to see her this afternoon."

Shep removed his hat and swiped his sleeve across his forehead. Despite the cool air, the beads of sweat congregated at his hairline. "Might not have been intentional. Someone as used to taking pills and drinking as much as Amber was…constantly need to increase their usage to get the desired effects. Her poor body just probably couldn't take any more."

"Shep, if you've got what you need, I'd like to take Karine home now," Omar said.

"Yeah, sure." Shep waved a hand absently. "As I'm sure you know, her car has to stay here. Part of the scene. Probably release it sometime this afternoon or evening. I'll call you when it's clear for you to come by and pick it up."

Karine nodded. "Thank you, Deputy."

Omar pulled Karine closer to his side. She was trembling slightly, and he wasn't sure it was due to the flimsy jacket she wore. They turned toward his pickup.

"Ms. Eloi," Shep called.

They turned back in unison.

The deputy's eyes had narrowed into beady little slits. "You aren't planning to leave town anytime soon, are you? I might have more questions for you."

Omar guessed it was too much to expect Shep to be decent for more than a minute or two at a time.

"I plan to be here for the rest of the week."

Shep nodded before turning and stomping up the walk to the house.

Karine twisted in Omar's arms, looking up at him. "Does that mean Deputy Coben hasn't one hundred percent bought into the theory that Amber accidentally overdosed?"

"I don't know about Shep, but I sure don't. Let's get out of here. We need to talk."

MARILEE'S KILLER WATCHED the commotion at Amber's place from the shadows of a vacant house across the street. No one noticed. The killer was good at going unnoticed. Always had been.

Amber. It was a shame, but had to be done. The killer thought Amber's silence had been bought long ago, but you really couldn't trust anyone nowadays. Amber had suffered the consequences of her attempted treachery.

But it still felt like the secrets of the past were bubbling to the surface now, and the killer wasn't sure what to do about it. One thing was for certain, the killer hadn't spent the last twenty-three years covering their tracks to fail now.

Hopefully, all Karine Eloi needed was a warning.

Hopefully for her, that was.

Chapter Seven

Omar drove her back to her house. As soon as she got inside, she put the electric teakettle on.

"You are buying Deputy Coben's theory that Amber overdosed, are you?"

"It's possible," Omar answered.

Karine frowned at him. Lots of things were possible, but plausible? She wasn't buying the accidental overdose line.

"It is, Karine." Omar sat at the kitchen table. "Amber had a problem. We all knew it, even if most of us preferred to look away," he added sadly.

Karin grabbed the kettle when it started to whistle. She poured the boiling water into two cups and added tea bags. "Okay, but don't you think that makes it less likely that she would accidentally overdose? I mean, if she abused drugs and alcohol regularly, she probably knew how much she could handle." She carried the cups to the table, sliding a mug of hot tea across the surface to Omar.

He wrapped both hands around the warm mug. "By that logic, no one would ever accidentally overdose, and we know that's not the case."

That drew another frown, yet she had to concede the point.

"But I can't say I don't have my suspicions. The timing

is just too coincidental for me. Especially following the break-in at your house the other night."

"Exactly." Karine punctuated the word by pointing at him.

Omar gave her a searching look over the top of his mug. "Don't tell me you plan on investigating Amber's death now too?"

"To the extent that it might answer some questions about my mother's, yes. There is something going on here. I'm not sure what, or why, but I feel like it's now or never for getting answers about my mother's murder."

Omar sighed heavily. "How do you plan on doing that?"

"Well, Daton used to be married to Amber. Maybe he has some idea about what she wanted to tell me."

"Maybe." Omar looked skeptical. "Daton and Amber's divorce wasn't amicable though. I doubt she would have confided in him."

"Is there anyone she would have confided in? A friend or family member?"

Omar shook his head slowly, thinking. "Amber has been kind of a loner since the divorce. She used to attend all the social functions, fundraisers and such for the church, and she chaired the Carling Lake Winter Festival during the years Spindler Plastics was the lead sponsor. But the divorce knocked her down a few rungs on the social ladder." He thought for a minute. "She does employ Fiona Kessler to clean for her a few times a week. I think I've seen them having coffee together at the café in town once or twice."

"Okay, Fiona Kessler. It's someplace to start at least."

Omar stood. "I have to get back to work. Are we still on for dinner tonight?"

She hesitated for a moment. It somehow seemed wrong to be making dinner plans when a woman had just died. But she and Omar would have to eat no matter what. And if she were honest, she was looking forward to dinner with Omar more than she probably should be. "Yeah, we're still on."

It was Omar's turn to smile. "Good. I'll pick you up at eight."

SHE ANSWERED THE door to Omar at exactly 8:00 p.m.

He'd changed out of his work clothes and into black slacks and loafers and a burgundy-satiny button-down shirt. It looked like he'd taken the time to shape up his goatee and the scent of his aftershave went straight to her core. She'd always known her best friend was good-looking, but the man standing in front of her wasn't just attractive. He was sexy.

"You look great," he said, giving her a brilliant smile that sent butterflies fluttering in her stomach.

She wasn't wearing anything fancy, a blue-and-white-flowered sundress that hit just above the knees and sandals, but she heated under his appreciative gaze.

"So do you." She locked the door and followed him past her rental, which she'd picked up once Shep had called to tell her he was releasing the crime scene, to Omar's pickup.

"There are a bunch of new fancy restaurants in town since you've last been here, but I figured you might appreciate just going back to our old haunts, so I plan to take you to Barney's Bar and Grill, if that's okay?"

"That's great. My parents used to take me to Barney's for special occasions."

Barney's parking lot was full when they arrived, but the hostess promised it would only be a couple minutes' wait while a table was cleared for them.

Karine excused herself to the ladies' room while they waited. As she made her way back to Omar, an older man with thinning brown hair and striking gray eyes homed in on her as she passed the bar. He looked vaguely familiar, yet the curl of his lips and the hatred in his eyes had her quickening her steps.

"Who's that man sitting on the third stool from the left at the bar?" she asked when she returned to Omar's side.

He turned and focused on where she'd indicated.

The man still stared unabashedly.

"That's Martin Howser. He used to be the high school principal at Carling Lake High. I guess he recognizes you as Marilee's daughter."

"I guess."

The man turned his back to them.

The hostess gestured for them to follow her then, and Karine put the man out of her head. Some people might not want her back in town dredging up old memories, but they'd have to deal with it. They settled into their table and perused the menu.

"Omar Monroe. Long time no see."

Karine looked up at the waitress who had stopped at the edge of the table. It took a moment for her to put a name to the face. Blanca Coben.

Omar shot Blanca a brief, polite smile. "Hi, Blanca. I've been pretty busy at work. I've been getting off too late to come to the restaurant for dinner."

Blanca ran her finger lightly across Omar's shoulder. "Now you know I'm here to serve you whenever you need."

That comment was overloaded with sexual innuendo.

The tips of Omar's ears reddened in embarrassment and he looked down at the menu in his hand.

Karine fought the urge to slap Blanca's finger away from Omar's shoulder.

Blanca, the head mean girl at Carling Lake middle school

during Karine's brief tenure there, had grown up. And from the looks of it, life had not treated her kindly. Blanca was skinnier than looked healthy and the smell of stale beer permeated from her body. Although the light in the room was dim, Karine could see that Blanca's eyes were blood-shot and her skin sallow.

"Blanca. It's been a long time." She couldn't say she really cared about the answer, but the question had the desired effect of pulling Blanca's attention away from Omar.

Blanca's smile dimmed considerably. "Karine Eloi. I heard you were back in town stirring up trouble."

She had no doubt Blanca had gotten that misleading piece of gossip from her uncle, Deputy Shep Coben.

Not taking Blanca's bait, Karine plastered a smile on her face. "How have you been, Blanca?"

Blanca snapped the gum in her mouth. "I'm just fine. Working. Taking care of my kids and my mother. It's not a fancy Los Angeles life, but it suits me just fine."

"Blanca," Omar said with a warning in his voice.

Blanca turned a smile on Omar. "Oh, Omar, I'm sure a big-city girl like Karine knows I am just teasing her."

"Well, stop teasing."

"It's fine, Omar," Karine said. She could tell by the look in his eyes that it was not fine with him.

"I think we'd like to order our drinks now?" Omar said pointedly.

Karine ordered a wine spritzer and Omar got a beer.

"She likes you," Karine said after Blanca sashayed away to put in the drink orders. She hoped Omar hadn't heard the touch of jealousy that seemed to her to have rung so loudly in her words.

Omar made a face. "Blanca is not my type."

Karine smiled. "Okay. Well, I haven't heard you mention a date and I don't know how long. So, what is your type?"

Omar arched his brow. "I could say the same about you. What's your type?"

You.

She gave herself a mental shake. Where did that come from? Omar was her friend. Just her friend. Although, if she could find a man as kind, caring and funny as he was who lived in Los Angeles, she might just marry him.

"Karine? Where'd you go?"

"Sorry. A work thing just popped into my head." A blush heated her cheeks.

Blanca returned with Omar's beer and her wine spritzer. She set the drinks down on the table in front of them with a sexy smile for Omar and not so much as a glance for Karine. She left a second time with a promise to return in a moment to take their food orders.

"Here are the rules for the night," Omar said, raising his beer.

Karine picked up her glass. "There are rules for the night?"

"There are now. Rule one, no talking about or thinking about work for either of us."

"That's a rule I can get behind." Karine held her glass up higher.

"Rule two, no investigation talk."

She tapped her glass against his bottle. "Agreed."

They drank on it.

"I do have a question though," Karine said. "What are we supposed to talk about?"

"We've been friends for over thirty years—"

"Hold on there. Your family moved in when you were

six, so it's just shy of thirty years. Don't make us older than we are."

Omar held up his hands with a laugh. "My apologies. Just shy of thirty years. My point is still valid. We should be able to find something to talk about besides work and murder. I, for one, want to circle back to this question of your type of man."

"I thought we were talking about your kind of woman." Were they flirting with each other? This felt like flirting, but to tell the truth, it had been so long since she'd been on a date that she wasn't sure. Not that this was a date, so it probably wasn't flirting. Probably.

Omar took another pull from his beer. His gaze locked on her face. "My kind of woman is intelligent, funny and slightly sarcastic. She's always thinking of others and has a strong sense of justice and right and wrong that guides her."

Something in Karine's belly fluttered. That had definitely seemed like flirting. It felt as if Omar was directing his words specifically to her, but he couldn't be describing her. Could he?

"A woman who, when she turns her beautiful brown eyes on me, it feels as if I've won the greatest lottery in the world," he added, his voice low and husky.

They stared at each other for a long moment. Karine's heart raced. Despite all the people in the restaurant, the music coming from the speakers, the laughter and chatter swirling all around them, it felt like they were the only two people in the room. Maybe in the world at that moment.

"What can I get y'all?" Blanca popped up next to the table with an order pad and pen in her hand.

Barney's wasn't fancy, but they boasted the best seafood platter in town. They ordered one to share.

Karine was glad to see that the charge bouncing between

them before Blanca arrived to take their orders was gone by the time she left.

They drank and chatted, catching up on the little details of their lives that had escaped telling in their phone calls and emails over the last six months. When the food arrived, they dug in. Lots of things may have changed in Carling Lake over the years, but Barney's seafood platter wasn't one of them. It was still amazingly good.

Barney's had expanded since she'd last been there to include a space at the back of the dining area for live entertainment and dancing. There wasn't a live band this night, but that hadn't kept many of the diners from taking to the dance floor and grooving to the music coming through the bar and grill's overhead speakers.

"Want to dance?" Omar asked after Blanca had cleared their empty dinner plates.

"Oh, no, I—"

Omar's eyebrow quirked up. "You've been tapping your foot and chair dancing since we sat down."

"Well, the music isn't half bad," she conceded.

"Come on." Omar stood and reached out his hand.

She gave in, taking his hand.

Mariah Carey's "Always Be My Baby" played as they hit the dance floor, but after a minute, the song faded. The first chords of Richard Marx's "Right Here Waiting" sounded from the speakers.

Karine started to turn away from the dance floor, but Omar caught her hand. She let him pull her into his arms. They were one of three or four couples on the floor. They swayed to the music, his lean, hard body pressed against hers.

They'd danced together before, at parties and clubs, but this felt different. Intimate.

She folded into his masculine scent, resting her head against his chest. She was pretty sure this dance, the feelings that she was experiencing at this moment, were a terrible idea, but she didn't pull away. The song ended and she opened her eyes, looking up at Omar.

"Are you okay?" he asked, his voice husky. He appeared to have been as affected by the moment as she was.

"Fine," she answered in barely more than a whisper.

"I should take you home." Omar's eyes bore into hers.

Her breath caught in her throat and all she could do was nod.

He paid the bill and they stepped out of the restaurant into the cool night air.

HE WANTED TO kiss Karine more than he'd ever wanted anything in his life. When he'd been on that dance floor, holding her in his arms, the world had just felt right. And he was pretty sure she'd felt it too.

Omar hadn't had any intentions other than catching up with his oldest friend when he'd invited her out to dinner, but maybe it was the right time to move their relationship forward. He'd been thinking about it for…years. But he was pretty sure Karine would have run. She'd never stuck with a relationship for longer than a few months. At least, not a romantic one. But it was getting harder and harder for him to pretend he didn't have feelings for her that went far beyond friendship.

They walked across the parking lot to his truck and he unlocked the passenger's-side door first. He turned to help her into the pickup. Inches separated them. The seconds ticked by, neither of them moving, their gazes locked. And then Karine went to her toes.

His mouth touched hers. The light tanginess of lemon

butter lingered on her lips. Her fingers skimmed down his arms in a touch so light he could barely feel it, which made it all the more exciting somehow.

He kept the kiss light, exploring her mouth.

Karine stepped back all too soon. Her eyes shone with surprise, desire and uncertainty.

He knew her well enough to know she'd need time to process the line they'd just crossed, so he took two steps backward, giving her space.

His eyes hooked on something over Karine's shoulder. A flash of metal. "Get down!" He grabbed Karine on instinct. They hit the ground hard enough to rattle his jaw.

The gunshot reverberated in the air around them.

He rolled, using his body to cover Karine as she cried out.

Tires squealed.

Omar raised his head, but the only thing he caught was the flash of red taillights. No make or model of the car or the person who'd shot at them.

"Are you hurt?" He was still perched over her, but he did his best to assess whether she'd been hurt in the fall. Or, God forbid, shot.

The doors to the pub opened and several people rushed to help them up.

"The sheriff is on his way," an overweight, balding man said as he offered his hand.

Omar let the man pull him to his feet and brought Karine up with him.

Deputies Coben and Bridges arrived moments later, followed by three more deputies. Once again, he and Karine found themselves giving statements to Deputy Coben. There was no question that this hadn't been an accident. Someone had shot at them. A group of diners had been leaving the restaurant when the shots had rung out and they'd seen the whole thing, backing up his and Karine's story to the deputy.

The parking lot was a crime scene, including Omar's truck. That meant they had to wait over an hour for the deputies to finish taking photos and searching the grounds before finally giving them the okay to head home.

Karine was quiet on the drive to her house. He worried that the events of the last few days were too much for her. As much as he wanted to be near her, if she was thinking about heading back to Los Angeles... Well, that just might be the safest thing.

It seemed she did have safety on her mind, just not her own.

She turned to him when he pulled into her driveway and shut off the engine. "I don't want you to help me investigate my mother's murder anymore."

"What? Why? Are you giving up on the investigation?"

"No." She shook her head. "I just don't want your help. It's too dangerous. You could have been killed tonight, and it would have been all my fault."

"Karine—"

"No, Omar." She unbuckled her seat belt and reached for the door handle. "I've made up my mind. I'm not going to let you put yourself in danger."

She got out of the truck and headed for her house.

He got out and followed. "Karine, wait." She kept walking.

"Wait!"

She stopped. Turned. "Omar—"

"No. It's your turn to listen." He stepped up to her and laid his hands gently on her shoulders. "I'm not going to stop helping you, no matter what you say."

"Omar, I can't risk…" She stopped, choking up.

He moved a hand to her face, stroking the pad of his thumb down her soft cheek. "You're not risking anything. I am. I know that there's a danger here. I was there tonight and the night before, and I get it. And I appreciate your concern. I wish you had more of it for yourself."

"If you were to get hurt, if I lost you, I don't know what I'd do." Her eyes shone with unshed tears.

Her words sent a flood of emotions through him. He lowered his head. "I know. I feel the same way about you. So, how about we keep doing this together? Watching each other's backs. What do you say?"

Her mouth turned up in a smile and she squeezed his hands in return. "Okay, together."

Chapter Eight

The high-pitched squeaking of the critters in the attic didn't keep her awake for long that night, but Karine did not find relief in sleep. In her dreams, she watched her twelve-year-old self creep down the second-floor hallway from her bedroom and peer through the stair railings. Her mother lay on the floor. *Why is Mommy sleeping on the floor?* She could hear young Karine's thoughts in her head, but she knew her mother wasn't sleeping. Her mother was dead. And the person who'd killed her was there. A shadowy form circled her mother.

She attempted to focus in on the shadow, but no matter how hard she tried, she couldn't see the person's face. But now she did see something she hadn't noticed in the dream before.

The fireplace poker.

It was in the shadowy person's hand.

Young Karine was trembling now. She shrank back, away from the railing.

The shadow turned, looked up...

Karine started awake, her heart thundering in her chest, the bedsheets twisted around her legs.

Sweat beaded on her chest and her head throbbed. She

pushed the covers aside and swung her feet to the floor, padding into the bathroom.

It wasn't the first time she'd had the dream, although being in the house where her mother had been killed seemed to have made it more potent. She'd also never seen the fireplace poker in the shadow's hand before, but that could have been a result of having viewed the crime scene photos.

It was getting harder and harder to know what part of the dream was real and what part she was filling in with what she'd learned about her mother's death.

Karine got into the shower and let the hot water wash away the dream, leaving the room in her mind to allow the memories of kissing Omar to flood in.

That kiss, which had been incredible…and a mistake.

Omar was her friend. Her best friend.

Sure, okay, there was an attraction there. They were both two healthy adults, so that wasn't unexpected, but letting that attraction take over was too much of a risk. What if they moved into the romantic zone and the relationship didn't work out? She'd lose Omar. She couldn't risk that. She didn't have a lot of people in her life who she was close to. He really was it. She needed him more as a friend than as a lover. He'd understand, right? Of course he would. He probably felt the same way. Their friendship was strong, certainly strong enough to withstand one little kiss. One little, amazing kiss.

She got out of the shower and got dressed, unsurprised to see Omar heading up the walkway toward her front door. She held the door open for him by the time he stepped on to the porch.

"I brought breakfast." He held up a white paper bag with OrganicSandwich written across it and a carrier with a cup of coffee for him and an English breakfast tea for her.

"You may enter," she joked, stepping aside and letting him pass.

They sat at the kitchen table and dug into the bacon, egg and cheese sandwiches he'd bought.

Awkwardness and something else—maybe a touch of anticipation—lingered between them. This was what she didn't want. She didn't want to feel uncomfortable around Omar.

Omar cleared his throat. "Listen, about last night—"

"If you're worried about how I'm doing after being shot at, you don't have to," she said in a voice that was a little too loud and a little too bright to her ears.

Omar must have thought so too. He tilted his head and gave her a look filled with concern.

"I just mean I'm fine. I've never been shot at before and I hope to never be again, but I'm okay."

It was quiet for a beat. Then another.

She was pretty sure Omar's "about last night" hadn't been about the shooting but about their kiss, but she wasn't ready to talk to him about that yet.

"You're fine. Okay. What are you planning to do today then?" Omar said.

She let out a breath, relieved that he wasn't going to press the kissing issue now. "I was thinking I'd go see Fiona Kessler. Maybe she can help me figure out what Amber was planning to tell me."

Omar frowned. "Fiona is…peculiar."

"Peculiar?"

He balled up the wrapper his sandwich had come in. "She's not particularly friendly, is all. I don't have to be at work for a couple more hours. I can go with you."

Karine gathered the trash from her breakfast and stood. "Let's go."

Omar drove them to a part of town Karine didn't remember existing when she'd lived in Carling Lake. Fiona lived in a neighborhood made up of modular homes. Fiona's was one of the larger ones, but from the grime on the siding and the dirt-packed lawn, it was clear she didn't put much care into the upkeep.

Fiona Kessler opened her front door wearing a pink housecoat, bedroom slippers and a wary expression. Her expression didn't change after Omar and Karine introduced themselves.

Okay, so not the friendly chat Karine had hoped for. Direct and to the point seemed like the best way to approach the situation.

"What can I do for you?" she asked without inviting them in.

"I was hoping you'd be willing to answer a few questions about Amber Spindler," Karine said.

Fiona's eyes flicked from wary to suspicious in an instant. "Are you a reporter?"

"No. I'm...well, I'm Marilee Eloi's daughter."

Fiona didn't seem surprised by the news. "I heard you found Amber."

"I did. Amber recently reached out to me. She said she wanted to tell me something about my mother."

"I don't see how I can help you." Fiona shot an uneasy glance from Omar to Karine and back.

"I think Amber was going to tell me something about my mother's death. I understand you and Amber were friends. You worked for her. I thought maybe she'd shared with you whatever it was she was going to tell me."

"I don't know why you'd think Amber told me anything. I cleaned her house for her. We weren't friends."

Fiona's inability to meet Karine's gaze made her question whether the older woman was telling the truth.

"Whatever it was Amber wanted to tell me seemed important. I'm pretty sure it was about my mother. Are you sure you don't have any idea what it was?"

"No."

Karine could feel the irritation rolling off Omar next to her.

"When was the last time you saw Amber?" Karine asked, keeping her tone light. They needed Fiona's cooperation. If Omar was right about Fiona's solitary lifestyle, she might have been one of the last people to see Amber alive.

"I already spoke to Deputy Coben. The last time I saw Amber was the day before...the day before you found her. I clean and cook three times a week. Monday, Thursday and Saturday."

"But I found Amber on Wednesday, which means you should have been there to clean the house on Monday, not Tuesday."

"Amber asked me to change my schedule this week. She wanted me to come on Tuesday instead of Monday."

Karine shared a quick glance with Omar before turning back to Fiona. "Did Amber tell you why?"

Fiona shook her head. "No. Not really."

"No or not really?" Omar barked.

Fiona took a step back from the door. "No."

Karine shot Omar a warning look. The last thing she wanted was for Fiona to slam the door on them.

"When you saw her, did she seem worried or upset?" Karine asked in an overly saccharine tone.

Fiona stuck her hands in the pockets of the housecoat. "Maybe. A little."

"Maybe or a little?" Omar pressed.

"Fiona." Karine jumped in to speak and hopefully cut some of the tension building. "Anything you can tell us about the last time you saw Amber, how she was, what she said, it might help us understand what happened to her."

Fiona's forehead scrunched in confusion. "What happened? I thought she took too many of those pills she likes."

"Maybe, but I'm not convinced and Deputy Coben…"

Fiona harrumphed. "Coben couldn't find his behind with a compass and a map. Has the nerve to be mad that we didn't elect him sheriff. We may be simple people in Carling Lake, but we aren't stupid."

Karine smiled. "You certainly aren't."

Fiona let out a deep sigh. "Look, I really don't know what to tell you. Amber seemed a little down. Maybe a bit agitated. She didn't tell me why but…"

"But what?"

"Amber didn't get out much, but she liked using those dating apps. You know, to meet people. Sometimes she'd meet up with some of the men online, like a video date. There was one guy lately who she seemed to like. A lot. And then he just stopped responding. What is it you young people call it? He ghosted her." Fiona chuckled. "I figured she was a little down over that, but like I told her, how much of a relationship could she really have with a person she'd never met in real life?" She shrugged.

"Did you cook for her on Tuesday?" Karine asked.

"Yes. A roast with baby potatoes, carrots and freshly baked bread."

"Do you usually make so much food just for Amber?"

Fiona tapped her chin. "No, now that you mention it. But Amber was very specific about the menu."

"Maybe she expected company," Omar said.

Fiona shrugged. "If she did, she didn't tell me. And I'd

have to say that's not likely. Amber doesn't have many friends, and she rarely entertains in her home."

"Rarely, but not never," Karine persisted. This could be good. If Amber had been expecting company, that person might know what she was going to tell Karine.

Or that person could have killed her.

"Rarely. Once she had a gentleman friend from one of those apps over for dinner, but it didn't go anywhere." Fiona's puckered lips said everything about how she felt about that date.

"Okay, so it's possible Amber was entertaining on Tuesday night."

"Anything is possible. Look, I really don't know anything else and I need to go." Fiona grabbed the door and took a step back.

"Wait. Is there anything else you can think of that was different about that day? Anything at all?"

Fiona paused. "Amber had me buy wine. Really nice wine. I had to go to this fancy store in Stunnersville."

"Wine?"

"Yeah. Sixty dollars a pop and she had me buy three bottles."

Omar shifted next to her. "And that was unusual?"

"Very. Amber usually drank Scotch and soda. Vodka. Rum. Gin."

"Hard liquor," Karine summarized.

"Very hard."

It wasn't much, but it was something. "Thank you."

Fiona closed the door without another word.

Karine walked beside Omar back to his truck.

"What do you think?" Karine said once they were in the pickup.

"It is possible Amber was expecting a guest, but it's really just supposition."

"Maybe so, but it's the best lead we have right now. If we can find the person that Amber was expecting to entertain the night before she died, they may know what Amber wanted to tell me."

The wheels spun as Omar pulled them away from the curb. "That's one possibility if this person exists and if we find this person."

"And another possibility?" she asked, although she was pretty sure where Omar was going with his line of thinking.

Omar braked at a stop sign. He looked into her eyes. "The other possibility is that the person Amber had over for dinner Tuesday night killed her."

Chapter Nine

Karine spent the rest of the day fielding work emails despite being on vacation and searching Amber's social media for her mystery man. It seemed likely Amber had a date, since what Fiona had described sounded like a romantic dinner. But Karine had no luck finding the mystery man.

By the time the sun went down, she had formed a new plan. Omar was at work, which was good because Karine didn't want him in danger. Deputy Coben had been quick to proclaim that there was no foul play and to declare Amber's death an accidental overdose. His main concern had been assuring the community that he had everything in hand in Sheriff Webb's absence. He didn't care about getting to the truth, but Karine did. She was going to break into Amber's house and search for clues to what Amber had wanted to tell her and maybe figure out who her mystery man was.

She wasn't exactly sure how she was going to get into the house. The police had probably locked the back door she'd entered when she'd found Amber's body. She'd cross that bridge when she got there. If she had to, she'd break one of the windowpanes in the fancy French doors, but she was hoping to find another way in, some way that wouldn't announce she'd been there.

Karine parked two blocks away from Amber's cul-de-sac and walked to the house. She'd dressed in all black and now did her best to blend into the shadows, just in case. It was late, nearing eleven at night, but you never knew who might still be up and glancing out of their window.

All three of the houses on the cul-de-sac were dark inside. Just as when she'd been there the day before, the neighboring houses appeared occupied. Still, Karine hurried around to the back of Amber's house, where she wouldn't be seen.

Just as she'd expected, the French doors were locked this time. She fussed with them for a moment, but they didn't budge. She pulled the small pinpoint flashlight she'd brought with her from her pocket and turned it on, scanning the porch or places Amber might have hidden a key.

She tried inside and underneath the planter by the door, to no avail. Above the doorjamb and windows, and under the cushions on the patio furniture. No key.

Just about to give up and go home, her eyes landed on a garish green-porcelain frog at the center of the flower bed that circled the porch. It was the only lawn ornament and decidedly out of place in the professionally manicured yard.

She hopped down the porch stairs, pocketing the penlight.

The frog was heavy. It took both hands and a considerable amount of force, but she was able to tip it enough to catch the glint of metal pushed into the soil. A key.

Karine used her knee to balance the frog while she reached underneath and grabbed the key.

Back on the porch, she unlocked the door then hesitated for a moment.

The last time she'd let herself into Amber's house, she'd been an invited guest, sort of, but this would be crossing a line. Trespassing. Breaking and entering. Deputy Coben was already unhappy with her. He'd probably take great joy in tossing her in jail if he caught her in Amber's house.

That was a risk she was willing to take. She had to know what it was Amber had wanted to tell her. There had to be a clue inside the house.

She pushed the door open and stepped inside. Once again, she pulled her penlight from her pocket, keeping the beam pointed downward as extra insurance against being noticed from the outside.

She had no idea what she was looking for, which made it impossible to know where to search. She wished she had insisted that Amber at least give her a hint, but she'd gone over Amber's email a dozen times and there was absolutely nothing there that pointed to what Amber had wanted to show her.

Think. Amber said she had something to show her. What could that have been? A note? A photo? The possibilities felt infinite. The only thing Karine could do was search the house, looking for anything that seemed important.

Karine moved into the living room where she remembered seeing bookshelves lining one wall. The living room faced the front of the house, but thankfully, someone had pulled the curtains on the front windows so she didn't have to worry about being seen here. Still, she turned off her flashlight and stepped close to the shelves, reading the spines of the books in the dark. A half hour of looking through and behind every book on the shelves and it was clear that whatever Amber had wanted to share with her was not there. Nothing else in the room seemed like it could be what Amber had wanted to show her either. Nothing jumped out at Karine as being in any way related to her mother's murder.

"Where else would you hide something important?" Karine whispered to herself.

To be thorough, she forced herself to look under the sofa cushions and under the sofa itself even though the memory of Amber lying there creeped her out. She searched the sofa and the area around it as quickly as she could then she moved to the formal dining room. The only place to hide anything in that room was in the sideboard, but she found nothing in there except fancy silverware and extra serving dishes. She searched the kitchen cabinets, the pantry and even the refrigerator and freezer. Nothing.

She moved back down the hall and climbed the staircase to the second floor.

Double doors at the end of the hallway marked the main bedroom. She headed for the room.

The hairs on the back of her neck stood up as she moved into the space. Instinctively, she knew that whatever Amber had planned to show her was in this room. While the other areas of the house were immaculately designed, this room actually felt lived in.

A gray, queen-size upholstered bed dominated one wall with matching, gray-washed wood nightstands on either side. The bedspread was a vibrant red and was stacked with a dozen pillows in all different sizes, shapes and colors. The matching dresser stood on the opposite wall in the space between the door leading into the en suite bathroom and the open door leading into the walk-in closet.

Karine started with the nightstands, finding one completely empty and nothing but a Dan Brown novel in the other. She checked Amber's dresser drawers quickly, feeling like a creep. The odds of finding whatever Amber had wanted to show her had been long to start with, but with every passing moment, it felt like she was just wasting her time while increasing the likelihood she'd be arrested for breaking and entering.

She stepped into the closet, looking behind Amber's clothes for a secret door or safe.

"A secret door. You're losing your mind," she whispered to herself. "No, you've lost your mind. This is crazy." She ran a hand over the neat stack of sweaters on the shelf above the hanging clothes and froze. There was something solid there between the cashmere layers.

She slipped her hand under the first sweater in the pile and pulled out a compact disc.

This had to be what Amber had wanted to show her. Why else would she have hidden the disc in her closet?

She tucked the CD under her arm and stepped out of the closet.

A bumping sound came from downstairs.

Her blood ran cold.

There was someone else in Amber's house.

Her penlight fell onto the floor with a thunk that sounded to her ears as if it reverberated around the room. Had the person downstairs heard? Did they know she was up there? Were they looking for her?

Karine grabbed the penlight and hustled back to the closet, closing the door and hunkering down in the far corner.

She heard footsteps climbing the stairs and making their way down the hall. The hinges creaked as the bedroom door opened. It sounded as if the intruder said something, but the blood pounding in her ears was too loud for her to understand the words. The intruder wasn't making much of an effort to be quiet, and that was as terrifying as anything else. Maybe he wasn't being quiet because he didn't care if she knew he was coming for her. Maybe he didn't plan to give her the opportunity to tell anyone.

Or the intruder could be Deputy Coben or another deputy. Maybe someone had seen her car or the beam from her penlight and called the sheriff's department. At this point, that would be a best-case scenario. Jail wasn't looking so bad compared to the places her mind was taking her at the moment.

Her heart thundered.

Her eyes darted around the closet for something, anything, to defend herself with, but there was nothing other than clothes and the CD she now clutched in her other hand. She realized too late that hiding in the closet with no way out hadn't been the best of ideas.

The handle on the closet twisted, the door opening slowly.

She may not have had a weapon, but that didn't mean she had to cower, waiting to be discovered. She had the element of surprise on her side.

She bounced to her feet and, with a war cry, launched herself at the figure standing in the open doorway.

She recognized Omar a millisecond before she crashed into him.

They hit the carpeted floor together, Omar on his back, she astride him.

She felt the air whoosh out of his lungs and stared down at him in stunned surprise.

They lay still for a moment, each of them appearing to be working through the shock of the moment.

"What are you doing here?" Karine finally asked.

"Looking for you."

"But why? I mean, how did you know I was here?"

"I was almost home, turning onto our street, when I saw

you peeling out of your driveway and take off in the opposite direction, so I followed you. Well, I tried."

His arms were around her waist, and it felt nice. She pushed the thought aside and focused on what he was saying.

"You drive entirely too fast. You were long gone by the time I got dressed and headed out after you. I drove around town, looking for you for a bit, before I realized where you must have gone. I saw your car when I drove into the neighborhood."

So much for being stealthy.

"That still doesn't explain why you're here," she said, rolling off him and standing. She fisted her hands on her hips. "Why were you following me?"

Omar climbed to his feet. "Because I know you. I wanted to make sure you didn't get yourself in trouble, or that you had backup if you did. Remember, watching each other's backs. We agreed."

Her pique thawed a little. "I didn't want to get you in trouble if I got caught breaking in here. I knew that wouldn't be great for you with your job and all."

"Getting arrested isn't great for anyone, regardless of their job. And on that note, can we get out of here?"

Karine threw up her hands. "That's why I didn't tell you what I planned to do. I wanted to protect you."

"Thanks for that. Come on." Omar headed for the bedroom door.

"Wait." She ran back to the closet and picked up the CD where she'd dropped it.

"What is that?" Omar said, eyeing the plastic in her hands.

"I'm not sure exactly, but I found it under a sweater in

Amber's closet. I'm hoping it is what she wanted to show me when she invited me over."

"Great. Not just breaking and entering, burglary. Shep will have a field day if he catches us."

"Then let's get out of here," Karine said with a smile and a sweep of her arm in the direction of the door.

Omar grumbled. "Woman, you are going to be the death of me."

Chapter Ten

Karine parked her rental in her driveway after they got back from Amber's and crossed her lawn to Omar's house.

He went straight for the fridge and grabbed a beer.

"You want one?" he offered.

She shook her head. "No. Not now."

He popped the top and took a long draft on the beer before turning back to her with narrowed eyes. "Do you have any idea how dangerous that was?"

He was furious, a rarity when it came to Karine. He could count on one hand the times he'd actually gotten angry with her over the years. She'd annoyed him for sure, but he'd always had trouble mustering real anger toward her.

That was not the case tonight. Her little stunt could have put her in real danger. But a small part of his brain also recognized that his anger wasn't just about the stunt at Amber's. He was upset that she was acting like their kiss hadn't happened. The kiss that had shaken him to his core. He knew she'd felt something, too, but she seemed intent on pretending that she hadn't.

She rolled her eyes at him. "The house was empty."

"There could have been an alarm, or a neighbor could

have seen you going in. They could have called the sheriff and we already know Shep isn't the brightest bulb in the pack. He could have shown up, guns blazing."

"Whoa." She held her hands up. "You are taking this way out there. First of all, there are no neighbors. It looks like most of the houses in that fancy subdivision are owned by part-timers who hightail it out of Carling Lake after Labor Day. Second, people who hide keys under ceramic frogs don't have alarms. No one in Carling Lake has a security system, not even you, Mr. Safety," she said, pointing out the obvious. "And third, yes, if Shep had caught me I'd be in jail right now, but this isn't the Wild West and, more importantly, he didn't catch me."

"That is not the point," he replied, emphasizing each word.

"Then what is the point?" she said with exasperation. "You know I didn't ask you to come with me." She stepped up close to him and pointed a finger in his chest. "You. Followed. Me." She jabbed with each word. "You didn't have to."

He caught her finger, holding it against his chest. "I know you didn't ask me to go with you. Instead, you snuck out without me because you knew I'd tell you it was a bad idea."

A current of annoyance and something else rolled between them before she stepped back and looked away.

"I knew you would have tried to stop me. And I had to see if I could find whatever Amber wanted to show me," she said quietly.

His anger dissipated some. "I would have tried to stop you and when I couldn't, I would have gone with you."

She looked up at him, her brow arched. "You would have?"

"Of course. I'll always have your back, even if the plan is reckless."

She let out a small laugh. "Thanks."

"So this compact disc you found in Amber's closet? How are we going to see what's on it?"

"I was thinking maybe you had an old compact disc player lying around," she said hopefully.

He shook his head. "Sorry, no such luck. But I may know someone who does. James West. I can ask him."

He pulled his phone from his pocket and sent James a text. He wasn't sure if he'd get an immediate response, given the time of night, but the three little dots popped up on his screen almost as soon as he'd hit Send. Less than a minute later, he had his response.

"James says he has a compact disc player in his office at the gallery. He'll be there early tomorrow morning if we want to come by."

Karine beamed. "Perfect. Would nine tomorrow morning work for you?"

"I have to work tomorrow, but I can do nine," he said, already typing a response to James.

Karine yawned. "I'm exhausted. I'm going to go home and get some shut-eye." She turned for the door then turned back. "Hey, O. Thanks for having my back tonight."

With more conviction than he'd ever felt before in his life, he said, "Always."

THE WEST GALLERY was located in a stone-and-brick building that took up an entire Main Street block. A gold-lettered plaque was mounted on the wall next to the double glass-door entry. The interior of the gallery was two stories of bright, mostly open space.

Dozens of pieces of art were spread throughout. Some

looked like traditional paintings while others seemed more like photographs, although when Omar read the descriptions next to them he learned that they, too, were paintings: hyperrealistic paintings, according to the explanations. Regardless of medium and style, they all showed extraordinary skill and talent.

James met them moments after they strode into the gallery.

"Omar. Karine. Welcome." James stepped forward and shook both their hands.

"Thanks for helping us out," Omar said.

"Not a problem. Like I said at the diner, anything I can do to help, you just need to ask. I may be the only person in town who still has a compact disc player. For work purposes, of course." James grimaced.

"Of course," Omar grinned for a moment before sobering. "We need to see what's on this." He passed the compact disc to James.

"You don't know?"

Omar shared a glance with Karine. "It may be nothing."

James's eyes danced between them before he started for the staircase leading to the second floor of the gallery, and Omar and Karine followed him, continuing the conversation. "But you don't think so."

"No," Karine said. "I think Amber was killed to stop her from showing me what is on that disc."

James's brows rose. "And how did you get this?"

"That doesn't matter," Omar said.

"I took it from Amber's house," Karine responded at the same time.

"I heard you were the one who found Amber."

"I was, but that's not when I got the CD. I went back to her house last night."

Omar shook his head.

"If he's helping us, he should know everything."

James grinned. "I appreciate the honesty. And I've hopped over the line of the law more than once. Don't worry. I'm not going to call the sheriff."

"Thanks for that," Omar deadpanned. "Shep is in charge until Lance gets back and I'm sure he wouldn't hesitate to throw us in jail."

They made a right turn at the top of the stairs into a large office space. One side of the room had large picture windows that looked out on Main Street. A cherrywood executive desk and high-backed leather chair had been placed in front of the window. On the other side of the office was another desk, this one a U-shaped computer setup complete with no less than three computer monitors and a laptop. A built-in shelf held assorted electronic equipment, including what looked like a state-of-the-art flat-screen television and a CD player.

"Okay, so let's see what we've got." James raised the hand holding the CD Omar had handed him.

He waved Omar and Karine into desk chairs in front of the computer monitors.

James slid the CD into the player and, after a moment of fuss on the television, it began to play.

It was grainy, but not so much so that they couldn't decipher that what they were looking at must've been footage from Karine's parents' home security system. It showed the front of the Eloi house.

"It looks like this must've been taken from a camera at the front of your home," Omar said, pointing to the screen. "That's your front porch and your front door, and you can even see a bit of my porch next door."

"Yeah," Karine answered in a nearly breathless whisper. "And the time and date stamp put this recording as the night my mother was killed. But I don't remember us having security cameras around the house," Karine said.

"Well, you were only twelve. It's probably something you just never thought about." Omar placed what he hoped was a soothing hand on her shoulder.

"I guess, but there must be something on here that's relevant. Why else would Amber have kept it all these years?"

The three of them continued to watch for several more minutes. A car passed the house and disappeared at the end of the street. A stray dog sauntered down the sidewalk.

"Omar, look," Karine said, pointing at a silhouetted figure that emerged from the shadows. The person was crouched down between Karine's house and his.

"There's someone there," Omar said softly.

"Can you rewind that a little?" she asked James.

James did as she asked.

They watched as the shadow moved through their yards. The person was dressed in dark colors and wore a coat with a hood pulled low over the head.

"This could be my mother's killer," she said with a shaky breath. The phone trembled in her hands.

"The video is too grainy and whoever this is, is keeping his head down. I can't even tell if it's a man or woman," Omar said.

They watched as the person disappeared around the side of the house. They knew from the police report that the detective on the case had identified the sliding-glass door from the back porch as the entry point for the intruder. The lock had showed signs of tampering.

James fast-forwarded the video, but the person didn't enter the frame again. Whoever it was must have left the house out the back door and cut through the trees behind the house to escape. The next person to show up on the video was Jean Eloi at approximately the time the police report said he'd told the detective in charge he'd returned home.

"If you leave this with me, I'll digitize it. Maybe I can clean it up a bit and get a clearer view of the person in the shadows. If I can't do it, I'll get the tech gurus at West Investigations to take a stab at it. If they can't do it, it can't be done."

"I'd really appreciate that," Karine said "And don't worry about the costs. I'll pay whatever West Investigations' fee is."

James waved away the comment. "Let's see if it can be done first, then we can talk about the fee." He tapped a few keys on one of the keyboards on the desk and the video zoomed in on one corner of the screen.

"There was no mention of a security video in the police report about my mother's death," Karine said.

Omar frowned. "They might not have known about it." He closed his eyes, bringing up a mental picture of Karine's house. "Given the awkward angle of the shot, I'd say the camera that recorded this was tucked into the eaves around your porch."

James nodded. "That would explain why the shot is so blurry and shadowed. It's almost as if someone put the camera there but didn't want the occupants to know it. Your parents may not have even known it was there." The implication of that swirled in the air.

"But who would have done something like that?" Karine asked after a moment. "And why? Certainly not my mother's killer. He or she wouldn't want the crime on tape."

Another question to add to the growing list of questions surrounding Marilee Eloi's murder.

"You guys should look at this," James said.

Karine leaned forward in her seat. "What are we looking at?"

James pressed a few more keys and the picture cleared a little more.

"That's the Portman house," Omar said, pointing to a neighboring house on the screen. "You remember Richie and his sister, Becky, Karine? They live across the street from us."

Karine's nose scrunched in thought. "Yeah, I remember them a little. Why are we looking at their house?"

"Because I'm zoomed in on a small section of the frame that showed your intruder sneaking around your house and—" James pointed to the Portman's second-floor window "—there's someone in this window."

"That means someone may have seen the intruder," Karine stated excitedly.

"Maybe." James looked between them. "It's worth asking your neighbors about it."

Omar shook his head. "The Nelsons lived there when Karine and I were young, but they've both passed on now."

Karine's phone rang. "Thank you, James," she said, fishing her phone out of her purse and looking at the number on the screen. "I'm sorry, this is work. I have to take it."

"Feel free to use my studio. Right across the hall," James said, nodding toward the door.

Karine answered the call and strode through the door.

James leaned back in his chair, an assessing gaze trained on Omar. "Karine seems pretty determined to investigate her mother's death. Breaking into Amber Spindler's house? That was quite a risk."

"Yeah." Omar ran a hand over his short hair. "She didn't

even tell me. It was lucky I saw her pulling out of her driveway. I followed her to Amber's place."

James gave him a look he couldn't read.

"What?"

"That was quite a risk for you to take too. I mean, you
are a state law enforcement officer. Breaking into a private
home? That could get you into some major trouble. Possibly even cost you a job I know you love."

"It wasn't much of a risk." Omar wasn't able to hold
James's stare as he spoke. "I knew the house was empty.
Well, except for Karine."

"Okay," James said.

Omar scowled. "What?"

"Look, I know we don't know each other very well, but
from everything I've seen, you're a man with a good head
on his shoulders. I know you and Karine go way back, but
maybe there's more than just friendship brewing between
you two."

"I...don't think so," Omar said. He wasn't sure what was
going on between him and Karine, but her seeming determination to ignore their kiss didn't bode well for a budding
relationship. In any event, he didn't want to discuss it with
James, especially not with Karine in the next room where
she might overhear.

"No? Are you sure about that?" James prodded, not taking the hint.

Karine walked back into the computer room before he
could ask James what he meant. Lines of concern were
etched on her forehead.

"Is everything okay?" Omar rose, crossing the floor to
her.

"Yeah. Fine. Just a work thing. I took the week off, but

my boss is acting like the place can't function without me. I guess I should be flattered, but it's kind of annoying too."

"Do you need to go back to Los Angeles?" Omar asked, simultaneously hoping the answer was no.

Karine shook her head. "I may have to do some work remotely this week, but I meant it when I said I wasn't leaving Carling Lake without answers. If I have to quit my job, I'll do it. Whatever it takes to finally get justice for my mother."

Omar studied the woman who'd been his friend for as long as he could remember.

She may believe that the answers were for her mother, but he knew that they were really for her. And he'd do anything for Karine, so if it was answers she needed, it was answers they'd get.

Chapter Eleven

Omar didn't have to ask Karine where their next stop was. James had made a copy of the security video for them, keeping the original for the West techs to work on enhancing. He'd also printed Karine a still photo of the person in the Portman's window.

She studied the photo silently on the drive back to their neighborhood. He drove them to his house and then they crossed the street and climbed the steps of the small concrete porch. There was no doorbell, so Omar knocked on the scarred front door.

After a long moment, the door was opened just wide enough for Richie Portman to stick his head out. "Yeah? The dogs get loose again?"

Omar had helped Richie round up his dogs more than once, but for the most part, Richie and his sister, Becky, kept to themselves.

"No, Richie," Omar said. "We're here to speak to you about something else, if you have a moment?"

Richie never seemed to have anything but moments. He and his sister had inherited the house when their mother died ten years earlier. If there was ever a father in the picture, it was before Omar's time. Becky worked at Rosie's diner part-time and Richie picked up the odd job here and there, but more often than not, he could be found at the Whiskey Wise, a dive bar on the outskirts of town.

Richie opened the door a little wider. He was only a few years older than Omar and Karine, but he looked to be a generation older. His dark brown hair had thinned so that a patch of pale white skin showed through where his hairline began. He was an inch or two taller than Omar's six foot one, but his beer gut hung over his belt and years of drinking seemed to have left his blue eyes permanently bloodshot. His fingers, rough and chapped, wrapped around a can of Bud Light.

"Who's we?" Richie scratched his chest with the hand not holding on to the beer.

"This is Karine Eloi."

Richie jerked, his eyes narrowing in on Karine. "Marilee's girl?"

"Yes. Marilee Eloi was my mother," Karine answered. "You might remember me from when my family used to live across the street."

"Kind of. I didn't pay too much attention to you two," he said, including Omar in his statement. "You were quite a bit younger than me."

Five years younger, not that much in the grand scheme of things, but Omar didn't correct him.

"What do you want to talk to me about?" Richie demanded.

Karine shifted nervously next to Omar. He squeezed her hand in support. "I have some questions for you about my mother's murder."

Richie's face registered surprise. "For me? I don't know anything about that except what I read in the papers."

"I don't think that's true, Mr. Portman," Karine shot back.

"Who all is at the door?" a woman's voice called from inside the house.

"It's the guy from across the street, Omar, and his friend Karine. Remember her?"

A hand pulled the door open wider. Becky Portman, Richie's sister, stood next to him. "What do you want?"

Karine seemed momentarily stunned by the woman's sudden appearance and abrasive demeanor. Becky was a lot to take in. Richie could be ornery, but Omar knew he was fundamentally a good guy. Becky, however, could be mean as a rattlesnake. Her bottle-red hair was teased into a bouffant that hadn't been in style since the 1950s. She was still in her uniform from the diner, but she'd accented it with large gold hoop earrings and a dozen bangles on each arm that clinked together whenever she moved.

"We were hoping to ask Richie a few questions about the night Karine's mother died."

A look passed between brother and sister. While Richie seemed to be more than a little hesitant to speak with them, Becky's lips turned down into a glower.

"I don't see how we could help, especially after all this time, but come on in then," Becky said, stepping back from the door. "You're letting the good air out, holding this door open."

The layout of the house was similar to his own, with the kitchen and dining area to the right of the entry, a long hall off to the left and the living room at the rear of the house.

Richie clomped into the kitchen and grabbed another beer from the fridge. Becky followed him and took a seat at the table. Omar and Karine followed her lead, leaving one empty chair for her brother to join them.

Richie remained standing, leaning against the short countertop next to the fridge. "What was it you wanted to ask me?"

Omar shot a look at Karine. It was her show. He was just there for moral support.

"You may have already heard that I'm looking into my mother's murder."

Becky scoffed. "Oh, we heard. It's about all anyone in town can talk about lately."

Karine cleared her throat. "I found a recording, a security video, from the night my mother was killed. And it looks like someone is standing in the window on the second floor of this house." She nodded at Richie. "I was wondering if it might have been you."

Richie shifted from one foot to the other. "How am I supposed to know? It could be. Probably is. I lived here after all. What's it to you?"

"The video is from around the time the police think my mother was killed—" Karine started.

"Hey," Richie said, pushing off the counter and waving the hand that held his beer toward the door. "If you're suggesting I had something to do with a murder, you can just get the hell out of my house right now."

Omar held up a hand while discreetly moving his chair so that Richie would have to go through him to get to Karine.

"Of course not," Karine said quickly. "If it is you in the video, that would be pretty solid proof that you weren't involved. You couldn't have been in two places at the same time."

Richie visibly calmed. "Damn straight, I wasn't involved."

"But I was thinking…well, hoping really, that you might have seen something. Maybe something you didn't even realize was important back then, but with time…"

Richie crossed his arms over his chest, his nose scrunched in thought. "I didn't see anything."

"Here." Karine pulled the still shot James had printed for her of the person in the window of the house. They'd agreed not to let on that the video showed someone skulking around the house. They didn't want to put the idea in Richie's head if he hadn't seen anything, but they also didn't know if they could trust Richie. If he had seen a person approaching the house on the night of Marilee's death, why hadn't he said anything in all these years?

"Could you look at this? Is that you?" Karine held the photo out toward Richie.

Richie made no attempt to cross the tiny kitchen and take it.

After a moment, Becky took the photo from Karine's hand. "It sure looks like it could be you. That's your bedroom window."

Richie came to stand behind his sister. "You can't tell anything from that photo. Might not even be anyone there. That could just be a shadow or some sort of glitch in your video."

"Whose shadow do you think it could be?" Omar asked, watching Richie closely. The man was too nervous. He knew something, but he'd been holding on to it for twenty-three years. He wouldn't give it up easily.

"I said it could be a shadow. Probably a glitch, like I said. All I know is it wasn't me."

"Are you sure? Could you think back to that day? Anything you remember could be of help."

"Look," Richie said, heading back to his perch next to the fridge. "I'd help you if I could. I'm sorry about your mom. She was…a nice lady."

Something about the pause Richie had taken made Omar sit up a bit straighter. He knew Karine had caught it too.

She leaned forward. "Please, if you, either of you—" Karine's eyes swept over Becky and then back to Richie "—remember anything about that night, you have to tell me."

Becky shot a look over her shoulder at her brother, then turned back to face Omar and Karine. "We don't have to do anything." She pressed her palms to the table and stood. "I think we've helped you all we can. It's time for you to go."

"Please—" Karine started.

"Let's just go, Karine," Omar said, reaching for her hand and helping her to her feet.

She shot him a glare that let him know she didn't appreciate his taking the Portmans' side. But he'd questioned enough suspects to know when to retreat and regroup. They weren't going to get anything out of either of the Portmans as long as they were together. Divide and conquer. That was the way to get the brother and sister talking. Richie was nervous enough that Omar didn't think it would take much if they distanced him from his sister. But that wasn't going to happen right now.

The front door slammed almost before they'd made it onto the little concrete porch.

"Why did you do that?" Karine stalked down the Portmans' walkway.

"Because we were getting nowhere with them," he said as they crossed the street to her house. "You aren't going to get Becky or Richie to talk if they don't want to."

"You don't know that," she growled.

"Yeah, I do." He stopped in front of her door. "This is Carling Lake, not Los Angeles. You're going to have to slow down. We can always approach Becky and Richie again. It will probably be better if we approach them separately anyway."

Karine stared at him for a long moment before letting out a huff. "Fine."

"Karine—"

"Really, Omar. I hear what you're saying. You don't have to worry about me breaking into anyone's house or doing anything rash. I plan to run some errands and see if there is anything in the house that I want to take back to Los Angeles with me."

She stepped inside her house and closed the door, leaving him standing on the porch alone.

Chapter Twelve

Karine knew she'd been a little snappish with Omar, but his suggestion that she slow down had irked her. Her mother's killer had been walking free, maybe in Carling Lake, for twenty-three years. She only had a week to find answers or to at least jump-start the sheriff's reinvestigation. And although she had more than enough banked vacation to extend her stay, she knew it would be a tough sell getting her boss to sign off on any additional time.

That meant slowing down just wasn't an option. But she had told Omar the truth about what she'd planned to do that day. She still needed to buy as many mousetraps as she could find and set them out in the attic. After a thorough consultation with the clerk at the hardware store, she returned home with traps designed to drive the little critters away.

She climbed the stairs leading to the attic and, with a bit of force, was able to push the warped door open inch by inch until there was a space big enough for them to slip through.

Karine froze, shocked. She knew her mother had used the space as a studio when she was alive, but she'd expected it to have been emptied out like the rest of the house when she and her father had moved out. Apparently, her dad had forgotten to instruct the movers to pack up the attic when they'd packed up the rest of the house.

She felt a shiver run down her back. Hesitant now to move too far past the doorway, she slowly turned in a circle, taking in the room. The sloped ceiling gave the space a small, cramped feeling in spite of the window opening out on a view of the Carling Lake Forest, a small section of the lake and the mountains. The view, Karine remembered, that had compelled her mother to turn the attic into her studio in the first place.

Stepping into the space felt like stepping back in time. Her mother's art studio hadn't been touched in twenty-three years. A half-finished canvas depicting a gloomy, almost macabre woodland scene sat on an easel. Next to it was a table with long-dried paints, stiffened paintbrushes and an empty mason jar. Several of her mother's paintings—some finished, some not—leaned against the wall, along with a stack of empty canvases. Her mother's smock hung on the wall hook next to the door. Everything was covered in several layers of dust and dirt. She felt a pang of loss for her mother and what could have been—her mother's potential.

"It's like stepping back in time," she murmured.

She ventured farther into the space, imagining her mother standing in front of her easel, assessing the unfinished canvas. Although the subject of her paintings was always nature, the mood Marilee Eloi had been able to convey was different with each one. The painting in front of Karine was clearly taking a darker tone. Leaning in close, she could see a woman in the thick of the trees, almost hidden. She appeared to be running, looking back over her shoulder with an expression of terror on her face, as if she were being chased by something, or someone, terrifying.

She couldn't help but wonder if that was a reflection of her mother's frame of mind in the days and weeks prior to her murder. Did Marilee suspect that she might be in danger? Could her last paintings somehow point them to her killer?

It was almost like her mother was there in the room with her, like she'd just stepped away for a moment, but planned to be right back.

But, of course, Karine knew that wasn't the case. Her mother would never hold her again and she wouldn't ever finish the painting on the easel or step foot in her studio again.

Karine couldn't get lost in grief. It was only natural that everything she'd been through in the last few days—being back in Carling Lake, getting shot at, the email from Amber and then her overdose—would dredge up a myriad of feelings, but she had to focus. Something in this attic might point her toward her mother's killer.

She took one more look back at the painting on the easel. Her mother had been really talented.

Too bad she hadn't gotten a lick of her mother's talent. Or her father's passion for plants. She'd gone out on a limb of her own with her interest in numbers and finance. Or really not gone out on a limb. Finance was safe. Steady. She was sure a therapist would have a field day exploring the connection between having lost her mother as a child and her desire for dependability.

She turned away from the easel. In addition to her mother's painting stuff, there was a large chest with four drawers on each side of a middle panel. A golden tree was painted on the panel, its branches reaching out and extending onto each of the drawers.

She remembered then how she'd loved that chest. Her

mother hadn't let her into the attic very often. She hadn't wanted her making a mess or destroying her paintings, but Karine had loved this golden tree. When she was little, her mother would take her on long walks in the woods behind the house and they'd search for golden trees. Of course, they'd never found one, but it was the journey, not the destination, that she'd treasured.

The scavenger hunts had come to an end after Karine had asked her dad if he could help her research golden trees and where she could find one. He'd told her that there was no such thing. Then her parents had gotten into an argument. Her dad thought her mother shouldn't have been misleading her about science. Her mother had countered that the walks fostered creativity and that maybe if someone had done the same for him, he wouldn't be so dull.

The memory came pouring back into her head as if it had happened yesterday. Along with other memories of her parents fighting. Her parents had quarreled a lot, she realized. How could she have forgotten that? But coming back to this house, stepping into the attic, seemed to have opened up a well of memories she'd locked away deep in her head.

Her parents hadn't really talked to each other as much as they'd argued with each other. She'd always remembered their family Friday night movie dates, as her mother had called them, for the quintessential family time, but now she tried to remember if they had ever talked to one another or looked at each other during those nights. With hindsight, it was almost as if they'd been going through the motions of what they'd thought they should be doing to be a family. They'd always made her sit between them and she'd thought it was because she liked to be in charge of the popcorn bowl, but now she wondered if it had been more to put as much distance as they could between themselves.

Karine shuddered out a deep breath as her memories seemed to twist and rotate to form a picture that was very different from what she'd always thought about her childhood.

She opened the drawers in the chest. The only things inside the first seven drawers were massive dust bunnies. But in the bottom right drawer, she found a plastic mood ring.

She gasped, reaching inside and drawing it out. Her old mood ring.

She held the ring out and inspected it. She'd loved that ring. Her father had won it for her at the Carling Lake fair when she was eight. She'd worn it every day for nearly a year. She'd totally forgotten about it.

She slid the ring onto her ring finger, back where it belonged.

Then she remembered something else about this chest of drawers. There was a secret compartment in the middle panel. It was part of the reason she'd liked the piece so much.

The release lever was in one of the corners, she was pretty sure. She pressed on the upper left corner, but nothing happened. She moved to the upper right corner, but still the panel didn't open.

"Could be rusted shut," she said out loud to herself.

Then, in a flash, she remembered. She pressed both corners at the same time, and the panel slid out. "Got it."

There wasn't space to hide much of anything, but her mother had stuck a thin notebook between the slats of the drawer.

Karine plucked it free and wiped the layer of dust clinging to the cover from it. She ran her hand over the gilded gold words on the front. She opened it, immediately recognizing her mother's looping cursive letters. Her mother's diary.

Based on the dates at the beginning of each entry, her mother had started writing in the diary about a year before her murder. The last entry was dated two weeks prior to Marilee's death.

"This is it. If my mother suspected she was in any danger, she'd have written it in here." She skimmed through the pages of the books. Nothing in it suggested her mother had been having issues with anyone.

A piece of yellowed paper fluttered from between the last pages of the diary.

Karine knelt. Opening the folded paper and reading, she rose. Her knees began to shake as she read.

The love letter trembled in her hand.

Her mother had been having an affair.

Chapter Thirteen

Karine hadn't known what to expect when she'd searched her mother's studio, but she certainly hadn't expected to find evidence that her mother had been having an affair. This must be what the note in the police report about "affair" had meant. Her mother had been having an affair. Who was her lover? And how long had it gone on? Had Marilee still been involved with the man when she died? Could her lover be her killer?

She flipped through the diary, reading as fast as she could, looking for the name of her mother's lover. There was nothing to even suggest whom Marilee may have had an affair with. Mostly, the diary detailed Marilee's hopes for her artist career. There were some references to Karine, and one or two about her father, but the diary was pretty benign. Boring even.

The question swirled in her head. Omar had warned her that she'd probably have to talk to her father, get him to open up, if she really hoped to find answers about her mother's death, and it seemed he was right.

She had to tell her father about the affair.

Six months ago she would have said that her father was going to be devastated by the news, but now, with her memories so jumbled, leaving her unsure of what parts of her childhood were real and what parts she'd glossed over, she wasn't so sure. Regardless of how her father reacted, he deserved to know the truth about his marriage, and she wouldn't have felt right keeping such a big secret from him.

Karine left the mousetraps in the attic and took a second shower. While she got dressed in jeans and a light sweater, she took the time to consider, then reject, the idea of asking Omar to drive with her to Connecticut.

It wasn't that she wouldn't have liked the company. She was finding that she more than liked being in the company of Omar, a feeling she was starting to believe she'd have to give some serious thought to at some point. But not now. She was about to spring some potentially upsetting news on her father, and she didn't want it to be any more uncomfortable than it had to be.

She shot Omar a quick text, telling him she was going to visit her father and would be back that evening, before leaving for Springtree. The bright sunny day was a contrast with the heavy feeling sitting in the pit of her stomach as she made the drive.

The afternoon traffic was light, and she made it to her father's brick ranch-style home just after three in the afternoon, having only made one pit stop for a quick lunch. The tall oak in the front yard still stretched up to the sky and the flower beds lining the front walk had been freshly mulched.

Her father had always taken great pride in the yard, no surprise, given his chosen career as a botanist. When she turned into the asphalt driveway and parked behind the sky blue Subaru station wagon, she also wasn't surprised to find her father in the yard, pushing the lightweight battery-operated mower she'd gotten him last Father's Day.

Jean Eloi had grown pudgy as he'd aged. Her stepmother's rich cooking hadn't done anything to help him keep the weight off. His gray hair was cut short all around, and his face was lined with its fair share of wrinkles. She smiled, taking in his attire. Khakis, a blue-and-white-checked, short-sleeved dress shirt and brilliantly white sneakers. He looked like the college professor he was even when doing yard work. That was her dad.

A smile bloomed on her father's face, and he stepped from behind the mower as she got out of the car.

"Well, this is a welcome surprise. I was wondering when you were going to get around to visiting your old man."

She let her father pull her into a warm hug. "I've only been on the east coast for a few days, and you are not old."

"Old enough that two days can seem like a lifetime when I haven't seen my beautiful daughter."

"Dad." She rested her head on his shoulder for a brief moment.

"Come on. Stephanie made fresh lemonade and I could use a cold drink."

Her father and Stephanie had married a year after her mother's death. Stephanie had tried to form a close, motherly bond, but Karine had been thirteen by then and the combination of having lost her mother and teenage hormones had made it difficult going.

In the years since she'd moved out of the house, her relationship with Stephanie had gotten better. They were not only cordial, but friendly most of the time. No doubt the three-thousand-plus miles that usually separated them had played a big role in mellowing the relationship.

It wasn't that she disliked Stephanie, her stepmother clearly made her father happy, and she was a nice enough woman. She'd done her best to be someone Karine could count on as she'd moved from teenhood into womanhood, but no matter what Stephanie did, she'd never be Marilee. She knew it wasn't fair to compare Stephanie to her mother, but fair or not, Karine couldn't help it. Deep down inside her, there would always be a little girl wishing it was her mother standing next to her father.

"Look who's here!" her father proclaimed loudly as they stepped into the kitchen.

Stephanie was at the stove. She looked up, blinking as if she wasn't sure of what she was seeing. "Karine. This is a surprise. A wonderful surprise, that is."

Karine had told her father of her plans to go to Carling Lake, although she'd left out the portion where she'd planned to look into her mother's death. All she'd told her father was that she'd wanted to get a good look at the house she now owned and make some decisions. She had no idea how much, if anything, Jean had relayed to Stephanie. It was quite possible her showing up like this was a total surprise to her stepmom. Her father could be a bit of an absentminded professor. Or an absentminded semiretired professor, now that he was only teaching one class per semester.

Stephanie wiped her hands on the apron she was wearing then stepped around the island stove to give Karine a brief hug.

"Hi, Stephanie. I hope my dropping in isn't a problem. Dad did tell you I was going to be in Carling Lake for a few weeks, right?"

Stephanie waved a hand. "Of course it's not a problem. This will always be your home. And yes, your dad remembered to tell me that you were going to be in our neck of the woods for a while." Stephanie sent an adoring smile her husband's way. "I'm so glad you found the time to visit."

Karine thought she heard the slight edge in the last sentence. It had been a while since she'd last made it to the east coast. Her father didn't like to fly, so his and Stephanie's visits to the west coast were few and far between. That left them video calling one another every few weeks, calls that they mostly kept to talking about work, weather and Springtree gossip even though Karine didn't really know many of the residents anymore. Nothing too personal or revealing about their lives. Sometimes Karine wished she and her father, and even she and Stephanie, had a closer relationship, and she got the feeling her father and Stephanie felt the same way, but none of them seemed to know how to forge that kind of relationship with each other.

Karine hopped up onto a stool to the side of the island while Stephanie took her place behind the stove again. It looked like she was making a sauce of some kind. It smelled delicious, like basil and garlic and something sweet she didn't have the culinary chops to name. One thing Karine had to hand to Stephanie, she was one hell of a cook. "I wanted to take a couple of days to get settled in Carling Lake before I dropped in on you."

"Yes, and how is the house?" Stephanie asked, stirring the pot.

Her father poured lemonade into two glasses and handed one of the glasses to Karine.

"It's fine. Better than I expected, actually. The trustee has been taking good care of it." Karine took a sip of lemonade.

"You'll probably get a pretty penny for it," her father said around a sip of lemonade. "Carling Lake has exploded as a vacation destination in recent years. You might even be able to start a bidding war. I know a couple of good Realtors."

"Maybe." Karine took another swallow from her glass.

Stephanie's sharp gaze landed on Karine, but her father kept talking.

"Now is a good time to sell too. Have you seen the way the real estate market is surging? You'd think after the calamity in twenty-o-eight people would be more cautious, but we never seem to learn." Her father shook his head. "Ah, well, it could be good for you though," her father continued, oblivious to her hesitation about selling.

"You do plan to sell the house, right?" Stephanie asked, still stirring the sauce slowly, her eyes trained on Karine.

Now Karine remembered something else that had vexed her about Stephanie when she'd been a teen. She could never get anything by her. If it had just been her father, she could have stayed out all night every night and Jean wouldn't have noticed. But Stephanie... Karine had often wondered if Stephanie had been a wild adolescent. She'd seemed to instinctively know what youthful shenanigans Karine was planning to get into and was always ready to head her off at the pass. She knew she should probably be grateful to her stepmother for that, but right now the old teenage irritation was back.

"I'm not sure what I want to do," Karine answered.

Her father's body jerked. "What do you mean you aren't sure? I thought you came back to the east coast to settle everything. Sell the property. Close out the trust."

"I did come to settle some things, but that doesn't mean I plan to sell the house."

"What does it mean?" Stephanie stopped stirring. "Are you thinking about moving back to Carling Lake?"

Karine felt herself revolt at the idea. New York winters, no way. She might have been born on the east coast, but she was a west coast girl through and through.

"I don't think that's in the cards." She couldn't be sure, but she thought she saw Stephanie's shoulders sag in relief.

"What does it mean?" her father pressed.

"I don't know exactly. I'm still figuring that out. Actually, I wanted to talk to you about some things." She cleared her throat, unsure how to say she wanted to talk to her father in private without offending Stephanie. It was her house, after all. "It's a little sensitive. No offense to you, Stephanie."

"No, no." Stephanie gave her a strained smile. "I understand there are things you and your father need to speak about. You two go ahead to your father's den. Karine, you do plan to stay for dinner, yes? I'm making sweet Italian sausages smothered in my famous tomato basil sauce."

Karine's stomach grumbled in anticipation. She gave her stepmother a genuine smile. "I wouldn't miss it."

Stephanie returned the smile before Karine turned and followed her father down the short hallway to the fourth bedroom that they'd taken to referring to as his den.

Her father sat in the leather executive chair at his desk, turning it to face the ratty old recliner that Stephanie had been fighting to get him to throw out for years. On one of their most recent video calls, her father had lamented that Stephanie had finally put her foot down and insisted that if he was going to keep the recliner, he had to move it into his den where she couldn't see it.

"Compromise is the key to a happy marriage," her father had told her, admitting the recliner had found a new home in the den.

It seemed that her father had taken the opportunity to freshen up his office too. The walls were still lined with the same photos of various flora and fauna, like they'd always been, but the dingy orange paint had been changed to more updated and neutral grayish-blue and the dark wood built-in bookshelves had been painted a fresh, crisp white.

"So," her father said after they'd both taken a seat, "what did you want to talk to me about?"

"I wanted to ask you some questions," she started hesitantly.

Her father's expression was curious but still open, which she took as a good sign. "Sure. Shoot."

It wasn't an easy topic to bring up. *Did you know that your wife, my mother, was having an affair before she was murdered?* Not something that a daughter usually had to discuss with her father. There was no YouTube video detailing the five steps for easing into the conversation.

"I was in Mom's studio earlier today and I found something."

Her father's brow furrowed. "Studio? You mean the attic?"

"Yes. You know Mom had it set up as a studio. There were several paintings still up there, one that she must have been working on when she was killed. It looked like it hadn't been touched since the day she died."

The lines in her father's face deepened. "I didn't know that. I paid a moving company to pack up our things. I couldn't bring myself to go back into the house after your mother's untimely passing."

Karine didn't think she'd ever heard her father refer to her mother's death as what it was. A murder. Or even that she'd been killed. He'd always referred to it as "her untimely passing."

And that had always irritated her.

Her mother hadn't just passed away. It hadn't been an act of God or even an accident. Someone had purposely taken Marilee Eloi's life. Someone who had never been brought to justice.

She tamped down on her irritation. "Well, I guess they didn't think to look in the attic, because I don't think anyone has been up there in more than twenty years. The door was locked, so I guess someone might have been, but nothing had been touched."

"Okay. Well, it shouldn't be too much trouble to clear the space out," her father said. "I'm sure you'd like to have the paintings that are there, but most of the stuff is probably trash, right?"

Karine nodded. "A lot of it can be thrown out and, yes, I'd love to have my mother's paintings." She already had several hanging on the walls in her condo. Her father had had the foresight to keep and store the paintings that had been on the walls in their home when her mother died. When she'd bought her condo in Los Angeles, she'd had them shipped to the west coast.

"But I also discovered a chest of drawers in the studio." She waited to see if the chest rang any bells with her father. His blank look told her it did not. "I guess you don't remember it—"

"I rarely went into the attic," her father conceded.

"I remembered that this chest had a special feature. A kind of secret drawer in the middle panel. When I opened it, I found Mom's diary." She reached into her purse and pulled out the diary. She handed it to her father.

A small smile sent the ends of his mouth upward. "I'd forgotten that Marilee wrote in a diary."

"So, it's hers."

"If it was in the attic, it had to be your mother's. Marilee had been writing in a diary since before we met. She had dozens packed away spanning years."

"There are more diaries?" She was surprised. She didn't remember her mother ever writing in a diary, but perhaps it was something she hadn't done in front of her young daughter.

Her father shrugged. "Sure. If you don't have them already, they are probably in a box in the basement or in my storage locker."

"Could you get them for me?"

"Of course. As far as I'm concerned, all of your mother's things belong to you now. It may take me a few days though."

"That's fine. Um… I didn't just find the diary."

Her father tilted his head, curiosity in his eyes. "No? What else did you find?"

She inhaled deeply. "There's no easy way to say this, but I found a love letter."

"A love letter?" Jean looked thoughtful. "I don't remember your mother and I ever exchanging love letters."

Karine pulled the letter from her purse. "I don't think the letter is from you. Dad, I think Mom was having an affair."

Her father studied her for a long second then laughed. "Honey, you must be mistaken."

"No, Dad. I don't think I am." She handed him the letter. "I found this in Mom's diary. I know it's not dated or signed, but it's pretty explicitly a love letter and it's pretty clear that Mom was having an affair with whoever wrote this."

Her father's face lost its color as he read the note. She felt sick. He didn't deserve this betrayal by his wife. For the first time in as long as she could remember, Karine was angry at her mother.

"Dad, I know this is a shock, but if Mom was having an affair, that could open up a whole new line of investigation regarding her murder. I mean, maybe she tried to break it off and her lover became enraged. Maybe he wanted her to leave you, us, and she wouldn't. Maybe—"

"Karine, stop!" Her father looked up, his eyes flashing with something she couldn't name.

"Dad?"

"This letter, it wasn't written to your mother."

She blinked, baffled. "But I found it in her diary."

"I don't know how your mother got her hands on it. She must have suspected and gone snooping in my things."

A nauseous feeling built in her stomach. "Snooping? Dad—"

Embarrassment seeded her father's expression. "Karine, your mother wasn't the one having an affair. I was. The letter is mine."

Chapter Fourteen

Karine couldn't move.

Her father had had an affair. He'd cheated on her mother.

Her skin prickled. "But the letter...it was in Mom's diary."

"She must have found it." He handed the piece of yellowed paper back to her. "I never realized it was missing."

She gripped the letter until her knuckles turned white. "She never confronted you?"

Her father shook his head, looking more than a little green around the gills. "She never said a word. I never even suspected."

She shook. A buzz grew in her ears. She'd fainted once before and knew she was close to repeating the experience again. She leaned forward, putting her head between her legs, gripping the arms of the chair.

"Honey, it was a long time ago. Your mother and I were having difficulties—"

Karine held up a hand, imploring her father to stop speaking. She felt like she was on the precipice of falling over a cliff. One more word and over she'd go.

Her father stopped talking. They sat in silence for several minutes.

When the buzz in her ears finally receded, she asked, "How long?"

"What?"

She sat up and looked into her father's eyes. "How long did the affair go on? When did it start? Was it still going on when Mom—" She couldn't bring herself to directly ask what she really wanted to know. Was he still with this other woman when her mother was murdered?

Her father's cheeks flushed and his gaze skittered away. "I don't think—"

"I don't care what you think. How long were you cheating on Mom?"

He sighed. "You have to understand, sweetheart—"

"Don't call me that."

Her father's back stiffened. He blinked and then his face took on an expression of resolve. "Okay, okay." He let out a breath. "It wasn't just an affair. It was a relationship. Your mother and I had been in a bad place for a long time. I didn't know she knew about the affair, but I was planning on asking her for a divorce. She was killed before I worked up the nerve."

"A relationship?" Even though she'd asked him for the details, she was struggling to make sense of them. And then it suddenly made all the sense in the world.

Karine glanced at the closed office door, bile rising in her throat. Her father and Stephanie had married a little more than a year after her mother had been killed. She'd always assumed the marriage had happened so fast because her father had wanted her to have a female role model in her life. A mother figure. But that hadn't been the reason at all.

"Oh, my—" Karine pressed a hand against her stomach, willing the bile in her throat to stay down. Her father had been having an affair with Stephanie. All this time, he'd been married to the woman he'd cheated on her mother with.

"Honey." He reached out a hand.

She leaned away from his touch.

Her father sat back. "Karine, all of this happened a long time ago. It has nothing to do with our lives now."

Karine glared at her father. "It may have been a long time ago for you, but it's happening right now for me." She shot to her feet. "I have to go."

"Karine—" Her father stood, but she was already through the office door.

Stephanie called out as she slammed out of the house, but she didn't look back.

Her entire body trembled, her hands shaking so violently that she dropped the car keys on the front walkway. She scooped them up and turned toward her car.

Omar.

He leaned against the rental, his legs crossed at the ankles, his arms crossed over his chest.

The dam of tears she'd been holding back broke at the sight of him.

He was at her side in a millisecond, wrapping her in his arms. "What's wrong? What happened?"

It was too much. It was all just too much. "Get me out of here. Please."

"You got it." Omar led her to his truck, helping her hop up into the passenger seat before jogging around to the driver's side. He started the engine and headed away from her father's house.

She wasn't sure how long they'd been driving when she finally got a hold of the emotions swamping her.

"Feel better?" Omar said once the deluge had ceased.

"A little."

"Want to talk about it?"

She nodded. "Could we go somewhere else though? I need to get away from here, but I don't trust myself to drive yet."

"Okay then. There's something I want to show you."

THEY WERE HEADED away from Karine's father's house, but in the opposite direction from Carling Lake. Omar didn't push her to tell him what had happened at her father's house. Whatever it was he could tell it had gotten to her.

"My father cheated on my mother," she said after they'd been on the road for a little while. Once she'd started talking the events of the day spilled out of her. How she'd found a love letter in her mother's things in the attic and had believed her mother had been having an affair when she'd been killed. Then going to her father and finding out that the letter had belonged to him.

He hadn't seen that coming. "Wow. How do you feel about that?"

Karine stared out of the front windshield. "I don't want to talk about it."

"Understood."

They drove in silence for twenty more minutes before Omar pulled off the main highway. He turned them onto a dusty little side road that looked like it hadn't been used in decades. A few minutes later, he turned into what had once been a popular drive-in movie theater.

"Where are we?"

"The former Stardust & Moonlight Drive-in Theater."

The screen had tears in several places, but it still stood like a sentry over the cracked parking lot. He backed the pickup in so the truck's bed faced the screen.

Karine quirked an eyebrow. "I don't think they're showing a movie tonight. Or ever again."

He chuckled. "No. This place closed in 2006."

"Sooooo, what are we doing here?"

He pointed at the windshield. "Looking at a different kind of stars. Come on."

The sky had already started to darken, and the stars peeked through what was left of the waning daylight.

He grabbed a blanket, a couple of power bars and two bottles of water from the go-bag he kept in the back seat of the pickup and got out.

He hopped into the truck bed and spread out the blanket before helping Karine into the back of the truck.

They sat in comfortable silence for a while. The stars had not only come out, they'd brought a full moon with them. It all gleamed brilliantly against the inky midnight sky.

"How did you even know about this place?"

"This is embarrassing. After you moved to Spring-tree, I learned everything I could about this place. I know there used to be a Mister Softee downtown and your violin teacher taught out of her house on Munkhouser Road, and that trash pickup was on Tuesdays in your zip code."

He waited a beat, fearing he'd said too much. In his twelve-year-old mind, knowing everything about the town where she'd moved had made him feel closer to her, but out loud now, he wondered if she'd think he was a preteen stalker.

She chuckled. "Wow, you really got to know this town."

"I missed you," he said.

"I missed you too." She reached for his hand.

They leaned back against the pickup's cab and stared out at the stars. The air was crisp, but it was a welcome coolness.

"I used to imagine bringing you here one day to watch one of those terrible sci-fi movies you love." The words he'd been wanting to say for...for years now, bubbled up inside him.

Just say it... I want to be more than just your best friend. I want to be your man.

I love you, Karine.

"*Barbarella* is a classic, and I will fight anyone who says otherwise."

He grinned. "I don't want to fight." Fighting was the last thing he had on his mind at the moment. Quite the opposite, actually. "I had a huge crush on you when we were teens."

She turned toward him, focusing her eyes on him. The moonlight created flecks like fireworks exploding in her light brown eyes. "You did?"

His heart pounded as if he'd just come back from a ten-mile run. "I did." He squeezed her hand.

She squeezed back. "I had a crush on you too," she said quietly, a shadow of a smile passing over her face.

He held her gaze. They were headed for potentially dangerous waters. Heaven knew he wanted to kiss her so badly right now that he could almost taste her lips on his.

As he searched her eyes, he was sure she felt the same way.

He let go of her hand and lifted his to cradle the sides of her face, angling her head up as he tilted down. He hovered for a moment, their mouths millimeters apart, savoring the moment.

He skimmed his lips across hers, drawing a small hum of pleasure from her throat that went right to his groin.

Karine reached out, her hands going to his waist, drawing him closer. The encouragement emboldened him and he coaxed her mouth open, deepening the kiss, their tongues tangling, dancing an exquisite dance. Desire pulsated in a current between them.

Karine moved her hands up, curling her fingers around his neck. He moved his hands down her back, cupping her bottom.

She sighed into his mouth then threw one of her legs over his so that she was straddling him.

He nearly came undone. He couldn't remember the last time he'd been this turned on by just making out. But then, Karine could turn him on with a look.

He scraped along the side of her breast. His body was begging him for more, and from the way Karine was grinding against him, she was right there with him.

The blast of an eighteen-wheeler's horn from the nearby highway shook the pickup.

They were too far away for anyone to have seen their hot and heavy make-out session from the road, but the blast of sound had an immediate chilling effect on the mood.

Karine swung off him, pushing her back into the side of the truck and putting as much distance as was possible in the limited space they had between them. "I…" She pressed a hand to her lips, swollen by his kisses. "I think you should take me back to my father's place to pick up my car."

She hurried to get out of the truck bed and around to the passenger's-side door. She was already strapped into her seat belt by the time he hauled himself behind the wheel.

"Karine, I'm sorry if—"

She held up a hand, her eyes flicking to his before skittering away. "Don't be sorry. I'm not, really. We just got carried away. It happens. No big deal."

No big deal.

He swallowed down the pain that arose with those words and started the truck.

No big deal. It felt like a big deal. A huge, life-altering deal.

Chapter Fifteen

It was just after nine in the evening when Omar pulled into his driveway just as his cell phone began to ring.

James.

He answered the call and exited the truck, watching across the expanse that separated his house from Karine's as she got out of her rental car.

"Omar? Are you there?" James's voice sounded through the phone.

He realized he'd answered the call, but hadn't yet spoken. "I'm here. Sorry. What's up?"

"I wanted to make sure you and Karine heard about Becky Portman."

He spun to look at the Portman house across the street. It was dark. It didn't appear that anyone was at home. "What about Becky?"

"She was attacked earlier today. From what I've gathered, she got home from work and she must have surprised a burglar," James said.

Karine must have clocked the concern on his face. She walked across their lawns and stopped next to him on the driver's side of the pickup truck. "What's going on?"

"Becky Portman was attacked in her house earlier today. James says it looks like a burglary gone wrong."

"Becky was taken to the hospital. Richie found her, and

she'd been hit on the head pretty hard. No updates on her condition yet."

Omar repeated what James said to Karine. His heart tightened at the stricken look on her face. Becky and Richie Portman were far from the nicest people, but he and Karine had known them both for most of their lives. They were fixtures in the neighborhood and in the Carling Lake community.

"I'm going to keep my ear to the ground," James continued, "but I wanted to make sure you'd heard the news. I'm sure you're keeping your eyes open, but with everything going on and you and Karine living right across the street..." He let the rest of the sentence fall away.

James didn't need to finish. A burglary at the Portman house hit more than a little close to home. Especially given everything else that had happened in the last few days and the fact that they'd just spoken to Becky and Richie about the night Karine's mother was murdered. Burglaries in Carling Lake happened, although they weren't common, and bad actors tended to target the tourists more than the residents. A sick feeling was growing in the pit of his stomach. The timing of this burglary did not feel coincidental.

He signed off the call.

"I'm going to go to the hospital," Karine said. "I'm sure Richie is there and whatever my issues with him and Becky, they are all each other has. I'm sure he could use some support."

Omar smiled, ever surprised by her kindness. "I'll drive."

Karine rounded the pickup and hopped in.

They rode in silence for several minutes before Karine spoke.

"Do you think...?"

"Do I think that a burglary at the Portman place is a little too coincidental, given we just confronted them about the possibility that they'd seen something on the night of your mother's death? Yes, the thought had crossed my mind."

Karine chewed her bottom lip. "But that would mean the attack on Becky was our fault."

"No," he said definitively. "It does not. The attack on Becky is the fault of whoever attacked her. No one else."

His glance across the cab told him his words hadn't convinced her.

The parking lot at the hospital wasn't crowded. Neither was the waiting room. Richie was the only person there. He sat, hunched over in a waiting room chair, with his head in his hands.

"Richie," Omar said.

Richie looked up with a mixture of hope and despair on his face. "Oh, it's only you two."

Omar let the comment roll off him.

"How is Becky?" Karine asked, taking the seat next to Richie. "How are you?"

Omar sat in the plastic chair on Richie's other side.

Richie scraped a hand over his face. It was pretty clear he wasn't doing well. He had a five-o'clock shadow and his eyes were bloodshot from crying. "The doctors haven't told me anything."

"Have you talked to the police?" Omar asked.

"Deputy Coben was just here, checking in on me and Becky, and Deputy Bridges took my statement while the EMTs got Becky ready to transport. I don't know much though. I came home and found her in the back room. She was lying on the floor…" He choked up. "There was so much blood. I called 9-1-1. That's it." Richie let his head fall into his hands again.

Karine rubbed his back soothingly. "Hey, Becky is tough. She's going to come through this."

"Deputy Coben said it looked like a robbery." Richie lifted his head. Tears showed in his eyes. He shook his head. "It wasn't a robbery. Becky, she regained consciousness for a minute while we were waiting for the ambulance to arrive."

Omar and Karine shared a look across Richie's back. "Did she say who attacked her?"

Richie shook his head. "No. She didn't say who attacked her, but she did say something."

The tense moment swirled around them.

Richie turned to look at Karine. "She said, 'Tell Karine she's in danger.'"

THE KILLER THREW the glass in his hand across the room. Becky Portman wasn't dead and Karine knew about the security recording of the night of Marilee's murder. A video that she had and was no doubt studying to find out who was on it. They could do amazing things with old videos nowadays.

A terrified shiver snaked through him.

The time for warnings was over.

He had to get the video and eliminate the threat posed by Karine. Her boyfriend would be a problem, so he'd have to go too.

Chapter Sixteen

Karine was relieved when she woke up the next day to a text from Daton Spindler, Amber's ex-husband, agreeing to meet her for coffee that morning. Her make-out session with Omar had supercharged the feelings she hadn't known were there for him. And now she didn't seem able to tame them. Her dreams had been filled with him. Kissing him. Touching him. Making love to him. She wasn't sure what to do with that, so she planned to ignore it for now. She had enough on her plate anyway.

She lucked out and found a space right in front of OrganicSandwich. The interior was trendy for Carling Lake but had a homey feel. A soft, jazzy song wafted from the overhead speakers and the entire shop smelled like freshly baked bread. She closed her eyes and inhaled the delicious aroma.

Daton was already at the café when Karine arrived. He stood as she approached the table and engulfed her in a fatherly hug.

He gestured to the cups of steaming coffee already on the café table. "I ordered both of us regular coffees because I wasn't sure what you wanted to drink. I don't have a lot of time before I have to get into the office. But I was so thrilled to get your text asking if we could meet up this morning."

She didn't tell him she didn't drink coffee. She'd texted

him the night before after getting home. She'd gotten so much new information over the last twenty-four or so hours about her parents, and she wasn't sure anymore if she could trust her father. There weren't a lot of other people who could help her make sense of what had been happening around the time her mother was killed. Daton was one of the few.

"You look so much like your mother," he said, taking the seat on the opposite side of the table from her.

"Really? You think so?"

He seemed surprised. "You don't?"

"I don't really know. I haven't seen a lot of pictures of my mother. I used to think my dad didn't keep them around because seeing her was too hard for him."

"But you don't think that's the reason anymore?"

"I don't know what to think right now." She swallowed hard, pushing down the emotion swelling in her chest. "I found out some things about my father and my mother. Things about their relationship around the time of her murder."

Daton looked at her with an expression of confusion. "What things are you talking about?"

"That my father was having an affair. My mother knew."

Confusion morphed into surprise on Daton's face. "Whoa, whoa, wait a minute. Marilee, Amber and I were pretty close back then. Marilee never said a word about Jean straying."

"He did." She ran a finger around the rim of the cup of coffee she wasn't drinking. "He admitted it to me after I found a love letter in my mother's diary. At first I thought it was to her. That my mother was the one who'd had an affair."

Daton shook his head vehemently. "No, Marilee had far too much integrity to treat a family like that."

"Well, apparently my father didn't," she snapped.

"I can't believe this. Your mother never said a word. I guess you never really know what goes on inside a marriage."

His comment reminded her that he had at one time been married to Amber. "I'm sorry. I'm bringing up all this stuff and I haven't even said I'm sorry for your loss."

He waved away the comment. "Thank you, but Amber and I haven't had any kind of relationship since the divorce more than three years ago now. To be honest with you, my comment about marriage was more about my first marriage than anything you've told me about your parents. It's no big secret in this town that my marriage to Amber ended when she found out I'd been having an affair with Valerie, my current wife."

It may have been common knowledge to the residents of Carling Lake, but it was news to Karine. She wasn't sure how to respond to it and, frankly, she wasn't feeling very forgiving toward cheaters at the moment, so she decided to move on.

"Can you tell me anything about my mother in the weeks and months before her death that might help me figure out why she was killed?"

Daton gave her a look that was half pity, half sadness. "Nothing. I'm sorry, but I've thought about that time, those weeks and days before and after Marilee's murder now. There was nothing unusual going on that I knew about before your mother was killed and I've had to come to the conclusion that it was just one of those tragic, horrible things that happens in life."

She couldn't accept that. "So you think the police are right? That my mother interrupted a burglar and was killed?"

"After so much time and no new evidence, no one speaking up, yes, I think the only logical conclusion is that someone, probably a tourist or one of the seasonal workers, thought the house was empty and was surprised by your mother." He reached across the table and took her hand. "I do know that Marilee wouldn't want you to spend your life consumed by her death. She would want you to move on. Fall in love. Start a family and give her grandbabies to look down on from heaven."

A mental picture of Omar popped into her head, but she shook it away. She didn't know if marriage, family and babies were in her future, but if they were, it was in the distant future. Right now, she had to find closure for her past before she could move forward. But she could tell from the look on Daton's face that he didn't want to hear that. Like a lot of people after a tragedy, he just wanted to move on. Get back to normal. But they never understood that life had not been normal for her since she'd been twelve years old. And it never would be.

Daton twisted his wrist to look at the Rolex watch on it. "I'm sorry, but I have an early meeting today. I have to go, but maybe we could get together again? Dinner at my house, maybe. I have tons of old pictures of your mother, Amber and I when we were younger. I can dig them out of my attic and you can take a look at them."

She gave him a genuine smile. She'd loved to get a glimpse into her mother's childhood. "I'd love that. Thank you."

She stood, and Daton gave her another hug. "I'll call you soon to set something up."

Karine watched him walk out of the café with the stride of a man who knew his place in the world.

She would definitely look forward to going through those pictures. Given how her investigation into her mother's death was going, they might be the only thing that came of her trip back to Carling Lake.

Daton may not have had time for breakfast, but Karine was starving. The café served breakfast and lunch, so she turned her attention to the menu above the counter and got in line.

"Karine? Karine Eloi?" Her head snapped to the left and her gaze landed on the woman behind the counter. It took a second for her to realize who it was.

"Meghan Foster?" Meghan had lived a few streets over and had been her regular babysitter when she was younger. She was only five or six years older than Karine, but she'd aged well. Her eyes were as clear and blue as the last time Karine had seen her, and her skin was clean, smooth and tanned, as if she'd just come back from days lazing on the beach. Her high blond ponytail swung as she wiped her hands on her apron and rounded the counter.

"I heard you were in town for a while." Meghan gave her a hug. "You look great."

"So do you. Wow, you look just like I remember you when I was twelve."

Meghan gave a hearty laugh. "I wish, but thank you."

"So, you work here," Karine said, taking in the apron with the OrganicSandwich name stitched across the front.

"I own it," Meghan said with a smile.

"Congrats."

"Thanks. My husband, Buck, and I started the shop several years ago. He'd been the manager at several stores around the county and he wanted something of his own. I wanted a job that allowed me some flexibility after our second child was born, so here we are."

"Well, it smells delicious. What would you suggest?"

"Today's breakfast special is a spinach, egg and cheese breakfast sandwich on a bagel."

"Sounds fabulous. I'll take it."

Meghan smiled and waved her to a table. "Have a seat and I'll bring it to you when it's ready. Would you like something to drink?"

Karine ordered a chai tea and grabbed the empty table by the front window. It was half past eight in the morning, but the shop was still doing a brisk business. Mostly takeout, but there was a handful of tables where patrons sat and ate too.

A younger woman who'd been behind the counter when she'd ordered brought her tea to the table. Karine scrolled on her phone until Meghan appeared with a plate in each hand.

"I hope you don't mind. I thought I could take a break and we could catch up."

"I don't mind at all. In fact, I hate to eat alone. You'd be saving me from some major embarrassment."

"Wonderful." Meghan set a plate down in front of Karine and scooted into the chair on the other side of the table.

They made small talk and ate for a while. Karine got the feeling that Meghan was working up to something and, when Meghan pushed her empty plate to the side and leaned forward, she knew she hadn't been wrong.

"The rumor around town is that you've been asking questions about your mother and the time period around when she was killed."

"That's the rumor?" Karine said noncommittally.

Meghan's smile was wry. "It is. I don't know if you knew, but I adored your mother. She was everything I wished my mother had been."

Karine had been pretty young, and not really observant

as to what the adults or even older kids like Meghan might have been going through when she'd lived in Carling Lake. But it had been common knowledge that Meghan's mom, Cindy Streeter, was an alcoholic and less than attentive parent. Cindy had been fortunate enough to inherit a house from her parents, but Meghan and her younger brother had largely been left to raise themselves. Meghan had been the go-to babysitter for Karine's parents and her friends' parents, which she now realized had been their way of helping Meghan and her brother, of making sure that at least there was some money going to them that their mother wouldn't spend on booze.

Karine reached across the table and squeezed Meghan's hand. "I know she thought highly of you and she'd be so proud to see what you've accomplished."

"Yeah." Meghan's smile brightened. "I hope so." She cleared her throat. "There's something you don't know. Something I've never told anyone."

Karine's heart skipped a beat. "Okay."

Meghan picked up a paper napkin from the table and twisted it between her fingers. "I don't know where to begin or how to tell this story. I've never told anyone. Not even Buck."

Karine reached for her hand again. "Just start at the beginning."

"The beginning. Okay. I guess, then, that would be my sophomore year in high school. I was a quiet kid. My mother's drinking and erratic behavior had already taught me how to make myself small, invisible. I did well at school, but didn't make any waves. I didn't want to stand out, you know what I mean?"

"I think so, yes."

"Except, I was a teenager, so I also did want to be noticed, you know. I don't know how to explain it exactly."

Karine chuckled. "You don't have to explain being a teenage girl to me. I remember."

Meghan laughed too. "I guess I don't. It was a confusing time, I guess is the best way to describe it, so when Principal Howser started noticing me, it made me feel good. I actually didn't think much of it at first, just like the principal saying hi in the hallway and stuff."

Karine's stomach turned, but she kept silent and just listened.

"And it was just that…for a while, hellos in the corridor between class or if he saw me after band practice. 'Hi. How was band practice?' 'Did you have a good weekend?' Like normal stuff. But I noticed that he always seemed to single me out. Like one time Vanessa Grey and her harpies—"

Karine made a face. The name didn't ring any bells.

"Right, I forgot you were so much younger. Vanessa Grey and her harpies were the Carling Lake equivalent of Regina George and the Plastics. The mean girls. Anyway, they were always kissing up to Mr. Howser and, frankly, he seemed to enjoy the attention. But all of a sudden, he was walking right past Vanessa and speaking to me in the halls."

Karine had a feeling she knew where this was going.

"Then he started calling me to his office. At first, I was terrified I was in trouble, but he said he was calling me in to 'check in.'" Meghan made air quotes. "But he never checked in on anyone else, as far as I knew. And he was doing it, like, a lot."

"Didn't any of the teachers notice?"

Meghan scoffed. "I'm sure they did. But no one ever said anything, not to me and not to Principal Howser, as far as I knew. He'd been hand-picked by the school board and you know how small-town power dynamics work. And I didn't have a parent who was going to go to bat for me."

She'd been vulnerable. The perfect target for a predator.

"Then he started touching me...nothing sexual," she hurried to add. "Just like massaging my shoulders. Patting my thigh. Brushing against my breast. I didn't know what to do."

"What happened?" Karine asked softly.

"Your mother." Meghan smiled wistfully. "I used to go into the woods behind your house just to think and be alone. To practice my clarinet because my mother hated the sound of it. I was in the woods one day, in a clearing that I thought only I knew about," she chuckled, "playing my clarinet. Mr. Howser had been escalating, and I was terrified of what he might do next. I didn't know what to do, or who to tell, or if anyone would believe me. It was eating away at me."

A single tear fell from her eye. "I don't know how long I was there before I eventually realized that I wasn't alone. Your mom was there with her easel, painting. I offered to leave, but she told me to stay because she'd enjoyed painting to the sound of music. I honestly don't know what possessed me to tell her what was going on, but it all just came out. We talked until the sun went down and then your mom walked me home."

Karine's heart pinched with love for her mother.

Meghan swiped at the tear. "Let me tell you, I was terrified of going to school on Monday morning. I knew your mom well enough to know that there was no way she was going to just ignore what I'd told her. But looking back now, I see that's exactly why I'd told her. Because I knew she'd help. I saw Principal Howser almost the minute I walked through the schoolhouse doors. I thought I was going to faint, but he took one look at me and turned the other way. Nearly ran down the hall in the opposite direction."

Karine's brow rose. "My mother did something."

Meghan raised her hands. "To this day, I don't know exactly what she did, but yes, she did something. That day, after I got home from school, your mom came by. She asked about my day and I told her that Principal Howser had steered clear of me. All she said was 'Good. You don't have to worry about him anymore.' She came by every day for the next couple of weeks. And then at the end of the month, the school sent home a notice that Principal Howser was taking a leave of absence to attend to some personal business. He never came back. In fact, I learned later that the school board had quietly voted to terminate his contract for cause and that Mr. Howser couldn't get a job with any of the surrounding school boards. That's why he took a job working construction."

And if Meghan was right about her mother having a hand in his firing, it explained the malevolence Martin had aimed at her at Barney's the other night. His dislike for her mother, no doubt, extended to her as well.

"He still practically runs when he sees me in town." Meghan's smile said she couldn't have been happier about that.

A scary thought bloomed in Karine's head. "Meghan, when did you say all this took place?"

"My sophomore year," Meghan answered somberly, giving her a moment to put all the pieces of the puzzle together. "Principal Howser was let go less than a month before your mother was murdered."

Chapter Seventeen

Karine hadn't answered the text Omar had sent her that morning, inviting her over for a pancake breakfast, and he'd taken that as a sign that she was worried about what had happened between them the night before. So he was surprised to find her on the other side of the door when he answered the doorbell.

"Karine." She was practically vibrating in front of him, whether it was with excitement or fear, he couldn't tell. "What's going on? Are you okay?"

"I'm fine. I ran into Meghan Foster at OrganicSandwich and she told me something about my mother."

He opened the door wider and Karine barreled past him and into the house. "Do you want some tea? Something to calm you down."

"I can't calm down," she said. "Meghan just told me that Martin Howser harassed her when she was a student at Carling Lake High and that she told my mother and that she thinks my mother got him fired."

"Whoa. Wait a minute. Slow down and start at the beginning."

She told him about meeting Daton at OrganicSandwich and running into Meghan, which didn't surprise him since he knew Meghan and her husband owned the organic sandwich shop. Her talk with Daton hadn't turned up anything helpful before he'd left. But Meghan had sat with her while she'd eaten breakfast and told her about Principal Howser's harassment, how Meghan had run into Marilee one day in the woods and revealed to her what was going on, and that Howser had immediately backed off, losing his job as principal not long after.

"Meghan said Principal Howser lost his job about a month before my mother was killed. Omar—" Karine grabbed him by the wrists "—this gives Martin Howser a motive to kill my mother."

"Slow down, Karine. We only have Meghan's side of the story."

Karine looked as if she was about to argue with him.

"And I'm not saying that she isn't telling the absolute truth, but even if everything she said is true, it's a big leap to accuse Martin Howser of murder just because he may blame your mother for costing him his job."

Karine glared at him. "What do you suggest I do, then?"

"Probably exactly what you've already planned to do. Talk to Howser. Confront him with what Meghan told you and see what he has to say. Gauge how he reacts."

Some of the anger in her eyes dimmed. "That was my next step, although, based on the dirty look Howser shot me outside of Barney's, I'm sure he isn't going to agree to meet with me, so I'm going to have to track him down first."

An ambush. Her plan was getting worse by the second.

"Okay. Well, I'm coming with you."

He'd expected her to say he didn't have to. That she could handle it alone. But instead, he got a relieved smile.

"Thanks. I'd appreciate that. Does that mean you don't have to work today? I know park rangers don't keep nine-to-five hours, but you've been helping me a lot these last few days. I meant it when I said I didn't want to get you in trouble."

"No, I'm off today and tomorrow. I'd actually planned to go on an overnight camping trek. I want to check something out in the northern part of the forest and it will just be easier to camp out and head back tomorrow."

She frowned. "It might rain this evening."

He shrugged. "It wouldn't be the first time I've camped in the rain. I have a waterproof tent. I'll be fine."

"Why the sudden desire to go camping?"

They hadn't talked much about his work since she'd arrived in town, but now he filled her in quickly on the possible water contamination.

"I've been a terrible friend," she said. "You have this major thing happening at your job and I didn't even know about it."

"You've been a great friend," he said, tripping over the last word. She was so much more than a friend.

"You have a lot going on right now and I get it. I just need to do this one thing and, like I said, it shouldn't take more than an overnight. I've been giving it a lot of thought and, if I'm right, about a pollutant—"

"You know the Carling Lake Forest better than anyone. If you say something unnatural is causing these animals to get sick and die, then something is."

He savored the sensation her belief in him brought on. "It has to be coming from the northern sector. It's isolated enough that if someone is dumping chemicals or something up there, no one would know. I'm not sure how they'd be doing it though." His body tensed with frustration. "It's nearly impossible to get through those dense woods on anything but foot."

Karine pointed at him. "Nearly impossible isn't impossible."

"True."

"How long has it been since you've been up there?"

"It's been a while."

"So someone might have cut a path."

He ceded the point. "It's possible. The main road is several miles away, but on an ATV, someone could cut a trail through."

"So we hike up there and take a look."

Omar's eyebrows rose. "We?"

"Yes. We. You've got my back. I've got your back. You've been helping me out with my investigation into my mother's death. This is the least I can do to repay you."

"You don't need to repay me. I want to help you."

She pinned him with her gaze. "And I want to help you."

A charged moment passed between them.

It was shattered by someone banging on the front door.

Omar opened a drawer in the side table next to the door and took out his service weapon. He shot a hard glance at Karine. "Go into the kitchen."

He waited until she did before he went to the door.

The person on the other side banged again.

He glanced out of the living room window at the same time that the person spoke.

"Monroe! Open up. It's the sheriff's department," Shep called out.

He exhaled a sigh of relief. He slid the gun back into the drawer and opened the door.

"Deputy Coben. What can I do for you?"

Deputy Coben scowled. "I've had a complaint about you and Miss Eloi. Tried knocking on her door, but no one answered. Do you have any idea where she is?"

"I'm here, Deputy." Karine stepped out of the kitchen and came to stand next to Omar.

Coben's smile turned into a smirk.

Omar fought the urge to wipe it off his face. "What can we help you with, Deputy Coben?" he gritted out.

"Richie Portman says you two have been harassing him."

"We spoke to him about what he might have seen on the night my mother was murdered and offered our support at the hospital. We did not harass anyone," Karine said.

Shep glowered. "I told you, looking into your mother's murder was a bad idea."

"And I disagree," Karine snapped back. "I'm not breaking any laws, so I don't see what business it is of yours, Deputy."

That statement wasn't entirely true, but Omar wasn't going to correct her.

"If Richie Portman had seen something relevant to your mother's murder, the sheriff's department would have found out and pursued it," Coben snarled.

"Except you didn't." Karine seemed on the verge of screaming.

Omar reached out and laid what he hoped was a calming hand on her shoulder. He didn't want her to say too much to Shep. The deputy couldn't stop them from investigating, but the less he knew, the better, as far as he was concerned.

Coben's eyes darkened. "What does that mean?"

"Nothing," Omar said.

"We found a recording that shows someone sneaking around my parents' house on the night of my mother's murder, and Richie, or someone in Richie's house, in a window, who might have been watching at the time."

Omar groaned internally.

"A recording? Where did you find this video?"

Karine seemed to realize a moment too late that she'd said too much. She shot a cornered glance at Omar.

He turned away from Karine and looked at the deputy. "I found it. In Amber Spindler's house."

"Amber Spindler's... What the hell were you doing in her house?"

"I wanted to take a look around. See if I could figure out what she wanted to tell Karine."

"You interfered with a crime scene," Shep growled.

"No, I didn't. The sheriff's department is treating Amber's death as a suspected suicide or accidental death. I presumed the sheriff's department had completed its search, as the house wasn't cordoned off."

"Oh, yeah," Shep said somewhat pathetically. "Well, I know for a fact the house was locked up. How did you get in?"

Omar hesitated, purposely keeping his gaze from straying to Karine, although he could feel her eyes on him. He didn't want to lie, but he wouldn't implicate her in a crime.

So, he remained silent.

"Where is this recording now? It's evidence in an open case, and you are obstructing justice by not turning it over to the sheriff's department."

Karine scowled, but reached into her purse and pulled out the disc copy, slapping it into Shep's hand. "Some people might ask why, in twenty-three years, the sheriff's department never discovered this recording?"

Shep's face turned purple and he pointed a stubby finger at Karine. "I'm going to tell you two this one more time. Stop sticking your nose where it doesn't belong or you might just get it cut clean off."

"It was my mother who was killed," Karine said. "I'd say my nose is right where it belongs."

"Deputy Coben, did Richie file a formal harassment complaint?"

Shep stared at Karine, but when she didn't back down, he finally shifted his glare to Omar. "No, which you should be grateful for. But I'm telling you to convince your girlfriend there to stop her snooping around before she crosses the wrong person."

"Well, you've delivered your missive like a good little messenger deputy. I think it's time for you to leave. You have a good day." Omar slid the door forward.

Shep slammed his hand against it, stopping it from closing. He was practically vibrating with anger. "You better get smart real fast, Monroe. If you don't, you and your lady friend might just find yourselves in a heap of trouble."

Chapter Eighteen

Omar didn't have any idea where Martin Howser lived, but he knew that the former principal now worked as the foreman at a local construction company. Karine hadn't been sure about approaching the man at his job, but Omar pointed out it would be safer to approach him in a public, or at least semipublic, place.

Omar drove them to the construction company's office, located in the industrial park off the main highway.

"You know I'm starting to wonder if there's more to Shep's determination to stop us from looking into your mother's murder than just keeping a lid on his shoddy police work," Omar said, making a right into the industrial park. According to his GPS, the company was located at the rear of the industrial complex.

"Something like what?"

"That's the question." He turned the pickup into the parking lot of Ace's Construction Company.

Howser walked out of the building in front of them and headed for one of the truck bays at the side of the building.

"There's Martin Howser."

Together, they got out of Omar's truck and walked toward Howser.

"Mr. Howser." She stepped in front of Howser, stopping him as he headed for the rear of the closest rig. "Karine Eloi."

He scowled, his gaze bouncing over Omar then back to Karine. "I know who you are."

"I'm wondering if I can have a moment of your time."

"What for?"

"I'd like to ask you a few questions. About when you were principal at Carling Lake High."

"That part of my life is over." He tried to step away, but Omar put a hand to his chest, stopping him.

Howser's scowl deepened. Howser may have been twenty years older than she and Omar, but his work in construction had kept him fit and muscled. The last thing she wanted was for this conversation to turn physical.

Since Howser wasn't inclined to give her time to ease into the thornier questions, Karine decided to dive into the deep end.

"Meghan Foster told me about what you did to her when she was in high school. And how my mother intervened."

"I don't know what Meghan Foster told you—" Howser took a threatening step forward.

Omar again pressed a hand to Howser's chest. "That's close enough."

"Meghan told me you harassed her. She told my mother, and you were let go from the school system soon after."

"That little—"

Omar made a noise deep in his throat, cutting Howser off.

Howser glared at them. "Whatever Meghan Foster told you is a lie. But your mother believed her and this town—" Howser shot a disdainful look around, but there was no one near except them. "This town adored your mother and grandfather. People around here thought they walked on water."

Someone hadn't adored her mom. Someone had killed her and, based on the venom coming from Martin Howser, he could very well be that someone.

"She convinced the board to fire me based on the word of a child," Howser continued. "Everyone knows how confused teenage girls can get. Especially girls like Meghan. No father in the home. Her mother is a drunk. Nobody pays her any attention, so of course when I show her the least little bit of attention, she misinterprets it."

"Misinterprets," Omar growled.

Howser continued to glare, but he also took a step back.

Karine crowded into Howser's personal space, taking advantage of his discomfort. "Maybe you decided to get back at my mother for ruining your career. You waited until you thought she was home alone and then you confronted her. Maybe you didn't even mean to kill her and things just got out of hand. You lost your temper."

"Now just wait a damn minute." Howser's face went red as a tomato. "I didn't kill anyone. I despised your mother for ruining my life. My wife left me. Took my son. I lost my job. My house. My family. But I'm not a murderer, and you better not be starting any rumors otherwise."

She looked Howser in the eye. "I'm not looking for rumors. I want facts. I'm going to find out who killed my mother."

"Well, I can't help you any more than telling you it wasn't me. Now, I've got better things to do."

Howser went to step around her, but Karine moved with him, blocking his way.

"You're a scumbag, Howser, and I promise you this. If you killed my mother, I will see you behind bars for it. You can count on it."

Chapter Nineteen

"Are you sure you're up for this?" Omar asked as they neared the turnoff that would take them to the trailhead.

"For the tenth time, I'm sure," Karine responded. "It will be good for me. I need time to think and process everything I've heard about my mother and her murder since I've arrived in town. This will be a good time to think."

"It's been several eventful days," he said, thinking about the kiss they'd shared.

The area of the Carling Lake Forest that they were planning to hike wasn't a popular spot for camping in no small part because of how difficult it was to reach. Omar drove them to the northernmost parking lot, which was empty. They got out and went to the back of the pickup. He'd put the cover on the truck bed, but they didn't need much. His job as a ranger meant he was as familiar with the forest as he was with his own home, but he and Karine had spent their childhood camping, hiking and exploring these woods.

They slung their packs onto their backs and started out.

He stole glances at Karine as she kept pace beside him. She wore a tight tank top that accentuated her ample breasts underneath a lightweight long-sleeved shirt. Well-worn blue jeans sculpted her tight behind. He found the mountain woman look sexy as hell. He found her sexy as hell.

"Penny for your thoughts." Karine was watching him.

"Oh, nothing," he said, feeling heat crawl up his neck. He hoped she hadn't noticed. "I'm just thinking about the best place to set up camp for the night. What about you? You've been pretty quiet."

They'd been hiking for more than an hour and they'd barely spoken a word.

"I'm just thinking about Martin Howser." She hesitated for a moment. "And my father."

"I wondered when you'd be ready to talk about that."

"I just can't believe he cheated on my mother."

"Don't shoot the messenger, but I hear that marriage can be hard," he said teasingly.

Karine rolled her eyes. "I know marriage is hard."

Omar raised an eyebrow.

"Not from experience, but you know what I mean. I just… I know my dad isn't perfect, but I wouldn't have ever predicted he'd betray my mother. They had their problems. I mean, they were an odd couple from the first, but my dad is like the most honest person I've ever met."

They stepped over a fallen log.

"You know your dad. Maybe he just made a mistake. He and your mom might have worked things out. Did you talk to him about it?"

She shook her head. "No, it… I was just so shocked and I wasn't sure what I was feeling. I just didn't want to be around him, so I left."

"I can understand that, but you know you're going to have to talk to your dad sometime."

"Sometime," she repeated.

But from the sound of it, sometime wouldn't be anytime soon.

They walked on for another hour, but the topics stayed out of the emotional or controversial areas of their lives.

They finally reached the stream that he wanted to take a sample from. It was one of the many ephemeral streams in the forest, but when its flow was heavy, the water had the capacity to travel quite a distance. It was also not far from the spot he'd picked out for them to camp for the night.

"So you think this stream could be feeding into other streams and creeks downhill and poisoning the smaller animals, right?" Karine asked, slinging her pack off her back and dropping it to the ground at the side of the stream.

He'd explained the details of his theory about the poisoned water on their hike to the stream.

"Pretty much." He was crouched down at the stream's edge, preparing to take a sample of the water. Fortunately, it was still full from the rain shower two nights before.

"But I thought you said the tests you'd had done on the downhill streams came back clean."

"They did," he said tightly.

"Sooooo."

"I just want to be sure. It's possible that because those larger water bodies receive incoming water from multiple smaller sources, there just wasn't enough contaminant to be detected in the water. Yet."

Omar put a cap on the second tube of water and tucked it into his pack along with the first sample he'd taken. Since John wasn't going to order another test, he planned to pay for the tests out of his own pocket. He'd have to call in a favor, but his friend who worked at a private environmental testing lab thought he could get the tests done. Omar just needed to make sure he had enough of the sample.

"'Yet,'" Karine parroted. "Have you considered sources of pollution other than water?"

He looked up at her from his crouched position. "What do you mean?"

"Well, I am admittedly not an expert, but I am the daughter of a botanist. Have you considered the soil?"

"The soil?"

"Yeah. The animals you mentioned you found, several of them are burrowers. And even the birds. They sometimes make nests in the hollow bases of trees or eat little creatures that are burrowers. If it's the soil that's contaminated, they'd be affected."

She was right. He'd gotten it into his head that it was the water that was contaminated because he'd found the animals near water bodies, but that could be a coincidence or an effect of the pollutant.

He'd brought more vials than he could have ever needed. He took two out of his pack and filled them both with soil.

"I'm not sure if my friend's lab can test soil samples, but even if his doesn't, I'll find one that will."

He packed the vials away with the water samples and stood, hiking his pack onto his back.

Karine reached down for her pack. Her right leg slid out from under her. Her arms windmilled.

He reached out, grabbed her by the forearms and steadied her, pulling her to him.

A sizzling awareness pulsated between them.

Karine's eyes were trained on his lips and he was pretty sure he was reading her mind.

She wanted to kiss him. Maybe as much as he wanted to kiss her right now.

Without thinking, he took a step forward at the same time she stepped back out of his arms.

"Thanks," she said, looking away.

He moved back.

She hoisted her backpack. "We should get going, don't

you think? It will be getting dark soon, and we still need to set up camp." She turned away.

He took a deep breath and let it out slowly. There was no cold shower in the forest, so he fought to get his libido in check. "The spot I have in mind is not far from here."

He led the way and they made it to the clearing he had in mind without incident.

Karine might have lived in the big city now, but she hadn't forgotten how to set up camp.

She took charge of setting up their tents while he made their dinner, soup and several pieces of artisan bread, using a backpacking stove.

"Ah, we have a small problem," Karine said.

He turned.

Karine held the two flaps of her tent. "The zipper on the front flaps is broken."

"I guess we should have checked them before we left. That's what I get for being in a rush."

"I could still use it, but if it rains tonight, it could get pretty wet inside."

"Even if it doesn't rain, it will be cold if you can't zip up. You can have my tent. I'll sleep under the stars."

"You'll sleep under the cold, rainy stars." She shook her head. "That doesn't make sense." She hesitated. "If you're okay with it, we can share your tent. It's big enough."

His tent was large enough for two, but it would be snug. His groin twitched at the thought of Karine sleeping a breath away from him.

"I'm okay with it."

They ate, sticking to neutral topics of discussion. But that didn't stop the sexual awareness from crackling between them.

After dinner, they washed up, securing their gear and

settling into their sleeping bags only minutes before the light pattering of rain drummed on the tent's roof.

He lay still and stiff as a board in his sleeping bag next to Karine, the smell of her perfume, which had always reminded him of the ocean, mingling with the scent of the forest.

Sleep was elusive. He couldn't turn his mind off. Or away from thoughts of taking Karine into his arms. Kissing her. Stripping her of her clothes and exploring her body thoroughly. He was sure she felt the electricity between them whenever they were alone. And he was equally certain that the same thing that kept him from acting on it had kept her from acting on it. Their friendship. He never wanted to lose her as a friend, but he couldn't keep pretending that he didn't want her as more either.

As he lay there listening to the rain, he realized Karine was struggling to fall asleep as well.

She shifted onto her side, looking at him.

"What?" he asked.

"What would you do if I kissed you right now?"

That had not been what he'd expected her to say.

She didn't wait for him to respond. She lunged across the tent, grabbing him by his shirt and pressing her lips to his. He gave in to the kiss, desire coursing through him.

She rolled so that she was on top of him. He ran his fingers through her hair, drawing her in as close as they could get with clothes between them. He knew she could feel how much he wanted her. He wanted to be inside her, but he had to make sure she was sure.

He pulled back enough to look into her eyes. "Karine?"

She gazed at him, desire darkening her eyes. She flicked her tongue over her bottom lip and said, "Yes. I want this."

That was all he needed to hear.

He took her lips again and stopped thinking about the wisdom of what they were about to do and started to just feel.

KARINE WAS BREATHING HARD. Excitement and desire coursed through her. Throwing herself, literally, at Omar was impulsive, but she'd wanted him for a long time. Longer than she was probably ready to admit to herself.

And now, here they were, limbs entangled, lips pressed together, the heat between them ready to combust.

Omar slipped his hand under her shirt and kneaded her breast beneath her bra. Her nipples tightened into tight beads under his touch. She moaned.

"You are so sexy," he said against her lips.

Her blood raced. She felt as if she were speeding down a steep hill without brakes. She was going to crash, but she didn't care. The ride was worth it.

Omar grabbed the hem of his shirt and whipped it over his head while she shrugged out of her top.

Omar eased her from the rest of her clothes then made short work of his own.

"You're perfect." His eyes roamed over every inch of her skin, sending electric shocks throughout her body.

He ran a finger over a birthmark on her hip.

She trembled. "If you keep this up, I might combust."

"That's the idea."

His fingers were like magic. Tickling, teasing and finally finding her core.

She arched against him.

It didn't take long before she felt the waves of ecstasy pull her under.

Omar sheathed himself as she breathlessly rode the last surges of bliss.

She didn't have time to catch her breath before he was back, braced atop her.

He seated himself inside her easily, as if he belonged there. As if he were home.

She shuddered at the weightiness of the thought. And then she wasn't thinking at all. She could only feel.

Pleasure rippled through her. She shifted to take him in deeper and they both moaned in synchronized ecstasy.

"Open your eyes, Karine. Look at me."

She did, the connection between them heightening even more.

She'd had intense sex before, but never like this. This, she knew, she'd only ever have with one man.

Omar.

Omar, who knew her better than anyone.

Omar, who knew all about her past.

Omar, who got her like no one else ever had.

Omar, who was right where he should be. With her.

He quickened his pace and she knew they were both close. He surged once, twice, and then her body tightened and she let out a sharp cry as he drove them both over the edge.

Omar collapsed next to her, pulling her to him as he did.

Her heart pounded hard against his. She ran her fingers through the hair on his chest.

She couldn't ever remember feeling shy after intercourse, but that was exactly how she felt now. Shy. Unsure.

Omar ran his hand over the birthmark on her hip. "I never knew you had a birthmark."

"You've never seen me this naked."

His body shook with laughter and her awkwardness eased.

"I've never seen you naked at all before, but you are one of the most beautiful things I have ever seen."

She stared at his very fine abdominal muscles. "I'm sure you say that to every woman you—"

He tipped her chin up with his index finger. "I have never lied to you and I will never lie to you. You are the most beautiful woman I've ever known."

She leaned up and kissed him.

He cupped her backside and she entwined her legs with his, feeling the fire ignite within her again.

Omar rolled her onto her back, but a fleeting thought floated through her mind before she lost herself in his touch for a second time.

What about tomorrow?

Chapter Twenty

Omar woke alone. He shrugged into his clothes and boots and pushed the tent flaps back, stepping outside. The sun had already broken over the horizon, its rays shining down on the forest floor through the trees. The rain from the night before had cooled the air, sharpening the smell of soil and pine, and softening the ground beneath his feet.

He scanned the clearing where they'd set up camp. "Karine?"

For a brief moment, he wondered if she'd gotten up early and left camp alone. But her pack and all their gear was still there.

"I'm here." Her voice came from just inside the tree line. "Out in a second."

He grabbed a sweatshirt from his pack, pulling it over his head as Karine stepped from the trees.

"Good morning."

"Good morning," she replied without looking at him.

His heart sank. Last night had been everything he'd dreamed of and more, but if she was having regrets… "Are we okay?"

"Yes, of course we are," she said without meeting his gaze.

Of course.

They ate breakfast and started the reverse hike out of

the woods in almost complete silence, and not the comfortable, friendly silence from their hike the day before. This was an awkward, cringe-inducing quietness that left questions swirling in his mind. He'd thought their night together had been incredible. After Karine had fallen asleep in his arms, he'd lain awake fantasizing about how they could make a relationship work. It hadn't entered his mind that she might not have felt the same way about crossing the line from friends to lovers as he did.

And if she didn't feel the same? Could he continue to be her friend, her best friend, when every part of him wanted to be more?

The questions bandied through his head as they walked. They were almost back to the truck when he couldn't take the questions any longer. One way or the other, he had to know what she was thinking. What she felt.

He pulled up short. "What happened between us last night?"

A part of him knew that things would never be the same between them. No matter what she answered, their relationship had changed and there was no going back. But he hoped...

Karine's gaze skittered away from him. "Last night was...a mistake."

Mistake. The word cut through him like a knife.

"Listen, what happened last night... We've been friends for a long time, like, almost thirty years. That's amazing and incredible. And I don't want to lose our friendship."

"Friendship."

His brain felt as if it had been filled with cotton. A mistake. Friendship. He imagined being shot would have been less painful than hearing those words from her after what he'd felt making love to her.

She let out a heavy sigh. "Yes, friendship. We're both adults and last night was…it was great. But it doesn't have to be a big deal. I'm going to go back to Los Angeles and you live here." She finally looked him in the eye, reaching out and pressing her palm against his heart. "This can be one amazing night we shared and that we remember fondly, as friends."

He recognized the unfamiliar pang in his chest as heartbreak. He'd done his best to avoid the feeling by keeping his romantic relationships with women at the surface level. It had been easy because he'd given his heart away years ago. To Karine. And he'd never gotten it back.

And now she was saying she didn't want it.

His entire body felt as if it had grown twenty pounds heavier than it had been just moments ago. Each of Karine's words had added a weight that he wasn't sure any amount of time in the gym would get rid of.

But if this was what she wanted, there was nothing he wouldn't do to make her happy. Even walk away from her.

Because that was what he'd have to do when she left for Los Angeles this time. Walk away. A clean break. He couldn't go on pretending that he just wanted to be her best friend when he wanted so much more.

How to do that without shattering into a thousand pieces himself was something he'd have to work out later. "Of course. You're right. Our friendship means too much to jeopardize it."

Karine's face flashed with something he might have pegged as disappointment under other circumstances. She gave him a tepid smile.

Neither of them spoke again until he pulled to a stop in

front of her house. He left the engine idling as he got out and retrieved her gear from the back of the truck.

She looked at him with a question in her eyes. "Omar—"

"I need to go," he said, cutting off whatever she was going to say. He wasn't sure he could stand to hear whatever soothing words she was going to trot out. He got it. She wasn't interested in being more than friends. Maybe he was being a little petulant about it, but it hurt.

"Oh, well... I'll see you tomorrow, then?"

He began backing toward the driver's-side door. "I don't know. I have to work tomorrow and I need to get these samples to my friend in Stunnersville." He turned to get into the pickup.

"Omar, please, wait," Karine said.

He faced her again.

"I don't want things to be weird between us. Can't we just pretend last night never happened and go back to the way things were?"

"What if I don't want to go back?" He slammed his palm against the side of the truck. "What if last night meant something to me, even if it didn't to you?"

"I—"

"I can't make you have feelings for me, but I can't pretend anymore that I don't have feelings for you. Because I do. I don't want to just be your best friend. I want to be your lover, your partner, your—"

He stopped himself. He'd never seen Karine look more terrified.

"I'm sorry. I... I just can't," she whispered.

He jumped into the truck, not waiting for her to respond. He didn't know how he was going to get through the rest of Karine's stay in Carling Lake, but right now he knew he needed space.

Space from the woman he wanted nothing more than to hold close.

Chapter Twenty-One

Karine grabbed the strawberry ice cream from her freezer and padded in her slippers and pajamas into the living room. She'd spent the day spinning her wheels regarding the investigation into her mother's death. She'd made no progress on identifying the person Amber had had dinner with the night she'd died. Martin Howser had a motive to kill her mother, but she knew that wouldn't be enough to jump-start the sheriff's department's investigation. And, if Becky or Richie Portman had seen anything the night of her mother's murder, they still weren't willing to share it with her or the sheriff. On top of all that, she'd been brooding about her argument with Omar.

She'd picked up the phone dozens of times to call him, but she'd never gone through with the call. What was there to say? He wanted to be more than her friend, and she didn't see him that way.

Well, that wasn't true. She'd definitely seen him as more than a friend the night they'd gone camping. She'd had lovers before, of course, but none of them had ever made her feel as much as she had in Omar's arms.

It couldn't work between them. She lived in Los Angeles and he lived here in Carling Lake. She wasn't a country girl and he wasn't a city guy. More than that, she risked losing him as a friend for a fleeting romance.

What if it isn't fleeting?

She'd never been good at romantic relationships. Too independent. Too career-oriented. She'd never had a relationship that had lasted beyond a year. She couldn't risk that with Omar.

They could get over this bump and back to their friendship. She closed her eyes and breathed through the ache in her chest.

They had to.

SHE SETTLED DOWN on the sofa and found *Krull* on Netflix, but not even a young Liam Neeson in one of her favorite sci-fi movies could pull her out of her funk. She glanced out the window as the final credits started to roll.

She rose and went to close the curtains.

A silver sedan rolled to a stop in front of the house. She was surprised to see her father unfold from the driver's side of the car.

He caught her watching from inside the house and waved.

She closed the blinds and went to open the front door.

"Dad, what are you doing here?"

He stopped on the top porch step. "I couldn't stop thinking about how we left things the other day. I didn't like it. Can we talk?"

She stood aside so he could step into the house.

He froze just inside the door, looking down the hall. She didn't have to imagine what he was seeing.

"Why don't we go into the living room?" She placed a hand lightly on his shoulder and guided him away from the memories of the past.

Her father let out a shuddering breath as they crossed into the living room. "This is the first time I've been in this house since... Everything looks so different. The furniture is all new."

She wasn't in any mood for small talk. She wasn't in the mood for a conversation at all with her father, but he'd driven for hours to talk to her and today seemed to be her day to have intense, emotional conversations with her loved ones.

"Dad."

"Right. I didn't come to assess the decor. Come. Sit with me." He sat and patted the spot next to him on the sofa.

She sat, and he took her hand in his.

Her father swallowed, his Adam's apple bobbing. "This is harder than I imagined it would be."

"Why did you cheat on Mom?"

"You know your mother was only twenty-one when we met. Fresh out of college. I was almost ten years older and, frankly, I hadn't had very much experience with the ladies." He chuckled. "We were infatuated with each other. And then we had you and we both fell in love with you."

"So you stayed together for me?"

"Yes and no. We stayed together because we both wanted what was best for you, certainly, but I think we stayed together because it was easier than being apart in a lot of ways. Easier than proving all the people who thought we wouldn't last right. And because we were scared of what our lives would look like on the other side of making a decision to separate."

Despite the anger she felt toward her father, his words resonated. Wasn't that exactly why she was hesitant to move her relationship with Omar out of the friend zone? Standing still seemed so much safer.

"That doesn't explain why you had an affair."

"I met Stephanie during a difficult period in my life, but meeting her was a blessing and we fell in love. I won't apologize for that." He looked her in the eye. "If you ever fall in love, and I hope you do, you'll see how hard it is to walk away from that person. How hard you'd fight to be with them."

Karine's eyes cut toward Omar's house even though there was no way she could see it from where she stood. Would she? Would she fight for the person she loved? All signs pointed to no. Maybe some people were always just too scared to take the risk.

Not that she was in love with Omar. She couldn't be, despite what they'd shared. They were friends. Best friends.

She forced herself to focus on what her father was telling her. That he'd had a reason to get rid of her mother.

"You were going to dump Mom. But I guess her murder saved you from having to have that uncomfortable conversation, didn't it?" She turned her back on him. It was difficult to look at him with the thoughts she had running through her mind. Questions she needed to know the answers to, but was terrified to ask.

Her father pushed to his feet. "Karine," he said, his voice hard, "I know this is a lot for you to take in, but I am still your father."

She spun around to face him. "Did you kill Mom?"

Her father looked stunned. "Karine, I can't believe you would ask me such a thing." Hurt flashed across his face.

She crossed her arms over her chest in an effort to stop the trembling in her body. She could let it go. His shock had seemed genuine. So had the hurt she'd seen flash across his face. But he hadn't answered the question. Not really.

And now that it was out there, the desire to hear him say yes or no was too strong to ignore.

"Did you kill my mother? Answer the question."

"No," her father snapped, his eyes hard pebbles.

She searched his face for a sign that he was telling her the truth. He looked angry enough to spit nails, but was that because he was appalled that she could even suggest that he'd killed his wife or because he was afraid she'd see through his lies?

She couldn't tell. Over the years, the distance that had grown between her and her father had made it nearly impossible for her to read him. And now she wasn't even sure she knew him at all.

After a long moment, her father let out a slow, deep breath. He seemed to shrink in on himself as the air left his lungs. "I know that you have had a lot thrown at you recently. I'm so sorry you found out about your mother's and my problems this way. You were so young when your mother died and after Stephanie and I married, I knew you never really warmed up to her. I didn't see any reason to drive a wedge further between you and her or me and you."

Was that all her father's omission was? An attempt to protect himself from embarrassment? She wanted to believe that, but there was no denying that the affair gave him, and Stephanie, a motive for wanting her mother out of the way.

"I need to get home," her father said. "This trip was a spur-of-the-moment thing and Stephanie will be worried about me."

He walked to the door and she followed.

Her father opened the front door, but turned back to her before stepping outside.

"I love you. You are, and always have been, the most important person in my life, and I'm sorry I haven't always acted like it, but I would never intentionally hurt you." He reached for her hand and this time she let him take it. He squeezed. "I'll call you in a couple of days, okay?"

His last words were said almost as a plea.

She didn't know how much she believed of what her father had told her, but she knew she wasn't ready to cut him out of her life, so she nodded. She watched him amble down the walkway and get into his car, wondering how it was that getting an answer to her questions had somehow only left her with more questions.

OMAR DROVE DOWN the highway, back toward Carling Lake. He'd turned the samples over to his friend, Brett, who used to work for the state crime lab, but had recently gotten a job at a large private lab that could run every kind of environmental and agricultural test known to man. Brett had assured him he could have the test results within twenty-four hours.

They'd also spent a few hours chatting over beers. Brett's wife had recently given birth to their first child, and Omar had had to coo over a lot of cute baby photos. Thankfully, Brett was so enamored with his new daughter that he hadn't noticed that Omar wasn't revealing very much about his own life. Omar was pretty sure Brett at least suspected his feelings for Karine were more than friendly, but he didn't want to rain on his friend's parade with the story of his disastrous love life.

He wound down the window and let the air flow over him, cooling the despair that heated his cheeks.

He'd bared his soul to Karine. Finally told her how he'd really felt about her, and she'd said "thanks, but no thanks." It hurt. It hurt so much it felt like the pain might kill him, but he'd have to get over it. The thing was, he didn't think he could get over Karine and be her best friend. That meant he'd have to let her go.

He would have thought his heart couldn't hurt any more, but it cracked into a million extra tiny little pieces. Karine would always be special to him, but he needed to learn how to imagine a future with someone other than her. Maybe then they could find a way back to being friends.

He pressed down on the accelerator and the pickup surged forward.

Maybe.

Chapter Twenty-Two

It was the smoke that woke her. She'd never been a smoker, so that was one way the smell was out of place. The other was that it didn't smell like cigarette smoke.

Karine opened her eyes and found a haze hovering over her bed. She swung her feet onto the floor and found it warm, although not unbearably so.

Something was wrong, but her brain was still too wrapped up in the fog of sleep for her to make out exactly what.

She slid her feet into slippers and shrugged into her robe before heading downstairs.

The smoke was thicker down there. One glance in the kitchen explained why.

Orange flames climbed up the walls and engulfed the cabinets.

The sound of the fire crackling and the wood it engulfed splintering filled the air, but the fire alarm was silent. She hadn't checked to make sure it was working when she'd arrived, and now it looked like she was paying the price.

She turned toward the front door, but pulled up short when she realized the flames seemed to have blanketed the front of the house too. She was boxed in by the fire. But that didn't make sense. How could the flames have jumped from the back of the house to the front without reaching the area where she now stood?

Logical or not, she had to get out. Now.

Smoke filled her lungs, sending a rough, hacking cough through her. Caution from a long-ago safety lecture ran through her mind.

It's the smoke that gets you, not the fire.

Out. She needed to get out now. If she couldn't go through the front or the back, what were her options?

She could go back upstairs, try jumping from a window. But the second-floor windows were quite a ways off the ground. She'd almost certainly injure herself. But a window wasn't a bad idea. Getting to the large front window in the living room meant going through the foyer, which, given the size of the flames, didn't seem wise.

But there was a smaller window in the formal dining room that might work.

A hacking cough gripped her. The smoke around her head was getting darker by the second.

Crawl.

Smoke rose and, in a fire, the best thing to do was to stay below it.

She went to her knees, the smoke still sending a wracking cough through her body.

Another memory from a long-ago fire safety lecture arose.

It doesn't take long for smoke inhalation to incapacitate a person.

She crawled into the dining room.

The smoke wasn't as thick in there, thank God, but she still stayed on her hands and knees.

Which wall was the window on?

Fear and panic joined the smoke in clogging her thoughts.

She needed to calm down. Panicking wasn't going to help. In fact, it might get her killed.

Karine pictured the room in her mind's eyes. She was at the door. The window was on the wall directly across from the entry. She just needed to crawl straight ahead and the window should be right there.

She moved forward, stopping once to take control of a hacking cough.

The smoke was getting thicker, she realized when she bumped into a chair she hadn't seen until too late.

The fire was coming for her. She was running out of time.

After what seemed like much too long, she finally reached the other side of the room. She ran her hand up the wall until she reached the windowsill and pulled herself up.

She flicked the lock and tried to push the window up, but it wouldn't budge. Years of paint, rust and who knew what else had sealed it shut.

A coughing fit threatened to take over. She shrugged out of her robe, ripped one of the sleeves off, and pressed it to her nose and mouth. The makeshift mask made it marginally easier to breathe, but she knew that wouldn't last for long.

She needed something to break the window with. She turned, but the room was cloudy with smoke now. She couldn't see more than a step or two in front of her.

"Karine!"

She turned back to the window. Omar was on the other side, his face a desperate mask of terror.

"It's stuck," she called back. "I can't get it open."

"Stand to the side of the window."

She did as he ordered. A moment later, a paving brick shattered the glass.

Through the now shattered window, she could hear the shriek of the fire engines.

Omar knocked the remaining shards of glass from the window with an arm he'd wrapped in his T-shirt. She snatched up her torn robe from the floor and helped him clear the last piece of the broken glass.

He grabbed her arms and helped her through the window.

Somewhere in the quest to escape the fire, she'd lost her slippers. Her feet barely touched the grass before Omar swung her up into his arms.

A fire engine screeched to a stop in front of the house, followed by an ambulance.

Omar carried her to the ambulance and lifted her inside after one of the EMTs opened the rig's rear doors. He sat her on a gurney and took the seat across from her.

"Was there anyone else inside?" one of the firefighters asked from outside the ambulance.

She shook her head. "No." The single word was enough to bring on a coughing fit.

"Don't try to speak," Omar said.

"He's right," the EMT, a beefy man with a mop of curly blond hair, seconded. "Let's get the oxygen mask on you. Breath deep." He fit the mask over her face.

Deputy Coben jogged up to the rig as the EMT fitted a clamp over her thumb. The machine next to the gurney began to emit quick, rhythmic beeps while two separate lines danced across the screen. Her heart rate and oxygen levels.

"Everyone okay?" Deputy Coben asked in a huff.

Omar stood and stalked, slightly hunched over, toward the deputy, but didn't get out of the ambulance. "No, everyone is not okay. Someone set fire to Karine's house and nearly killed her!"

Deputy Coben threw up his hands. "Whoa, there now. We don't know for sure that this was arson."

The deputy's word hit her like a punch to the chest. *Arson.*

"We don't? When I saw the flames, I tried getting into the house by the front and the back doors," Omar said. "There were flames at both ends of the house. How do you explain that?"

All four of them turned to look at the house. It was all but engulfed now. Impossible to say where the fire had started without an expert opinion, but she had seen the flames first-hand. Omar was right. The fire had been in the front and back of the house, but not at the center. That didn't seem possible unless...unless someone had purposely started two separate fires with the intention of trapping her inside.

Karine's stomach knotted into a ball. Someone had tried to kill her. More than likely the same someone who'd killed her mother.

"Let's let the fire department do its job," Deputy Coben said.

The look Omar shot the deputy was enough to send the man backing up a step. Or two.

"If you'd done your job years ago, maybe there wouldn't still be a killer out there. Maybe this wouldn't have happened."

Deputy Coben's face pinked and his eyes narrowed to slits. "Now you just wait a damn minute, Monroe."

"Stop!" Karine said as forcefully as she could through the mask. "This is not helping anyone."

Omar shot one more venomous glance at Deputy Coben before reclaiming his seat across from Karine. She reached for his hand and gave it a squeeze. She could see that his anger at the deputy was partially fed by fear. "I'm okay."

He squeezed back.

She turned to watch the fire brigade attempt to save her house, but knew it was a lost cause. The few things she'd brought with her from Los Angeles, her mother's paintings, her mother's diary, which she'd tucked into the nightstand next to the bed...she'd probably lose them all.

But she was safe, she reminded herself. At least for now.

THE KILLER WAS growing desperate. Karine had escaped every single trap he'd laid.

She was smarter than her mother. Much smarter than the killer had given her credit for, it seemed.

But self-preservation was a strong motivation. He couldn't make it in prison.

The plan was risky, but he didn't see any other way. A more hands-on approach was needed.

Face to face. Direct.

It was time to put an end to Karine Eloi's meddling.

Chapter Twenty-Three

The EMT insisted on taking her to the hospital to be treated for smoke inhalation. Omar held her hand the entire way and only left her side when the doctor demanded he do so. Deputy Coben stopped by to take their statements and relay that the fire had been put out at her house. The second floor had come through relatively unscathed, but the main floor had suffered extensive damage. A city engineer would have to sign off on the building's structural integrity and the house would require thousands of dollars of renovation before she could move back in. And, in an uncharacteristically kind move, Deputy Coben had brought her a change of clothing, Crocs, her purse, and her phone, both a bit waterlogged, but because they'd been in her second-floor bedroom, still usable.

After hours of oxygen, blood tests and waiting around, she was finally discharged at half past midnight with instructions to take it easy for a couple of days.

James West was waiting for her and Omar outside the hospital in a sleek black four-door.

"I called him for a ride," Omar said. Her arm was tucked through his as he led her to the car.

"That was a good idea," she said, the cool night air singeing her lungs. "He can drop you off at your place and then I can ride with him to the B and B. I'll need to take a room there until I can figure out what to do with the house."

Omar stopped walking. "You'll stay with me."

She peered up at him. "I can't ask you to put me up. Not when things between us are so—"

"Karine, things will never be so bad between us that I won't be there for you when you need me."

The feeling behind his words struck her so forcefully, especially after the last twenty-four hours they'd spent together, that her knees threatened to buckle.

Omar caught her around the waist. "Are sure you're okay? Maybe we should have the doctor check you out one more time."

"No, no, I'm fine. Just tired."

The expression on his face said he wasn't convinced, but he guided her the rest of the way to the car.

James drove them back to Omar's house. Karine did her best to avoid looking over at the charred remains of her childhood home, but she couldn't help stealing a few glances. It looked like Deputy Coben had downplayed the damage to the house. It would take a lot of time, work and money to renovate. She'd seen the name of the homeowner's insurance company in the papers her lawyer had sent her when he'd transferred the title to her name. She'd look into all that later. Right now, she just wanted to sleep.

James left Omar to fuss over her, and he did an admirable job. The nightgown she'd been wearing was a lost cause, but Omar loaned her a T-shirt and, after assuring him at least a half dozen times that she was fine, had finally left her alone in his guest room.

As tired as her body was, she could only seem to sleep in snatches of time. Her dreams were a slideshow replay of the night she'd spent making love with Omar under the stars, the hurt she'd seen reflected in his eyes when she'd told him she couldn't be more than his friend, and the fear she'd felt when she'd thought the fire and smoke in her house might overtake her. Her father's words rang over and over in her head, accompanying the montage.

If you ever fall in love, and I hope you do, you'll see how hard it is to walk away.

She awoke, tangled in the sheets, her breath coming fast, burning her healing lungs. She reached for the glass of water Omar had left for her on the night table.

Even after everything they'd been through, he was by her side, taking care of her. She was terrified of moving her relationship with Omar from friendship into romance, but what if she was on the cusp of losing something even more precious? Because almost being burned to a crisp had made one thing crystal-clear.

She loved Omar.

And not as just a friend.

She'd loved him for a long time now, years in fact, but she'd been too much of a coward to do anything about it.

You'll see how hard it is to walk away.

Just the thought of walking away brought on an excruciating pain.

She swung her feet to the floor and stood, buoyed by the need to tell Omar how she felt. To fix what she'd broken.

He'd poured his heart out to her, and she'd said no.

The memory ripped a low groan out of her.

She had to make things right between them.

She shot a glance at the bedside clock: 5:05 a.m. Omar was an early riser, but five in the morning was probably pushing it.

She padded from the room and down the hall, each creak of his refinished hardwood floors sounding like the blast from a bullhorn to her ears.

Omar's door was slightly open, but she couldn't see the bed from the hall. No sound came from inside his room though.

He was still asleep, which made sense after the night they'd had. It had taken her years to get to the point where she was ready to admit to him and herself that she loved him. She could wait a few more hours.

She turned back toward the guest room, the floor creaking underneath her feet again.

"I can see your shadow. I know you're out there. Hovering. Are you going to come in or not?" Omar called from inside the room.

She pushed the door open.

He sat up in the bed, bare-chested, his reading glasses on and his phone in his hand.

"I didn't want to wake you," she said, suddenly shy.

"I've been awake for a while now. How are you feeling?"

"Fine." The word came out as a croak. She cleared her throat. "I'm fine. Fine."

He gave her a wry smile. "I'm glad to hear you're fine, fine. Are you hungry? I can make us some breakfast." He set his phone on the bedside table and placed his glasses next to them.

"No, I'm not hungry," she said, stepping into the room as he swung his feet to the floor, preparing to stand.

"Okay." He shot her another curious look. "Do you need something? Is there something I can get for you?"

"I love you." The words burst out of her, unwilling to be contained any longer.

Her declaration appeared to have shocked Omar into silence.

She took advantage of his temporary speechlessness and continued. "I love you and I was afraid. You have been the one constant in my life. The one person who was always there. Who understood me. My best friend. And I was afraid of that changing. But then there was the fire, and my father said something about how hard it is to walk away from someone you love, and he was right." She was babbling, she knew it, but she didn't seem to be able to stop herself.

"Ever since you drove away from me yesterday, I haven't been able to stop imagining my life without you in it, and it was more terrifying than being in that fire because I knew that you would move heaven and earth to get me to safety if you could, but if you weren't even there? If you weren't even in my life anymore? That, I couldn't stand. And then I realized that the reason I couldn't stand it was because I love you. I've loved you for a really long time, to be honest. So long, I don't even know when it started. Maybe forever." She took a breath. The deluge of words had given her healing lungs a bit of a workout, but she did want to end on a positive note. "So, yeah, I love you."

Silence seemed to hang between them for an interminable amount of time before Omar spoke. "So you're not afraid anymore."

"I'm terrified. But I'm more afraid I'd lose you, and I think that's what would happen if I didn't tell you how I feel."

Omar sighed and the faint smile that had been turning up the edges of his mouth died. "Karine, I don't want you to say anything because you think you'll lose me."

"No, that's not why..." She crossed the room and sat next to him on the bed. "I'm messing this up completely. I love you. I am more sure about that than I have been about anything in my life ever. It was always easier to pretend my feelings were just platonic because you were here and

I was in Los Angeles. But now, I don't want to pretend anymore. I don't even think I could after the other night."

The sexy grin slid back onto Omar's face. "I was that good, huh?"

She slapped his chest and rolled her eyes. "I'm pouring my heart out here."

He grabbed the hand she'd hit him with. "Yes. I'm sorry. Continue," he said with faux seriousness.

"I love you and I don't want to go back to just being friends." And there was nothing faux about how serious she was.

Omar leaned forward, kissing her softly.

She tried deepening the kiss, but he pulled back. "I want nothing more than to ravish you right now, but the doctor said you need to take it easy."

She eyed his sculpted abdominals. "What I have in mind can be very relaxing."

Omar laughed, but shook his head. He scooted back on the bed, taking her with him. "Neither one of us got a lot of sleep last night. I think I'd like to just lie here and hold you." He lay down, making room for her to stretch out next to him. He wrapped his arm around her, pulling her in close.

She hooked her leg over his, her hand caressing his chest. "How long do you think we can stay like this?"

He dropped a kiss on the top of her head. "I was thinking forever. What do you think?"

"Sounds good to me."

Chapter Twenty-Four

Omar's side of the bed was still warm when she awoke later that morning, but he was gone. In his place was a note.

Results on the water and soil samples came in. Didn't want to wake you. Back soon.

Karine was annoyed that he'd gone to see his friend without her.

She dressed, considering whether she should give Omar a call and meet up with him and his colleague, but decided against it. This was part of his job, and she was sure he would bring her up to speed the moment he got back. And she could read him the riot act for leaving her out of the loop then.

She slipped her sockless feet into Crocs and headed downstairs.

Karine filled the electric teakettle, then turned to see what she could find in the fridge for breakfast, and yelped.

A face stared at her through the windowpane in the back door. It took a moment for her brain to catch up with her vision and put two and two together.

"Daton?" She put the kettle on the warming plate and

switched it on before marching to the door. "Daton, you just about gave me a heart attack. What are you doing?"

Daton raised both hands in the air, an embarrassed blush flushing his cheeks. "I'm sorry. I didn't mean to scare you. I rang the doorbell. No one answered, but your car was at your house and... I guess I got worried. I heard about the fire at your place and with everything that's been going on and the situations you've found yourself in lately, I just wanted to make sure everything was okay."

Her heart was still beating furiously, but she felt her mouth turn up in the beginning of a smile. "The situations I've found myself in, huh? I guess I can't argue that I have gotten into a bit of trouble lately. Come in." She stepped aside to let him enter. "I was just about to have some tea. Or I could make you some coffee. Would you like to join me?"

"I would love tea." He beamed.

The water for their tea was already beginning to boil. She reached into the cabinet over the sink and drew out two mugs and two tea bags.

"I am sorry I startled you. How are you doing?"

Karine carried the mugs and tea bags to the kettle. "I'm fine. Frustrated. I guess I might have expected too much when I came to town. Finding new information about a twenty-three-year-old murder... I knew it wouldn't be easy, but I didn't realize just how hard it was going to be." She poured the boiling water into the mugs and passed one to Daton. "Sugar." She pointed to the bowl next to the kettle and pulled two spoons from the drawer to her left, handing one to him. She used the other to shovel two generous spoonsful of sugar in her cup. She took a sip and let the hot, soothing scent and taste of the chamomile engulf her.

Daton dipped the spoon into the bowl and sprinkled half

a teaspoon of sugar into his cup. "Could I trouble you for a little milk?"

"Sure." She turned her back to him and went to the fridge.

"I have to confess, I'm kind of relieved your investigation hasn't been as fruitful as you'd hoped," he said.

"Why?" She grabbed the milk and turned to him with a frown.

"Because whoever killed Marilee is out there and you asking questions is clearly putting them on edge. I think you should consider leaving the investigating to the proper authorities."

Karine slid the milk across the counter, her frown deepening. "You're not the first person to suggest that." She took another sip of her tea. "But it feels like the answer is right there in front of me. I just can't fit all the pieces of the story together in a way that makes sense."

"The pieces of the story?" Daton wrapped his hands around his mug.

Karine took another long drink from her mug before she answered. "That's how I think about it. Like the story behind what led to my mom's death. There's the love letter I found, and mom's intervention into the situation between Principal Howser and Meghan. And, of course, the email from Amber that started this whole thing." She yawned, a sudden desire for a nap overwhelming her. She felt loose. Not so much tired, but like she wouldn't mind a quick nap. She shook her head to clear her mind. "I can't help but feel that if I just knew what Amber was going to tell me, I'd have the answer I needed."

"Yes, I'm sure you would," he said carefully.

A warning prickled at the back of her neck. "This tea seems to really be taking effect. Let's move into the living room where we can be more comfortable and, if I fall asleep while we're talking, you can just leave me on the sofa," she joked.

Daton didn't smile, but he did follow her into the living room.

She didn't make it to the sofa though. The curtains on Omar's large picture window were open to the street. The driveway was empty, as was the space on the street in front of the house.

"Daton, where is your car?" she asked, leaning against the window as much to hold herself upright as to get a good look up and down the street. No black Porsche in sight.

"I parked on a service road about a quarter mile from here. And I didn't drive the Porsche. It's too conspicuous."

The warning tingle turned into a warning torrent. Karine looked at Daton. Two Datons actually. Her vision swam. "What did you do to me?"

"Just a sedative. Oops." Daton reached out, grabbing her teacup before she dropped it with one hand and her arm with the other. He led Karine to the sofa. "You should sit before you fall down."

"You drugged me."

The two Datons sat next to her on the sofa. "Yes. It will be easier this way."

"Easier." She blinked and he came into focus. She fought to make sense of what was happening, but her mind seemed to be moving too slowly. "Why?"

He sighed, a sad smile playing over his lips. "Because you are too much like your mother."

"My mother?" His words weren't making any sense.

"Yes, your mother. I didn't want to kill her, either, but she wouldn't just mind her business. Well, you've seen how she was. Sticking her nose in Principal Howser's business and everyone else's around town. She was just so self-righteous. So sure she was always right. There was never any gray area with her, just black and white. Well, life isn't just black and white. There's a lot of gray. I tried to make her understand, but she just wouldn't."

Karine had to fight to hold her head up. She couldn't believe what she was hearing. The man she'd thought was her mother's friend had killed her. "You killed my mother."

"Yes, I did." He nodded solemnly. "You should understand that I didn't want to, or even mean to. I went to the house to try to talk some sense into her. To appeal to her as a friend. But, like I said, self-righteous. I lost my temper. It was an accident, but if I'd called the police and said that, then everything else would come out."

"What…out?" She wanted to hear the whole story. She deserved answers, but she wasn't sure she could remain conscious for much longer.

"The dumping."

Her head fell to the side, which Daton must have taken as a sign of her surprise.

"Yeah, the dumping your boyfriend is looking into. Spindler Plastics has been burying waste in the Carling Lake Forest on and off for years. Decades, actually. Not all the time, but it was a good way to cut back on expenses during a hard period. Your mother was always in those damned woods. She saw something she shouldn't have. I'd just taken over the company less than a year earlier and she figured I must not know about it. She came to me because she thought I'd take care of it. She believed in me." He sounded wistful. "It never occurred to her that I knew about it. I'd authorized it."

"Why?" Just getting the one word out had felt like a Herculean task. She was fading fast with no idea what

Daton planned for her once she was unconscious or how she'd get out of it.

Omar. If she could just get to her phone. He'd said he'd be back soon. How long had he been gone?

"Because my father was a terrible businessman and my mother spent money like we were printing it in the basement. The company was going to go under, and then we'd have nothing. Everything my grandfather had worked for, the family name, everything I'd planned for my own future would have been gone. I couldn't let that happen. I tried to explain that to your mother."

"What...do...with me?"

Daton trailed a finger down her cheek.

She shuddered at his touch.

"If I thought I could convince you to keep quiet, I would, but like I said, you're just too much like your mother. Too tenacious. Too determined. I tried, I really did, to get you to walk away from this misguided investigation. A break-in. A fire. Nothing worked."

It was all coming together now.

"Amber."

Daton's lips twisted into a scowl. "Amber. Yes, I killed her too. She knew about the dumping. Had for years. It's hard to hide something as big as murder from someon you're living with. She put the pieces of your mother murder together and came up with me. She didn't care.

Her heart cinched, and bile rose in her throat. All of people who'd been closest to her mother had betrayed

"As long as the company made money, *I* made mo Amber didn't care," Daton continued. "But when I for a divorce, she used the video and the information the dumping to get a very nice settlement out of me. A she'd just left it at that, I wouldn't have been forced to with her. But what do they say about a woman scorned?" He nearly growled the words. "When I told her about Valerie's pregnancy, I could see it in her eyes. I mean, she already hated Valerie, but now she was giving me the child Amber and I couldn't create together. I think it tipped her into the deep end. Luckily, she was a loose-lipped drunk. She called me the night before she was going to meet with you. Taunting me about how she was going to tell you everything. It wasn't difficult to make her death look like an overdose. Too bad I can't do the same for you."

He picked up her mug and stood. "Don't worry. I'm going to clean up everything before we go. Can't leave any fingerprints. Hopefully, your disappearance will distract Omar from his investigation into the pollution in the forest. I'd hate to have to take care of him too. I don't think he'd be quite as easy to dispose of as you and Amber." Daton sighed heavily. "Oh well, no use in worrying about it. I'll cross that bridge if I get to it. Now, you just sit there and pass out. I'll only be a moment."

He strode into the kitchen.

Karine willed herself to find the strength and focus to get up. The front door was only steps away. If she could just get outside, maybe one of the neighbors would see her and come over to help.

But the sedative was too strong. In the end, she did just what Daton had instructed her to do.

She passed out.

Chapter Twenty-Five

Omar met his friend Brett at a café midway between Carling Lake and Stunnersville, where Brett lived and worked. It was their usual place to meet whenever they carved out a few hours to catch up, although that had been happening far less frequently since Brett and his wife had had their first child.

Brett was already there when Omar arrived. He stood, and the two of them engaged in a quick bro hug before settling in. The waitress came by and took their drink and food order at the same time.

"Thanks for helping me out," Omar said once they'd placed their orders and the waitress had moved away from their table.

"Not a problem. I mean, you are paying for the tests, but I did put a rush on them for you." Brett grinned. "No charge."

Omar laughed. "Thanks. It pays to have friends in high places."

Brett's grin fell away as he reached for the file folder in the empty seat next to him. "I tested the soil, and it came back positive for high levels of methyl ethyl ketone or MEK."

"MEK." Omar frowned. "Karine was right then."

"Karine." Brett perked up. "Isn't that your best friend slash secret crush from Los Angeles?"

Omar rolled his eyes. He and Brett had been friends long enough that Brett had heard most of the Karine and Omar childhood stories, even though he and Karine had never met. Somewhere along the way, Brett had picked up on his feelings for Karine and he'd been gently teasing and alternatively pushing him to make a play for Karine ever since. Since he'd spent years telling Brett that he and Karine were just friends and that was all they'd ever be, he expected to take a bit of self-congratulatory ribbing when he told Brett that the relationship had moved out of the friend zone. Brett didn't disappoint.

"I knew it." Brett clapped. "It was written all over your face whenever you talked about the woman. You love her."

Omar held up a hand. "Whoa. Slow down. I mean, of course, I love her. She's my best friend and, yeah, okay, I have, and have had for some time, strong feelings for her. We're going to explore that, but I don't know," he said, letting his uncertainty hang out there for a moment. "She lives in Los Angeles. I live here. I don't know how we make a long distance relationship work."

"What are you talking about?" Brett said incredulously. "You've been making a long distance relationship work with Karine since I met you. But, look, if you don't want to do long distance, I don't blame you. But, my friend, take it from a happily married man. If this is the right woman for you, do whatever it takes to keep her. They hire park rangers in California, too, or so I hear."

The waitress returned with their food and they took a few minutes to eat.

Omar thought about what Brett had said. Could he really move to Los Angeles? He'd always imagined himself working until retirement in Carling Lake, but, really, there wasn't much keeping him in his hometown. Yes, he had many good friends, but his parents lived in Arizona now. Moving to California would actually put him closer to them than he was. And he did have an acquaintance who worked for the parks department in California. It had been a while since they'd spoken, but he could reach out to him, see what the employment layout around Los Angeles looked like.

Whoa. He slammed on his internal mental brakes. *Getting way ahead of yourself, Monroe. You and Karine literally just...*

Well, they'd literally just had an incredible night. And had agreed to see where a relationship went. Planning a move across the country might be just a bit too fast. But the seed had taken root. It felt fast, yes, but it also felt right.

He finished half his sandwich and requested a refill on his cola before he forced himself to focus on the task at hand.

"Tell me more about this MEK," he said, getting the conversation back on track. "I don't think I've ever heard of it."

"You might have heard it called butanone."

Omar shook his head. "Nope, never heard of it."

"It's a colorless chemical that only occurs in nature in small amounts."

"Yet the tests found high levels of this butanone in the soil samples I sent you."

Brett nodded. "Off-the-charts high. No way this is occurring naturally. Or by accident, in my expert opinion."

That meant he'd been right all along. Someone was dumping the chemical in the Carling Lake Forest.

"Could this kill small animals?"

Brett tipped his head. "I did a little research after the results came in. I couldn't find a study specifically looking at the effects of MEK on the environment, but acetone is a close chemical cousin to this stuff, and it definitely causes harm. In animals and in humans, if ingested in large enough quantities."

"So it's probably safe to say that this butanone is also dangerous. Certainly to smaller animals."

"If I was in your place, I certainly wouldn't dismiss the possibility. More testing would need to be done, but I'd say you found your pollutant."

"So, I know what is poisoning my forest, but I still need to find out who is doing it and where the chemical is coming from." Omar pushed his plate to the side and pulled out the map he'd taken down off the office bulletin board after John had ordered him to drop the investigation.

Brett had already inhaled his entire lunch, so he pushed his empty plate to the side as well.

Omar spread the map out between them. "Here are all the places where I found affected animals." He pointed to the multiple red Xs that replaced the pins.

Brett studied the map for several minutes. "So we know the water isn't affected. It's just the soil."

"Yes. Karine suggested that I test the soil because something hazardous might have seeped into it and the animals are affected when they burrow into the soil."

"Or eat plants or insects that have absorbed the chemical." Brett looked thoughtful. "It's not a bad theory, but it's way out of my expertise."

Omar's, as well, but he did know someone who might be able to help. Karine wouldn't like asking her father for help though. He'd cross that bridge when he got there.

Brett leaned back in his chair. "So, what are you going to do now?"

"I don't know," Omar answered honestly. "My supervisor doesn't even want me on this. I have to have irrefutable proof of soil contamination before I take it to him."

Brett frowned. "Is this the same supervisor who supposedly sent the water samples to the state lab for testing?"

"Yes. Why do you say 'supposedly'?"

"That was the other thing I wanted to talk to you about and didn't want to put in an email or say over the phone. I called a friend of mine who still works at the state lab to confirm something on the water test results you sent me with the soil sample. My friend couldn't find any record of the lab having conducted the test on water sources in Carling Lake."

Omar sat stunned for a moment. "That can't be right. I sent you the test results."

Brett held his hands out. "All I can tell you is my friend says the test didn't come from the state lab."

The implication of the information hit him. "John falsified the report."

That meant there was a good possibility water sources could also be contaminated. And that John was aware of it. He knew about the contamination, knew who was causing it, and was probably taking a bribe to keep that information covered up.

Omar flagged down their waitress and asked for the check. He needed to get back to Carling Lake and figure out his next steps. He'd have to go over John's head, but he had no idea how far up the corruption went. He'd have to be careful.

His phone rang just as the waitress dropped the check off. He dug his phone and his wallet out of his pocket, answering the phone without looking at who was calling first.

"Hello?"

"Omar, it's James West."

Omar dropped enough cash to cover the bill and a generous tip on the table then stood. "James, can I call you back later? I've got a developing situation on my hands."

He said a hasty goodbye to Brett, who waved him off in understanding, then exited the restaurant.

"I don't think this can wait," James said. "The techs at West Investigations were able to clean up the video of the man skulking around Karine's house on the night of her mother's murder. They got a good shot of the intruder's face and I'm sending you a still shot of it now."

Omar put the phone on speaker and opened the new text message from James.

"Omar, Karine might need to brace herself—"

He should have heeded James's warning as well.

"Damn it," he said as the face in the photo registered in his brain.

The person creeping around the Eloi house on the night of Marilee's murder was none other than Marilee's close friend, Daton Spindler.

Chapter Twenty-Six

The first thing she became aware of was her throbbing head. The second was the fact that she was in a car. One was related to the other since her head was bouncing against something, not exactly hard, but not exactly softly either.

Karine tried to open her eyes, but they felt like they'd been glued closed. It took effort, but she finally forced them open.

She was definitely in a car. She raised her hands, surprised to find them bound together tightly with rope.

She turned her head slowly, her brain still thick with fog, but becoming clearer.

Daton.

His blurry figure was behind the steering wheel. He was taking her somewhere. Where? She couldn't remember. Had he told her?

He glanced across the car at her.

"You're awake." He didn't sound pleased.

Her mind was clearing slowly. Daton showing up at Omar's and drinking tea with her. Daton drugging her. Daton confessing to having killed her mother. And now he planned to kill her too.

Her limbs still felt like lead. She looked out of the window but could only see the road and trees. She didn't know where they were exactly, but it appeared to be remote.

Daton's phone was on the charger on the dashboard, but she doubted he'd let her make a call.

"Where are you taking me?"

Daton glanced at her again. "Someplace where no one will find you."

She pulled against the ropes. She had to get out of this car. She glanced around for a weapon, something, anything, to use to defend herself. She didn't see anything.

Bright lights flashed in the rearview mirror. A small compact car was barreling down on them. The driver honked, leaning on the horn.

Karine turned in the seat, her head throbbing. It was hard to see, but the driver…it was Richie Portman.

Richie honked again.

Daton looked in the rearview mirror. "What the…?"

"It's my neighbor. He must have seen you kidnapping me. I'm sure he's called the sheriff. You'll never get away with this. The only way out is to stop this now and turn yourself in."

"You think that's the only way?" Daton scoffed. "I've come too far to let a nosy neighbor get in my way."

He pulled a gun from between his seat and the console.

Karine shrank back, pressing herself to the door. "What are you doing with that?"

Daton didn't answer. He rolled his window down and reached his left arm out, holding the gun.

Pop. Pop.

There was no way the bullets could have hit Richie, not with the angle Daton was holding the gun, but the shots had their desired effect.

Richie's car fell back a bit, but didn't stop following.

"Damn it," Daton snarled when he saw Richie still following. He stomped on the brakes.

The car skidded to a stop.

Richie swerved to avoid hitting them and sped past.

Daton hit the accelerator. He stuck his hand out the window again, and this time the bullets whizzed forward, slamming into the back of Richie's car.

Karine screamed. Richie was out there because of her. To help her. She couldn't let Daton hurt him.

Without thinking, she reached across the console and grabbed the steering wheel.

"Let go!" Daton yelled, trying to knock her hands away.

She fisted her hands and smacked him in the face.

"Damn." Daton brought a hand to his bloody nose, letting the gun fall into the footwell.

The car veered toward the trees at the side of the road. Karine grabbed the wheel, attempting to bring them back onto the asphalt. But Daton snatched the wheel, too, and he was stronger.

The front of the car dipped and then they were tumbling. Rolling over. Once. Twice. She thought a third time before the car stopped, upright.

"Ugh!" Her head felt like it had split in two.

Daton was unconscious, but she could see the rise and fall of his chest. He was alive.

Karine tried her door. It was jammed. But Daton's window was still open. It would mean crawling over him, but that seemed safer than staying in the car. As long as he didn't wake up.

She crawled over him, holding her breath and praying he'd remain unconscious until she was out. Richie had to have seen the wreck. If she could make it back to the road, they could drive to safety and send for help.

She was finally able to extricate herself.

"Karine!"

She looked up the incline. Richie stood at the side of the road, looking down.

"Karine. Hang on," he called again, sliding down the hill.

She started up, meeting him halfway.

Richie wrapped an arm around her and helped her the rest of the way. "I already called the sheriff," he said when they made it to the top.

She could hear the sirens, although they still sounded to be a ways off.

Richie glanced back down the incline at the wrecked car. "I guess I should call for an ambulance too." He loped off toward his car.

The sirens were getting louder, but it wasn't a sheriff's cruiser that turned the curve first.

Omar slammed his pickup into Park and jumped out, running to her. "Karine. Are you okay? Where is Daton?"

She pointed down the hill.

Omar glanced at the wreck then back to her. He cradled her face. "Are you sure you're okay? Did he hurt you?"

"No. I mean, I'm a little banged up and my head is killing me from the combination of the sedative and the accident, but no permanent damage."

A breath gushed out of Omar. He pulled her to his chest, wrapping her in his arms. "Do you know how scared I was? When James called to say Daton was the man in the security video from your house and then Richie called the sheriff to say he'd seen Daton carrying you out through the woods behind my house. I thought—"

"I'm okay. I'm—oh!" Omar shifted her to the side. Threw her, really. "What?"

And then she saw.

Daton. On his knees at the edge of the road. He'd come to and crawled out of the car. And he had the gun.

Omar snatched his own weapon from its holster at his hip.

Karine screamed as the sound of gunshots exploded around them.

She crouched on the asphalt road, her hand covering her head.

"Karine, baby, it's over. It's over," Omar's soothing voice said next to her.

She raised her head. Daton lay in the grass beside the road. Completely still.

Omar helped her to her feet.

"It's over," he repeated.

This time, she believed him.

Epilogue

Karine stood on the street in front of her family home. Dealing with the arson inspector, the insurance company, and getting bids for repair and renovation had been grueling, especially since she'd had to do a lot of it long-distance. Omar had been an immense help there and, thankfully, the actual work that needed to be done to get the home in livable condition had begun a couple of weeks earlier. She planned to put her family home back together again and then put it on the market. It was time to move on.

Omar joined her in front of the house. He wrapped an arm around her shoulder and pulled her close to his side. "Are you doing okay?"

She looked up at him and smiled. "I'm better than okay."

And she was. The moment was tinged with sadness and nostalgia for what had been and what could have been under different circumstances. But mostly she felt hope and excitement.

She glanced at the house next door.

The For Sale sign in front of Omar's house now had a big red-and-white Sold sticker crisscrossing the Realtor's face. When she left Carling Lake in a few days, Omar would be leaving with her. He'd gotten a position with the California state park rangers and they were going to try to make a go of their relationship.

Daton had survived the gunshot injury to the shoulder and confessed to the attack on Karine on her first night in town, shooting at her and Omar in the parking lot of Barney's, killing his ex-wife, Amber, and bludgeoning Karine's mother to death. He'd also confessed to attacking Becky Portman after Shep had told him about the security video from the night of Marilee's murder. He'd had plans to make sure Richie also had a tragic accident, but events had spiraled beyond his control before he could get to it. Thankfully, his sister, Becky, had made a full recovery.

Daton and Spindler Plastics were facing a host of state and federal crimes arising from the environmental pollution Marilee had stumbled upon and ultimately lost her life because of. It turned out Daton was nowhere near the businessman his father and grandfather had been. Twenty-three years ago, the company had been headed toward dire financial straits when Daton came up with the idea of cutting costs by burying some of the chemical manufacturing waste deep in the Carling Lake woods. Unfortunately, Karine's mother had stumbled upon his men when they'd been engaged in the crime. She'd gone to her friend, believing he could not have been aware of what others in the company were doing and that he'd put a stop to it immediately and fix the issue. Once she realized that Daton had not only known about the pollution but condoned its illegal disposal, she'd decided to go to the authorities. Her mistake had been in telling her friend what she'd planned to do. Daton had tried everything he could think of to keep her from going to the police, but Marilee had loved Carling Lake too much to let anyone destroy it.

Daton said that on the night of her murder, he had only

gone to try to talk Marilee into forgetting about what she'd seen, but that he'd lost his temper. He'd struck Marilee with the fireplace poker. He swore he hadn't meant to kill her and that he hadn't realized that Karine was home. The one good thing that had come out of her mother's death was that Daton had been so terrified that someone would discover what he'd done and why that he'd ceased the illegal dumping of waste. At least until six months ago when tough times had befallen the company once more and, feeling safe from ever being outed as Marilee's killer, he'd gone back to his illegal dumping scheme to save Spindler Plastics money.

Daton also hadn't known about the new, small, unobtrusive security cameras Marilee had installed in an attempt to catch her husband with his mistress. Nor had he known that she had confided in her friend Amber, who'd gotten the security recording and been stunned when she'd recognized the shadow creeping toward the Eloi house as her husband. She'd kept quiet for years, not even telling Daton about the video until he'd announced he'd wanted a divorce. Then she'd used it to extract a very generous settlement. But her conscience had begun weighing on her in the months before her death. She'd made a tragic mistake the night before her meeting with Karine in calling Daton after she'd been drinking and using pills. She'd let spill her plan to tell Karine what she knew and Daton had decided she had to go.

Deputy Shep Coben had known about the security cameras. He'd admitted to feeding Daton confidential information for years, not just about Marilee's case, though that was the initial reason Daton had made the alliance. Lance wanted to initiate formal disciplinary proceedings, but Shep had resigned and moved away from Carling Lake before he could be fired. Shep had bigger problems than losing his job, though. The prosecutor was planning to bring charges against him for misuse of public office, bribery and obstruction of justice, among other charges.

Karine knew in her gut that Shep at the very least must have suspected Daton of her mother's murder. She couldn't get it out of her head that maybe Shep hadn't missed the security camera at all. But her gut wasn't evidence, so it looked like Shep would get away with whatever crimes he might have committed.

John Huyton, Omar's supervisor, had also been let go for taking bribes from Daton and falsifying water testing reports. Word around town was that he had already made a deal with the state and federal prosecutors to testify against Daton.

Things between her and her father were still tense, but she'd told him everything she'd discovered about her mother's death, and Jean had vowed to be in court every day of Daton's trial. Her parents' marriage hadn't been perfect, but she'd seen how much her father had cared about her mother. And how much having people believe he could have been involved in her death had affected him. Omar was right. People made mistakes, and she wanted to have a relationship with her father.

She shook away the memories of the last several months and looked toward her future. She looked at Omar. "You ready?"

He leaned forward and pressed a kiss to her mouth. "Absolutely."

* * * * *

COMING SOON!

We really hope you enjoyed reading this book.
If you're looking for more romance
be sure to head to the shops when
new books are available on

Thursday 15th August

To see which titles are coming soon, please visit

millsandboon.co.uk/nextmonth

MILLS & BOON

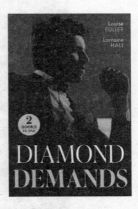
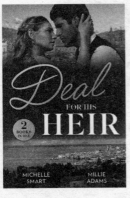

LET'S TALK
Romance

For exclusive extracts, competitions
and special offers, find us online:

f MillsandBoon

X @MillsandBoon

O @MillsandBoonUK

♪ @MillsandBoonUK

Get in touch on 01413 063 232